Erotic Fantastic

The Best of Circlet Press
1992 - 2002

edited by Cecilia Tan

CIRCLET PRESS, INC.
CAMBRIDGE, MA

Erotic Fantastic
edited by Cecilia Tan

Copyright © 2003 by Circlet Press, Inc.
Cover art © 2003 by Janet Bruesselbach

All Rights Reserved

Printed in Canada

First Edition May 2003

ISBN 1-885865-44-9

Circlet Press is distributed in the USA and Canada by the SCB Distributors.
Circlet Press is distributed in the UK and Europe by Turnaround Ltd.
Circlet Press is distributed in Australia by Bulldog Books.

For a catalog, information about our other imprints, review copies, and other informtaion, please write to:

Circlet Press, Inc.
1770 Massachusetts Avenue, #278
Cambridge, MA 02140

http://www.circlet.com

CONTENTS

INTRODUCTION

People sometimes ask me what it takes to become a publisher and my answer is usually this: a stapler, a P.O. Box, an ISBN prefix, and a dream. I started Circlet Press in 1992 by publishing a tiny chapbook of stories I collated myself on the floor of my apartment in Boston. It was called "Telepaths Don't Need Safewords" and combined three erotic science fiction stories I had written into a forty-page booklet.

The decision to self-publish was one of necessity, really. There were no markets I could send those stories to for publication. They were too long, too kinky, too plot-driven for the men's glossies, too bisexual for either the gay or the lesbian magazines, way, way too graphic for the science fiction magazines. I thought I'd sell a hundred or so copies, at science fiction conventions or leather/SM parties and events I went to. I took that first hundred with me to Lunacon, a science fiction convention near New York City... and sold them all. Within a year I had sold 600 copies, and a curious thing happened. Manuscripts began to land in my P.O. Box from science fiction writers and erotica writers alike. The letters usually went something like this: *Dear Ms. Tan, I recently picked up a copy of your book and thought you might be interested in publishing my erotic science fiction which has been languishing in a drawer...*

It seemed I was not alone in my taste for the erotic mixed with the fantastic. There were authors writing it, and bookstores asking for it, and it just took someone to be the go-between. I had been working in book publishing for three years already at that point and knew when Fate was staring me in the face. I was the person who could, and would, do it.

Within a year Circlet was publishing trade paperbacks and our titles were being distributed nationally. Excellent reviews and nice write-ups in publishing trade journals followed. And a bonanza of brilliant, edgy, sexual science fiction and fantasy continued to land on my desk.

What you have here is the best of that crop. Out of the forty or so books and anthologies Circlet has published in the past decade, I have plucked the stories that were, to me, the most memorable, the most affecting, the most rewarding to read. It was difficult to winnow them down, actually, to the ones represented here. If economic times were different, perhaps I could have squeezed a few more in. But I am pleased with the gluttonously rich feast I am providing here. If you find you want more, there are many other volumes to choose from.

Enjoy.

Cecilia Tan
Cambridge, MA

MILAGRO
Francesca Lia Block

From the time she is very young, all Plum wants is this: to be loved for who she is with complete and awesome devotion. She tries to dress herself the way she feels inside so that the love of her life will recognize her easily. Which means that in elementary school she wears as many barrettes as she can fit in her long black hair and shortens her skirts daily, letting them down again before her mother sees. In junior high she staples rhinestone studs to her clothes. In high school she chops off all her hair, to her mother's horror, and spikes it with gel. She designs clothes covered with zippers and chains and does her eyelids like various flowers and insects—orchids, dragonflies.

This is when she meets Santiago. He recognizes her by her radical hair and the clothes she has designed and made. Her soft voice and delicate hands and the way she comforts him when he calls to tell her about how his father tried to beat him again.

Santiago wears make-up and jewelry. He is so beautiful that no one except his father gives him shit. Everyone is infatuated with him, whether they know it or not—the popular girls, the shy girls, the jocks, the gay boys. Plum is the one who gets him. He is all she wants. She gives him haircuts and does his eyeshadow. He looks like a supermodel. They take ballroom dance lessons and go to punk gigs and do the tango in the pit. They are so charismatic together that instead of being shunned because of how eccentric they are, they are elected "Cutest Couple" in the yearbook. Plum realizes that this means everyone thinks they are sleeping together, and that maybe that is another reason why Santiago doesn't suffer (except from his father) because of his appearance. She also wishes that it were true—the sleeping together. They have never even kissed although they hold hands and when they are dancing, pressed up against each other, hearts slamming—it is like what she imagines it would be like to make love.

They go to the prom together wearing matching black zippered satin and leopard prints and boots and sporting matching bleached blond hairdos that contrast with their dark features. They do their punk tango and sit at the table with all the "Class Bests." They feel like rock stars. Plum realizes that she is in love with Santiago when he feeds her dessert with a spoon and tells her that he is not going to go back east to school the way he had planned because she is so beautiful.

After the prom they get in Santiago's old Cadillac and drive to the desert. On the drive they listen to their favorite B-52's tapes really loud, open the windows so the warm winds lash their faces, and scream into the night like banshees. Plum feeds Santiago grapes and chocolates as they speed down the highway.

In Desert Hot Springs there are natural springs running under the desert floor. The motels were built around them over the years. There are little mom-and-pop places decorated in blond wood where Swedish moms and pops give deep tissue massages, pink and turquoise 50's style places, fake Roman set-ups with bad replicas of David and Venus around the pool, and broken down deserted bungalows that seem haunted by lost desert ghosts when the sand blows through. Then there is Villa Milagro. The pale blue bungalows surround a mosaic tiled pool and a glassed-in jacuzzi. There are large chunks of crystal and candles and garden shrines and silk flowers in the garden.

When Plum and Santiago get there in the still, hot, coral-colored desert dawn, Milagro, wearing beads and a long caftan decorated with birds, checks them in. Plum can't tell if Milagro is male or female. Milagro says, "What a beautiful couple you are." Plum and Santiago are shown to their bungalow decorated in Chia pets, clown paintings, beaded curtains, glass baubles, fabric printed with ferns and daisies, strands of fake roses and throw rugs covered in sunflower designs. It is fresh and smells like clean desert air. They collapse on the butterfly-adorned comforter and fall asleep almost right away. They sleep straight through till the next evening.

When she gets up, Plum goes to find Milagro. Milagro is sitting by the pool wearing a caftan decorated with ladybugs. Plum asks where they can get some food and Milagro takes Plum into Milagro's bungalow which is afire with glass objects refracting the light. Milagro prepares avocado sandwiches and fresh figs.

Milagro stares at Plum silently until Plum winces.

"You have a gift," Milagro says.

Plum thinks Milagro is talking about how she designs clothes and applies make-up but she realizes that she is only wearing her bathing suit and her face is bare.

"The love gift," Milagro says.

Plum feels shivery and assumes it's from the swamp cooler blasting rosewater scented air at her neck. The love gift. Does this mean she has found her love? She thanks Milagro for the food and says she has to get back to Santiago.

He is sitting on the bed wearing his swim trunks. His rippling deep amber colored body is even more glowing in desert light. He grins at her.

The sky is pink with sunset, a neon motel sign flashing in the distance, a cluster of palm trees, otherwise just desert everywhere around the pool. The air warm and sparkling. They put their feet in the soft glow of blue water and eat the avocado sandwiches and figs. The sky changes to blue-violet and a crescent moon comes out with her stars.

Plum tosses the towel away. "Are you going to swim with me?"

She jumps in the water. It slides over her body like a warm slip of silk. She floats and splashes, looking up at the glint of moon and smelling the burnished sweetness of the desert night.

"What's that smell?"

"Creosote."

"It smells like rain."

He dives in. The water ripples out from the force of his body. She feels it rush against her abdomen, forcing her bikini bottoms away from her pelvis. A current rushes between her legs. They swim around and then Plum slips through the little entrance into the glass Jacuzzi.

Santiago comes in after her. In their own private cave of steam. Milagro has lit some candles along the outside rim and the crystals are throbbing in their light. There is also incense that has a light scent of vanilla and exotic flowers. A collection of mermaid statues are poised ready to splash into the water. Plum presses back against the lowest jet. She is afraid to turn around because if the jets hit between her legs she thinks she might start coming. It's being around him and seeing his bare chest and it's the heat and the air and the sky. Santiago lies back and closes his eyes. The water stutters against Plum's tail bone. Between that and seeing Santiago lying there with his brown arms floating above the ripples of water she thinks she might come even without turning around. She moves closer to him.

He says, "You look like a mermaid."

He switches places with her so his body is up against the low jet.

She says, "Give me my jet."

He laughs. "I don't have your jet."

"Yes you do!"

She wants to reach out and stroke him under the water.

Later, in the kitsch paradise, their bodies still whir with heat from the water as if someone is tracing spirals on their skin. The coolish night air comes in through the window, caressing. They lie on the bed drinking the cold beers they'd managed to score before they left town. Plum feels calm and brave. Milagro told her she has a love gift. She says, "Wouldn't you be more comfortable without those?"

He laughs. He gets under the sheet, takes off his wet trunks. She reaches under, puts her hand on him, cradling his balls.

"Is this okay?" He nods.

They lie like that for a long time.

"Do you want me to move my hand?" He shakes his head.

"That could mean two things," and they laugh but Plum doesn't think he wants her to move away or try to get him off because he isn't stirring and she can see a little vein beating at his temple so she kisses it and then whispers, "May I go down?"

He nods but there is some tension in the curve of his lips. Plum stays where she is, kissing his temples and forehead and cheeks, cradling his face in her hand, her other hand on his cock.

She says, "No erections now, whatever you do."

He smiles and his mouth softens. Plum moves down slowly and rests her face against his hip. His groin is flat and smooth. She moves her mouth against him and touches his tip very softly with her lips, then she kisses his shaft and around his groin.

He still isn't responding and he seems a little tense so she comes back up and fits herself into the warm cradle of his arm, her head on his bicep.

That is how they sleep in Milagro's villa, with the beaded glass curtains tinkling in the desert breeze. Deep in the night or is it early morning Plum is lying curved around him, her bare breasts sticking to the breadth of his back, and she finds her hands moving down over his hips and stroking him. He stretches back so that she can touch more. His penis stirs toward her hand and she grasps it. It makes a slapping sound against his flat belly. She moves her hand up and down along the shaft and he sighs softly. She does this for a long time, breathing with him. Then he flips her so she is on top of him with his cock upright in her hand between her legs. He arches his upper back and she keeps going, the skin moving quickly in her palm. He thrusts with his hips and Plum hears him breathing. Sweat pouring off of them. Plum throws back the covers and feels the desert air. She kisses the side of his face to let him know he could keep going as long as he wants even though her hand is starting to cramp. He comes in a huge burst, crying out and gripping her shoulders. She is so relieved that she hardly notices the empty ache between her own legs.

In the morning she opens her eyes in the shadowless flare of light and sees him watching her with the most tender smile all over his face.

"Magic," he says.

She traces her finger along his cheekbone, to his throat, his clavicle. She leans over to kiss him but he pulls away.

"You know, right, Plum, this place is magic?" he says.

"Yes," Then, "You are."

He sits up, drawing the sheet around him. He looks even browner against the white linens. "No, Miss Plum. I'm gay."

She isn't shocked, of course. It's like she's always known. She just hasn't wanted it to be true. He has promised not to go away to school because he loves her. He has come on her belly. It is still sticky there.

"Don't be upset."

"What just happened?"

"I know. I love you. What happened was beautiful. But it's not going to happen again. I didn't mean to hurt you."

She wants to say, but you did hurt me, it's been a year of you hurting me, but she doesn't. Because it isn't really true. He never pretended anything else. Somehow she just didn't want to think, he never kisses me, he wears mascara. What she wants to think is—burning wind, blue pool, neon sign, pink sky, wind chimes, heaving chest, dense muscles, amber skin, avocado sandwich, tango dancers, cutest couple, Villa Milagro. These are the things she wants to hold onto instead.

"Have you been with a guy?"

"No."

"So how do you know?"

"I just do. I've wanted someone so badly. The strange thing is, after what just happened, I'm not afraid now."

Plum thinks about this, isn't quite sure how to take it.

"Not because it wasn't great," he says. "It was so healing. It was like you were comforting me."

She doesn't say anything but she knows that he can see by her eyes that she needs him to comfort her now. He takes her hand and presses his lips to the thin skin. "I'm sorry if I hurt you, Plum."

The love gift, she thinks, is the gift of giving love.

On the drive back they are quiet. The Cadillac doesn't have air conditioning so they leave the windows down and it's too loud to talk much anyway. Plum wants the hot wind to blast her mind, blast away the sand in her throat, obliterate the invisible "S" tattooed on her chest.

"You are going to find him very soon," Plum says, over the wind, after awhile.

This, she is beginning to realize, is her gift.

WILDERLAND
Reina Delacroix

I'm free again. I run across the plain into the wind that whips my ruff against my neck. I brush against the thorny bushes as I lope, to let the sharp branches work loose some matted fur on my shoulder.

The world is full of scent and sound. The pumping musk of a nearby herd of caribou overpowers the tartness of onion grass, and the wind does not quite mask the characteristic clump of their hooves as they move to the riverbank. Summer has come to its full height on the tundra, and my prey are dusty, thirsty, tired and hopefully careless.

The near bend of the river lies over a crest some strides away. I halt, ears pricked to catch the faintest sound of alarm, but they are unaware of my presence. I lower my profile as I stalk to a familiar ledge that overlooks an eddy pool, where it will be easiest for the caribou to drink and cool themselves in the water. I can wait and watch until I sight the weakest among them, which will be my target.

The sun has passed from overhead to halfway towards the mountains that form one border to my territory, opposite to the river boundary I crouch near. I know my prey now. It is a caribou calf which stands on its legs steadily enough but nearly falls as it attempts to trot with other calves. Its mother keeps a close, nervous eye on it. Her instinct tells her I am near, prowling, and her offspring is the most vulnerable of the herd.

But her instinct is not enough to give an alarm.

I wait, patient as a glacier that moves all before it, for the time to strike.

The sun is nearly to the mountains now; the shadows have gotten long and the light plays tricks. While the caribou are more wary as the light dims, the dusklight offers false security. I am ready to strike from the sunside, the wind in my face. I tense my legs, and spring.

The leggy creatures run in all directions, and the calf gets cut off from its mother in the melee. They bleat to find each other, but my nose finds the calf first. As young as it is, it knows my sharp teeth and claws mean death, and it runs from sheer panic. The treacherous legs give out on the muddy ground, and I close quickly, almost too quickly to clamp my jaws on the throat and begin to tear the flesh—

The scenery flashed white twice and a small red mailbox incongruously posted itself to my immediate right. My computer system at home had just received urgent mail. I sighed and, with my juicy prey still struggling in my teeth, swiped the mailbox twice with a clumsy paw.

Everything went black.

A monitor and keyboard warped out of space and surfed to a stop in front of me. Once stabilized, the monitor linked to my visor and the keyboard to my gloves.

Ordinarily I wouldn't interrupt one of my rare sessions in Wilderland, one of the new virtual reality areas in the vast Network, for anything short of actual world emergency. But I needed a job to afford to enter Wilderland, as well as to provide unimportant things like food and shelter, so I had to pay attention to mundane reality.

> to joanna@washline.connect.com
> from kate@netware.amaterasu.com
>
> Just saw your old partner Word Smith in the halls, who mentioned that he has taken a freelance offer from Amaterasu to work on documentation for some of our VR offerings and is looking for help. Apparently we're coming out with upgrades to Tourland, Parkland and Wilderland, and when I mentioned the amount of time you spend logged on to alternate reality his ears pricked

up. So go for it!! (And don't forget who recommended
you—if this works, I expect a victory dinner.)

Oh, Kate, I thought, if you were here I would kiss you, and I'm not
even a lesbian. And Word Smith, too, though I'd have to ask Damask's permission first.

I hesitated to log off Wilderland. The excitement of the chase, the taste
of salt and blood on my tongue as I ripped the throat of the young caribou, tugged at me. It was the land of my dreams, my true self, and I hated
to leave my kill unfinished.

But the storage charges to save a VR program for future return at the
precise moment of exit accumulated in megabytes per millisecond and
mounted all too quickly to ruinous expense. I didn't have that kind of
money to spare, so I pushed aside my regret, consoling myself with the
knowledge that if I got the job, I wouldn't have to exist on tuna fish for
a week to afford an hour a day on Wilderland.

Since Kate worked at Amaterasu, I would be one of the first on the
scent... but this was a prime opportunity and there would be others in
the hunt. I had to hurry. I cancelled the rest of my Wilderland session,
pulled up my resume from storage in my home system, changed my
cover letter date to May 13, 2004, and zapped it to Carter C. Smith at
both his work and home addresses.

Then I stripped off the gloves and unlocked the VR helmet, an all-in-
one assortment of goggles, earphones, and rebreather for rudimentary
scent production. The chaos of Dave's Sight & Sound Arcade assaulted me.
Machine gun rattle, the ping of crossbows and the snackt! of kung-fu
kicks warred with the roar of flamethrowers and sizzle of neon arcs as
some ten-year old destroyed the entire Xannax attacking force.

The owner hastened over to take the equipment from me as if it were
the Golden Helmet of Mambrino rather than fused sand, wires, and a
plastic shell the color of unpainted model airplanes. Dave's plump dark
face glistened with sweat despite the air conditioning.

"Any problem, Joanna?" he said as his nervous hands fiddled with the
input cable and air hose connected to the Network terminal area.

"No, nothing's wrong, Dave."

"I mean, you stopped early, and I was worried maybe the helmet
conked out."

He was a small operator, and the few VR helmets he owned repre-

sented a lot of capital outlay. Yeah, they were reconditioned first-genera-
tion tech from 2001, but the engraved Roman-style VR inside the
Amaterasu sunburst logo attested to their original quality, while the
cheap Pakistani knockoffs already lay in piles of silicon slag in the recy-
cler plants.

"Everything's fine. I just got a message over the board there might be
a job for me."

"Hey, great!" His smile split the grey stubble on his face. "Don't forget to come back and spend time here. You know I'll always give you
what discount I can. I'll even save your favorite helmet for you."

His high school ring rapped on the purple-grey styrene, near the deep
scratch I had given it one day as my reflexes followed the in-helmet
action too enthusiastically and I sprung...only to collide with the casing
of the Intergalactic Wrestling machine.

I grinned at the memory. The thrill of catching my first deer had made
the following day's nasty headache worth it. "That's a lucky helmet for
me. This time I nearly caught a caribou."

"Working up to bigger game, huh? Rabbits aren't enough anymore.
You'll be a Big Bad Wolf any day now, Joanna," he kidded me as he turned
to put the helmet in its locker in the utility closet.

"Hey, it takes a lot to feed a growing timber wolf," I retorted. "They
don't let us wild animals in the corner market, and I haven't figured out
yet how to use my claws to dial for pizza delivery."

I heard him chuckle as I sprinted out the door.

By the time I got home, Word had already skimmed my resume and summoned me to appear at Amaterasu, before he wasted his time interview-
ing anyone else.

He grinned at me as I navigated through the piles of printouts that
mined his office. "I almost didn't recognize you, Jo, you look so strange
in that getup."

I stroked the fabric of my lightweight heather-grey wool suit—colored to set off my copper hair and blue-green eyes, and tailored to fit my
tall, angular body. "This old thing? Oh, I just had it lying around... in case
I was so desperate as to look for work at some place with a dress code.
How've you been, Word?"

"Fine, fine." He ran his slender fingers through hair the color of
maple syrup. We'd kept in touch over the Network since we'd worked

together at Aurora/Phoenix, but I hadn't seen him in some years. He looked great, thinned out a little, brighter-eyed and bushier-tailed than ever.

"Life with Damask suits you."

His hazel eyes greened in intensity. "Jo, I wake up every morning in ecstasy. Damask is everything I ever wanted."

"Good to hear. Where do you wake up, anyway? Last I heard, it was on the floor at the foot of the bed."

He lowered his voice, but his grin widened. "You haven't heard the latest, then. We had a bed specially constructed with a cage hidden underneath. She locks me in there every night. It's wonderful."

"If you don't mind being caged, that is," I retorted.

Word didn't take offense at that, knowing my sense of sarcasm too well. "Hey, I'm a domestic animal, not an untamed creature like you. Belonging to someone is more important to me than being free."

I sighed. "Is it too much to ask for both?"

"Joanna, I'd say you are a hopeless romantic... if I didn't know you'd claw me to shreds for saying it," he added swiftly as I mimed a playful swipe. He swiveled away, the motion a seamless flow into a courtly bow, and the accompanying arm-swing waved me to the only chair in the office that wasn't playing Leaning Tower of Pisa with reams of paper. "Have a seat and I'll go find Darrow—he's the designer/owner of the VR programs, Amaterasu just distributes them for him—to come and meet you. I just need to finish this paragraph."

He bent back to his terminal and busied himself with corrections, muttering curses at the myriad ways techies bent the English language. This familiar scene brought back memories of when Word and I worked together before.

One late night at Aurora/Phoenix we were trying to reconstruct a tech manual that had been translated from Japanese by way of Xhosa, and we ended up drinking sake at 4 AM and playing lawn darts with my beanbag chair. We talked about our dissatisfaction with our "normal" relationships, and I became so boldly drunk I showed him some of my milder erotic fiction.

I had tried to use the jargon of D&s (master, slave, cuffs, whips, etc.) as a metaphor in stories to express my own deeper wild-animal fantasies, but it was an imperfect fit at best. In my stories, slaves were obedient yet proud, and their masters used them in ways that enhanced rather than degraded them.

Word found my lighter fiction much more interesting than I myself did, and shared some of his more traditional sexual-slavery stories with me in return. He also told me about the "D-ring-nets," the Dominance/submission computer networks MasSlaNet and Dungeonmasters, with their dozens of sideboards on specific sexual fantasies—bondage, foot worship, piercing, and the like.

I had never dreamed there might be others out there as imprinted with childhood dreams as I had been, and the leap of hope I felt frightened me. I was not as resigned to my solitude as I had hoped; part of me was still a social animal.

We were just drunk enough that night to dare each other to post our latest works on the nets; once we sobered up, our skewed senses of humor helped us enjoy even the most pathetic and/or obnoxious of our correspondents.

My lighter sex-stories brought some inquiries, but none sparked my interest in return and my replies were polite but negative. My one attempt at something deeper was called "Speaking in Tongues," a story about a werewolf enslaved by a human, filled with violent sex and sexy violence. "Speaking" sank into the nets without a trace, and I never knew if anyone had even read it.

In contrast, Word got lucky within a week and connected with Damask, a tall dominant woman who resembled the twentieth century singer Cher. His intense involvement with her made my own failure to connect with anyone all the more painful, and I split up our partnership to freelance.

Discouraged, I dropped off the public nets completely and narrowed my life to the point of isolation. I worked enough to get by, but my internal world was more compelling than anything outside me... until I found out about Wilderland.

Touted as an alternative to actual wilderness trips for the disabled (or just plain lazy), Wilderland hooked me when I discovered it would allow me to discard my human persona and assume an animal one. My wolf skin fit far better than my human one ever had.

Still, it was a lonely pleasure; even in Wilderland, it seemed, I could not belong to a "pack." In two years, I had never seen another wolf, and I wondered if that was a design in the system, to prevent competition between "players," or just another example of my independent nature subverting my conscious desire.

Or was it as simple as no one else, anywhere, wanted to become a wolf?

Sometimes at sunset, I sat in the high grass above my lair in the mud-brown foothills near the border mountains, and raised my muzzle and howled again and again, in protest at my bitter isolation, and in quest of an answering cry.

Was what drifted down from the peaks then just an echo, or another of my kind straining its voice to reach me through the thin air?

I looked up at that moment to meet a pair of grey eyes set in the unblinking stare of a mature wolf, flat and wary, but curious. I shook my head to clear the cobweb lure of Wilderland memories, but the eyes were still there. They belonged to a thin, loose-jointed man in his mid-twenties, with unruly rust-brown hair and the broad cheekbones of a Native American, who stood in the doorway and watched me while Word's voice rose from its murmur in greeting.

"Darrow, I was just about to get you. This is Joanna McDonnell. Joanna, Darrow Northwalker."

The eyes didn't blink, didn't move, didn't react; he simply stared at me. I suppose I should have been self-conscious, even uncomfortable, under that silent gaze. But I felt no threat from him, only a sense of recognition as he considered me.

So this was the architect of my desire!

"Welcome," he barked, and then the door was empty.

I raised my eyebrows at Word. "Does he always behave that way?"

He shrugged. "Sometimes Darrow can be harder to interpret than his code... but I think that means you're hired."

While my job at Amaterasu helped my bank balance, the day-to-day contact with other people had the unfortunate effect of transmuting my manageable aloneness into not-so-tractable loneliness.

One Friday the scent of Darrow's prized deerskin jacket, dampened by a sudden shower, made both my mouth and eyes water. I felt stirrings in my crotch that even Wilderland could not help me ignore. Though I found Darrow intriguing, I had always followed the time-honored tradition of "not shitting where I ate," or more prosaically, not dating in my workplace. So I went to a human hunting ground.

Squares was a well-attended gathering place for computer folk in Seattle. The owner, a former programmer, designed it to appeal to the computer-friendly: an abundance of video monitors and game machines, free outlets and cables for those who wouldn't leave home without their laptops, networked glassed-over tabletops for those who would.

Eventually I made my selection. Marshall was a technophile, rather than an actual "techfreak" like me. He worked in the marketing department at my old place, Aurora/Phoenix; though our times there didn't overlap, we knew a lot of the same people. He said he liked to hang out with the computer geeks after work as well—told me he found them "creative."

That statement, coupled with his fawn-brown hair, lanky body and a tentative quality I had always found appealing in men, made him a promising target. I cut him neatly out of his group, suggesting we go back to his place because it was closer.

His condo was sterile, like a laboratory. It had bandage-white walls, polyurethaned pine floors, and wire-frame Scandinavian furniture. Everything was so clean I could almost smell the reek of disinfectant. Even his New Age makeout music sounded thin, empty, with no meat coating its synthesized bones. And, in the best tradition of lust-crazed mad-scientists, Marshall liked to experiment in bed... but only in an acrobatic sense. His idea of variety was to change positions every few minutes, and if he'd owned something so ornate as a chandelier, I'm sure he would have suggested we swing from it.

I did come, twice, as he took me from behind, my pubic bone pressed by his athletic strokes into a bunching of the corduroy bedspread, and I bit the pillow to muffle my howls. Yet it was mere mechanics—my wild spirit remained untouched.

He, on the other hand, was impressed with what (to him) were our sexual pyrotechnics, and began to plan future dates with a satisfied smirk.

His assumptions made me feel trapped. I snapped at him, he lashed back instinctively, and the resulting shrewishness reminded me why I didn't try getting laid very often.

His parting kick at me, as I walked out the door, was, "You bitch, you were just using me to masturbate!"

As I trotted the twelve misty blocks to my home, I began to laugh. Marshall was right; of course I had used him (though the same comment could be applied to him as well). But I had been a fool, to imagine that some civilized and hygienic human could ever be the kind of lover my fantasies demanded.

Footsore and heartweary, I unlocked the door to my basement efficiency. I didn't bother with the overhead switch; the glow-in-the-dark stars on the ceiling cast enough light for me to make my way to bed.

"Bed" consisted of a tangle of pillows, blankets, and thrift-store furs over an area equivalent to a full-size mattress. I crawled into them, and reached under the pillow backrest in the far corner for my collection of playtoys. I kept them in the beaded canvas parfleche which I had hand-crafted long ago in my Indian lore class, a neat package which my fingers could untie and unfold from memory.

My tail was a small latex butt plug with a padded wire affixed to the flange end by epoxy; knotted into the padding were hundreds of horse-hairs. I slathered the plug with lubricant and pushed it into my asshole so that it would swish from side to side as I twitched my rear.

The scene had to smell right, so I sprayed musk oil from the small crystal atomizer into the air, onto the covers, and finally onto my fingers so I could paint the oil into my cheek hollows.

I stroked my tail to disperse the last of the scent from my hands. The kind of lubricant that I used on the plug warmed up over time, and I could almost feel musk glands burning where the tail joined the spine.

Next came the "wolf paws," modeled as realistically as possible by wrapping rabbit fur around a dowel. I had carved their claws from horse hoof clippings I found sold in a pet store as dog chews. I grasped them with my hands and laid back in the pile of cushions, imagining it a bed of pine needles and spongy moss. I rolled in it, and the dampness of the soil beneath matted my coat. The paws caressed my chest and teats, claws raising red streaks on my skin until I whimpered, dropped them, and rolled over onto all fours.

I rammed the inflatable butt plug into my cunt and pumped it with the valve closed, so it steadily expanded inside me. This simulated the "tie" when the wolf's cock balloons inside the bitch and locks them together. My lips and interior walls were still slick with a combination of condom lubricant and lingering arousal, so the imitation cock penetrated me without resistance, but it wouldn't lock in place until it distended my cunt well past the normal inch in diameter. The pressure was so strong that I could not close my legs completely.

As I reached for the hair clips that I used to imitate bites, I braced myself for the weight of the other wolf's body and rolled onto my side to snap at him.

Teeth nip my neck, my teats, my haunches, and I writhe with the pleasure of being filled. I roll and roll, to one side and the other, but I cannot shake him loose, nor do I really want to. It is simply part of the battle that is mating.

Back on all fours, I arch my back and hang my head in submission. As I raise my muzzle to his, I see a pair of grey eyes set in the unblinking stare of a mature wolf, flat and wary.

Gods! I know those eyes, even in fantasy.

The brindled wolf has me trapped and pinned; I bare my teeth and loose a howl that I cannot stop. Darrow curls around me, licking and caressing me, as I quiver, spasm and jerk into unconsciousness.

That weekend I holed up in my lair, knowing better than to go outside in my out-of-control state. Every time I woke from my fitful sleep I was possessed, physically and mentally, by Darrow in the guise of a wolf. I wore the inflatable plug all weekend, removing the tail plug only when I had to defecate. I kept a rubber sheet and paper towels in an unused corner of my bathroom for times like this, when my wolf nature consumed me. Feeling the piss trickle around my swollen cunt as I raised one leg over the absorbent material, my eyes watered and my cunt burned and even before the last drop had passed I had my legs in the air and one hand rubbing my slit raw.

I lost track of the hours I played with myself, the times I came. But I could not lose those eyes.

I tapped the final keystroke. "Finally. The manual for Parkland Two is done, finished, gone, out of here. Hurry up and print it, before that perfectionist comes up with another 'just one more' feature."

Word shook his head, his hands plunged into the entrails of our balky printer. "Not yet, Jo. I need ten more minutes to fix this, twenty minutes with the final diagrams, and another fifteen to produce the camera copy. At minimum."

"Forty-five minutes?" It was past midnight as it was. "Darrow might revise the whole system in forty-five minutes, Word, unless we tell him we're done with this manual and any other changes have to wait until the next version."

"Go distract him, then," sighed my exasperated partner. "Get him talking about Wilderland; he hasn't discussed it yet with me and we ought to get started on it tomorrow. You're good at getting shy people to talk."

I snorted. "The man of monosyllables? He isn't shy; he's downright closemouthed. Especially about Wilderland."

"Then take him out for Chinese food—bring me back some while you're at it. Anything. Just get me forty-five—" a loud snap issued from a newly broken gear in the printer. "Better make it at least an hour. Go!" he yelled, "before something else goes wrong."

I trotted out the door and down the hall to Darrow's office. He didn't answer my knock, so I pushed the door open slowly.

He lay curled on the floor, the VR helmet locked around his head. I rushed to him and shook his shoulder, worried that he had fainted.

He flew awake and, disoriented, clawed at me. I backed off immediately. His chest heaved for a moment, and then he unlocked the helmet and threw it off to the side as if freeing himself from a leg-trap.

His eyes were dark, dazed and wild.

My arms burned where he had touched me. I backed away farther, forcing normal breaths to calm myself.

"I'm sorry, Darrow. I thought something was wrong."

"Sometimes I sleep like that," he said, and tossed his hair back out of his eyes. It wasn't an apology, just a flat statement.

"I wanted to tell you that we're printing the manual for Parkland now." A little white lie never hurt anyone. "Word asked me to check and see if you had had dinner."

"Yes—I mean no." His smile twitched. "Not in real time."

I motioned to the helmet. "There?" He nodded. "Where were you?" I asked, curious.

His eyes flattened at my question, a sign I had seen often in the two months we'd worked together. Whatever it was, he didn't want to talk about it, and I didn't want to press him when he looked to be finally opening up a little. "Never mind, Darrow. Are you hungry? The Golden Lion up the street is open until one."

He glanced at the clock, then the window. "It's past midnight? I had no idea."

"It's easy to lose track of time in Wilderland," I said deliberately, to see if I could get a reaction. "Perhaps in the next version you should include clocks on the trees."

His instinctive response was, "Animals can't read clocks," and then he caught himself. His eyes turned to shifting, yet impenetrable, smoke. "You know that time doesn't matter in Wilderland," he challenged me in return. "Carter says you journey a lot in there."

"The sorry state of my bank account will confirm that," I replied, as I picked up the helmet and handed it to him.

He smiled ruefully as he turned it in his thick, short-fingered hands. "I put a good dent in it this time." He displayed a pyramid-shaped pockmark where it had clipped the corner of his desk in its flight. "Hope I didn't break it."

I snorted. "That's nothing compared to the gouge in the one I use at the arcade, where I crashed into a game machine cabinet. Trust me, Amaterasu helmets are indestructible."

He tilted the helmet up, checked the viewscreen, and nodded. "Good, because this is the best of the third-generation prototypes, and the engineers will have my hide if I break it before they get a working copy."

He slid open the security locker and began to place the helmet with reverence in its raggedly-cut foam cushion. Then he glanced at me. "Did you really say you've been using Wilderland from an arcade?"

"Yeah, my pusher—I mean supplier—is Dave at Dave's Sight and Sound. He has a TacBoard link to the main system, and reconditioned VR 130 helmets."

He exaggerated his wince. "Not only expensive, but clumsy like an ox to boot. Look, why don't you use the system now, while I'm not on it? If you're that familiar with Wilderland One, you can document the changes I've made already. And maybe you'll have some suggestions for Version Two. It's hard for me to be objective—I'm too close to it."

"If you're not afraid I'll break your helmet..." I kidded.

"I'll make sure to tell the engineers it was your fault," he replied, handing over the helmet. "I'll go fetch some food for Carter, and then—not that I don't trust either of you—but I want to proofread that manual. I might have some changes..."

I groaned. "Somehow I knew you were going to say that. You can do whatever you want, Darrow, but I'm going to get some sleep. I can't work all day and howl all night, like some programmers I know."

He grinned, showing his teeth. "Before he left my mother and me in Ottawa, to return to his tribe, my father taught me a basic rule of the wilderness during our outdoor trips: Nap when you can."

"At TacBoard rates, I've never been able to afford to nap."

The grin widened. "Then try it. Waking up in Wilderland is very restful, and really intensifies the experience."

As if I needed that! I decided dinner could wait as I trotted back to my office and its VR interface with the helmet clutched in my hand.

No moon yet, but starlight burns in every direction. The crickets sing in the low lands as I climb, ears pricked and aware. The grass is dry, and the storm it desires but a distant rumble beyond the high ridges.

I seek another wolf, no longer a phantom echo of my voice but a separate—therefore real—presence. The notes ring out this time on their own, scaling low to high, then dropping into a moan. I hear howls in the mountains, mournful, aching, desirous, calling me, and I go.

Up into the black sky I climb, as the moon rises past the river. I come closer to the sound, stepping along narrow ridges of sheared, weather-blunted slate, eyes watchful for a glimpse of shadowy fur or the gleam of eyes in the silver light.

My fur bristles as all my attention focuses on the guiding whine: less than a thousand strides, I judge. I creep forward.

Silence. The howl has stopped. Frustrated, I raise up and launch all my breath into one long reply, a single downward trail from high-muzzle to low-throat.

The underbrush explodes, paws crashing in a panicked flight. Once again I have noise to follow, and I begin to close on the other wolf, who will have to run through a low, narrow cut in the ridges to gain the snowline.

I make the overhang of the cut in time, but before I can gather my feet under me, a flash of fur streaks by, nose held high. Its tail, held at level, almost brushes my own nose with its fur. I spring, but miss, and sprawl on the lichenous ground as my ears hear the fade of his retreat and his smell lingers in my nose.

The system became a ghostly gray, a superimposition against the sightless black interior of my helmet, and then Darrow glared at me. I had dozed off inside the prototype he'd loaned me, so he had to be using one of the other helmets. I could see a ghostly image of a wolf surrounding his human form, braced to defend his territory.

"So it was you I've been hearing at night," he accused. "How did you get in here, anyway? You're not supposed to be here."

The sensation of lost breath, after my fall, had not yet left me, and his tone made me angry. "What do you mean, how did I get in here? I went into TUNDRA and typed TIMBER WOLF at the selection box, like I always do."

"But that's impossible!" he shouted. "I'm the only wolf in here. There aren't even many human visitors in TUNDRA. It's not 'popular' enough; they stick to the safe, familiar temperate areas."

"I didn't know it was impossible when I did it," I interjected, as the adrenaline rush of the chase lessened and my sense of humor returned. "And as far as other wolves go, why should you hog all the fun?"

He ignored me, absorbed in the wiggle of his fingers in mid-air—a pixel-mapped duplication of touch-typing hands on a keyboard only he could view.

"The point is, Joanna, you shouldn't have been able to select TIMBER WOLF in the first place, not even from my helmet. It's not on the menu list." His fingers tapped away as he glowered at me.

"Oh, that not-on-the-menu bit is easy to explain, Darrow: I can't stand them. I've seen enough systems now that I just use the selection box and type in what I want."

"You went outside the menu?" He looked horrified.

"Never even looked at it," I admitted with a cheerful grin. "Users aren't all sheep, Darrow. We don't always follow the rules you programmers set up. Besides, you know what they always say."

"What?" he snarled, intent on his typing.

I had caught him unawares, and sprung the oldest line in the computer worker's jokebook to try to make him laugh. "It's not a bug, it's an undocumented feature."

His subvocal growl made my hair bristle. His earlier friendliness to me had completely vanished. "Well, this is one feature you won't be using anymore. I've put in a password to keep you and any other hackers from trying this little trick in the future."

I couldn't imagine why he was so angry with me. "Wait! Darrow, I've been looking for this place all my life. I didn't know this was a private dream of yours. But don't you see, we share the same dream!"

His feral grin was ugly, like that of a little boy hit moments before in the mouth with a rock. "Oh, I doubt that. You're just another one of those romantics idolizing the natural state, thinking it's cute to roam through the woods. Well, it's not really very romantic being a wolf, Jo. This isn't a dream on my part: it's my real life. I've been half-frozen, and starving, and injured, and fought my way through it because that's what wolves do: survive.

"I gave up expecting you humans to understand me years ago. All I ask is that you leave this particular wolf out of your plans to shape the wilderness to your own ends, please."

He stopped for a moment, out of breath. He had just dug up for me my own gnawed bones of discomfort and discontent, the hurt of those years and years of uneasily buried feeling: I am the only one of my kind, and no one will ever understand.

If I'd been thinking, I wouldn't have said the absolute wrong thing to him then.

"And Wilderland isn't shaping the wilderness to your ends?"

Trying to show our similarities, I had flung too much indigestable truth at him. He either had to deny it, or deny the purity of his motives.

He turned tail to flee.

"Wait! You can't just shut me out like this!"

"No? Watch me." He whirled, as swiftly as the west wind of Wilderland twisted mica dust at nightfall. The grey twinkled to black, like a shake of fur rolled in the dust, and he was gone.

I logged off and swore as my copper hair caught in the helmet. The empty feeling in the pit of my stomach reminded me of my missed dinner, so I wandered down to the employee cafeteria to force down some breakfast.

But the empty feeling refused to leave politely; filling my stomach with food didn't drive it away at all.

I had lost Wilderland, or at least that part of it I knew and loved.

What had Darrow been afraid of?

When I got back to my office, I found out.

The helmet I had left was gone. For that matter, so were all the prototypes, and all the background papers and disks, and oh yes, Darrow as well.

Word, still very much present, and not so much angry as querulous, was more than ready to tell me his side of the story.

"Now let me get this straight, Word. You complimented him on his Grand Canyon and he got mad at you?" The morning sun made my eyes hurt.

Word sighed. "Nearly bit my head off. Said he would rather have done Canada's Nahanni. 'I'm more familiar with it, and its canyons make that overrated hole in the ground look shabby. But they wanted well-known, American parks.'

"So I tried to reason with him. 'Amaterasu has to think of what will be most popular,' I argued. 'Perhaps it's just as well you didn't do Nahanni. Maybe the average Parkland users wouldn't appreciate it the way you do.'"

Poor Word! Considering how protective Darrow was of his creations, I was surprised only that his throat was intact enough to tell the tale.

I shuddered. "Of course they wouldn't. I suspect Darrow would have a very... unique perspective on Nahanni and would hate to see it misused. You would have hit quite a nerve with that statement."

"Did I ever! Darrow gave me this spooked look, and said in a really bitter tone, 'You may be right at that, Carter. If I did Isle Royale, I bet they'd want the wolves to act like dogs and come when called.' And then he stalked out."

I felt much as if an elk had kicked me in the stomach with its powerful hindquarters. Had Darrow seen me as little better than a tamed dog? No wonder he condemned me without bothering to listen.

"I saw him later in his office, but he was in VR, so I assumed he was working and left him alone. Then I went back to his office half an hour ago and he'd cleaned out everything like he'd never been there."

Another hoof thumped soundly into my stomach, as I thought of my ill-timed attempt to show Darrow our common ground. "What about the programs?"

"Oh, they're still mounted on his system. Mr. Secretive had already put up Wilderland Two without telling us, so we can work on the documentation for some time while Amaterasu transfers it to the public system." He punched me playfully in the arm. "So don't look so worried, Jo—we're still employed."

"What about Darrow? Will Amaterasu go after him?"

Word shrugged. "Why should they? Everything they wanted him to do right now is done. Far as they're concerned, he can be as eccentric and unsociable as he wants to be and they won't bother him, because if he's unhappy he'll just take his programs back when the contract ends in a few months."

And I had delivered the very speech that made that once-remote possibility highly likely. Had I no hope of ever getting near him, or seeing Wilderland again?

I chewed that thought over during both the rest of the day at work, and the long walk back to my apartment. If I chased him, it would scare him farther off; he was not prey that would freeze in fear, after all, but a mature predator.

An elusive, skittish wild animal may be lured near humans, but Darrow was now a frightened, if not angry, wolf who trusted nothing that smelled of the human world.

On the other hand, I recalled Word once describing his pursuit of Damask—quite the mature predator herself—as "chasing her until she caught me." So I logged onto the nets and did a little research on the characteristics and habitat of the elusive Darrow Northwalker, hoping for some inspiration.

Even congenital loners leave some tracks in the electronic forest. In reading about his parents (father Red Lake Chippewa, mother English Canadian, divorced and both dead before he reached majority), his past (rootlessly misfit, almost a mirror of mine) and his present (unmarried and very much active on the Nets), I found my plan.

I uploaded "Speaking in Tongues" out of my archives and, while leaving my real name and date written on it, e-mailed it to all of Darrow's online accounts. The email's subject line contained the only words I thought might tempt him to read it rather than just hitting the delete key: *Mah een gun*, "timber wolf" in his father's native language.

The trap was baited with something juicy: would he bite?

Dave hurried out of the air-conditioned office as I walked into the arcade two weeks later. "Jo! Long time no see. Listen, thanks a lot for getting your friends at Amaterasu to pick my place to test those new helmets. The kids are crazy about them."

I almost said "What new helmets?" but I was so stunned my tongue froze. What he held up to me so proudly was the third-generation VR 330, and I knew they weren't in general production yet.

I hadn't sent them, but I had a good idea who did.

"The use of my VR system has gone up ten times in the last week!" The arcade owner was ecstatic. He would gain not only increased business from the new helmets, but increased prestige—and the two elements often pursued each other into an upward spiral of success.

"So, are you so busy that there's no room for me?"

Dave sputtered. "Joanna, I owe all this to you. I got one helmet reserved solely for you, in a padded and soundproofed booth no less... so you don't crash into any more of my machines, of course."

He motioned me into a 6 x 8 plywood booth that nestled between the Network machine and his office. "You ought to put a lock on the door, so the person in VR won't be interrupted," I pointed out.

He nodded distractedly as he plugged the cables and rebreather into the jacks set into the booth wall. "I've been so busy I just haven't gotten around to it," he said, with a guilty glance at the utility closet that held his toolchest.

He handed me the helmet and gloves. "When I talked with the guy who installed everything, he said this helmet was special to you."

I didn't have to look; my finger found the distinctive pyramidal dent in the helmet he handed me. "It is," I breathed, and strapped myself in without hesitation.

It smelled like a trap, but it was a trap I had to enter. Darrow wouldn't have gone to all the trouble and expense of giving Dave the helmets without a reason. I trusted his vision—our shared vision—and my heart rose in anticipation.

The first box opened immediately.

CHOOSE DOMAIN>

and I typed in TUNDRA X

The next box opened in the darkness.

CHOOSE PROJECTION> TIMBER WOLF

And I ENTER Wilderland.

The rain pelts down; mingled with it are sharp cold pellets of hail that sting even through the thick winter fur I have yet to shed. It is early, very early spring on the mountainside, but the storm strikes with all the leaf-lashing fury of the rolling thunderclouds that threaten and bluster in summer.

I fight the wind to climb the mountain and follow the trail. My nose sniffs each clump of dirt, desperate to hold to the scent.

I gain the ridge and find fresh spoor, barely an hour old, in the pine groves. I cover each urination with my own mark. If Darrow retraces his path, he will smell me. I will not sneak up on him and frighten him, but make my presence known as widely and vocally as possible.

I feel stronger and heavier than before, and I notice as I pee that the stain is more pungent than last fall—signs of maturity driven home by the taste of blood as I nuzzle my crotch in investigation. A sign that Wilderland is coming of age.

The rain seems endless in its vigor and intensity, but it lessens to a steady drizzle as I approach the clearing of the rabbits. The scent of Darrow is especially strong here. Various intensities of marking, and dozens of muddy prints, give me a clear image of the other wolf pacing, howling, and rolling in the grip of strong emotions.

I lift my muzzle and howl. I am prepared to do this as long as my throat holds out, but almost at once an answer comes from upwind and uphill. It rises, in a mixture of surprise and happiness, and I hear the invitation in it: "Join me!"

I bound joyfully towards the direction of the reply, and find myself on the banks of the rapids. The other wolf stands on the far bank, and we look at each other, across the chasm that separates us.

He barks in greeting, and makes for a fallen tree upstream that spans the rapids by less than his shoulderheight. He is more surefooted on the rain-drenched trunk than I would trust myself to be in this unfamiliar weight and size, and I settle on my haunches to wait for him.

A tangle of branches, mud and small rocks swells the river at a bend above the tree. Flash-flood! I bark in warning, but he cannot hear me over the crash of the rapids.

Even as the dirty water smashes the tree and engulfs him, I spring forward into the dark flood. I hear a frightened yip as he paddles to keep his head above water, then silence. I swim into the flood towards the last sound. Everything is swirling and collapsing in the green-brown froth atop the river.

A thump-splash of a wet, furry body against mine, and I sink my teeth into him to hold on while I strike out for where I think the shore is. The soil of the banks erodes under my feet as I scramble, burdened with Darrow's weight, to climb out of the raging river.

Then I feel him twitch with life and scrabble with his paws on the slick slate just underwater, finding toeholds under his own power. I unlock my jaws thankfully, and my four paws push my weary body onto safe ground.

Our skins have cuts from jagged rocks and splintered branches, but they are surface wounds. Too cold and tired even to clean ourselves, we curl together into a small hollow on the north edge of the rabbit clearing. It offers some shelter from the sleeting wind as the eye of the storm moves southward and the backlash begins.

There, we sleep, nose to tail for warmth, as the winds howl.

I awaken in the quiet night to the soft caress of a cool nose, and hot tongue, under my tail. The glands around my anus ooze an oily yellow scent that he licks eagerly.

His hind feet cuff my head as if we are cubs playing together. But we are full-grown now, and the childish gesture takes on new meaning. I slap his feet away with a lazy paw, and roll over so that I can press my muzzle to his in submission.

He whines as I butt my nose against the short fur of his snout—unsure, even with instinct full in him, whether I am his mate. He leaps out of our shelter into the moonlight, droplets of silver flying from his fur as he quivers and shakes in tension.

I follow, determined that he shall not leave me behind again. Once more I croon to his muzzle, pushing so hard that the lip bares the teeth, begging him to accept what I am—no, to accept what we are.

He moves away again, but not as swiftly as before. It is not a rejection, but rather his disbelief that our desire may run along the same trail. He is afraid to trust me.

I roll my shoulders into the matted needles of the clearing, to expose my throat and belly to him. From my upside-down view, it is as if I look at a reflection of Darrow in a still pool, outlined against the black sky and crowned with a few bright stars. The moon over his shoulder dusts his ruff with glimmers of white and silver.

He edges closer, wary and shy, expecting me at any moment to rear up and snap at him. I remain still, even when his breath is hot on my throat, his bared teeth one easy bite away from my death.

He nuzzles awkwardly along my throat and ruff, the increasingly insistent pressure a sign that I should stand.

He backs away a few steps, and mimics my former position on the ground, as he presents his vulnerable areas to me in turn. He bares himself to me, terrified and hopeful, his longing plain to eye and ear as the short pants of his breath heave his slender flanks. His eyes are round and a soft pleading whimper beckons me closer, closer, so that I smell his fear and desire together.

Nose, throat, ribs, belly, penis and anus all receive my gentle lick of the tongue, as I taste the savage flavor of my new mate.

Since I did not attack him, he grows bolder now and springs up to put his paws on my shoulders, pressing me flat against the ground. I feel his penis shove against my tail, and I twitch it aside so that he can mount more easily. His nose is wet against my ears as his hind legs press forward and he enters me. A gush of hot fluid comes immediately, along with the swelling tie that will bind us together physically for some time. (But time does not matter in Wilderland, I remember Darrow once saying.) He jets, and jets, and jets, and we whine and whimper in the joy of our union.

As I unstrap the helmet in the dimly-lit booth I feel how I am drenched with sweat, and my panties are soaked in my own overflow of musk. "But it's not real," I whisper to myself, forcing a return to reality while my whole body screamed to return to my wolf self. Never had I felt so alone; never had I longed more for my imagination to be real.

"It's as real as we are," came a voice from just behind me.

Shy wolf eyes peered into mine, glinting red in the glow from the monitors. I smelled pine, and musk, and machine oil, and semen, as a trembling paw—hand—brushed my hair away from my neck. From Darrow's other hand dropped my old helmet, its cable plugged into a second jack hidden under a lip of the padding.

Caught.

STATE
M. Christian

The building floated on Kyushu harbor. Once part of a sprawl of temporary industrial units meant for a Korean-owned nanochip factory, now forgotten like an obsolete power tool, it had been stuck on a shelf and left to rust. As far as Fields knew—and could see—rust still really managed the property. Rumor said that Mama had scored the old building for cheap and found some hungry jacks to scalp juice from the main grid. And the girls? They came from wherever lost girls always came from: the cramps of hunger or addiction, the Devil of father. They came and Mama fed them, sprayed them when they were sick, and put that rusting roof over their heads. In return, they worked.

Friday nights weren't usually so busy. Tonight there were rumbles from Mama's office that Fields might be called down from her box to work the cribs with the pie-faced girls. But someone asked for the special of the house so she was spared watching the ordinary flatscreen with the rest of the girls. She was the special, so she had a while to get ready, time enough to watch the end of Don't Drop It (her favorite) on the antique Hakati tank—and yum!—relish the show's new host.

The Hakati took a long time to power-down, and she felt that thrill-tingle of worry that some client would come in and see the spray/wash/float of green/blue/red hanging in front of the cheap holo

35

print of Tokyo At Night that hid the unit and would ponder a bit too long over why a Mitsui Automaton was watching a game show.

The streets, and common knowledge, said that Autos took a while to power up, boot up their software, get their circuits warm and ready—though never really willing: the perfect love doll. The perfect toy. The real fact was that it took Fields time to get completely into her Act.

Her friendly gray robe went first, into the hidden closet behind the false wall of phony blinking tell-tales and dummy flatscreens playing loops of technical gibberish. The robe hung on a hook next to the rest of her reality: vid discs, street clothes, wigs, pills, towels, creams, sprays, and plain-faced bottles of special dye.

Very special dye, she applied the binding polymer each morning. Incredibly durable stuff, but she always examined every inch of herself in a roll-up plastic mirror, lathering on the thick blueness at the faintest signs of her real pinkness, before the light over the door flashed green. Her hair, every brown strand, was months gone—and kept at an imperceptible level by a chilling spray of tailored enzymes. Sure, she could wear any of her wigs, and sometimes did for those who couldn't handle a too-inhuman Automaton, but for the most part she liked going smooth and streamlined: they paid for the machine. And her little yellow hexagon pills had about another two hours to go—her skin texture and temperature would be just that different. Not quite human, but almost machine synthetic. Anyone, of course, who knew the real Mitsui would know the reality of pink skin-and-blood Fields under the blue, behind the contacts, beyond the re-engineered body. But then the Autos were very rare, their legends and rumors huge, and who would know the real thing in the dim shadows of big, sprawling, bad Kyushu?

Fields' body was a gift from Mama, really an investment: those long days two years ago with the Osaka Scalpers had taken what nature had lucked her with and shaped her into an almost perfect Auto Class B—still one of Mitsui's most popular models. Strong shoulders, round face with high, almost too-wide-for-nature cheekbones, tiny, pert, full lips, huge crystal blue eyes, high, wide and moderate tits, huge against her small frame, with aggressively large nipples—some of it was really hers, some was machine made for her machine act. Her looks, real or made, would be good and profitable as long as the real unit was State-of-the-Art . . . and the rumors of how good, and how hot, kept flying.

Fields' cortical jack was a gift from Sammi, now long gone. His gift of matched wetdreams through cheap Kobe scalp implants was also gone, one quick brain-trip with the tall and lean New Tokyo hustler had been enough for the pre-teen Fields—spasms of her riding him, his impression of nothing-but-sex nothing-but-sex and her always on fucking top running/stomping all over her images of that one time, that one good time, at that Osaka shrimp stick stand when he had just smiled at her oh so special. The jack was the one and only thing that really remained of him. It was important to the Act, so she kept it polished and in good repair. The clients knew, if they knew anything, that no one had shrunk the hardware for the Autos enough for them to be self-supporting. They expected and got her—Regulation Blue, hairless, eyes also blue but without irises, slightly cool, perfect little ass, perfection tits, and trailing her braid of cables: a love-doll lifted from a Japanese collective consciousness, a manga sex-toy—all eyes and ass and tits and mouth and cunt. Pure fantasy, rolled off the assembly line to a male libido's factory specs. Her body was flesh, tricked by drugs and chemicals—the jack on the crown of her head was real, the line was dead, but she was still State: the perfect whore, the perfect trick, perfect in her Act.

And, god knew, she liked it. Like it a lot—

The tank's fountain of basic colors died, and with it Fields' ritualistic fear of discovery. She sat on the stool, made sure one last time that she was jacked into the dead line, and that her breathing was cool and calculated. Mama buzzed her as she was supposed to, that the client was coming up the stairs.

Green light over the door.

He was nice. She had been there, in that maze of old modular sheeting and drop-in offices, long enough to know it. That night, that Friday, she was tingling with work lust, and she liked it. Don't Drop It had that great new host, the one that rang of Sammi, her Tokyo hustler, when he was cruising and straight, and she had enjoyed a quick little jill while watching—running a blue finger up and down her little blue slit, bathing her blue pearl with her own juice. No cry, no come, not enough time for that. But a trembling thrill up and down her, up from her blue pussy, vibrating her back and jigging her leg. She was wet for the client, always wet for him (Mama schooling), but she was going to be really wet for this one.

And he was going to be a good one. Mama school and her years there clicked through her as he opened the door and came in. Shy and kind of reserved. He looked everywhere but where she sat on her stool in all her blueness, the Act full blown: a square room, walled with semi-transparent white plastic, bare save for the stool, a simple futon, one wall the brains of the Mitsui Automaton (closet, bathroom, etc.), and the "Unit" itself sitting on that black and chrome stool waiting for the Job—almost lifeless, almost perfectly human (Regulation Blue, so if they should impossibly break free they could never pass), waiting to do just what you wanted. Anything. At all. Your heart's desire, your cock's (and sometimes clit's) desire.

She stood up and took a neutral position, making sure her legs were just-so parted enough so he could see her blue slit and the dot of her blue clit. Her nipples were hard from her near-jill and Mama school, and she knew her scent was filling his nostrils. Perfectly lifelike. Perfect imitation of a machine that was supposed to be better-than-lifelike.

He was a surprise. A type, but still a surprise. Away from the Company tour, maybe? Shy and inside about this, maybe not wanting to be seen with the rest of his Contacts diving into perfumed pools and being given tepid blowjobs by bored/hungry girls? What better way to do the same without the examining eyes: find someone who didn't care, who couldn't shoot him down with a bat of dull, professional eyes.

"Stand up and come here." Stone, gravelly, deep. Young, yeah, but childish, no way.

As Fields stood and walked, in that special loose-hipped caricature that the Autos walked, she took better stock of Johnny. He was youngish, maybe mid-thirties. His synthetic suit was simple and professional. The tie, though, was real silk and the scenario changed. And the tone, the strength, the gravel: maybe he was one of the managers, out to do something special with someone who couldn't complain or say no... to anything.

She didn't believe it possible, but Fields got wetter. She liked it rough and fast and maybe metal-tinged dangerous when she liked it. And she was in the mood, anyway.

"And how can I please you, sir?" It had taken her a while to get the voice right: just enough of a non-inflection. Mama School. The Medicos. And something that was just part of the Act.

The programs were varied, and rumors circulated. The Units, the Autos were soft and hardwired to be the best, they could surprise you, so Fields was loose in her Act. Without waiting for his commands, she got up and walked to him, listening to her cables sing across the futon. A tinge of fear again: maybe he suspected, maybe the dye was wearing thin, maybe he knew the real thing. But he didn't move, just let her come forward, drop to her knees and breathe on the tent of his pants. "Will you allow me to pleasure you?"

He shook his head and moved past her to sit on the stool. "Come here—" patting the fine synthetic of his suit leg.

The tone was just right and the Act reached beyond even Fields to click her into it. Like a dancer who knows the right moves to get from one end of the stage to the other, Fields moved her head just so to untangle the trailing decorative umbilicus, a debutante's hair toss, a flirt's bat of shaved eyebrows, and a step, walking an invisible line to get her hips and bare breasts enough of a sway. Her lip got jutted: impertinent and pouty, her hands ran through her non-existent hair and, instead, tugged a bit on the cables to make sure they didn't grab or snag. Across the room now, in front of the Client now, she stuck a finger under her chin, lowered her eyes and shuffled her feet.

She made a move to make a noise ("Daddy?") but caught it in her throat at the lights in his eyes, the firm tent in his finer pants. The Act had her then, and it had him. His fire and need leaped the gap as she moved closer, putting him into her heat—letting it wash over him.

"Come here," he said, patting his knee.

She nodded, her age now lost somewhere between naughty girl and playing strumpet, and moved towards him, letting the tingling of his excitement bathe her. Her eyes batted, part Act, part his excitement.

On this Now Daddy's knee, she turned and looked at him. So close, so close, the heat of him, this was his treat, this was what he'd come for. She didn't pretend to know (his hand lifted and traced a fingernail line up the side of her arm and across her left shoulder) what drew them to this with an Auto, but they came. Maybe this was something tight and shut and secret within him, maybe he had suggested the game to someone else and they'd shut it down further so now the only person he could tell this heat to was someone artificial and consciousless. Supposedly.

On Daddy's knee, she arched her back just a bit. One thing they always did come for was the fresh enthusiasm. It was perfect for Fields, she really looked forward to each and every chance to refine the Act. An Auto would treat each and every client as if they were the only Client, man, woman, in the world. They matched: the fact of what she was supposed to be, and what she was.

His breath was hot and faster, it warmed the side of her left breast. The nails turned and glided under: her nipple tightened and knotted in front of his eyes. His breath tingled her nipple and she ached to reach around his head and draw his hot and soft (she knew, she knew) mouth to her nipple, to reverse the play and become mother to him. But she resisted, and let him take the way.

The hand dropped to her thigh and rested there. She resisted again, trapped in the Act. Fields was in bondage to her performance: Think like the machine, be the machine and let the Act take its way.

I like being the machine, she thought, her mantra as he pushed a bit against her tight thighs, so she took the cue and spread them just so. I must be the machine.

The terror came as he brushed his fingertips up along her slit, tickling the bead of her clit. The Act: she responded a bit late, a second after the thrill itself, the wave itself, went from pussy to head. A second delay. A second second, and she moaned slightly. She wanted to turn and slip off his leg, turn and face him, spread her legs to let his fine, smooth fingers (nails trimmed professionally short) to touch her, to explore her. She wanted to be free, but the Act was around her, close and confining. Invisible bondage of acting.

He said something. Something lost in the heat.

"Pardon, sir?"

"Have you been keeping clean?" he said. His voice was constrained and hard, but broke with a crack of excitement. These were his lines, and the fact of it actually happening was taking its toll on him.

"Yes, Daddy" she said, tones of slight shame, embarrassment. Resting her hands on her own thighs, she spread her own legs a little wider on the balancing Act of his knee.

"All over?"

"Yes, Daddy"

"Even your coochie?"

"Yes, Daddy." (Machines do not laugh, machines do not laugh, machines do not laugh... you sweet, crazy guy.)

She knew the next: "How did I tell you to do it?" but that didn't stop the tingle when he really did say it. Leaning back into his arm, tucking herself under his arm, she put her head on his shoulder: a silent language I'm embarrassed.

He stiffened somewhere else, and she could tell that a wave of shock had made its way through him. This was almost, his thoughts almost ringing through her head, too real. The fear made him soften a bit under her leg, made his posture twist. Too real, too real.

Time to bring him back, to let him go. Give him his money's worth: she whispered her adolescent fear into his shoulder again I'm embarrassed, Daddy and let him stroke her back, tsk-tsking her into comfort.

"I use a washcloth on my private place," with small hands over her slightly-spread thighs.

It took him a while, coughing it up from his own real embarrassment through his brain via his now-hard steel/rock cock. "...careful to clean everywhere?"

"Yes, Daddy."

"Especially your pearl."

Quiet, shushed. "Yes, Daddy."

Knew the next line, too, but let it come from him real and quite strong: "Show me how you do it—how I told you to do it."

Dropping her hands into her lap, she spread a bit wider, balancing herself on his knee, leveraging herself on the ridge of his cock. Her clit was a tiny button under her finger, and the first touch was almost too much, too hard and chafing. The finger went down lower, scooping up a shine of her own juice, and returned to her knot. The first stroke was clumsy and childish, in character: a quick, hard rub up and down with the meat of her hand, pressing up and in. The feeling tore, rather than washed over her. It was a near-kick in the clit. It was too much too hard too soon and she had to use her Act, use the breathing of the machine to keep from making a noise. State of the Art, she thought, gripping herself inside to keep from making noise, tightening her thighs too much. State of the Art—

"That's it, that's it—" his voice a deep whisper in her ear "—it feels good to clean yourself, doesn't it?"

That was the way she would have started, if she was what he really wanted, so she had given it to him. But that was the Act, that was the realism that he wanted from a machine. Now what he really wanted, what she really fucking wanted: the next stroke was leisurely and circular. She cupped hand in another hand and moved them slow counter-clockwise, cupping and working her cunt with her fingers. One thumb stroked and ringed her hardening and hardening clit while the other fingers and the other thumb worked into her cunt itself, relishing the muscularity of her, the rings of her muscles, the little no-man's land between cunt and asshole.

Under her, behind her, Fields felt him tighten, and caught a whiff of the metal tang of his excitement. The gates had been passed, and the Act was running smooth. A quick jill come climbed up out of her cunt in a series of throbbing quakes, Her legs, her thighs, her tummy jiggled with the coming wave, and she pressed harder and moved faster, and chanced a quick skirt right across the top of her clit.

The orgasm was real—it reached out of her cunt, through her gut, up her throat in a low moan, finally spilling out of her lips.

Leaning back, she twitched and quaked in his arms. She let herself fall only so far, not letting him have to support her entire weight. She was, after all, supposed to weigh something like five hundred pounds.

Propped, balanced on his leg, she let herself slide down to a crouch on the floor. His hand was on her shoulder, stroking her. His fingernails were lights gliding through her closed eyes. A good performance, a fine come. Act 2:

Turning, she pulled herself now back up, pulling with all her real weight on his pants, climbing the fine suit with clenching hands till she was where she needed to be.

Rubbing the bar in his pants, tracing with her first and little fingers the crown of his circumcised head, she admired it, lost herself in her contemplation of it, getting off on its length (average) and hardness (the Act was really working, it really was). She was contemplating, working herself up with another hand between her legs (and the sweet slick noise of her cunt juice, and her hard clit swimming in it), and she was feasting on his cock without really touching it.

Sign: his hand gently rested on the back of her head. "Clean Daddy now."

With fluttering skill, she found the zipper and glided it down on its nylon-Teflon teeth. His underwear was peach and also silk. A dark, salty-smelling dot ended at the tent of his ridged crown.

The material was clean, with the fine wine of his sweat and the tingle of a few pubic hairs poking through the fine material. She washed it with her tongue, bathing him, tasting the salt of his pre-come. Fields pulled back and admired her work: a darker spread on the fine peach: his cock becoming visible through the damp fabric.

His pants came down: fingers snaking up, she hooked his belt with one hand, unbuckling with the other. With a hiss of Tokyo tailoring mastery, and the creak from the stool as he stood, they came down.

Dimly, as she pulled down the peach and licked and kissed his hard cock, she was aware of him undressing over her. Tongue around the head, tasting salt, and salt, and skin and skin. Hands in his short, almost shaved pubic hair, fondling his balls, feeling the wrinkled sacs, the bristling hairs.

Too quick maybe, too sudden probably, but he was hanging way down, his breathing was quick and deep, his legs were columns of meat and tension. He slid down her throat: the head rubbed against the ridges of the top of her mouth, hit the softness, smoothness, warmth of the back of her throat. She swallowed and pulled him close, and kept swallowing him down and down, using those hungry, swallowing, eating muscles to draw on his cock, milk it, and work it inside her.

Dimly, through all this, she became aware that her other hand was back inside her, three fingers deep and working her own reverse throat, playing with the twitching, clenching muscles of her cunt. Her clit was a tight singing, throbbing, pulse between her legs. She soothed it and calmed it and bathed it with a circling thumb, pressing on that special spot just to the right of her slit, hitting her special come button at just the right instant—

—and somewhere, he was standing over her, his hard, hard, too-hard cock down the back of her throat and she was consuming him, swallowing it down deep—

—and somewhere was the room, somewhere was Fields and her trailing umbilicord prop in a small room in an old factory building in the old, bad part of Kyushu—

—and here was Fields in the Act, connected and linked to this man, this man who came to her, who let it down and showed it to her, and she played with it, and made it real safe and fucking hot. State of the fucking Art—

—and he came, a shudder and two hands hard on the back of her head, not pushing, not forcing, just holding himself there. The jets (one, two, three, four—good boy—five, six...) were beyond taste but his body relaxed and oozed the come out of his skin. He broke out in a head-to-toe shine of sweat and giddy release.

Opening wider (was it possible?) she eased him out and kissed and licked him clean, then let her own deep and rumbling come, a thigh-trembling and spine arching (was that her head on the floor, was that his hand on her hand, steadying her, easing her rough ride?) spasm that left her panting almost out of Act, almost to the edge of mumbling "Fucking grand, man—"

Final Act, lady and gentleman: She got to her legs in a supreme Act of control (without a quake, without a mumble, no hand to reach to steady herself) and walked to her private corner of the room.

With the stainless steel bowl of warm water and the soft cloth, she bathed and cleaned his cock and balls. She let him prattle a bit, his "Oh, Gods!" and such washing over her. Applause. Applause. Applause!

Cleaning done, she helped him dress: cocksucking whore to Geisha in one quick move. The Act for him was over, the orgasms tasty and filling. The Act, though was not quite.

Fields showed him to the door, and concluded with a "Thank you, sir. Please come again," in the voice, in the Act. The tones of coolness, not of boredom, but of very, very expensive circuits. Stance slightly stiff, slightly posed, more than slightly mechanical.

She closed the door behind him and stretched out on the futon. The applause of her come, the applause of his come, the applause for the Act. This was someone, and something, she really, really, enjoyed, and could do a really, really long time—

The purr interrupted her quick sleep—just long enough for her head to rest.

Mama glowed, a wrinkled goddess with a thin black cigarette, as always, between broken tombstone teeth. In chopped English she woke Fields up—

—the message worked its way through ("Okay, Mama—okay..."), "He say he want you—"

"That's great, Mama. I'm broken, though, right? Little Miss Robot busted for the night—"

"No, no, no, he want you. Buy you. He want buy you."

Fields smiled back at the broken, smiling, teeth. "Good night, Mama."

Applause, applause, applause...

...to sleep.

THE BRIDE'S STORY
Lynda J. Williams

Eeee!"

"Von! It's Von!"

Blue and yellow knee-length dresses flouncing, six Demish girls jumped up and down trying to get a glimpse of their visitor.

"Girls!" Matron drove them away from the door, radiating disapproval. The girls would see him soon enough at the bride's party. On the eve of her arranged marriage, a Demish bride celebrated with her peers. Matron still remembered the games and the beautiful, highly skilled courtesans who came to perform for her, but in her day, the courtesans were all female. Today, seventeen-year-old Princess Lillan would spend her bride's party with five girl cousins and one male courtesan, Von. The girls' pale cheeks were flushed with excitement and Matron waved a hand at them. "Back in you go now! I must have a word with him."

Von was a rising star with the old women of the court and Matron knew it well. She considered it a dangerous vogue that the girls now demanded their favorites from rumors told by servants and loose-lipped older relatives. She herself was ninety years old, but like most Demish widows in the long, stable stretch of Sevolite adulthood she had avoided commoner-style aging. She looked to be a well-worn but healthy thirty. Despite her resilient physique, Matron did not enjoy her extended youth

45

with the abandon of her aunts and sisters. She disliked men—particularly courtesans. At least the pompous selfishness of Demish men was honest.

Matron shoved at the little one trying to peek around her legs. "Ow!" the child objected.

"Lillan!"

"Come on." Princess Lillan reluctantly reclaimed command of her party guests. "Matron won't eat him. He'll still be there to look at in five minutes."

"But—"

"We've already waited—"

"Is he pretty? I've never seen a man that's pretty. Will he look like a girl, then?"

"Hush!" When she had her younger cousins in control, Lillan made to join Matron in delivering Von's instructions, but Matron turned her away with a frown, leaving her as vexed with the delay as all the others.

In the hall, Von cocked a thin eyebrow at Matron from the shadows of his hooded cloak.

"Come" she barked, and marched him into an anteroom across the foyer. Matron eyed the courtesan as he stood just inside the door, a lithe shape draped in soft black folds, out of place among the embroidered throws and racks of porcelain ladies in a constellation of sedate positions.

"Let me see you," she ordered.

Von shed his traveling cloak. His off-white tunic and lounge pants looked touchably soft, the tunic sporting a loose fold across the chest, trimmed in gold, with a braided belt of the same pliant material. He was barefoot, his shoes with the house porter, where they were left on his arrival.

"You come with good references," allowed Matron. "You've performed at other children's parties without incident. But I've heard the gabbing of those satisfied clients with which I am, unavoidably, acquainted." With practiced control, Matron allowed the politeness of her voice to show her distaste. "These girls are innocents. The men expect them to be that way, and demand its blessing until marriage is forced upon them. So do not imagine you know what is expected here because you have been in the beds of their bored aunts and grandmothers. The only men they've much to do with at all are frightened servants and foreboding uncles. Do you understand what I am saying?"

"I think so, Your Grace."

She frowned as if at something slimy. His intelligent understanding had the air of a gift about it, which she heartily resented for a parlor trick. "What is it you specialize in?"

'Sword dancing."

"Too provocative. Do you sing?"

"Yes."

"Tell stories?"

He nodded.

"Stick to things of that nature." She gave him another once-over. His hair was jet, his lips pastel, his features finer than those of her porcelain maidens. Add to that a dancer's grace and strength, and eyes like cut gems of gray crystal. He was dangerous. A carefully tutored false advertisement, an icon for an adult society Lillan and the rest did not know the truth of.

"Remember," she warned, frowning. "Be careful."

She led him back to the children waiting in the room bedecked for the party. They were dancing in a circle. When the door opened they dropped hands and swarmed around him.

"This is Von, of Den Eva's," announced Matron. "Von, this is tomorrow's bride, Princess Lillan."

The girls fell silent. Matron watched them stare at him like a piece of breathing sculpture, his beauty worn with a studied carelessness.

Lillan curtsied and Von raised her gently. "You mustn't do that, Your Highness. I'm commoner."

Lillan was wide-eyed. "But you're so beautiful."

As beautiful as the romantic prince-hero from a court ballad, Matron thought and shook her head. These girls' real lives would be far removed from that. Simsa was shy; she would be her husband's willing decoration. Danda was insipid. Both of them would take up with courtesans in their middle years because their peers were doing it. Fifteen-year-old Vrassa would be one of the trendsetters. She and fourteen-year-old Ola were already competing. When they were older, they would try to outdo one another's wickedness. Tala, at eleven, was all bounce and boldness and too young to predict. But Lillan she felt the most sorry for. Lillan the romantic.

Von was smiling at them all. "Thank you for having me to entertain you. What shall we start with?"

"Dance, please?" Tala begged. "I want to see sword dances!"

Matron watched his answer carefully as he flicked a glance toward her. "Oh," said Von, "to sword dance I would need a trained partner. Besides, I would rather learn your dances. Can you teach me?"

The girls eagerly dragged him to the center of the room and began a round of dancing tag. They circled and circled until the ring broke in a mad scramble.

"One—two—three—four! You lose!" cried Tala, as each girl tagged the unprepared Von.

"Oh, so that is how you play this game," said Von. "Let us have another round."

And so they did, the girls petting him like a tame dog. A flush, a touch, too much body contact...

By the fifth round, the girls piled upon him.

Matron rose, clapping her hands to be heard over the shrieks of laughter. "Lori!" She summoned the serving girl to divert them. "Refreshments!"

Lori hurried in with a tray, long legs scissoring and dishwater-dull eyes downcast.

Von evaded Vrassa's efforts to help him straighten his clothing.

"Tell us a story," begged Lillan.

"That's a good idea," Matron said, glad of a change from such physical games. "Something quiet."

Lillan took Von's hand. "Tell us the story of Princess Demora."

"That's mushy!" Ola objected.

"It's about love," Von allowed, catching Ola's hand to draw her toward Lillan. "Demora began much like Lillan" he began, "a girl obliged to marry by contract. But, she already loved another." He placed Ola's hand in Lillan's, casting them as hero and heroine. As he recited the story, he cast each of the other children into the roles of Demora's in-laws and others. They listened spellbound as he directed them with the magic of the story and gestures. Lori's platter went unnoticed by everyone except Matron, who eyed the sliced fruit and wafers with annoyance.

There were tears in bright blue eyes when the hero received his mortal wound, redeeming Demora from the false accusations of her in-laws. Ola lay on the floor with her head in Lillan's lap as Vrassa, in the part of the husband, stood by frowning and Tala, playing the physician, looked up to pronounce with Von, "The wound is mortal."

Lillan sobbed aloud.

"That's enough," Matron said, and stood over the troop on the floor. "Clear the things, Lori. The party is over."

Von broke off, blinking, as if jarred himself to be robbed of the story's sentimental ending. Simsa, Danda, Ola, and Lillan flocked around Matron, whimpering their protest.

"Can't we finish?"

"He's only been here an hour!"

"It's so sad... Poor Demora."

"Such nonsense!" pronounced Matron.

A movement caught her eye. It was Vrassa. Matron parted the crowd of skirts and golden locks around her in time to see, but not stop, the girl from throwing herself at Von with vigor.

She'd caught him off guard as he stooped to gather up some props they'd been using in the drama. He fell over, with her on top of him.

She shamelessly kissed him on the mouth.

Danda screamed in alarm. "You'll get pregnant!"

Von began to disengage himself from Vrassa. Tala made as if to help him up. Matron crossed the room in two strides, and caught Tala by one hand even as her other slipped between his parted thighs. "Tala!"

"It's soft," the child said, sitting back on her knees, unrepentant. "How could he stick it through you?"

Von chuckled. Matron stiffened. He stifled the chuckle and said in a soft voice, "No one gets wounded."

"Oh, Tala," Lillan apologized in a fluster. "How awful. She's so brazen."

"What *does* happen?" Vrassa demanded.

"I thought *you* knew!" Ola remarked.

Tala pulled her hand free of Matron. "Tell us?"

Matron never expected what happened next. After all her warnings to him, Von had the audacity to answer. "Don't do what you don't enjoy. Enjoy all that you're able to. That's the best I—"

"On your feet!" Matron snapped, pushing Danda away from her.

Von stood and the girls peeled away from him.

"Lillan," Matron ordered. "Say goodbye to your guests, and call their escorts. Then come see me. We've things to discuss before your wedding."

"Matron's going to tell *her*," complained Ola.

"Shh." Lillan started to herd them off. She paused to glance over her shoulder. "Goodbye, Von. And thank you. It was a great party."

Matron saw the wan smile on his lips. No doubt he realized he was in trouble.

"We will take this up in private," she told him. "Lori! You will come also."

"But I didn't—"

"I did not say you did anything, girl. Just do as you are told."

Matron hurried them down the hall to her apartment. They passed through her office, into the lounge, then the private dining room. She opened the bedroom door. Dark hints of the polished wood and russet reds of the furnishings showed through the doorway, formal and foreboding.

Von stood still. Matron held the door wide for both of them. Von's left hand flexed. Lori was fidgeting. "Inside," Matron told them both, impatient. Lori darted in with a little moan. Von obeyed silently.

Matron pulled the door closed, then paused with it open a mere crack. The two of them were talking. What could this courtesan have to say? She listened while she waited for Lillan to join them.

Von's voice was soft as he said, "You'd better calm down."

"I—I—"

She heard water being poured from the pitcher beside her bed. "Drink this. You'll feel better."

"It's different for you," Lori blurted. "People want you. You have talent. There's nowhere to go if I'm thrown out! I'd just starve. I'm nobody."

"I've met worse people," he answered with kindness. Was he trying to seduce the girl? Matron wondered.

Lori sniffed. "How can you be so calm?"

"I'm not. I'm a good actor."

Lillan arrived, still wearing her frilly party dress. Matron took her hand. "Come with me, dear."

Von was sitting on the chest at the end of Matron's bed. He sprang up. Lori put her water glass down guiltily. Lillan look at Matron in surprise. "I thought we were going to talk about men," she said, clutching Matron's hand harder.

"We are dear," said Matron. "Von, stand up on that chest."

It was one easy step. He faced Matron, his waist now at eye level. The bed's russet canopy brushed his head.

"On my wedding night," Matron told Lillan, "I had absolutely no idea what a man was. You will." She untied Von's belt.

Lillan pressed a fist to her mouth. "What are you doing?"

"He's a courtesan," Matron said blandly. "He does what he's paid for."

"Don't!" Lillan caught Matron's hands as she started to jerk Von's breeches down.

"Very well, then," said Matron. "You do it."

Lillan bit her lip. The soft cloth of Von's tunic moved with each breath he took. She put her hand on it. She held her breath. Matron watched her eyes travel up, and frowned, but Von avoided eye contact. He was looking across the room.

"At first, men struck me as ugly," Matron informed her, guiding her hand lower. "Then ridiculously vulnerable." Lillan resisted and she released her. "Take your clothes off," she instructed Von. "All of them."

Lori turned her head with a tiny gasp.

Von stripped off his soft tunic.

"Oh!" sighed Lillan.

"You can see as much on any statue in a public corridor," Matron reminded him. "It's their tender spots men keep to themselves, so they can frighten you with them. She jerked down Von's breeches. He flinched slightly.

Lillan's lips parted. She stepped back and stared. "What... is it?"

Matron sorted out organs through Von's fine mesh of pubic hair. At her rude touch, Von braced himself with a hand on either post of the single bed. "These are testicles. They're tender. You can disable a man if you hurt him here." Von obliged her with a muffled sound as she gave an experimental squeeze. He closed his eyes.

"This is what gets rigid," Matron continued her inventory. "He can't do it at will, but you can make it stiff easily with handling. It's what they put inside you."

Horror showed on Lillan's face. "But—where!"

"Lori!"

"May I dress?" Von asked quietly.

"No. Come down here." Matron pulled Lori toward him as he stepped off the wooden chest. "Demonstrate," she ordered him, "on the servant girl."

"No!" Lori tried to escape. Matron caught her by the arm. "Don't be a silly girl. There are princesses who pay a great deal for this."

"I don't think I can, Your Grace," Von demurred.

"Don't be silly. By all reports you are as tireless as royalty."

"It's not that—it's—if you could find someone willing? I mean the girl."

Matron squeezed Lori's arm. "You're willing, aren't you?"

"Yes, Matron," she whimpered.

"There." Matron thrust her at the naked man.

Von gathered her against his chest, her tears and runny nose wet on his skin. "Have you done this before?" he asked. She shook her head from side to side. "It might hurt," he said, "but it will be worse if you are tense and frightened."

Her voice climbed toward a wail. "I can't help it!"

He kissed her on the edge of her lips. "Pretend that you're dreaming," he whispered and she clung to him. "You will not get pregnant," he promised. She nodded against his chest and he rubbed the back of her neck.

Matron decided this was taking too long. "Do it on the floor. There's no need to soil the bed."

Lillan was surprised again. "Does it make a mess?"

Von eased Lori onto the carpet.

"Too slow and too gentle," Matron hissed. "It won't be like that for Lillan tomorrow."

But Von loosened Lori's clothing, advising her to touch him as he massaged some flexibility into her rigid limbs. "Like this, it helps." She stared up at him, hanging onto his advice and terrified of him all at once. He kissed her, using only his lips. She relaxed slightly, only to grow brittle as his hand moved up her thigh.

"You see that?" Matron pointed to Von's stiffening member.

"Is it really hard like a sword?" Lillan wondered.

"Touch it."

She looked at Matron and Matron urged her with her eyes. Lillan slipped down to the floor and reached out her hand toward Von. Von was wise enough to help. No sooner did she touch him than she snatched back her hand and scrambled away, proud of her courage but half upset.

Lori had curled up into a ball. Von began coaxing her open once again.

"Do it fast," Matron ordered. "She must know what it's going to be like for her. The first time is the worst. But, like childbirth, it would be easier if she knew what to expect."

He took a deep breath. For a moment, Matron thought he was going to resist, though she couldn't imagine why. This could hardly be difficult work for him. Finally, he took Lori's shoulders and forced her to lie back. He used his knee to separate hers. She began to pant with fear.

Von rocked back, a hand fisted near his waist.

"What's the matter?" Matron folded her arms in exasperation.

"I can't!"

"You look perfectly capable," she said, noting the state of his organs. Why would a courtesan be so reluctant? She thought she had it. "Of course, you will be paid extra."

"No." He looked her in the eye. "I can't do it."

Matron matched his stare, expecting his to break. But his jaw was white with anger and other emotions. "You'd both be ill advised to spoil this lesson," she said coldly.

"I'm willing!" Lori bleated. "I really am willing, please!"

Von gave the servant girl a hot, resentful look. "You're slightly more willing than you are to starve to death!" He was losing his erection and closed his eyes briefly. When he opened them, he concentrated on Lillan using a sweeter voice. "Perhaps there are things I could tell you, or show you, without—"

"Lori!" Matron pointed to the chest. "There's an old sword in that chest. Get it out, in its sheath." The sword had belonged to Matron's father and would be a suitable instrument. "And you, Von, lie across the top of this chest. Let her sheath-whip you, if you'd prefer that to doing what you are asked for reasonable compensation! You *are* a good actor. But I am not as easily manipulated as a crowd of virgin girls. We will do this on my terms."

Lori stood hugging the jewel-studded saber in its heavy, velvet-covered sheath, inhaling with little, sharp hiccups and staring like a mad woman. Von's stare, though, looked sullen. Matron ordered, "Get on the chest."

He balked. Lillan interrupted. "Oh no, Matron!"

"He's just playing a role to raise the price," said Matron. "He'll change his mind before he'll take a beating."

"He's protecting poor Lori!" Lillan countered.

"A sentimental courtesan? Lillan you have much to learn. Hit him where he stands!"

Lori swung wildly. Von evaded the blow easily, snapping out his hand to grab the sheath. Lori pulled back and drew the sword. They faced one

another, Von with the sheath and Lori with the naked blade. Lori looked
as though she might drop the blade. Matron snatched it away from her
and slapped at Von's head with the flat of it. He parried with the sheath.
"Drop that!" she railed at him. How dare he fight back! Here, where she
had all the power!

Her rage shocked and frightened him. He held out the sheath. "Don't
use the sword," he said. "You'll kill me." She jerked the sheath from his
hand and struck. He had no rights here! He would not turn the tables and
make her the villain. This was for Lillan.

He defended his head with his naked arm and she beat him across the
back. He went down and she struck again, the metal tip of the sheath
raising a welt that began to bleed.

"Stop it!" Lillan grappled with her, shrieking. "Stop!"

Matron dropped her bludgeon and caught Lillan's arms. "You don't—
understand—" she gasped, trying to make Lillan see that her horror was
misplaced. "Husbands... are animals. Courtesans are paid. That's all there
is. Just lies! No heroes."

"He wouldn't hurt her, and you beat him because he wouldn't hurt
her!"

Matron sighed. Lillan still did not understand. "Lillan—"

"It was nice of him! It was brave! Even if he's just a commoner!" The
young princess tore away in an explosion of tears and fled noisily, the
door slamming shut behind her.

Matron swayed. Where had the lesson gone wrong? Von straightened
up, on his knees, and Lori blubbered. Matron spoke numbly. "You may
leave, Lori. There's a good girl."

Lori gave a sob and, following Lillan, ran from the room and
slammed the door.

Matron sat down in a carved upholstered chair.

After a long, quiet minute, Von asked, in a small voice, "Can I get
dressed?"

"Stand up."

He made a throaty noise as he climbed to his feet, less graceful than
before but with no sign of crippling injury. There were marks coming up
in welts, and there would be bruises. Matron snatched a dressing gown
from the chair and hurled it at him. He caught it, but did not put it on.

"Why wouldn't you do it?"

He did not answer.

"Tell me!"

He drew the gown around his shoulders, dragging it through the ooze of blood on his back. His left hand gripped his right forearm. The rest of his stance slowly relaxed, but he seemed to have lost his voice.

"I could put it about that you molested Tala," Matron said. "You'd never work near Demish girls or their mothers again."

He looked up at last. "Don't!"

"Then, tell me. And make it convincing."

"I've... been raped."

She let out the breath she had been holding. There was a long silence while he forced himself to inhale and struggled with his composure.

"Come here," she said. He approached, without limping, and stopped within easy reach of her if she leaned forward.

"Look at me."

She watched as he struggled to keep his feelings off his face.

"How old were you?"

He swallowed. He tried to speak, but started to shiver and paused to gain control of that first before he began again, eyes focused past her. "I... don't know. A child."

"By a man?"

He nodded. "Often."

"I see." She waited out another minute of silence. "I was a child myself."

His gray eyes lifted, surprise and compassion in them.

"A child bride," said Matron, "like Lillan."

He knelt down in front of her, sinking like a sigh despite his bruises. His eyes stayed with hers.

"I try to prepare my girls," she told him. "I try to ready them, so they won't face it without weapons. Knowledge. Hatred to help them through it. It's cruel help at best."

"You are not wrong," he said, his voice offering gifts of understanding. "I have heard about Demish husbands. And I am paid." He touched her knee, lightly.

She took his hand. His fingers were long and clever, a smear of blood on his palm. She rubbed the blood away with her thumb and set his hand onto her knee again, holding it quiet, beneath her own.

"Would you like me to talk with Lillan?" He spoke as if they had known each other a long time and shared this problem.

"Yes." Matron let his hand slide free and immediately missed its warmth and pliant strength. In his eyes shone the promise to learn, to teach, and to keep the results private. He rose to dress.

"And come again," she said, in a rush, as he made his way to the door. "For the next bride's lesson?"

"For the bride of long ago, who missed her lesson."

He smiled freely at her then. "I can do that, yes."

CYBERFRUIT SWAMP
Raven Kaldera

Don't you hate it when the phone rings right as you climb into the shower? I mean, it's like they *know*. Hiss of hot water over your shoulders, your body relaxes, and you've just dumped a handful of shampoo on your head when they do it to you. Ringggg, like a demon's screech, and you curse, and try to leap out, and trip on the wet floor, and end up sliding through the filth in the hallway, and hit the phone stand with your shoulder, and grab the thing just before it cracks you in the skull, and scream "What!" into the receiver. Whereupon a taped voice informs you that you are behind on your insurance payments, and to disregard this notice if you have already sent in your bill.

What do you mean that's never happened to you?

Of course, it wouldn't have happened to me either, if I hadn't been waiting for Chakti to call. I'd have let the voice mail get it otherwise, but I wanted to hear her pretty voice in my ear in realtime. I was pretty sure we had a date, but I'd called her the day before and her roommate said she was out of town with someone named Pito. Never heard of him/her. "Well, I'm supposed to get together with her tomorrow; do you think she'll be back by then?"

"I have no fucking idea," said her roommate angrily and hung up on me. Not a good omen, oh great chief. Let's maybe disembowel a couple more pigeons to be sure of the intestinal portent. I dialed her beeper and left a message. "Chakti, honey, maybe I made a mistake, but I thought…" Well, it's the next day and I'm sliding around on the floor to get the phone and she still hasn't called back. Okay, sweetie. There are other winktis in the world. Effing hangouts full. Time to change my plans, definitely.

I finish my shower, dry off and dress to hunt. The age-old ritual—are you watching, class of Anthro502? The native shaman clothes themself for the possibility of mate attraction. I have to have a sense of humor about my hobbies, or I'll start taking them seriously, including the rejection part. Which is the road to madness.

I almost wish there was a class of students watching me. I've gotten myself to the point where I like my body, finally, after so many years. Oh, yes, according to the Cynthaians, you're supposed to get to love your body the way it is, part of all their love yourself chickenshit. Well, I hated being a round weak little genfem. I love my flesh now—hard, muscled, drifts of hair over my arms and legs that catch the light. I can sit and watch my body hair glisten, and it doesn't matter that my car blew out a hoverjet last week. I can touch my firm pectoral muscle, trace the curving snake tattoo that covers where the lasers carved my tits off, and it doesn't matter that I can't replace the hoverjet till next month and I'll have to ride in to work on the skybus. I can stroke the beard on my chin and cheeks—beards are a great toy to play with and chew on, I've discovered—and it doesn't matter that I still have the huge bill for my surgery and testosterone implants because I've been blowing all my money on APPles. When you're at home with yourself, everything else can be dealt with.

I slide into my pants. Black and malachite green deadleather—meaning it's constructed to be indistinguishable from the real stuff, which is so expensive as to be out of my reach. Hundreds of slashes decorate them, with puffs of green deadsilk. When the fashion tommyhaws started borrowing from Renaissance German Landsknecht mercenaries, I knew that for once I'd been born into the right era. I leave my torso bare to show off the tattoos, throw on the doublet-cut deadleather jacket with its matching slashes and puffs, and black spacer's boots (Okay, I've never been off the planet, but they look good) and transfer my wallet, credit chips and Paki blade from my other jacket. I also detach the chain and fasten it around my shoulder, through one of the slashes.

The chain is what's really important. Gold means you're looking for a genguy—a genetic male—and silver is for a genfem. Rose gold or copper means a winkti—used to be genguy, now a girl—and black iron means a kurami, like me. I used to wear gold and silver chains twined together, even before I Tranzed, but not any more. Gave them away, I just can't seem to trust people who are onlymen or onlywomyn. I mean, they can be nice people, and most of my friends are male and female, not to mention most of my ex-lovers, but they just don't get it like a nachtlei does.

We nachtlei—winktis and kuramis and a few nonspecific folk right in the middle—we didn't used to date each other. We were supposed to date gens, to prove we weren't freaks. But it's been thirty years since Dis Sybil was assassinated and the TranzPride movement got underway. Now my chain is copper-and-black twisted, with my antique Tranzpride pendant and my nachtlei basket-and-bow symbol. Mind you, it's not justabout solidarity or politics. If you're both, like me, my head snaps around so fast my neck almost breaks and my APPle flares up like a magic charm. I used to call myself pansex, but men and womyn, though they're great at first, they get to thinking. Thinking. Wondering what they are in relation to you. Queer. Straight. Husband. Wife. Then they get uncomfortable. So when I fill out the forms for the Net personals now, I check off NQ— Nachtlei Queer. I only sleep with my own kind. It's safer that way.

Time for the final touch. I open the drawer where I keep my precious APPles, all seven of them. "Why don't you just hang them on the wall, you love them so much," my last gen lover had said nastily. Yeah, yeah, but some things are too blatant even for me. Why seven of them? Different moods, different lover, different orifices. Besides, since I can't afford the rare transplant surgery to get a natural-flesh cock, why shouldn't I have the next best thing—and have a variety as well? I mean, it's one of the few bennies about Artificial Penile Prosthetics, also known as APPles, CyberCocks, Freudbusters, and some other less flattering terms.

Which one for tonight... hmm. Puck, small and thumb-size, no balls, really an enlarged clit, for virgin assholes. Mjollnir, realistic but small, four inches or so (song cue: Thor had a hammer that was a hand too small!) for slightly larger assholes. Legba, shiny and plum-black, bought on a whim to match a dark-skinned genguy lover. (He wasn't amused.) Coyote, with a special trick, an inlaid vibrator. Wapiti, nested in fur and feathers, masturbation only. Pan, perfect and realistic, about eight thick uncut inches when hard. And finally, Asmodeus. Nine cut inches when hard, glinting with gold piercings—the Prince Albert at the tip, three dydoe rings along the back of the head, an ampallang, several jingling hafadas in the scrotum. People have been known to fall to their knees at the first glance at it. (They've also been known to run, so if I pack Asmodeus I usually bring another just in case.)

I think that'll be the plan tonight, I tuck Pan into the inside pocket of my jacket and undo my codpiece. The base of Asmodeus fits up against my pubic bone, and I find the implanted metal socket among the coarse hair, just above my clit.

Asmodeus is warm, pulsing, alive-feeling in my hand. I guide the plug in; there's that moment of grinding sensation that I hate and then all I feel is my own hand on my cock, stroking it. No matter how many times I've done it, it's still magick.

So I go out and kick my bike into gear and hit the streets. It's raining, but only a mist. Not hard enough for the Public Works to send up the Precipitation Dome. Which is fine, because I'm too chicken to ride all this leather through an unDomed rain and the Nachtlei hangout that I like best, the Black Sun, is outside metro lines.

My luck doesn't hold. The rain steepens and I pull off under a store awning of fragrant bioengineered plantstuff to watch the pearly curve of the Dome rise. Damn. Do I try for Black Sun even in the wet—damn that busted car!—or go for something in town, an unknown quantity? A gleam of violet/periwinkle light catches my eye and I see a Hangout I've driven by before, the Camshaft. Supposed to be mostly pansex, but my winkti co-worker Alphonsine said it's mostly overrun by the male type. Wait, didn't she say that she also picked someone up there? Maybe it's worth a try.

They have a cheap bike rack, which is good. If your bike isn't racked and guarded in this town, it'll be gone in two minutes flat. Which is why I have to take the hoverbus to work. Inside, it's the usual low light for flattering aging looks, music, cubbies with people talking, bar for drinks. A few winktis—oh how, I love the little winktis, drool, drool—but they all seem to be with someone. The only loner looks at me, smiles, then sees the TranzPride logo and looks away. Shopping for a gen tonight, eh, honey? Fine, your loss.

I take a seat next to a genfem with crescent eyebrow pendants and order fizz'n'citrus. No substances yet, I want to be alert for the next hour in case there are no prospects and I have to drive out of here. The genfem looks at me, is just about to dismiss me as a genguy when she sees my advertising. Then she looks disgusted. Probably a Cynthaian, by the preponderance of crescents. They think what we do is unnatural, especially kuramis. By her lights, I've committed a crime of mutilation against a woman's body, never mind that the body in question is mine. She's probably also pissed because she's just realized that if I hadn't Tranzed, I might be someone worth picking up to her. Life's a bitch, honey.

Maybe it wasn't worth it to come here at all.

That's when I see the Boy. No, not a guy, a Boy. She's staring at me as if I was—what? No, now she's ducked her head and is looking away. I can smell her desire from here, see it in the curve of her shoulders under that androgynous jacket and ripped pants, baggy to hide the hips under them. She shuffles her feet in their scuffed runner's shoes and tries desperately not to look at me again. No genfem dresses that grungy in a bar these days unless they're dipping a toe into the nachtlei sea.

She gives in for a moment and glances my way again. This time I'm staring at her over my fizz and she draws in her breath sharply, reaching too fast for her drink and inadvertently knocking it over. Someone next to her snarls something and she turns to apologize, face scarlet. I keep studying her. Let her turn and see me, see that her clumsiness is irrelevant to me, that I'm more interested in her ass. I know when I was just starting out, first wondering whether this was the path I wanted to take, I would have given anything for an older, experienced kurami to accost me in a bar and say, "Okay, kid, this is what you're gonna look like, and this is what it's gonna be like, and your sex life will be better than ever. Now bend over."

No chain, no pendants, no signs, but I'm sure she can see mine from here, and she'll know what I'm looking for, and be able to guess what I am. I expect this will be a kind of formal initiation for her. If I'm an NQ, and she goes with me, it'll mean she's one of us, she's taking the first step from the silver to the black. Which'll it be, Boy? I ask her silently. I can't hang out here all night staring at you. I'll get bored, or maybe that winkti in the amethyst skinsuit will get bored first. You never know. Better make up your mind, kid.

Five minutes crawl by as she hunches over her drink. I'm just about to give up and order another fizz when she slowly turns. This time, when our eyes lock, I don't let her look away. (I mastered that trick a while back.) Go to her? Nah. She made me wait. Let her come to me. I jerk my hand toward the empty stool next to me that the Cynthaian has evacuated. Get your ass over here. She does, oh thank you gods below. Phew.

"You know what I am," I snap at her as soon as her ass touches the seat. Small talk is for people with time to kill.

Her eyes widen and she doesn't speak for a moment. "Kur—kurami?" she squeaks, finally. "I wasn't sure... You can't tell, looking at you. You look just like..."

"A genguy," I say, relieving her of having to say it. "That's the way it works. You might work for one of us, and if he's not political, you'd never know." Kuramis are a little luckier than winktis in that regard, but I don't mention that. I zoom in; no sense in wasting time. "And how many souls do you have?" The line is old, stereotypical, but it works.

She looks caught. "If I said... two... what would it..." She trails off in a whisper.

"Entail?" I ask.

"Mean," she says quietly.

"I've asked myself that a lot," I say. "We all do, and we all come to the conclusion that nobody would claim to be one of us if they weren't. I can usually smell my kin, anyway." I'm leaning closer to her as I say this.

She draws in her breath, nostrils flaring. It's a neat habit, sexy. "And am I your kin?" the Boy asks.

"Do you want to be?" I return, almost in her ear.

She closes her eyes and shivers, just once. "I think I'd kill for that." Her eyes open and she looks at me, worried. "But I'm not sure I'm ready to commit to any... changes."

"Neither of those," I assure the back of her neck, "are necessary to letting me fuck you. That is, if the idea appeals."

I swear she almost faints. I get the Boy around the waist, shove them up against the bar (I think this boy deserves the plural nachtlei pronoun now) and press Asmodeus, rapidly hardening, into that shapely chicken-kurami ass that I've been noticing. The Boy is not fainting now, but is pressing hard against me. I reach around and grab, opening the seal of a fly, find a cheap silicon pants-filler prosthesis and a wet boy-cunt. I get a little carried away at this point, and I'm glad the Boy's head is now down on the bar because the people staring might give them an attack of stage fright. I yank their pants down, undo my cod-piece, and am just about to release a straining Asmodeus when there's a tap on my shoulder.

It's the bouncer. "Not in here," she says. "There's a stall in the john for that kind of thing." Gestures over her shoulder toward the back. No point in arguing. I grab the Boy by the back of the jacket and yank them toward the bathroom.

Stall, eh? She must have meant the one without the door, I guess. Oh well, life is short. The Boy gets slammed up against the wall and kissed, brutally, thoroughly. Their teeth finds my lip, gnaws momentarily on my beard, my throat, the collar of my jacket, and sinks lower until they're chewing on the front of my pants. Not wanting them to wreck the leather, I pull their head away by the hair and get the last sticking point on my cod-piece. My cock slides out into my waiting hand, piercings glinting in the bright, bald lighting. The Boy opens their mouth reflexively, and takes me without even commenting on size. Manages to take nearly the whole thing, up to where it form-fits to my upper vulva. Manages to get fingers up where fingers shouldn't be without explicit permission.

I grab the boy's wrist, digging a nail between the tendons as a warning. They make a muted noise around my cock and glance upwards, brow furrowed. I yank the hand out and check the manicure. Good. Back to the quick. "All right," I growl, letting them know that this is a privilege. "But you better be good at it."

The Boy's eyes get that I'm-going-to-faint expression again, but they don't stop sucking me. Three fingers slide up behind my balls, into wetness, and it takes about two minutes for me to come. (Okay, so one of the nasty truths I learned about myself within 24 hours of acquiring my first APPle is that I'm a premature ejaculator.) My pelvis bucks, shooting come right down that pulsing throat.

There is stuff you can buy, four bucks a can, to fill the reservoir in the cyber/testes that completely mimics human semen in looks, taste, and smell. At least that's what they say, but I find it has a faint metallic odor that just isn't quite right. I did have a girl complain about it, the only time I used it, so I don't bother. Besides, one-hundred-twenty proof vodka keeps it cleaner internally and is much more of a surprise.

Minutes later, we curl up in one of the cubbies together. I order a felissium inhaler, thumb on the heater, and take a hit. The Boy is telling me about the last scene they did with their last lover. "It was a big party, all these people watching, and she had me tied to a support beam, and got this branding iron really hot with a blowtorch. All I could do was stare—I mean, we d never done anything that heavy before. Just some light whipping, and one pretty heavy caning once... Anyway, she went around behind me. I don't think anyone in the place made one sound at that point. And then I felt it."

I stare at them, half mesmerized, trying to picture it. "The brand?"

Their shoulders droop. "No. Cold. She had a second brand back there, in a bucket of frozen nitrogen. It hurt for a second, and then I realized it was all just a mindfuck. I started to cry, in front of everyone."

"In relief?" I ask.

"In disappointment. I had really wanted her to do it. She was embarrassed and got really pissed off, and we broke up two weeks later."

"In other words," I say, thumbing on the heater in the inhaler and keeping it on until it glows cherry red—which burns up the last of my felissium, but what the hell—"In other words," I say, holding the flame half an inch away from their forearm, "don't threaten you with anything unless I'm willing to come through on it. Is that it?"

The Boy flushes, but their eyes are on the flame. "I didn't mean it to be... impertinent, sir."

I turn the inhaler off and leave it on the table. "But you hate being whip-teased. Or cock-teased, I take it. And I did say I was going to fuck you, didn't I."

The Boy is wary, searching my face, unsure of what I want. My hand goes out like a striking snake (it's a trick I learned a while back) and closes on their throat, pressing just hard enough so that they can't move their head. "I always keep my word," I tell them. "But I do it in my own damn time, and I won't be rushed. Understand?"

Tries to nod, can't, says, "Yes, sir," in a whisper. I let go and stand up. "Come with me, Boy."

The underground parking garage—cities are so much nicer now that all the parking is underground—contains cars and racked bikes from several shops above. I'm just about to get my bike when I notice the car parked next to the rack. Large, expensive, covered in stickers from retro-conservative groups, including Nature's Front. My jaw immediately clenches. The Nature's Front goons are pushing for legislation to make prenatal hormone blockers mandatory. You know, the implants that block the variable fetal hormone showers that create people like me. Something evil boils up in me and I grab the back of the Boy's jacket again. "Bend over on the hood of that car, Boy."

It takes only one look at at the stickers for the Boy to to realize that it isn't mine. "The cameras are on," they remind me, not sounding as if they care much.

"I'm counting on it," I mutter, slamming them down on the expensive silver finish. I undo my codpiece again, and realize I have to change dicks to fuck this Boy properly. It's one thing to deepthroat Asmodeus, but quite another to take him up the ass. Besides, Pan is specially built to ooze lube when squeezed. I make the change in full view of the cameras—go ahead, let the guy in the booth have some jollies—although I wince a bit at the replugging . The Boy is watching sideways from under their fringe of bangs, wide-eyed. I can almost hear the wheels turning over in their head. This is one who'll go home and cry over their bank balance tomorrow, unless that retro grunge garb is an affectation.

I get the knife out of my pocket and give it the flick that makes the blade appear like a flash of red and white light. I like the way it runs along their shoulder, their scapula. The Boy turns their head obediently so that my knife can slide a hair's breadth above the fine skin over the carotid artery. Ah, such a picture. Lovely.

I yank down those ragged pants and slide a few fingers up underneath that wet boy-cunt and its owner moans, humping my hand vigorously. "Hold still," I say sternly, pressing down on their tailbone with my hand. The Boy tries, valiantly, but it's no use. The squirming starts again, and I make a snort of disapproval and withdraw my hand, wiping it on the car hood. Pan is hard and ready, throbbing in my other hand, my hips moving involuntarily with pleasure as I press against the Boy's asshole and release some lube, slowly inching my way in. My little chicken-kurami pants and makes muted howling noises, trying desperately to hold their ass still and not hump my cock, fingernails scraping the gleaming enamel. (Good.) I hold the knife within an inch of their throat, and pound hard into their ass, and I'm just about to come when a voice sounds through a portable police loudspeaker. "All right, don't move. There are three K38A2's pointed at you. Step away and put your hands behind your head."

Oh, crap, crap, crap. Me and my stupid ideas. The guy in the parking booth probably called the cops. Well, it would be really stupid not to do as I'm told at this point. It's a serious effort to pull my throbbing cock out of the Boy's ass, but I do it. As I lift my arms, a hand grabs my wrist and relieves me of the knife. Shit. That one was a gift from an ex. Now I'll probably never get it back. My arms are twisted behind me by the two cops I can now see by turning my head. "Hey," I protest. "At least let me get my pants up." The cops ignore me and snap on the restraints. They're filming everything; I can see the small mirrors on their hats.

The Boy is hustled out of my field of vision; their face is white, but the last glance at me is worried, not accusing. Then I can't see them and there's a yell, "No! Not at all! No! Stop!" Keep calm kid. We'll get through this. My attention focuses on the medcop in front of me, brandishing a cotton swab as if it were a deadly weapon. Huh? He takes a sample from my bobbing dick, which is rapidly going soft. I'm a little confused. All this for at best a vandalism arrest? Then, as he takes out his med-scanner, pointing it at me to check for drugs in my system, it dawns on me and I start to laugh near-hysterically. The idiots think it's a rape! The booth worker must have seen the knife and misinterpreted. Big time.

I laugh even harder when I see the expression of the guy holding the medscanner to check me for drugs. My flesh will show up in shades of red, but my APPle will look bright green. Cyberflesh. His eyes leap to my face, and I sag in the cops' grip, I'm laughing so hard. "Shut up or we'll have to trank you," snarls the guy locked onto my left arm, and that manages to sober me up a little, but I'm still shaking silently.

There's a two-hundred-year-old law in this state that nobody's gotten around to changing yet. It isn't rape unless it's done with a real penis. Of course, it's all made irrelevant in a moment as the Boy comes hurtling back around and flings their arms around me, yelling wildly, "Don't! Don't you hurt him!" The medcop rolls his eyes and heaves a big sigh.

Two hours later, I'm released from the cell I've been in, sitting alone on my ass. The jerks decided to charge me with vandalism so as not to have wasted their time, but they confiscated both my APPles anyway. Maybe they thought I'd sit here in my cell and masturbate. Hell, I might have. The look on that one cop's face when he got Asmodeus out of my jacket pocket was enough to put me into another spasm of laughter, which didn't do much for my case.

The Boy is waiting for me by the desk when I'm let out. Looks worried; I'm touched. I guess I'd expected that when the cops chose not to arrest them they'd hightail it home faster than a jackrabbit, but instead the kid runs over and throws their arms around me again. "You okay?" they ask. "They didn't put you in a cell with real rapists or anything, did they?"

I gently disengage them from my neck. "Nah, nachtlei get separate cells. It's policy. I'm okay. It was a stupid stunt anyway. I'm sorry I dragged you into all this, kid."

The kid grins. "It's all right. I called Mom and got your charges dropped. It won't even be on your record. And I got back your stuff." Holds up a clear sealed bag with my wallet, keys, two lovely curved cocks, and wonder of wonders, my knife. The kid's eyes are twinkling, and I notice the sullen expressions of the cops behind the desk as they glare at me. "It was the least I could do," the Boy is saying.

I blink. "Who in hell is your mother?" I ask, almost afraid of the answer.

"County commissioner." Complete innocence in those big eyes. "Sir."

Shit. The kid must have raised one gargantuan stink to spring me. Now I'm going to have to deal with gratitude, and obligations. The police station suddenly feels terribly oppressive, and the force of all those glares pushes me right out the front door, the kid at my heels. I find I really don't know what to say. I mean, a one-nighter is a one-nighter, but... I owe this kid big, and it makes me vaguely uncomfortable.

My bike is in front of the cop station. I take a step back in surprise. "What—How?"

"I had it towed here, sir."

"That must have cost a lot."

The Boy shrugs. "No big deal, sir." The honorific helps. I glance over. Those eyes are still on me.

"Thanks," I say. "I appreciate everything. Really. A lot."

The eyes drop. "I... I hoped you wouldn't consider it too impertinent, sir. I mean, I know you can handle your own problems. I didn't want it to seem... interfering."

The kid is trying really hard not to smile throughout this self-effac-ing speech, and that breaks through my shell of discomfort and makes me chuckle. Okay, so I've been dumb more than once tonight. One more test, and then they're off the hook. I rip open the bag and pull my keys out. "Guess it's time to go," I say. The Boy doesn't say anything. The way-too-new sneakers scuff the ground.

I straddle my bike and start it. Then I look up, scrutinizing the figure who stands there, hands jammed into pockets. "Well?" I say, jerking my head in a command. "Do I have to tell you everything?"

The Boy's face breaks into a big grin, relief, and joy and—something else? I don't know. They scramble behind me onto the bike. I freeze them with a grunt, and hold out the plastic bag, holding everything I value in it. "Think you can take care of this on the ride home?" I ask. "Keep it safe in your coat, not drop it on the highway? 'Cause if you lose my dicks, I'll have to kill you. Not to mention that you won't get fucked."

The kid takes the bag gingerly, as if it's a treasure, which it is, and tucks it inside their jacket like a baby. Then their arms go around me, just as gingerly, as if it might not be allowed. I chuckle again as I put on my helmet. "You'll have to hold on tighter than that. I wouldn't want to lose my valuable cargo." The arms tighten into a bear hug, and the Boy puts their head on my shoulder. Valuable cargo. As I kick my hoverbike into gear and roar off, I wonder for a moment exactly which I was referring to.

LIKE A REFLECTION IN A MIRROR WITH NO GLASS
Renee M. Charles

From her semi-prone position on the Syntho-Mate-Inc. recliner (head and upper torso resting flat, hips and pelvis raised, legs conveniently spread on separate, swing-out platforms), Tanja could barely see this session's Syntho-Mate surrogate resting on its matching recliner—her gravity-flattened breasts, under the thin drape, obscured her view—but Tanja did notice that this particular model was a Euro-body, with light-complexioned "flesh" and almost ludicrously butter-yellow hair on top, which contrasted sharply with the artfully arranged merkin of black curls below.

The designers must have been hung up on suicide blondes, Tanja decided, as she waited for the Mechi-aide to prep her before this latest Bio-donation, her seventh (or was it the eighth—after a while, especially after the indignity of the first session had worn off, she'd found it hard to keep track) this year alone. Long ago, Tanja had stopped jerking reflexively with fright as the Mechi-aide made its abrupt appearance through the Bio-'nation chamber's swinging metal doors, but no matter how many times she went through the prepping procedure, her heart still yammered in her chest when the wheeled, four-limbed, headless robot whirred over to her head, and deftly applied the brain-link sensors to the thumb-sized shorn spots on her scalp (after the first session, when the Mechi-aide sheared off most of her hair, Tanja learned to pre-shave those areas, and kept the rest of her hair at a uniform half-inch length, so all she had to endure was the application of the sensors), then whirred down to the spot between her legs, and sheared her outer labia, before applying the remaining sensors to her shorn skin, the already hairless folds of her inner labia, and the pearl-like nub of her clitoris, using that almond-scented, slightly oily, and definitely sticky substance to bond the sensors to her skin, completing the link between herself and the life-like plastiod covering of the latest Syntho-Mate resting on her own splay-legged recliner, before it rolled itself back through the still-moving swinging doors.

Then, another, albeit briefer wait, while the technicians (none of whom Tanja could see, even though they definitely could see her through the banks of two-way, smoke-tone mirrors which lined the walls and ceiling of the small, overheated chamber; as it was, the only live people she ever did see at Syntho-Mate-Inc. were the female attendants who supervised the undressing-briefing area—it was no secret that a woman desperate enough to endure a Bio-donation session might also be desperate enough to rifle the contents of unguarded clothes-belongings lockers—or the gal who gave Tanja her money after the session was over) did whatever it was they did to establish a link between Tanja's living, feeling flesh, and the synthetic, receptive "flesh" of the nearly-programmed Syntho-Mate, prior to activating the Stimu-probes...

I'll bet they take their sweet time just to make sure every one in the room gets a good, long look at the donor, Tanja thought with surprisingly little bitterness; that particular emotion had long since mellowed into a cynical black humor after she'd taken to checking out each finished Syntho-Mate prior to getting off the recliner and hurrying back to the undressing area. Despite surface differences in each 'Mate (black skin, delicate Oriental hues, artificial tan lines permanently dyed into the "flesh," all in readiness for the company's world-wide clientele), all of them wore an identical, vacuous expression, like a reflection in a mirror with no glass, which belied absolutely nothing of the sexual responses she'd just donated... No wonder they want to get a look at the donor... no matter how pretty they make 'em, no matter how they wiggle their hips and twitch their labia, they're not much of an improvement over those blow-up fuck dolls from my grandfather's day. And the folks who

manufactured those things didn't have to pay volunteers for every automated twitch and wiggle...

For a time, Tanja had a so-pay-me-for-nothing attitude; remembering
how her own grandmother had to pose for nude pictures to work her
way through college, Tanja went through her period of indifference... but
always, just before she scurried across the nubby-carpeted chamber floor
on her way to get dressed, she'd feel that stab of disappointment when
she saw her Syntho-Mate just... lying there, expectant and uninvolved, a
waiting vessel for some man's self-involved, self-satisfied physical out-
pourings. Only, unlike the latex sex dolls with the vibrating vaginas, these
'Mates did have computer brains. With fuzzy logic, if her roommate (and
on-off lover) Ingrid could be believed—and, after all, Ingrid was dating
(for money, to be honest) one of the technicians who did whatever it was
that they did behind those murky mirrored walls... (Although Tanja did
find it ironic that the man preferred real flesh-sex, albeit it for hire, but
since Ingrid was so much prettier than Tanja, the irony wasn't so hard to
swallow...)

Stealing another glance at this latest Syntho-Mate, with her luxurious,
glistening waves of aureate hair, and her just-pinched-pink nipples surmounting the artfully asymmetrical mounds of her pearly-pale breasts,
and the coiled arabesques of hair framing her puckered labia, Tanja
thought, What I wouldn't give to look like that, before reaching up to
slowly peel the tissue-thin paper drape off her torso. Looking above her
in the mirror, she appraised her own body, taking in the small but neatly formed breasts with the slightly oval nipples, the just barely convex
stomach—now rippled into a creased dewlap by her upraised pelvis—
and the semi-bald stubbled labia just barely visible from this angle; not
bad, but not... mythic. Not dream-like in its fantasy contours; certainly
not direct-flesh saleable, like Ingrid's. Her legs were still draped, but she
knew they were serviceably long and lean, a little skimpy in the calf, but
then again, the people at Syntho-Mate-Inc. weren't programming the
'Mates to jog... But Tanja's main dissatisfaction was with her face and hair;
true, she had good Germanic bones, and her hair—if let to grow—was
glossy, but had she been born in her great-grandparents' day, she never
would have been considered to be an ideal German woman. Like Ingrid,
she found herself thinking, as a part of her still stung at the injustice of
her situation... true, in hard times like these, any work is desirable, and
after all, Ingrid did warn me that being a Bio-donator takes... how did

she put it? "A certain talent for removing yourself from the situation." But do you need to remove yourself from the flesh-sex sessions with your "date" I wonder? True, sessions with him aren't nearly enough to keep either of us sheltered or fed, but... but you never have needed to give a Bio-donation, no matter how much better they pay, have you? You've never lacked for flesh-sex requests, Tanja mentally harangued her roommate, even as she felt the flicker of wanting for Ingrid stir deep within her own partly hidden sex. And, after all, it was no one's fault that Ingrid was a natural-born blonde...

But then again, this Syntho-Mate's not a real blonde, either. But yet... perhaps something within her could be real, Tanja found herself musing, as the Mechi-Aide finally made its unannounced appearance, first pausing by the Syntho-Mate and gathering up its tendril-like sensor-wires dangling from the prone 'Mate's head and labia in one robotic arm, then glided over to Tanja's own head (the bare ovals of shining skin there resembled a tribal pattern against the roan covering of her hair) and began to apply the first of the sensors linking her brain—her feeling, but also thinking, needing brain—to that of the waiting 'Mate, first squirting on a daub of adhesive, then securing the sensor... but this time, Tanja mentally advised her latest Syntho-Mate, not even knowing for sure if her words would or could be heard:

Go ahead, enjoy this... you may be more beautiful than I am, but you're not just a tool. You're the receiving end of all this, you're the one he's pleasuring, no matter what he thinks... or you can simply pleasure yourself, if you've a mind to.

And as the aide's moist, sponge-tipped adhesive-spurting arm bore down on the next shaved-clean oval on her scalp, Tanja's mind drifted inward, as she completely, wholly concentrated on that long-ago day when—

—she and her best (and prettiest) friend Marthe were sitting in Tanja's bedroom, trying on the swim suits they'd just bought with their saved-throughout-the-winter allowances, even though the water still wasn't warm enough for swimming anywhere save for in the indoor municipal pool, "—and who wants to go there?" Marthe had pouted (and somehow, pouting seemed to suit Marthe, while it just seemed childish when Tanja did it), as she wiggled into the bottom of her new ruffle-trimmed suit-panty behind the tall, shirred-fabric-covered folding screen which occupied the eastern-most corner of Tanja's room.

There was just enough sunlight coming in through Tanja's western window that she could see Marthe's lithe, slender body silhouetted through the tight gathers of the pink-flowered fabric covering the open framework of the screen; despite the distortion, she could easily make out the nub-like buds of Marthe's breasts, and the slight swell of her bottom, as Marthe stepped out of one suit panty and bent to pick up the other new suit she'd purchased shortly after their half-day Saturday classes let out.

Both girls were only in the sixth grade, too young yet for shower-afterwards-gymnastic class, but Tanja was already beginning to feel curious about how her friends' bodies looked in comparison to hers—Has their hair started coming in yet down there? Have any of their nipples gotten hard when their blouses rub against them?

From where she sat on her bed, Tanja could see her reflection in the three mirrors, one long, the others shorter, surmounting her vanity table, only each reflection was slightly different, showing her body at incrementally non-identical angles, but she liked the view in the middle mirror the best (it chopped off her bare feet, which she thought too big), especially since she could also see the fabric-distorted reflection of Marthe's shadow in that one... and as her eyes drifted from her own nearly-naked reflection to that of Marthe, her right hand began to drift toward her lap, until she'd unconsciously peeled down her modest suit bottom, until the first reddish curls of hair were visible—

"Oh, you have hair too... I thought I was the only—"

Marthe's voice made Tanja jump in place; when she looked toward her friend, Marthe was wearing her one-piece suit, but she, too was pulling aside the stretchy fabric along one leg, to reveal a dark-brown feathering of hair covering her mons. Her own heart now fluttering in her chest, while her mouth became too dry for her to speak, Tanja just nodded, while Marthe padded over to her and then reached down with a tentative hand to grasp the waistband of Tanja's swim suit, as she asked, "Can I see?" even as she pulled the panties out of the way, until all of Tanja's matted-down vaginal hair was revealed. The sunlight streaming into her room touched the nest of curly hair, turning the reddish locks a fiery golden-orange. With a barely-pressed down finger, Marthe felt Tanja's mound, then wiggled out of her own suit, to reveal her own rounded corners triangle of pressed-down pubic hair—along with her budding breasts, and concave belly below.

Without needing to ask, Tanja lightly ran her hand over Marthe's mons, before giggling, "If only the hair on our heads was so curly!"

"No more need for permanents," Marthe agreed, before she sat down next to Tanja and said in a low whisper, "My older sister says that when her boyfriend... touches her, down there, she gets all slippery, but even when she doesn't, he uses lotion, which she says feels even better..."

Both girls were headed for Tanja's vanity in a second, looking for a suitable hand lotion, but Marthe found the bottle first, so Tanja hurried to her bed, and laid down, with her legs over either corner, so that her bare mons was supported by the corner of the bed itself. Closing her eyes, and picturing Marthe's boyfriend in her mind (even though she'd never seen him), she found her breath coming in short, hard gasps as Marthe squirted a dollop of the nutty-sweet-smelling creme onto the spot where her wrinkled inner lips met at the top, then—using her first and second fingers in a slow, circular motion—Marthe rubbed the lotion onto Tanja's labia, then used her other hand to gently knead the curls-covered skin over her labia, while Tanja's lower legs hugged the sides of the bed tightly, and her own moisture began to mingle with the lotion, until all Tanja was aware of was the warmth of the sun across her bare middle, the musky-nut-like smell in her nostrils, and the ripples of throbbing pleasure which radiated outward from her now-slippery vagina like rings moving outward from a stone tossed in still water...

The metallic scree of the Mechi-aide's surgical razor-tipped arm moving into position brought Tanja back into the now with a jolt, even as the memory of that schoolgirl masturbation session remained as a warm glow in her mind; glancing above her, she saw the now-humming razor approach her stubble-covered labia, but as the Mechi-aide's arm made contact with her skin (the tingle of the vibrating cutting edge felt uncharacteristically delicious this time, unlike any of the previous sessions), Tanja instead saw—

—her curls-framed vagina in the reflective circle of the hand mirror her boyfriend had handed to her, as he placed the towel under her pillows-supported bottom, and spread the fabric taut between her spread-open thighs, and despite the fact that Tanja had seen how she looked in private, when she'd examined her genitals in her own bathroom after taking a bath, what she saw now was somehow different, mostly because this was how she looked to Peter, so it was like she was looking at the mons of a stranger, a person outside herself. For a moment, she was reminded of that afternoon with Marthe, and how she'd looked with that drizzle of pale pinkish lotion covering her tight, supple lower lips. That day, the sight of Marthe's openness had been strangely exciting to Tanja... as the sight of her own openness was this evening.

She and Peter had spent several nights together, but tonight was to be different; first he'd shave her, than she'd shear off his fringe of curls around his organs, since they'd read in one of Peter's sex magazines that the experience of bare flesh caressing moist nakedness was incredible...

But now, as she lay on his bed, with her softness exposed and slightly parted, so that her vagina gaped a little at the bottom, hinting at the slippery depths within, and Peter busied himself with his scissors, disposable razors, and can of shaving foam, lining everything up neatly on the dresser-top next to where he was sitting (likewise naked, with his penis already semi-erect) across from her, Tanja felt a rush of pleasure-fear: Suppose he nicked her? Or the scissors caught the hair instead of cutting it? The unexpected vulnerability of her position was a little intimidating; while she'd been spread open during gynecological exams, her doctor hadn't had barbering items at the ready...

"Ready?" he suddenly asked, as he approached her mound of Venus with his hair-cutting shears, and—keeping her mons in view of the mirror she held out at an angle to her body—Tanja just smiled up at him, and nodded. The scissors snicked as Peter alternately grasped (very gently) tufts of her hair, snipped off the curls close to her skin, then set the shorn locks on the towel, before lifting and holding the next tuft, and cutting again. Getting the hair closest to her anus trimmed did pinch a bit, but Tanja smiled anyhow, and watched Peter's seemingly disembodied fingers and the sharp-pointed blades as they freed her now stubbly labia and mons of the reddish curls she'd been so proud of only a decade before, that day with Marthe...

Once she was trimmed, Peter ran his palms against the grain of her hair, until the short bristles stood upright, like an uneven crew-cut on a misshapen, cloven head, and while he shook the can of foam, she reached down with her free hand and felt her close-cropped skin; the sensation of her skin touching the stubble was ticklishly pleasant. Before spreading on the foam, Peter meticulously snipped off a few stray longer hairs, then touched the nozzle of the can against her lower belly, allowing the minty-cool white creme to billow out in a frothy puff that crept into her mirror-view like a wind-scudded cloud. And Tanja felt herself growing moist as Peter smoothed the creme over all her clipped hair; as the head of the plastic razor appeared in her mirror, taking away the foam and the hair beneath in narrow swaths, she found it hard to hold the mirror steady...

Only when she saw the reflection of a smooth, knee-cap bare mons in her mirror did she relax fully; not a drop of blood could be seen, only softly contouring pale skin surrounding the now deep-pink inner labia and gently throbbing, twitching clitoris. The warm air of Peter's bedroom suddenly seemed cooler against her denuded skin, and the overhead light glinted softly off her still-moist curves and deep folds. Slowly, she tilted the mirror so that she could see the rest of her body along with her freshly shorn mons, as if to reaffirm her disbelief that such a shell-like, beautifully wrinkled and deeply concave bare softness could really belong to her. Reaching down once more with her free hand, she caressed her slippery smoothness, until she felt Peter's head next to her hand, and she moved her fingers to the back of his neck, as his tongue flickered along her hairless labia—and she turned the mirror toward her pelvis, to better see what was happening, until the swell of sensations became too much for her, and her eyes closed of their own accord, and her vision was a red-veined screen before her—

Tanja's eyes snapped open as the swinging doors swished shut behind the departing Mechi-aide; glancing down at herself, she noticed that she'd been trimmed more extensively than usual, until only a tonsure-like thin fringe of curls remained along the upper edge of her mons. More sensors than usual were attached to her down there. Must be a special-order Syntho-Mate, she reasoned, whoever is getting her must've paid extra for the increased sensitivity levels. (Ingrid had once told her roommate about the special-order models; supposedly they had increased memory-capacity, to better serve their owners... if that's the case, Mr. Lucky Owner is really going to get his money's worth, Tanja decided with a smile in the direction of the prone, mute Syntho-Mate across the room.)

And, as a further departure from the normal Bio-donation sessions, the recliner began to vibrate slightly, the only sign she ever had that the automatic probes were about to be released from the enclosed pedestal-like base of the recliner—they're never this fast, her mind protested briefly, before another, more primal part of her brain countered, And you've never been this ready for it...

Not needing to watch the coiled metal probes with the flexible, slightly yielding syntho-flesh ends emerge from the bottom of the recliner, and—after a fine misting of oily liquid from the one nozzle-tipped probe was sprayed on her bared inner softness—bear down with slight, but firm pressure on her labia, her exposed clitoris, before the main probe slipped into her, Tanja narrowed her eyes as she tilted her head in the direction of the still-oblivious Syntho-Mate, and intensely thought at her:

Put those fuzzy little data banks and ROMs of yours to work... you're only getting one chance at this...

And as the first of the probes made contact with her flesh, applying stylus-like even pressure on the gently rounded folds of her upper labia, Tanja mentally added, Feel what I feel... see what I saw... experience it all—

"You've never done it with another woman, have you?" Ingrid's voice was casual, but Tanja caught the slightly taunting edge to it, as she pulled her head away from Ingrid's pillowing breast, and replied defensively, "I've been with girls... once, a friend of mine and I, we were trying on swim suits, and—"

"But not a woman," Ingrid teased, as she traced the outline of Tanja's right nipple with a pale-pink painted fingernail, letting the pointed tip of the nail lightly graze the puckered darkness of Tanja's areola, then spiraling around the darker oval of flesh until it reached the tender opening of the nipple itself. The sensation was so similar to what Tanja did with her own breasts while she was wet and slippery in the bath water, that she gasped from the feeling of deja vu. As if seeing that shock of self-recognition in Tanja's eyes, Ingrid whispered, "Were you and your little girl friend pulling the crotches up against your labia, or were you giving each other pussy-massages?"

Her face growing hot, Tanja lowered her eyes and mumbled, "Yes... with hand-lotion—" at which Ingrid laughed that throaty, purring chuckle of hers, as she reached down to lightly tickle Tanja's mound of Venus, until her fingers burrowed deeper through the re-grown reddish mass of curls, and Tanja found herself gasping and panting as her room-mate lazily circled her clitoris with a light, teasing motion. Tanja flipped on her back, arching up her pelvis as Ingrid increased the pressure on her clitoris while simultaneously rubbing the area in ever-widening circles, until the lack of stimulation on the sensitive nubbin of flesh made Tanja's thigh muscles quiver with excitement, but Ingrid's fingers grew even more coy, now drawing lazy figure eights along Tanja's entire labia, paus-ing briefly in the vagina itself, before arcing back to flick past the clitoris, then starting the cycle anew.

And, as if from a very long distance, she heard Ingrid's teasing voice ask, "Do you even miss the lotion?" and in answer, Tanja shook her head No against the pillow, sending her hair streaming out in ray-like strands of burnished red, while her belly and pelvis arched reflexively before Ingrid finally resumed the slow circling motion on Tanja's now blood-engorged organ, and Tanja felt the ripples of her orgasm envelope her, until the last of the ever spreading ripples washed from her conscious-ness, and she opened her eyes to see Ingrid propped up on one elbow next to her, her breasts shifting to one side like stacked pillows, while a wicked tight smile played on her lips.

"Was this better than little-girl rubbing? Little girls, they know only the tickle and the itch... a little scratch, a bit of rubbing, and it's all bet-ter," she cooed in that slightly mocking, yet softly tender voice, before she held her hand up, the fingers shiny in the room's dimmer-lowered lights, "And they need to add water—"

Coming back to her sense of self, Tanja chided, "I got wet on my own that time... my friend did, too... We weren't 'little,' either... we had hair and all—"

Ingrid laughed again, as she peered down at her own shaven mound, and the clear bubble of moisture welling deep within her; before her roommate could tease her again, Tanja added, "And I've been shaved... by my boyfriend. Before I did it to him."

Languidly rubbing her own bald mound, Ingrid asked, "And who liked it more? You or him?"

Taken aback by Ingrid's shift away from taunts about her lack of expe-rience, Tanja found herself buying time by looking at their paired reflec-tion (only their heads and the rising curves of their bare hips were visi-ble from this angle) in the dresser mirror; she hadn't really thought about it that night, since she'd been so intent on not nicking or cutting

Peter with his razor, but now that she really thought about the experience, it all came back to her:

Peter kept craning his head up, as she carefully snipped away the tufts of his light brownish hair, asking, "How close are you to the skin? Don't pull too tight... is there much left to go?" but she'd been too nervous to answer him, for fear of losing concentration and cutting his testicles or penis with the tips of the scissors, and once she'd shorn the longer hairs, he propped himself up on his elbows, until his usually taut stomach was a mass of rolls of flesh, so he could supervise the actual shaving, and even then, he kept up his worried stream of directions—"Not so much foam, be sure you can see the skin underneath... pull the razor with the grain... ouch, not so close... be careful, he's very attached to me... wait, that scrapes... there, you missed a patch..."

And afterward, when she had him in her mouth, and was rubbing the newly bare flesh around his member with her fingers, he chafed under her, until she had to stop and go get some lubricating jelly from the tube in his dresser drawer, and slather his shorn flesh until it glistened, and only then could she resume caressing his flesh with her tongue, but by then... all the orders and admonishments and requests had turned the evening somewhat sour...

"Well?" Ingrid was now playing with Tanja's breasts, cupping each in her dry-skinned palms, and squeezing them gently for emphasis, until Tanja admitted, "I did... but I suppose it was because I knew he was used to shaving his own face—"

Ingrid's mouth puckered into a moue at that; releasing Tanja's breasts, she shook one finger teasingly in front of Tanja's face, as she said, "Since when does a man have a face contoured like a woman's pussy? No, you simply trusted him with your essence, while he feared for a slip of the razor. Do you think I let my boyfriend shave me? Even if there were no vaccine for AIDS, do you think I'd fear it if he cut me, or if I clipped him... blood is as natural as sex. Your boyfriend was obsessed with his own needs. Do you think you'd have enjoyed it more, shearing him, if he'd let himself enjoy it?"

Tanja merely blushed at that, remembering how she and Peter had stopped making love for as long as it took for their hair to grow back, as if their continued baldness was a reminder of that not-quite-perfect sensual experiment... but when she felt Ingrid's fingers caressing the coiled locks of hair on her mound, she placed a staying hand over Ingrid's and asked, "Why does what you do to me feel so much better than what Peter, or even my own hand does down there?"

Brushing off Tanja's hand from her own, before she resumed that exquisitely lazy circling and moving away motion, Ingrid smiled and said, "Because I know what feels good on me... and since you've got the same organs I do, it's like pleasuring yourself without bending your wrist in the wrong direction... besides, if a man did have a vagina, and a clitoris, and labia too, he'd better understand us... and vice-versa," she added, with a wink, before extracting a vibrator from beneath the covers.

Tanja stared at the peach-colored wand of plastic, which was covered with a disposable, realistically wrinkled sheath, and argued, "But it's not real," to which Ingrid replied, "But at least I know where it will feel best for you," before switching it on.

And, true to her word, Ingrid was able to position the gently throbbing faux penis at just the right, clitoris-rubbing-as-it-entered-her angle, sipping it swiftly and evenly in and out of her moisture-sheened depths, then allowing the entire vibrating length of it to linger against her labial folds, before teasing it along the length of Tanja's belly, and under and around each breast.

Afterward, Ingrid whispered, "If a man were to try that, his poor back might break," before she handed over the still-quivering wand and a freshly opened sheath to Tanja, then flipped on her own back and arched her smooth-skinned mound toward Tanja's descending hand...

As she traced the tip of the vibrator against Ingrid's yielding flesh, Tanja let her own memories guide her (memories of probing fingers and penises wielded by others she'd thought knew more about pleasuring her by virtue of their imagined-to-be-superior looks, or supposedly superior sex), and—buoyed by a new-found sense of confidence—even added some variations of her own as she felt the throbbing motion of the plastic wand move along her hand and arm, then spread over her entire body; once she was through using the vibrator, she clicked it off, then ran her own tongue along Ingrid's slippery, musky folds, as she pictured her own freshly-denuded mons and labia under her own, flicking, probing tongue—and to hell with Peter, I don't need him to feel something this deeply, she'd mentally added, as Ingrid moaned, then shifted around under her, seeking out Tanja's own hidden inner softness—

When she heard the metal-against-metal *zuuupt* of the probes retracting back into the base of the recliner, Tanja opened her eyes... and immediately saw the glistening clear pool of moisture spreading out in front of her sensor-trailing vaginal area in the overhead mirror. And the deep, sated redness of her organs, and of her eyelids, was unmistakable... and utterly different from her previous Bio-donation sessions, the early ones during which she'd allowed herself to be distracted by her petty, mostly self-perceived inadequacies. As if it were my fault, or Ingrid's, that she'd be better suited to flesh-sex for hire than I am... as if I should take personal offense that men like her Tech-date choose to only look at the outside of a woman. As if pleasure can't come in any package...

And she was both surprised/not surprised to see how mottled her breasts were, from kneading and rubbing them as she'd relived that first, pivotal lovemaking session with Ingrid, back in the days when times hadn't been quite so tight, and Ingrid had little need for seeking out flesh-sex buyers—or Tanja hadn't been so willing to take Ingrid up on her "you might not like it, but it is a job—and a good-paying one" suggestion. But times had grown so tight, and jobs were so scarce, and neither of their university-sponsored jobs were quite enough anymore... but that didn't mean that the roommates still couldn't make time for each other, outside sex-jobs or not—

Maybe next time, I'll ask her to shave me completely before we make love... or I do another Bio-donation, Tanja mused, with more eagerness on both counts than she'd ever felt before, as she sat up on the slippery recliner, and allowed her legs to meet for the first time in over an hour (the stiffness in her hips was still there, as usual, but then she remembered the pre-need-for-sex-selling time when Ingrid snuck her into the university dance practice room, where they'd done naked splits and leg-on-the-bar stretches in the drapes-drawn, mirror-walled room, and as much as her hips had ached after that night's lovemaking, she'd been eager to make yet another visit to that echoing, parquet-floored room), perhaps I'll even take her up on that offer to shear off all my hair... she's always teasing me about the "dots" on my scalp, even as she keeps assuring me that I do have a beautifully-shaped head... no matter how much I tell her I don't...

Finally confident in Ingrid's assessment of her looks, Tanja was so absorbed in imagining what a complete shaving session might feel like, how the weight of Ingrid's razor wielding hand would feel going over the lathered curves of her perfectly-shaped skull, that she almost missed the first subtle motions of the Syntho-Mate on her recliner... but when that unexpected movement appeared in the corner of her eye, Tanja found herself standing, still sporting the sensor-pads linking her to the 'Mate like multiple umbilical cords (only who was really born just now, you or me?), and staring mouth-agape as the gloriously golden-tressed Syntho-Mate slid her elegantly long, tapered fingers through and under the springy locks of her merkin-like mons, the fingers moving with exquisite slowness and purpose while the 'Mate's blue eyes were nearly closed in ecstasy, their lids just beginning to flush with a faint tinge of quite realistic red...

Watching the masturbating Syntho-Mate, as the newly Bio-donated construct took pleasure in herself, for her own sake, Tanja felt a glow of self-satisfaction ripple through her own body; for once, she felt like a total sexual being, one not dependent on mere looks (or her imagined lack of them) alone, or the reactions of others to her... she stopped feeling twinges of envy over Ingrid and her flesh-sex-buying "boyfriend" (who might very well be sitting on the other side of that one-way glass at this instant, not quite earning enough money to even afford a Syntho-Mate of his very own), for didn't Ingrid still seek her out, when all Tanja could pay her was satisfaction for its own sake?

And I finally passed that on to a Syntho-Mate... that thing in me that transcends the need for the exchange of mere money, she thought triumphantly, her face and body glowing from within with a sense of confidence and inner-peace she'd only felt in brief, incoherent snatches before... only now, Tanja knew that she could call upon this totality of feeling which transcended any single sexual act any time she so desired... and I even get paid for the pleasure of experiencing it. Before she pulled the sensors off her head and her mons, Tanja thought/told the Syntho-Mate, Don't ever forget this... no matter what your owner expects of you... whatever you feel is yours, to keep. Remember, that's a greater gift than whatever you happen to look like... looks are only important as long as you have a mirror handy.

Then, hoping that the had-to-be-watching technicians didn't pay too close of attention to her as she exited the room, sans the paper drape she usually wrapped around her nakedness like a bath towel, Tanja made sure that she walked close enough to the Syntho-Mate to be able to surreptitiously run her own hand along the freshly programmed 'Mate's symmetrically-tufted mound of Venus—and see, out of the corner of her departing eye, the Syntho-Mate's lips turn upward in thanks, their motion mirroring that of Tanja's own smiling lips.

And as she dressed under the watchful eye of the dressing area attendant, Tanja was already looking forward to her next Bio-donation—and the fee she'd get for it (a fee far bigger than any flesh-sex Ingrid might hope to earn) was the last priority on her mind...

You were the first, she mentally advised the activated blonde 'Mate, the first of many, many more. I have memories to spare, and my future memories will be even better, because I know what I have to give others is well worth the receiving now... what I give is good for others, but even better for myself, and for remembering—

And all of you 'Mates will have forever to relive my memories and enjoy them, as you enjoy yourselves...

TEMPORARY INSANITY
Thomas S. Roche

I lived in health clubs among glittering mirrors and dropped by mansions when I wanted to relax. I posed for a trillion nude photos, a skin flick slut seduced by the photographer—and generally his or her assistant(s)—at every shoot.

I lost my virginity a thousand times, spread like succulent marmalade on canopied king-sized beds, tangled in satin sheets and caressed by baby oil and vibro-fingers massage. I did red hot virgins whose need consumed them. I took on cruising bimbos three at a time. I seduced the neighbors (all of them) while my husband was at work, sunbathed nude twenty-four hours a day, owned two thousand black garter belts and a million pairs of fishnet stockings, eighty leather jock straps, a hundred split-crotch panties and forty thousand pushup bras. I had a fifty foot cock and a pair of hundred pound tits. I invariably deep-throated on the first try, and juices were constantly running down my thigh. I went to a tanning salon at eight, noon, six, and midnight, serviced each time by the helpful massage therapists in their skintight tank tops and nylon gym shorts.

I haunted bars replete with domestic cigarettes and hard alcohol, a cocktail waitress who didn't own underwear. I was, perpetually, a freshman in college with enormous breasts and/or blonde pubic hair. I spent most of my time in Southern California, occasionally dropping by Hawaii for the weekend. I was going for my PhD in Sexology and used this as an excuse to seduce every hot young stud and flirtatious virgin in my class. I used my position as CEO of an enormous corporation to get me pussy. I drove around pedal-to-the-metal in Daddy's Porsche 911 convertible, cruising for hot young flesh.

I was badder than Satan. I turned out porn novels faster than a printing press turns out wedding invitations. I ate latex double-headed dildos at sundown and shit tiger-striped nylon jock straps just before dawn. I pissed French Roast and slept with my boots on.

I was the god(dess) of Sleaze, the Damned Thing, the Pornographer, a vision of Sex with its tits on backwards.

I had a stack of published porn novels twice the size of my roommate, all with my name on them (or someone else's, I forget whose). Half again that many books were in transit awaiting publication. I was paying the rent. Nothing could touch me.

The publishing house I had been writing for had gone out of business, taking several of my porn novels with it before I knew what was happening. I was left with a credit-card balance approaching infinity and a stack of unpublished pornography that was now almost worthless. I was in the death-grip of capitalism, and the end of the month was approaching.

I got wind of a shady outfit in Brooklyn that published original novels, hardcore S/M she-male and bestiality books for an absurdly low fee provided you sent it on disk so they didn't have to retype it. I could not work for such shitty wages, and resolved to starve rather than prostitute myself thus.

It was thus that I submitted, with a sick, curious pleasure, to the ultimate degradation beneath the booted feet of the System.

I submitted myself, wrists crossed, to temporary insanity.

So it was that I came to stand before the dark tower, dildo in one hand, begging bowl in the other, tie loosely knotted, to the foot of the forty-story building to answer phones for $12.50 an hour. I was greeted by a middle-aged woman with a frilly white shirt and a wool blazer with an "I LOVE SF" button on it. Her name was Deirdre. She led me through miles of winding cubicles, under fluorescent lights, through the valley of the damned. I was not afraid. She spoke to me about the duties I would be fulfilling, but she seemed to be speaking ancient Greek.

Finally, we reached my cubicle, deep in the belly of the beast. There was a Garfield doll hanging from the light fixture, and a computer in one corner of the tiny cubicle.

"Susanne is on vacation," Deirdre told me. "She normally answers this phone. People will be calling in if they have problems on the network. They'll get put on hold in a queue at the service desk. If they want to speak to someone immediately, they hit the pound key, and they'll be transferred to you."

"And what do I do with them?"

With a straight face, she told me: "Ask them to wait a moment, and transfer them to the service desk."

The hum of the fluorescent lighting grew in volume until it filled my entire being. The phone had not rung at all. The boredom was like a fine espresso or a cigarette I savored but did not enjoy. The minutes grew exponentially longer. 11:23 lasted for eight years.

My tie seemed to be choking me. The polyester pants, all I could afford on such short notice, was a field of ants crawling over my balls.

I stared at the black computer screen.

I couldn't. I wouldn't. It was crazy.

Tentatively, I switched the Damned Thing on.

Around four, Deirdre dropped by to make sure I was doing okay. I quickly switched screens and sat there grinning nervously.

She regarded me as if I were a maniac. Her gaze gradually softened, and her lips parted slightly. I noticed that her tits had gotten larger, her eyes bigger and more seductive. Her gray-streaked hair was now bleached, teased in an inviting mane of an unearthly color. She breathed deeply, her breasts heaving, as she sat on the arm of my chair.

Deirdre's palm grazed my cheek as she gazed into my eyes. Her own baby-blues were shaded by mascara-black palm fronds.

She spoke in a low, harsh whisper.

"How is the day going?"

"Fine," I mumbled.

"Do you have any... questions?"

"Sure," I mumbled. "Do... uh... do you need me back tomorrow?"

"Oh," she sighed. "We couldn't do without you. We need you back for the rest of the week. Susanne doesn't come back until next Monday. You're doing great. Everybody here likes you."

I was a bit confused, since I couldn't recall having met anyone, but I let it slide. "You can go ahead and pack up to go home," said Deirdre. "We don't get many support calls in the last hour of the day, so just go ahead and leave at five..."

I didn't have the heart to tell her that I hadn't gotten a single call all day, except for a wrong number around noon.

After she left, dancing in perfume and hallucination her way out of the cubicle, I turned my attention back to my computer, and the novel in progress that lay within.

I was the she-male, an androgyne with a flawless pair of silicons and a foot long schlong undamaged by hormones. I was a creature of desire.

I cursed. I hadn't brought any floppy disks, and there were none to be found in the office. Chapters One and Two, where the she-male in question visits a weight room and thereafter an ice skating rink, were on the hard drive.

There was nothing that could be done, so I secured the files, turned off the computer, and left.

All night long, I was tormented by visions of some perverted hacker working his way into the office in the middle of the night and feeding random combinations to the word processor until he found the password to those files.

But when I arrived the next day, the two chapters were still there, intact, and the hair I'd placed on the keyboard was on the same place. Some people tell me I read too many spy novels.

I went back to work. There were a lot of calls that day, particularly during the particularly steamy scene involving the she-male and a kitchen full of pastry chefs wearing nothing but aprons that said "KISS THE COOK."

The phone rang like an avalanche of Tibetan wind chimes.

"Hello," I mumbled incoherently, sweat pouring down my back and soaking my undershirt. "I mean...Technical Support, can I help you?"

"I can't get my machine running," the young woman on the other end of the line said breathlessly. "It seems to be giving me error messages. Do you think it might be going down?"

I had to think about that one. "If you'll hold for a moment, Ma'am, I'll transfer you to the service desk."

"I don't want to be transferred to the service desk. I want you to help me." It was said with husky, breathless desperation.

"Can you hold?"

"Oh... I guess so."

I transferred her away into nothingness and went back to Chapter 4, introducing a phone call on the kitchen phone from a woman desperate with need. The she-male invited her over and the bread was effectively kneaded while the chefs kept doubly busy on biscotti with unusual shapes.

The she-male finished off with the pastry chefs, leaving them caked with flour, spread out across the kneading table.

The phone rang again.

It was a panting, desperate being of questionable gender, but the voice was rough and whispered. "My terminal tells me access denied, but I know the password's right. I need to get in. I need in, right now—open up? Please open up and let me in? I want to enter...at the highest possible baud rate...open up! Open up for me, She-male!"

I frowned. I seemed to be suffering from intermittent hallucinations, something numerous colleagues of mine had experienced. I shrugged.

"If you'll hold a moment, Ma'am?"

"That's 'Sir' to you, punk! On your knees and give me access! On your knees, She-male, and take my data stream right into that steaming hole!"

Things had gotten serious.

"Hold please," I said. "I have a hallucination on my other extension." I transferred him away. "Technical support," I said to the next caller.

He responded with a desperate plea. "Need it! Want it! Gotta have it! Help me get it running! I need my access! Lines closed up! Need them opened! Please! Please! Open me up—wide!"

"Oh shit," I said. "Let me get you the service desk."

"No, oh God, please," he wailed, his voice crumbling into a dancing desperate moan. "Not the service desk—they're limp-dicked pansies! I need you! I need the she-male! Bring me back on-line!"

"Holy fuck," I muttered. "Hold on a minute."

I transferred him.

Again and again, three lines at once.

"She-male! Fuck my tits and help me reestablish my carrier!"

"Jesus Christ. Uh...wait a minute... hold please..."

"Oh God! Fucking oh my fucking God, She-male, put those luscious lips together and give me the 800-number for 9600 baud access, now! I need it now... oh please give me the number..."

"Um, excuse me, but you'll have to wait... holy fuck..."

"Swallow it! Swallow it, baby, and cough up the terminal type, cough it right into my ear, baby, I need it!"

"Shit!"

"I'm sitting here naked at my terminal, she-male, and I've got my cat in my lap. I want you to put that collar on and meow like you've never meowed before..."

"Oh son of a bitch... hold please..." There was nothing to be done. The calls would keep coming until She-male gave in to the desire of the callers and became their eager-dreaming pleasure pumpkin.

"Let me swallow your hardware... let me tongue your software..."

The she-male laid her bed of satin sheets and switched to speaker phone.

At the end of the week Deirdre signed my time sheet with a puckered red kiss of her blackberry-slathered lips across the words "Supervisor Signature," and with a friendly wave bid me farewell.

I carried home the better part of "She-male Software Slut" secreted away deep in my valise among ancient Guardians and dog-eared Paul Bowles novels.

I finished the novel sitting at my computer at home playing Lydia Lunch's "In Limbo" at top volume. Her erotic moans evoked the desperate hallucinatory dreams of people trying to reestablish their carrier.

She-male ended up in a villa in Switzerland, sharing it with three dozen nuns, two Russian construction workers and a German Shepherd.

I sold the novel, all rights, to the aforementioned shady outfit in Brooklyn for the colossal sum of $200. That roughly approximates the $1 a page that Henry Miller made some half-century ago. I started work on something a little slower-paced.

One morning after working all night I walked a mile or so to the edge of North America and watched the sun rise like an acetylene holocaust over the Golden Gate Bridge. Sea-birds screamed their war cries far beneath me as I chain smoked Pall-Malls at the crumbling edge of the cliff.

The fluorescent sun rises above acres of cubicles with faceless pimpled creatures laboring pathetically and dancing their unmoving death-dance here at the frozen moment of the forty-story apocalypse. I thought about that and smiled.

I had danced for real.

A demon wind sprang up from the ocean and put out my cigarette.

SHAYNA MAIDEL
Laura Antoniou

Kiva sighed as she took the freedom rings from around her throat and hung them from the hook on the back of the closet door. "It's not going to be that bad," Shari consoled from across the room. "It's only for a few days. And really, I've wanted to meet your family anyway."

"As my roommate," Kiva groused.

"As your special friend. When you're ready to come out, I'll be ready too." Shari was as patient as ever, her dark, sapphire eyes showing nothing but acceptance, security and love. It never took long for those eyes to make Kiva smile, and she eventually did, her lips tight in a sharp grin.

"Well, wait until you experience the High Holy Days at Temple Hillel," Kiva teased. "Every stereotype of Jewish culture, right there in front of you, and half of them coming from my relatives. Women in fur coats, trying to make matches while comparing the cost of cars, weddings and jewelry."

"I just wish I could bring my talis."

"Me too, baby. But I don't think Rabbi Feldman will be very up on women in tallit. And I don't expect he'll have some interesting interpretation on the vidui, and I don't think we'll be hearing a woman sing the Kol Nidre, either."

Their regular synagogue was a very liberal congregation, with a heavy gay and lesbian membership. Shari, since her conversion, was a much better Jew then Kiva when it came to observing the customs. Yet, because of Shari's fervor, Kiva had rediscovered the beauty and serenity of the Sabbath, and the comfort of the seasons and their celebrations. Time could easily get to be abstract without those reliable markers.

"We'll make do, sweetie," Shari said. "Bubeleh." She giggled.

"Don't start with me," Kiva warned. With another long suffering sigh, she pulled a dark skirt out of the closet and began to fold it. "Just don't start. I'll sic my mama on you, and she'll have you married and pregnant before Sukkot."

"Oh! Kayn aynhoreh on that!" In a fit of giggles, Shari almost fell off the bed. When she recovered, she noticed that Kiva hadn't joined in or offered a pithy comment. Instead, the darker woman was holding an old gray wool shawl, embroidered with fine stitching and worn around the edges. She had it bunched up under her nose, breathing in the scent of old perfume and smoke and piety.

"I wish you could have met her," Kiva said, breaking the silence.

"I wish I had."

Kiva folded the shawl carefully and put it in her suitcase. Maybe this year, she would wear it in front of the rest of the family, and solve the mystery of what Baba Chanah had done with it before she died.

But then, maybe she wouldn't. Kiva drew in more barren air and compressed her body to expel it, falling into the rhythm as she continued to pack. She was a little out of practice. Baba Chanah had told her not to allow these things to fall away, but it was so easy to forget. Especially when she had the headache of a family reunion after all these years. And during the Days of Awe, of course. The fast was going to make her very touchy. All this, she had explained to Shari months ago, but Shari was firm. It was time for Kiva to go home, even for a visit, and time that she met the family. It was only fair—Kiva got to meet Shari's parents last year, during Christmas, when they had to deal with their daughter's conversion and her new lover.

But fair doesn't mean bubkes when you have a family like mine, Kiva thought. And without Chanahleh there to smooth things over. . .

There were definitely times when lacking the ability to cry was a blessing.

"I've come to tell you a story, Akivaleh," Baba Chanah said as she slipped into Kiva's bedroom. Kiva pulled her head off the pillow and smirked.

"Baba, I'm eighteen years old. Don't you think that's a little grown up for bedtime stories? And what are you doing up so late?"

"You don't think an old woman like me hears things, like young women sneaking into the house at three in the morning?" Baba Chanah humphed in her elegant, knowing way and sat down on the edge of the bed.

Unlike her sisters, she had not grown rounded in her age, staying slender and almost a little bit fragile, her pale skin tight over her long fingered hands. She was always a small woman, but strong, and when the sisters gathered in family emergencies, it was always Chanah who was consulted and heeded. Kiva's mother had once told her that Chanah had always taken care of the entire family, men or no, and always would.

"I'm sorry I woke you," Kiva said immediately. She meant it.

"Tcha, tcha, I don't need all this sleep. I need to tell you a story. Now, will you be quiet and listen to your old Baba, or talk, talk, all night?"

Kiva sat up and drew her legs under her. If Baba Chanah wanted to tell her something this much, it must be important. She looked into the older woman's sharp eyes and wondered if Baba Chanah felt she was going to die. She was never ill, never weak. But she was much older then she looked.... Kiva bit her lip to hold back the wave of pain that swept through her and took Chanah's hand.

"Is it about the family?" she asked. "Is it about you?"

"Yes, of course!" Chanah patted Kiva's hand reassuringly. "It's time you were told about Michal."

"And this couldn't wait until morning?"

"Tcha! It's morning enough! Now listen:

Back in the old country, under the Tsars, our family lived in a village where nothing stands now, in a place where people do not remember that a Jew was ever there. And Michal, the girl with the strong name and a temper to match, was the oldest daughter of Akiva, for whom you were named, and who was the finest weaver for miles and miles.

"You never say anything about the men, Baba Chanah."

"Ah, men. They tell their own tales. These tales are ours, Akivaleh. Now, listen!"

As I was saying; Michal was the eldest of three daughters and two sons. There are men for you, all right? And this was back in the days where we Jews lived only by the whim of the Tsar—one day, we are valuable, and the next we are nothing. There might be peace for a year, for three, or five, but then the Cossacks would stir up the filthy peasants who hated us and they would burn and steal, and drive us away from our homes, what little land we had. They would cut down men in the street and take the young girls and do as they wished to them. They burned down our synagogues and spat upon the learned men and the Torah. And there was nothing to do, no place to go! There was no police precinct to complain to, because the police were the peasants, ready to take what was ours. We had no—no—civil rights?—not like here in goldeneh medina.

For many years, my mother's village was quiet. A little beating here, a little fire there, some ruffians breaking windows and stealing chickens, that was all.

Now, also from this village was a loose woman, a kurveh—

"Baba Chanah!"

"Well, she was! You're not a child, you can hear such talk."

"Mama would die if she heard you say that!"

"Your Mama, dear heart, should be so lucky that she gets a story like this one from me. Are you going to listen now?"

"Yes, Baba."

—this woman who had a reputation, nu? But more then that, she had a profession, and she didn't come to the synagogue, and no one spoke to her. Except for Michal, who had been her friend in their childhood and never forgot that, even when this woman turned her back on our ways and went to ply her trade among the goyim. And not a few of our men as well, I might add! But they never talk about that, only that she was shtupping the goyim for rubles. Never mind the giggles, Akivaleh, just listen!

It happens that one day, Michal goes into the fields to the secret place where she meets her old friend, and instead of gossip and young women's thoughts and dreams, they share terrible news. This outcast, this woman, had heard (don't ask how) that men were coming to this village, soon, tomorrow maybe! They were going to do this pogrom, do you know what that was? Of course you do, you're a good girl, a good scholar. They were going to burn the village and chase all the Jews out, maybe even kill them.

And now, Michal knew. But there she was, with her younger brothers and sisters, her mama, and the whole village to think of, what could she do? She was only a girl. If she warned them, they would not defend themselves—there were no shops to go buy guns, and our people, sadly, were not great fighters in those days. Chachemin, yes, but Lions of Judea, no. They could only run away, and hide, and hope that the troubles would be over soon.

Michal did what she thought was right; she ran home as quickly as her legs could carry her, through the fields and down the roads, and to all she passed, she cried, 'The Cossacks are coming! The Cossacks—

"What, what's so funny? This is a serious story I'm telling!"

"I'm sorry, Baba. Please, go on."

And the word spread through the town. Many people put their candlesticks and holy items under boards in the floors of stables and in their houses. They hid their valuables—what little they had—and they sent many of their daughters on wagons to another town to the east, where there was no trouble that day. But Michal's mama would not separate her family—together they would stay, until the troubles were over. Carefully, they took up their shawls and the smaller children, and some milk and bread and cholent in an old iron pot, and they went off into the woods, where no one knew the trails. Akiva (for whom you are named) was a wise woman to do this, but foolish as well. They left the morning of the pogrom, and slipped into the trees and vanished, a family together.

When the animals came the following day, they did the things they are known to do, and worse. They smashed windows and they smashed people. They carried off furniture and books and chickens and children, the girls for—hurting—and the boys to go into the army. And they burned down not only the synagogue, but the three shops and the mill and the spinning house where all the women of the village went. And when they discovered that many people were missing, they became enraged and set out into the fields and onto the roads, and yes, into the forest, to look for them.

They did not like being outsmarted, these Cossacks and their peasant slaves. Now, they wanted to kill as many Jews as possible, to teach them a lesson.

Deep in the woods, as dusk fell and no one from the village came to look for them, Akiva became worried and sent Michal back along their trail to try and find out what had happened. Michal didn't have to search long to realize that the woods were full of drunken peasants looking for the escaped Jews! She hurried back to her mother and her brothers and sisters, and took two children up in her arms. Leading the way, she brought them further and further into the woods, never losing the sounds of these terrible men coming after them. It was a nightmare, one shadow on another, strange cries and noises, and so many kinder to look after. Soon, they all became tired, and Michal had them take shelter near a stream. As they drank their fill, Michal looked at her mama and said, "I must go and get help."

Akiva didn't argue, only kissed her daughter and sent her on her way. You might ask, what help was there? As I said, there was no police, no FBI, no men to come save them. And this Michal knew also, yet she thought that there was one chance.

Through the woods she went, now to the north, now to the east, now to the west—each way, she looked and listened, and kept moving— always ahead of the searching men, always watching that some drunken momzer doesn't come and catch her.

And then suddenly, she sees a clearing. And in that clearing is a house, built in the old way, with logs and straw on the roof, and round windows without glass. There is no path leading to the heavy door, because that house doesn't sit still for much time in one place. But there were three large rocks by the door, because the house didn't sit on the ground. No, on both sides of the house were big, fat legs. The legs of a chicken!

"You like laughing at old women?"

"Baba! You're mixing Russian folktales with Yiddish ones!"

"Tcha! This is a story in Russia, yes? And she is being chased by Russians, right?"

"You didn't tell me this was a fairy tale."

"Because it is not a fairy tale, Miss Smart Mouth. Are you going to listen or not?"

"All right, Baba Chanah. So, she meets Baba Yaga."

No, not Baba Yaga, as though there is only one. One of the Baba Yagas, perhaps a young one, perhaps an old one. To her eyes, as she climbed the stones and reached for the door and it opened by itself, to her eyes, Baba Yaga is a baba, a little grandmother of a woman, with bad teeth, and round black eyes like saucers and hair like a bird's nest. Baba Yaga reaches out for Michal with one huge hand like a shovel and brings her into the hut on chicken legs and sits her down by the fire and gives her a nice cup of tea from a kettle that sings old Volga songs. Michal takes the tea and sees that her chair is made of bones, but she drinks the tea and says, 'Hello, Grandmother. Peace be unto you.'

You see, even being chased by those momzerim, she was still polite.

And Baba Yaga laughed in the way of old women, and sat down in a chair piled high with the skins of unclean beasts and picked her crooked teeth and nodded. 'Greetings, child of the Chosen People. I have never received a visit from your folk before!'

'And I have never met one of your folk before,' said Michal.

'What is it you wish, Daughter of Sorrows? A charm to win the heart of the Rabbi's son? A potion to rid a woman of an ill-gotten babe? A cow that gives golden milk, or the horn of Cheslav the Wicked, which brings the dead back to life once during a battle and once during a wedding?'

And Michal shuddered to hear of such things, because she was a good girl. She said, 'No, Grandmother, I have no need of such things, thank you. But I am in need of something to save my family with.' And so she explained about her mother and brothers and sisters hiding in the woods with the Cossacks and the peasants getting nearer.

'My magic can only help one person at a time,' said the old witch, rubbing her bony hands together. 'Tell me what I can give to you so that you might save them instead.'

Michal thought and thought, but couldn't come up with the answer. All she could think of was asking for some great weapon out of the past, but she was a young woman, she knew nothing about any weapon save the Ark of the Covenant, which she would not even mention before this goyisher magic woman. And in despair, she cried, 'I wish I had the power—the strength and cunning to protect my mother and all of my family from harm, forever!'

And Baba Yaga laughed again and spun in her chair and cracked her knuckles like gunshots. She sprang up and leaned over Michal, her breath like spoiled meat, and said, 'By your God, I swear that I will give you this power in exchange for a kiss and an oath!'

'I will not swear before God to do anything without knowing what it is,' Michal said wisely.

'You will have the power you seek forever,' promised the old witch. 'But you must consume what is forbidden to your people in order to do so!'

Michal's stomach turned at the thought of eating pig. (For that was what she thought the old women meant.) But to save her family? Yes, this she would do.

'I swear that I will consume as you direct if this power is true,' she said.

'Then come for your kiss, Daughter of the Book!'

And Michal closed her eyes and leaned forward. But instead of kissing her on the forehead (as her mama did), or on the cheeks (like Russians did) or on the lips (as lovers did), Baba Yaga kissed Michal on the neck.

After that, Michal could hardly remember what happened. She saw herself putting the teacup down and thanking the old woman for her gift. She remembered walking out of the hut and patting one of the fat chicken legs absently as she turned to the south. She knew it was night, but she could see as clear as day. And although she knew that there were still men running through the forest looking for her and her family, she was no longer afraid.

When she came upon one, who was carrying an old sword and a pistol and a bottle, she almost ran away. And as he came to her, unsteady and filthy, grinning like a wolf, she wanted to fall to the ground and cry and shake.

But instead, she waited for him, her entire body full of something, she didn't know what. Not until he touched her did she move.

His neck was broken in a blink of an eye!

Yes, Michal, the daughter of the weaverwoman, had taken a grown man up and broken his neck—snap!—like a dry branch. And instead of letting him fall, she caught him, and pulled him to her, because like Baba Yaga, she wanted to give him a kiss. But not on the forehead, or the cheeks, or the mouth. Michal kissed him on the throat, and took into her the most forbidden trayf!

"Are you saying that Baba Yaga made Michal into a vampire?"

"Are you going to listen to the rest of the story, or ask questions?"

"Baba Chanah—why do you have to tell me this in the middle of the night?"

"Shush and you'll learn."

Michal was terrified of course. She had heard legends of creatures that drank blood, but they were things of the Christians, the goyim, not of her people. (Well, there's Lilith, but she's a demon, so she doesn't count. Besides, she really wasn't Jewish.) Michal wanted to run away at once and kill herself, but she knew that her family was depending on her. So, she dropped the body of the man who would have raped and killed her, and went in search of her mama.

During that long night, Michal did what she had to do to keep her family safe. And when the dawn came, she roused them and took them back to their village, without explaining what had happened to her or how it was that they were never found. 'It was surely God's will,' she kept saying.

But when they got back to the village, matters had become even worse! For all the Jews were being forced to leave, at once, and they no longer had a house to return to, nor mule nor chickens. They had to join another family as almost beggars, and go onto the road alone in the world, after a night of horror.

"But Baba, the sun was up."

"The sun shouldn't be up in the daytime?"

"But Michal was a vampire! Didn't she have to sleep in a coffin or something?"

"Gevalt! Didn't she have enough tsuris, without this Dracula nonsense? Obviously, the vampires in Russia are different than the Romanian ones, what can I say? Oh, Michal didn't like it out in the sun, but it was a fashion to wear a shawl in those days, even if you were a pretty, young, unmarried woman, a nice shayna maidle like you."

"What about crosses?"

"She was Jewish, Akivaleh, what do crosses have to do with her? That's goyisher mishegoss."

"Okay, okay. So, they're on the road, fleeing the village."

That night, Michal slipped away, and went into another part of the woods, off the side of the road. Before long, what with going this way and that way, and this way and that way, she found her way to the hut with the chicken feet underneath. This time, Baba Yaga was outside, picking mushrooms.

'You must undo this gift,' Michal said right off.

'Oh, but you swore,' the old witch said back, taking a large pink mushroom and munching. 'Have I not given you the power to keep your family safe, forever? And is not the price that you must eat a forbidden thing? Or drink it!'

Michal wanted to say that she was wrong for asking for the gift, but when she thought about how many families back in the village that were missing people, girls and boys gone forever, she knew that no bargain she made to save her family could be a bad one. She was resigned to live with it—but forever?

'Before Hashem, it would be an averah to live more years then Moshe,' she said finally. 'I beg you to limit my life to 119 years only. Surely that will be long enough.'

Baba Yaga considered as she munched and munched. 'Forever is forever, Daughter of the Hebrews, as you well know. But I will give you this; before your 120th year, should you find a daughter of your mother's blood who will accept your place, you may die a true death and be judged as your God wills. But if you wait for one day past the start of the 120th year, you shall stay as you are forever, and be cut off from your people when your Messiah comes!'

'And if there are no girl children of my blood?'

The old witch cackled. 'When there are no daughters, there are no babies! But I will allow this—if there are no girl children to pass this gift on to, then surely it will pass away.'

Michal bowed her head. She knew she would get no better then that. And she returned to her family and stayed with them and guided them to safety, eventually, in Poland.

"A lot good that did," Kiva said bitterly. "Think of what you had to do to get the family out of there!"

"Well, I was only doing what Michal told me to do before she died, alecha ha-shalom. When I had to became the guardian of the family." And Baba Chanah sighed and patted Kiva's hand. "And now, I'm thinking that

119 years is a long time for a woman to walk the earth. Eighty one was enough for Michal, and I'm thinking that eighty-seven years is long enough for me. And Akivaleh—you are the only daughter of my blood."

Kiva eyed her old aunt with tired skepticism. "Baba—none of this makes any sense, you know. You're only talking about two generations going back to pre-revolution Russia. And you're sixty-seven, not eighty-seven."

"And this is so, bubeleh—according to the records in this country. We age slowly, we Sovetski women. Especially the cursed ones." She sighed and patted her niece's hand absently. "I am the only daughter of Michal's youngest sister, Leah. So many died in Poland. I was our protector, but only of those of our blood—so wives, husbands, they were taken—it was our blessing and my curse that we were able to survive, some of us, and come here to be safe again."

"Wait. I'm losing track here. You're not my aunt?"

"I'm your grandmother, Akivaleh."

"Does mama know?"

"Of course she does! What child doesn't know her own mother?"

"But—why lie about it?"

"That was my idea—when Baba Michal finally went to her rest, I thought we could change the records and make it seem like I had no daughters. I could just join my child with her cousins, and say that they were my sisters. Perhaps the curse would end there! But blood tells, and your Mama was supposed to be the one I asked to become our next strong woman. But Akivaleh—you know your Mama, my sweet Leah, my tender Lily. Nice, she is. Bright, oh, she's bright as a button! And very kind, full of charity! But strong? Strong, she's not. So, anyway, here we are. And Akivaleh—you might be the one to end this forever! We don't need guardians anymore, in this new country. We have a nice family—all boys! And, honestly, I don't think you're planning on having any babies, are you?"

"Baba Chanah!" Kiva blushed and then rapidly paled. "What—what do you mean?"

"I mean that you're a nice young woman who's not interested in men, nu? And to think, I'd be happy that my own granddaughter is a faygeleh! But, that's what you get for having children. In this case, it's a blessing from God, I'm sure. You'll be the guardian, and when your time runs out, the bargain with Baba Yaga will be over, and we will be free."

She brushed her hands briskly together in her "That was easy!" gesture and smiled.

Kiva lowered her gaze at her newly discovered grandmother and chewed her lip. "So, you're a vampire."

"Yes!"

"And you want to make me one, because you think I'm a lesbian. And when I do become a vampire, you can die. After that, I'll live until I'm 120 years old and then, because there won't be any more women of your blood in the family, I'll die."

"Yes!"

"Baba Chanah," Kiva said softly, "have you ever heard of Prozac?"

It was a long night for both of them.

"Kiva! Kiva, sweetie, over here! There's my baby!"

Kiva sighed and shifted the garment carrier on her shoulder. She pointed at the waving figure covered in fur and mouthed the word "Mom" to Shari.

"I guessed," Shari said, smiling. They nodded and waved as they made their way through the checkpoint and toward the baggage claim area where the excited woman and two beaming men stood waiting.

"Kiva, Kiva, look at you! My little bubeleh, so thin, so pale! Look at her, Henry, she's thin as a stick! Are you starving in your fancy schmancy condo in Chicago?" Lily Birnbaum held her daughter at arm's length and then drew her in for a flurry of kisses. "Oh, it's so good to see you, my baby, my poor skinny baby!"

"It's a co-op, ma," Kiva sighed. "Ma—Ma, it's okay, I'm fine!" She laughed and kissed her mother gently on the cheek. "You know, I'm not alone—this is Shari, my roommate."

Shari darted forward and shook hands with Lily. "It's great to meet you, Mrs. Birnbaum. Kiva's told me all sorts of things about you."

"It's good to meet you too, Shari, welcome to New York. Well, come on, let's get these poor girls someplace warm—Kiva, you're as cold as ice! I've got some nice chicken soup for you—your favorite, with the noodles, just like when you were little! Did she tell you how she made us always put the noodles in the soup instead of matzah, Shari! Oh, how she liked her noodles!"

Meeting the men was a brief clutch of hands, and the girls were swept into the car and onto the roads in a flurry of nostalgia. During the ride,

Kiva smiled and clutched Shari's hand carefully, and tried to remember to breathe.

"You didn't tell me about the noodles," Shari whispered accusingly.

The house was full, not only of people, but of scents, rich, heavy scents of long simmered soup, pungent aromas that made your mouth water, like the garlic touched drizzle that spoke of fat, green pickles, aged in barrels. In preparation for the fast, lunch was catered from the local corner deli. In addition to Lily's soup, there were hills of burgundy colored corned beef, peppery pastrami, pale roast turkey, slow cooked brisket. And the hills led up to a veritable mountain of potato salad and cole slaw, and were surrounded by islands of potato and kasha knishes. Tributaries of sour and half sour pickles led you to bowls of pickled tomatoes, stuffed derma, kasha salad with bow-tie noodles, and then finally to a lake of chopped liver, wide and deep enough for the skewered herring— not the cream sauce one, but rich with marinated onions—to swim in— if they were in any shape to swim.

Men were everywhere. Shari was introduced to Uncle-this, and Uncle-that, and this cousin and that cousin. She had always understood that Kiva was the only girl in her generation, but never really though of how isolating that could be. Wives were present, yes, and even one girlfriend for one of the younger boys. But no sisters, other then the three who led this clan. No girl cousins. When she did spot another 20-something girl, chatting at the other end of the room, she asked who that was.

"My Uncle Mike married a divorced woman after his divorce," Kiva explained, politely turning down an offer of a taste of chopped liver, nicely spread for her on a cracker. "That's Trudy, her daughter by her first marriage. No blood there. Unfortunately for Mike, no Jew, either. Trudy was baptized, and although Aunt Eileen did convert to marry Mike, Trudy hasn't yet. Gee, let's move away from the food again, okay?"

They had discussed the fast before. Last year, the day long fast for the atonement of the sins of the Jewish people was meaningless to Kiva, who didn't eat much anyway. Oh, she could, if she wanted to—put some mass in her mouth, chew and swallow it. But it was rarely worth the cramps as her body tried to figure out what to do with this foreign matter. It also wasn't very palatable any more, no matter how she used to love it. No, in order for the fast to be meaningful, she had to abstain from what really served as her diet for at least a week.

Now the only trick was to hide this special fast from the rest of her family for the two days before Yom Kippur.

"Eat, bubeleh, eat!" That was Aunt Sarah, now known to Kiva as not her mother's sister, but her cousin.

"I had some in the kitchen," Kiva gamely lied, patting her flat stomach. It had been like this for hours. She eyed Shari with a different kind of hunger, and the two women surreptitiously touched. Shari's warmth, her vitality, her sheer force of life made Kiva hunger in ways that her body could not process. From this desire too, she was abstaining. It was a vacant hope against hopes that some sacrifice would serve to open the proper gates this time. She sighed and turned down an offer of some more chopped liver.

"Your roommate, she's not seeing anyone, not engaged?" Sarah whispered, passing the liver off to someone else. "Two nice girls like you! Listen, you go to temple, I'll introduce you to my friend Paula's son, Harry, he's a graduate of Yale! I'm sure one of you will get lucky!"

That night, Shari slipped into Kiva's bed, Kiva hearing every move as her lover eased back the sheets and tiptoed across the room. They were sharing the guest room, the one with one single bed and a folding cot that smelled of mothballs. They had considered moving them together, but decided not to tempt fate.

"I miss you," Shari whispered unnecessarily as Kiva gathered her into an embrace. "Maybe you were right, this is too hard. I'm so sorry, sweetheart, I didn't realize there'd be so many people here—and that we'd never get any chance to be alone—"

"Shhh, it's okay," Kiva consoled, letting her lips touch Shari's forehead. "It's almost over. Tomorrow starts the fast, and we'll be heading home right after it's over." They touched, slowly, their hands exploring, cool and warm, soft and hard, until Shari moaned and broke away.

"This is the hardest for me," she said, turning away. "I want you so much it hurts."

Kiva smiled her thin smile and touched Shari's back with one cool finger. "Aishet kayyil..." she murmured. A woman of valor...

"...I have found. Her worth is far beyond that of rubies," Shari responded automatically. She turned halfway to kiss that finger, went back to her cot. Finally, the two women rested, each in her own way.

It was still daylight when they entered the temple, surrounded by well dressed men and women, some of the men carrying decorated tallis bags, others looking vaguely lost. In her white blouse, with Baba Chana's shawl around her shoulders, Kiva looked more pale than ever, and Lily had agonized over it all through the ride and into the actual temple.

"You shouldn't fast when you're sick," she lectured, eyes whipping back and forth to greet friends and rarely seen acquaintances. "The rabbi said so, last year."

"I'm fine," Kiva insisted. In fact, she did feel a little weak. But that was the point, wasn't it? The daylight shining through the windows gave her a pounding headache—she practically had to let Shari lead her to a seat and settle her. She tried to ignore the steady stream of humanity that passed her by, their pulsating heat, the rich scent of their bodies, the sound of their heartbeats echoing against the walls. When she saw the ushers herding people to their seats and the white-clad cantors ascend the bima, she almost felt like singing. It took a while to figure out how to do it, though, so she passed.

It was so familiar, not only to her, but to the memories bound by blood which lived inside of her. The relief that the Days of Awe were almost about to close, the anxieties of communal sin about to be washed away by communal repentance—all the burdens of humanity against humanity examined and stripped and held up for judgment. And now, on this holy of holies, the burden of humanity's crimes against the Ineffable. Not so much crimes of blasphemy and law breaking—but that of the making of vows which should not have been made.

The shortest cantor was the one with the biggest voice. As he pulled his pristine kittle in place around his rotund body, the entire congregation stirred and then stilled.

"Kol Nidre!" he sang, his voice quavering in that beautiful, haunting melody which compelled silence and attention. He was surrounded by two other men, holding Torahs, for this was not a prayer as much as it was a legal statement.

Shari had learned that much in her religious studies. The Kol Nidre asked that forgiveness be granted for vows made and not fulfilled, and that any vow made falsely or under duress will be considered null and void. These vows could not have been made specifically to other people—they had to be vows before or to God. There were all sorts of theories about where the Kol Nidre came from, and why it was part of the ceremonies of Yom Kippur, but it had occurred to Shari that it might have real meaning for Kiva.

"Who knows?" she had said, urging consideration of her idea. "At worst, you'll be hungry for a while. At best..."

Kiva didn't think about what might happen for the best. She cleared her mind and allowed the words of the Kol Nidre to penetrate her, fill her, and as it was repeated two more times, she swayed with its passionate rhythm and resonance. Slowly, the sun began to set and the evening services continued, just a hint about the marathon of prayers and reflection which would come the next day.

The afternoon sun was merciless as the millionth repetition of the al chet had Kiva staggering to her feet and beating her chest with genuine anguish. This list of community sins, cried out in the plural, as the entire congregation confessed to them, was a central part of the Yom Kippur daytime services. It was even repeated within the solitary prayers. She dimly realized that many members of her family were shocked, not only by her appearance, but by this apparent religious fervor. To Lily, religion was fine, a good thing to have—but not in abundance. Luckily, Shari situated herself between them and Kiva, and made it difficult for any of them to reach over and ask what was going on.

Shari gives me strength, Kiva thought, sinking back down into her seat. I need her so much! She glanced at the swelling body of the woman in the row in front of them, and then reeled back a little and closed her eyes. The pulsing heat of her, the hypnotizing scent, it was worse than being tempted with food. Food didn't fulfill your soul—food didn't give you the purity of oneness, that moment when a heartbeat becomes yours.

Just a few more hours, she thought, clenching her fists tightly. Then, I'll slip away and... or maybe not! Maybe this will end it all—the gates of heaven will open, and this injustice will be over! God will see that a deal made by a frightened girl with a crazy old witch should never have gone this far!

A tiny part of her mind stubbornly avoided the issue of what kind of God would allow this sort of thing to happen to begin with.

The service droned on, through the story of Jonah, through still more recitations of the al chet, and then, finally, the late afternoon saw the part of the ceremony called Ne'ilah, the Closing, representing the closing of heaven's gates, open for only so long.

Souls gathered in that temple, earnest prayers of release and relief, mingled with mumbled echoes of bad Hebrew tinged with annoying hunger pangs, thirst, and caffeine and nicotine withdrawal symptoms.

Kiva's withdrawal was making her itchy—her mouth and stomach ached, her head pounded. She needed to get out, and soon. But still, she prayed and sent her prayers into the setting of the sun, toward those gates which could surely send her case directly to the Creator, the Originator, to her Shekinah, the female essence of God. Hear me! she begged, not even realizing that she had fallen back into her seat.

When she felt Shari's hand on her shoulder, she started and almost leapt up. "Come on, honey, everyone's outside!"

Kiva licked her tongue across the top edges of her mouth and this time did execute a perfect sigh. Her lips were cracked, and there was a unique, sharp agony buried deep in her jaw that tingled and pounded at the same time. Shari was looking at her with compassion, guilt and worry written all over her face. "It's time to go," she said softy. There was nothing else to say.

Kiva got to her feet and stretched. Food or no, it was night, and she was stronger at night. Carefully, she made her way down the stairs, into the back seat of her mother's Buick, where she waved off the panicked suggestions that she need medical attention.

"Food!" Lily declared, throwing the car into gear. "She needs some nice, hot food! Chicken soup, with noodles, we have some at home in the fridge."

The very thought made Kiva's stomach lurch—or, what passed for such a reaction these days. The heavy, cloying smell of chicken fat, the pale golden color, the thin liquid, the high temperature—she closed her eyes and gripped Shari's hand, wrapping her fingers in icicles. Time was running out. If she didn't find a way to get out of the house, she would start losing it. That much she knew—her limitations had made themselves clear many times before. On two occasions, it was Shari who had saved her—Shari, with her beautiful, unselfish, unwavering love, Shari, who held her up and never, ever doubted or condemned her—Shari, whose pulse seemed so loud, drowning out the engine, the wind, the sounds of Kiva's aching soul.

Past the front door, she burst upstairs, Shari in close pursuit. An echo—"We'll be down soon!" seemed like jackhammers in her ears, and the startled cries and tsks of the relations were like the retorts of gunshots. Once in the room, checking the window, no, the fall wouldn't be that bad, she could hit the ground running. What a damn shame old Michal hadn't bargained better, the ability to become a bat or a wolf would be nice at moments like this. She threw the window open and groaned as her body shuddered in a great spasm of hunger/hurt.

Instantly, Shari's arms were around her. "Don't, don't," Shari murmured, her heat wrapped around Kiva from behind. "Lover, love, stay, don't leave me. God, I want you so much, Akiva..." Little kisses, sweet as a Rosh Hashanah apple, dripping with the honey of her tongue—Kiva turned in the embrace and wrapped her arms around her lover, unable to resist.

Their hands were everywhere at once, sweeping over their backs, curling over arms, twisting in hair. Their skirts rode against each other, and slid up, as their thighs crushed together, their bodies melded. Always like this after a period of abstinence, but worse now, because Kiva was lost in hunger, lost in the bitterness of a bargain left intact, a price so heavy it couldn't be spoken of.

"I can't do this to you again," she whispered, groaning, into Shari's ear. She nibbled on that earlobe, sucking it, a tease that made her teeth ache. Even as she spoke, she felt the shift in her mouth, and the preparation of her body to receive what would sustain her. "Three times, isn't that what they say? Let me go, I can't—I can't—"

"I'm not afraid," Shari whispered back. "I want you, now. I want you in me, lover, I want all of you." She pressed her own short, grinding teeth against Kiva's throat, and Kiva shuddered and whimpered in sympathetic agony. The sweeping power of her body's response made her growl, and forced the final change—that inner—click—that told her she was ready to feed. She grasped Shari's hair in one hand and swept the other fingers across her chest, tearing pearl buttons open, revealing Shari's beautiful breasts, nipples taut with excitement.

"I love you," Kiva growled. And she bent forward, scent and heat and need driving her, until she could feel the touch of needle to flesh, feel the sweet heaviness of the impression, taste the heaviness of the skin's own sheen—and then the door opened.

"Kivaleh! What is going on in here? You don't answer—Gevalt!" Lily Birnbaum stood in the doorway, still clutching a mug of her bracing chicken soup, her mouth open, and her eyes sharp. Next to her was Aunt Sarah, and then behind her was Aunt Reba. The triptych of their astonishment might have been amusing had it been caught at that moment and gone no further.

Kiva and Shari, caught in the act, stared back at the three old women at the door. They were still entangled, their skirts hiked up past their thighs, Shari's blouse gaping open, Kiva's rumpled and loose. And worse—far worse for Kiva, who swayed as she realized what was on her lips, she had done more than tease Shari's flesh—a little trickle from one successful puncture was stark against the white of her throat and her blouse. A drop—a single, cursed drop!—was shooting through her mouth, screaming for company.

"Close the door!" Lily snapped, stepping in. Still, her grip on the mug was unwavering—not for nothing had she managed Passover Seders and High Holy Day meals for over thirty years! Her "sisters" stepped in as well, and were busy shaking their heads in amazement.

"And just what is going on here?" Lily demanded, her voice just hitting the lower range of her scale.

Shari grabbed the sides of her blouse and shrieked as she realized that her throat was a bit messy. She turned away, blushing and shoving her skirt down over her upper thighs again. Kiva drew herself up, hard when she was so dizzy and one of her shoes had fallen off. The pounding of her hunger and the pain from her disappointment had made her bold. How dare her not-strong-enough mother barge in on them like this? And why did she care what this ungrateful family thought about her anyway? To hell with being the guardian, to hell with it all! She had been about to have amazingly tasty sex with the woman she loved more than she had loved life, and she couldn't even do that...!

"I'm a vampire, mom!" she shouted, baring her still extended—and now truly agonizingly hurting teeth. "Just like Baba Chanah was, and Michal before her! To save this stupid family from the Russians, from the Nazis, from those pathetic skinhead creeps that attacked cousin Nate when he was a kid! That's right, a stick my teeth in someone's neck and drink their blood vampire! And You're driving me crazy with your 'eat this, drink that, you're so skinny and pale'—dammit, I'm undead! We're not supposed to look like the very picture of health!"

Aunt Sarah made tsking sounds as she shook her head. "So, that's what Chanah did!"

Aunt Reba nodded. "That old fool, alecha ha-shalom. She couldn't tell us? What did she think we'd do, tell the world?"

"Always with the mysteries," agreed Sarah with a sigh.

Shari turned back, her breasts recontained and the trickle now smudged into a pinkish smear on her neck. She looked at an equally confused Kiva and then back at the three women at the door. "You—knew?"

"Of course we knew, what are we, idiots? Children? You think we don't know what's what in our own houses?" Lily asked indignantly. "Am I some stupid yutz who doesn't even know what her mama is doing? Apparently so, because here I don't know what my own daughter is doing! Akiva, why did you do such a thing to this nice girl, your roommate! Don't you know, this is only for mamzers, the scum outside? What did mama tell you, nothing at all? What a way to treat such a shayna maidle, and to do this on a Holy Day, besides!"

"I'm not—but mom—" Kiva stumbled over her words and sat down, missing the bed entirely and sliding to the floor. She looked up at Shari for help, advice, anything, and Shari pressed her lips together and nodded.

"Kiva wasn't hurting me, Mrs. Birnbaum," she said carefully. "I wanted her to, um, do what she was doing. I've done it before. You see, we're more than good friends—we're lovers. I don't mind when Kiva takes a little blood from me—she can have it all, if she wants." She looked down at her befuddled and starving lover fondly and then back at the relatives. "I love your daughter, Mrs. Birnbaum."

"Lesbians?" Lily's fingers loosened, and all that good soup spilled over the worn shag carpeting, the cup bouncing harmlessly aside. "You're a faygeleh?" Her voice scaled up two more octaves, and the sisters behind her began 'tsk-ing' again. "I don't believe it—go raise children! This is how they treat you—they run off and become homosexual!" She threw her hands up for good dramatic effect and shook them accusingly at the sky. "Curses aren't enough, you have to do this? Go raise children!"

With that mighty wish aimed at the Almighty, Lily Birnbaum stalked to the door and threw it open. "So, be a lesbian! If that's what you want! Don't give a thought to your mama, who loves you! I'll just go back and cook some more now, don't pay any mind to me!"

"She knows about—?" Kiva waved her hand limply over her mouth. "She knows?"

"She'll get over it, this lesbian thing," Sarah counseled, picking up the mug. "Oy, what a mess. One of you girls will clean this up, okay? It's okay to call you girls, right? Of course right. Just don't go marching with those drag-boys, yes? You stay at home and just keep out of trouble. And don't worry about the family. You come down later, when—you're feeling better."

The two young women nodded, in shock, and Sarah took a breath to start advising them some more, but caught an elbow from her sister.

"Don't talk, go," Reba snapped, pushing Sarah out the door. "Lesbians!" the girls could hear her say, as the door swung. "And such nice girls, too!"

FOR THE MORTALS AMONG US
Robert Knippenberg

The forest below the house was dark and forbidding, the greens too verdant, the huge gnarled trunks of the trees made even blacker by the rain. The tires grumbled on the long gravel drive as though satisfied to have arrived at last. Finally we stopped in front of the huge old house. It at least seemed resplendent in the foggy air, its tall columns like the masts of a great white ship plowing blindly onward into the mist.

"What do you think, Shell?" said father, utterly failing in his attempt to sound cheerful. He always called me "Shell" when he was trying to be nice.

"It's beautiful," mother said, joining in the charade. I could hear the brittle tears just beneath the surface of her voice.

"It looks like it has been raining here forever," I said. It was an observation, but mother started to cry anyway.

"This isn't easy for us, you know," said father, turning in the seat.

Any ordinarily perceptive person would have caught the edge in his voice, but of course I understood as well his deeper feelings, and even though it was all in the past, all the times he had made me happy in bed counted for something, so there was no point in reacting to what another might take for anger. Besides, he really isn't a bad man despite what we had done, and he's been good to mother.

"It is beautiful, father," I said, smiling at him, and it was enough. He didn't want to fight. He just wanted to get on with his life, hoping now that I would no longer be a threat to it, and that he would eventually stop feeling the guilt he carried around with him like a lodged bullet. He sighed, got out of the car and went to get someone to carry in my things.

My room was on the second floor in the front and was even larger than my bedroom at home. It had a great bay window that looked out over the vast rolling lawns and formal garden. From here I could see down into the maze of clipped hedges, and the tree line seemed further away than it had been from down below in the Rolls.

I sat in the window seat and stared out, letting mother and the maid unpack my suitcases and trunks, knowing she was grateful to be doing something tangible and motherly. She had brought almost everything I owned, as if she expected me to stay here forever. Later I would rearrange it all anyway.

"You know this is for the best," she said standing beside me finally. "Everything we've always done has been for your own good. You do know that we both care very much for you, don't you?"

Mother had always had trouble with the word "love," and as I turned to look at her, for a moment I was almost tempted to tell her about all the ways her husband had showed me how much he "cared."

But as always, her pale sad eyes prevented me from saying anything. She is not a stupid woman, and well aware of her own fragility. And often she would look at people like this, her lips asking questions, but her eyes desperate, pleading for answers other than the truth. And since she did this most especially with me, sometimes it was all I could do to keep from telling her just how different I was from the daughter she wanted me to be. What stopped me was that she wouldn't have believed me.

I stood up and hugged her instead. She had caught me in her bed with three boys, and I doubted now that stricken look in her eyes would ever go away. Afterwards I concluded that this uncharacteristic careless-ness had been deliberate, that I was as desperate to leave as father was to have me out of the house. At that point I could no longer stand his side-long glances, or her trying to forgive me for the gossip she was begin-ning to suspect, despite her best efforts, was true. I had already given up trying to forgive her.

"Let's go Sylvia," said father from the door. "I have to pack yet, and my train leaves early tomorrow. There's no point in prolonging this."

Once things changed between us, father too had begun to be suspicious, and this had become another reason to be somewhere else. Still, there is an inevitable connection between two people who have found joy in each other's arms, and behind his relief there lurked a regret that made me feel more sympathetic toward him then I had felt in quite awhile. I decided not to upset the poor man by kissing him goodbye as I had planned.

"Promise me you'll do what the... ah... doctor says," she said, pulling her arms out from under mine.

"I will, mother," I said, trying to sound reassuring. I had given up blaming her as well. In fact the question of whose fault anything was had become irrelevant at about the same time as had the issue of who should be forgiven.

That was two years ago. I was fourteen then and had just seduced father for the first time, although who seduced whom would probably have been a wonderfully tangled legal question, if it had ever come to that. I had thought it about for awhile, reading up on the law, imagining the courtroom scenes, picturing myself in all the various roles, judge, prosecutor, defense attorney, jurist. It would have been great fun, but turning him in would have destroyed mother.

Besides, I had not yet fully discovered myself at that point, and wanted to do it again. Of course father blamed himself entirely, and was terrified, and I had to hint I might tell to make him cave in.

The next time, despite his fear and guilt, he had made me come. He is an experienced man, and it was delightful for about a year. Then I discovered the fun I could have with the inexperienced boys my own age, and with some of the older ones at the nearby college, and I had to use the same threat to keep him at bay.

She leaned to kiss me and I turned to let her thin dry lips, so unlike the lips of her husband, briefly brush my cheek just as I sensed Doctor Blandon in the hall.

Doctor Blandon. His name fit him, and he came in smiling the same pleasant and eminently qualified way he had the first time I met him. He had the same kind of handsome professional face as father, warm, gracious and absolutely convincing. I have discovered that most adults have faces like that, or try to. They use them to shut out the world, thinking they can keep themselves secret.

"Welcome to Greensward, Shellina," he said, positively beaming as he took my hand. I had read the notes he had written during our interview, when he left the room to get mother. He had written, in a hand remarkably clear for a male doctor, "affective disorders, nymphomania," and quaintly I thought, "la belle indifference."

We had not talked for long, and his intelligence was impressive. Nor was his diagnosis unexpected. It was a matter of his perceptions, for which I could hardly blame him. I'm not in their books, and no psychiatrist is capable of understanding me.

He touched me for the first time, and instantly I felt his surprisingly quite genuine enthusiasm. He had undoubtedly been doing some thinking and perhaps some further research since the interview. I could tell I no longer fit neatly into his original categories, and he liked that, and since I enjoy challenges too, this made me feel even warmer towards him. Of course, I could also sense he was affected as most adult heterosexual men are. It is practically impossible for them not to be when presented with a sexually precocious young girl whose body has begun already to develop into that of a woman, and, framed by the kind of perfect blonde hair you see on dolls, a face as beautiful and virtuous as a child's.

I smiled back at him, not quite as innocently as he expected, and sensed a sudden flicker of desire, clamped down on so quickly he would have been just as genuine in his denial of it, but it was enough to make my pulse quicken, and I thought, "Maybe this won't be so bad after all."

I was introduced at dinner in the large ornately Georgian dining room. Dinners were always formal at Greensward. Doctor Blandon believed that this was therapeutic, it made us more like a family. As the soup was being served, each said his or her name in turn around the table.

Either all people have names before they are born, or the names they are given affect what they become. In any case, as always, I found their names fit them for the most part. I have done enough reading in abnormal psychology to be able to guess which labels had been applied to each of them just from their names and from the feelings I got as they said them. As usual, the closer they were, the more certain I was about who and what they were. Later I would touch each of them and confirm or revise my diagnoses.

Vicky sat on my right. She was a darkly pretty, thin girl, several inches taller and a year or two older than I. She had obsessive-compulsive tendencies, was a lesbian, and liked being disciplined.

Sidney on my left, was a fat disgusting boy of fifteen. A pathological liar and a fetishist, he was already planning to steal a pair of my underpants to masturbate with.

All the others were similarly afflicted with one or more psycho-sexual problems of one sort or another, although it was more difficult to determine the exact nature of those furthest away across the huge table.

Only one boy, Paul, at thirteen quite the youngest and shyest of the group, was particularly interesting. He kept looking at me throughout the meal whenever he thought I wasn't aware of him. He was mildly gender dysphoric as befit his fair pretty face, but there was a flicker of intensity in his intelligent pale blue eyes, and other secrets that went beyond his charmingly harmless (in my opinion) desire to wear girls clothes that made me think he might be worth getting to know better.

All in all, it was quite a little group Doctor Blandon had on his hands. Ten sexually disturbed young people, all the unhappy children of even unhappier (how could this happen to us?) rich parents, all secreted away in his little private sanitarium in the countryside.

I made eleven, but of course I didn't really belong here. I have never been unhappy with myself. It's just that everyone else was.

I was politely distant, as was expected of me, for the first few sessions. It was a question of whether I would stay or not, and for how long. As far as I was concerned, that depended on whether or not I liked it more than any supposed therapeutic progress.

Of course, there was also the problem that I had nowhere else to go, but that was not insurmountable. The world is a huge and varied place, and if I should decide to go whereever I wished in it, I am confident I would find a way to reach my destination, and a way to live once I got there. It was simply a matter of making up my mind.

But until I did, there was no point in being uncooperative. The living conditions at Greensward were lavish, the grounds huge and ripe for exploring, the company interesting, if a bit self involved, and the good doctor an attractive and benevolent tyrant.

Besides, there was the matter of Paul. He had proved to be more intractable than I thought possible. He was fond of me of course, and didn't avoid me or do anything else so obvious. It was just that I couldn't read him easily beyond a certain point, and that was new to me. It was as if he too was using his reason for being at Greensward as a disguise, a costume for averting suspicion. And we were similar in other ways as well.

I'm small for sixteen, and he is tall for thirteen, and we look enough alike in our rosy cheeked fairness that the casual observer (and most people are incapable of being anything else) could easily mistake us for brother and sister.

The stimulating discovery that he was far more complex than anyone, including all the adults I had so far met in my life, made me more determined than ever to uncover his secrets. I had become fond of him as well, and sympathetic to the point that I anonymously left him one of my lacier nightgowns under his pillow. His smile of thanks at breakfast the next morning told me he knew it was mine, but it was not sufficient to break down the walls. Happily I realized he was going to make me work harder than that to find out what was going on inside him. I knew I would succeed eventually, but that it would take a while and some effort would only make my success that much more rewarding.

In the meantime I amused myself with Vicky. I had known from the first that she longed to have me seduce her, and although I am not a lesbian, the prospect nonetheless interested me.

My ability to sense the needs and desires of others, and especially during moments of intimacy to share their actual physical responses, had given me an understanding of how males experience the sexual act. The cliche that "they are all after the same thing" is only superficially true, and then only because so many of them have been taught to believe it. I have found that each of them experiences sex differently, and in different ways at different times. In general however I had concluded that the perceptions of men are much different than my own, and I had become curious to discover if other women experienced the same kinds of sensations I found in myself.

Vicky's masochistic tendencies were also interesting to me. I had always wondered why so many people (mother is a classic example) take so much pleasure in hurting themselves all their lives, and although Vicky expressed her desires physically rather than emotionally, I was sure that the same underlying phenomenon was at work.

So I "tuned in," as I call it, to her, watching her closely to determine the best way to accomplish her surrender. A quick glance around her empty room (the doors were never locked at Greensward) gave me the key, and after cutting one of my silk blouses into strips one afternoon, I stole her beloved stuffed teddy bear, then waited that night for her to come.

Finally she rapped softly at my door.

"Shelly? Are you awake?" she said.

"Come in, Vicky," I said, my stomach already fluttering with the lovely hollow feeling of sexual anticipation.

She was wearing a satin nightgown unbuttoned down the front almost to her waist. The moonlight streaming in the bay window made the white of her gown glow, and her pale skin translucent, so that the ebony blackness of her hair tumbling down seemed like midnight come alive.

"Please. Have you seen Alfred? I can't find him."

The lower lids of her eyes were bright with tears, exciting me further. She was also afraid, not quite aware of the rules, or even that we were beginning a game, but her heart was excited and I could tell she was willing.

"Yes, Vicky. I have. In fact, I know exactly where he is. He came to me to complain. Apparently you have not been paying enough attention to him."

I flipped off the covers then and let her see the bump beneath my silk nightdress. The large ratty toy was lodged with its nose between my thighs so only the ends of its legs stuck out from beneath the hem.

Her large eyes widened even more. "Oh," was all she could manage.

"On my dresser you will find some strips of cloth. Bring them to me."

"Yes, of course," she said. She returned and laid them gingerly on the edge of the bed. She was already deeply into it, and she stood obediently waiting.

"Now undress."

The words alone made her arousal soar. Quickly, she pulled her gown over her head and threw it to one side. She stood with her head bowed, her hands behind her, the nipples of her small pointy breasts hard and dark. The lovely blue shadows in the hollows of her neck and shoulders, hips and knees accentuated the milk white of her skin, making her appear even thinner, and her slender pubic delta was a black crow at dusk, shivering in the snow.

"Kneel," I said. She obeyed, and I could feel her moisture seeping.

After propping Alfred up against my pillow so he could "watch," I got up and tied her hands behind her back with one strip and then used another to secure her ankles. I used a third to join the two, pulling it taut so she was bent slightly backwards.

It was similar to scenes I'd only read about, but had never tried, and I began to understand her better, and something about myself as well, so that I savored the moment.

The words I spoke then came naturally, a product of both our imaginations.

"Tomorrow, we will go riding. Meet me at the stable after lunch. Be sure to bring your riding crop, and we will find a private place for your punishment. But first you must thank me for taking care of Alfred."

"Yes, Shellina," she murmured.

We were both quite excited, and standing before her, I lifted my nightdress, holding it with my chin as I spread my legs and held myself open with my fingers. She shuffled forward and her eager tonguing made my knees tremble so I had to hold on to her shoulders to steady myself.

Father, and most of the boys I'd had sex with, refused to do this, and those few who were willing didn't really like it, so I had never had a mouth attack me so ardently.

Taking little steps, I moved backwards until the bed was behind me. In a single motion I took off my nightgown and lay back. She'd followed me, never losing contact, and I wrapped my legs around her to hold her tightly. She alternated, licking inside, holding her breath, then flicking her tongue quickly over my clitoris.

"Alfred wants to play horse," I said, straining to reach him. I put his legs around her neck and pulled, and her excitement nearly matched my own as she moaned and mashed her mouth against me.

I came. Then, anxious to see if I experienced the same delight as she in the act of cunnilingus, I freed her, only to tie her ankles and wrists to the bed posts. I knelt between her legs. Her female odor was quite powerful, but as I did what she had done, the slipperiness of her vulva in my mouth and the sour odor/taste became more than enjoyable.

In moments she was trembling, and not just her hips and belly against my mouth and hands, but inside, and in my head—she was on the brink—and I put two fingers inside her, ramming them roughly in and out the way she liked, while using Alfred's worn nose on her clit, which I knew had many times, by her own hands, brought her happiness.

She moaned as she came. It was hard and physical, like little bottles bursting in my/her head. It was unlike any orgasm I had ever experienced, and although not qualitatively superior, it seemed to go on for a very long time.

I untied her, and she sat up on the bed. Exhausted, not only from our orgasms, but from the effort it always took to share another's feelings, I collapsed face down next to her.

"Shelly? How did you know?" she said incredulously, somewhere in the sudden fog in my brain. "It was perfect."

Struggling against the petit mort, I was unable to open my eyes. "Yes, it was lovely," I replied, wanting her to go so I could sleep.

I felt the bed move as she got up. But instead of the sound of her footsteps and the door closing, I heard the silence of her staring at me.

Then I felt the gentlest kiss on my buttocks, her lips and tongue down my leg, as softly as a butterfly walking. She lifted my foot and more tiny kisses tickled my instep, and her tongue wet my toes.

"Goodnight, Shelly," she said finally, drawing the blankets over me.

Later that night, I rolled over and discovered the lump under the covers with me was Alfred.

There is something about sex that makes the world seem almost normal. The next morning's session with Doctor Blandon went very well; I know he was happy with it.

Each time I learned more about what to say and how to say it, and our quiet rhetorical exchanges were like foreplay. I could feel him repressing his desire, for in spite of his reserved professional facade, he was a very sensual man, and I found him quite charming. I knew if I had to seduce him in order to get him to let me leave when I was ready, I would have to do it carefully, because he was also a very strongly principled man, and I had no wish to destroy him.

I had used sex as a weapon against father, but that was my first time, and I was ignorant of my power. That may sound callous, but where would any young woman be without her unfairness. Her heartlessness protects her, and besides, up until that point I had thought all men were more or less invulnerable.

And while I enjoyed the verbal charade of our sessions, I did not lie any more than I had to. I had discovered early that the world is almost consciously hypocritical when it comes to the truth. Not only do most people say what they are expected to say, but most hear, and even trained listeners like Doctor Blandon are no exception, only what they want to hear. And some have the ability to encourage others to say what they want them to say as well.

Doctor Blandon was very talented in that respect, and so I gave him just enough to please him, and yet I could not help but taunt him at the same time. I could feel the child in him delighting at the game, and it's this I find attractive. After all, it's the child in all of us, not the adult, that is the source of our true sexuality.

As a child learning to talk I had thought at first everything was a game. Later, when I realized how serious everyone was, I was frightened by the vast conspiracy in which everyone except the people on television seemed to be involved. It was only after I began to understand that others could not do what I could, and what my own limitations were, that I began to realize how alone I really was.

Knowing their true feelings made it difficult to pretend, and to participate in the games all toddlers play, the cute little mimicries that parents smile at, and which are so necessary for adaptation to adulthood.

Still, I didn't understand why my playmates either picked on me, or shunned me, until one day I chanced upon a nest of two young birds in a low bush outside our house.

In the beginning they were twins, except when a parent came to feed them. Then one chirped louder and more stridently than the other and I noticed the adults helplessly responding to its raucous cries by feeding it first. I watched it grow visibly larger as the days passed, and soon it was able to physically push aside its now smaller and weaker nest mate whose tiny dispirited peeps were almost totally ignored.

One morning there was only one, and nearly fully fledged it sat bright-eyed in the nest learning how to sing by mimicking the notes and trills of the nearby adults.

Searching through the tangle below, I finally found the other. It was almost dead, but still warm in my hand as I carried it to show the others, anxiously hoping that finding something interesting would ensure my acceptance.

I shall remember forever their feelings. They surrounded me, staring and prodding at the trembling bit of feathered flesh in my hands, and their revulsion, pity and fascination with death poured through me.

I ran home terrified. But mother wrinkled her nose in disgust and made me take it out of the house, so that I sat in the backyard with it for a long time, until finally, angrily, I wrung its neck. Burying it, I wept, vowing over and over that this would not be my fate; I would learn how to sing.

Vicky was waiting at the stable as we'd arranged. She looked sweet and slim in her tight riding pants and black frock coat. Her nervous smile and the way she tapped her riding crop against her high shiny boots as I approached made me tingle.

It's odd how the privileged seem to be able to master useless skills so easily, and yet often fail at living. All of us except Sidney and Paul were accomplished riders, and we were allowed to ride by ourselves over the well marked trails through the woods on the southern part of the estate.

Vicky spurred her horse to a gallop as soon as we were out of sight, and I chased her, both of us laughing and ducking our heads as we skimmed around the bushes, and under the trees growing close to the path.

Later she said, grinning meaningfully, "Don't you think the horses deserve a rest and a drink?"

I laughed and nodded, and we left the trail. We picked our way through the woods to the little stream that meanders throughout the many forested acres that comprise most of Greensward.

We watered the horses then led them to a little clearing where they could graze. Vicky took some small rawhide strips from her saddle bag, and blushing now, held them out. Without a word she began undressing. She had not worn any underwear. I let her excitement seep through me, adding to my own.

Again the words, the pictures came quite naturally. "Put your boots back on," I said.

As she sat on her coat tugging at them, her pubic patch was already glistening.

I saw not too far away a smooth barked deciduous tree that had been knocked over by the wind. It lay at an angle, propped up by its branches. I walked toward it, and Vicky followed.

She lay face down along the trunk, and as I tied her hands and feet underneath with the leather strips, I tuned in to her, marveling at how the sensation of being bound made her guilt melt away, her body tremble. Having never indulged in this particular variety of sexual activity, her anticipation of the pain made it difficult to breathe much less talk, but once again the words seemed to come to me.

"Alfred and I made love all night long. We discussed your punishment afterwards, and Alfred said that he would forgive you, and take you back if you promise to do whatever I say from now on, and to love me forever."

"I promise," she said huskily.

I was amazed at how this excited her, and myself as well. I went on. "We thought that thirty was sufficient. But he said they must be hard, and that I was not to spare you no matter how much you begged."

"I understand," she said. "Shall I count them for you?"

"That would be nice," I said, thoroughly enjoying my new role.

At fifteen I switched the riding crop to my other arm, and moved to the other side of the tree to redden the other buttock. On the twenty-fifth stroke her pain suddenly changed to pleasure, like a switch had been thrown inside her. The sensation of her orgasm was so overpowering I had to struggle to deliver the final five, and then sit down on the ground to regain my breath, my senses.

A few moments later, her sobbing had softened, and as I untied her, she sighed musically, "Thank you, Shellina. What would you like me to do for you?"

Immensely pleased, I leaned down to kiss the welts I'd given her, still as aware of their sting as she, and in the dappled light playing over her reddened skin the shadows seemed the memories of the crop, still rising, falling. Suddenly I was saddened, realizing for the first time that for all my life another could never know what he or she had given me. Dizzy, and nearly in tears, I leaned back against the tree.

Then, remembering her tender kisses of the night before, I said, "Take off my boots."

We changed places. She knelt and I sat up on the tree and held on while she struggle with them.

"You have beautiful feet," she said, after she had rolled off my socks.

I lay back as she kissed them, and then she licked and sucked my toes, alternating between my feet, and wetting both so thoroughly the heat of her mouth on the one was made even more intense by the coolness on the other.

Although I have the kind of body men and boys seem to need to worship, I had never had my feet adored, and I discovered how remarkably intimate and delightful an act it could be. The sensations went all through me, arousing the Sapphic desires that I had experienced with her before, so that I longed to have her sweet mouth moving eagerly against me.

I unbuttoned my pants and she giggled as she helped me wiggle out of them. She took off my panties and kissed and licked her way up my legs before cupping my ass in both hands and tonguing my clitoris hard and fast.

As I came, I pushed her head lower, and she sought me deep inside, so that the contractions became even more intense. I had to hold on to the tree with both hands to keep from falling off.

She took my hand as we walked back. She took off her boots again, and I stripped off the rest of my clothes. We both giggled as we crouched in the stream to pee and splash ourselves clean with the chilly running water.

Among un-ordinary people there is a network of understanding. Perhaps it is born of sympathy, a grateful recognition that despite the differences which isolate them, we are all reluctant members of an exclusive club that it has cost each of us much too dearly to join. Or perhaps, more simply, it is a matter of the propinquity of shared incarceration.

I'm sure that Vicky did not actually tell anyone about our night together or the afternoon that followed, but afterwards I could tell that the others liked and respected me. This was new to me, and I was flattered even though I disagreed with the assessment of my emotional health their acceptance implied.

Certainly Paul was less aloof. He sat next to me at dinner that night and every night afterwards, and although he did not say anything more or less than usual (less would hardly have been noticed by anyone except myself), I could tell he was at last willing to let me peek in, if not open the door to himself completely.

I decided to let him make the first move. Granted I am not your usual sixteen year old girl, but I selectively enjoy some of the rights our society permits female adolescents. Besides, it would be good for him.

It was a warmer than usual spring evening when he finally approached me. It was not a casual meeting even though we had not planned it. I had merely mentioned to him how peaceful it was in the little ornate gazebo at the far end of the garden, and I had been sitting there for at least an hour before he finally wandered around the last of the high square-trimmed hedges of the maze.

At first he feigned surprise, but he did not hesitate to sit down on the bench across from me. He looked at me for a moment then down at his feet.

"Why are you here?" he asked.

An ordinary person might have been confused. I knew he meant Greensward. "For the same reasons all of us are, I suppose," warming up to the provocation.

"No, you're not like the rest of us. You are what you are because that's the way you want to be."

"And you think that you aren't?"

He looked up, and smiled. "Not entirely anyway. That would be too simple wouldn't it?"

"I didn't say it was simple, but ultimately it must be true. The doctors can't change us really, short of lobotomies and shock treatments, and they don't do that anymore. That's all their therapies can do, is make us want to change."

"Do you want to change?"

"No."

"That's good," he said, getting up and walking to the railing.

His back was to me now. It meant I could be more personal. "Do you?" I asked.

At the time, I wasn't sure what the words he spoke so softly meant:

A virgin girl upon her knees,
the three quarter moon above the trees,
aches to be fulfilled.

While frantic bats below her fly
weaving shadows in the sky,
with threads of invisible insect death.

The midnight thickets, secrets keep
from mortal souls who stay asleep
dreaming of their lives unwilled.

But each night my one true love awaits
gauzy-winged at the fairy gates,
beckoning, she takes away my breath.

He was looking at the forest, and the moon hanging huge above it like a promise.

"The meter is odd, but I like it. Is there more?"

"Yes, but I haven't finished it yet. Do you like poetry?"

"Yes, as long as it's not too romantic."

"What's the matter with romance?" he said turning. His smile was different now, and I couldn't place it anywhere among all the smiles I'd ever seen, and that explained, I thought, the sudden thrill of anger I felt.

"It's not the truth," I said.

"Is that what's important to you? The truth?"

"I didn't say it was important. It's just that's all we have."

"Ah, I see," he said, sitting down again.

I doubted that he did. How could he if he wasn't even comfortable being a boy? I wondered if he had ever had sex with anyone, of either gender. "Are you a virgin?"

"I don't see what that has to do with anything," he said.

It was clear that he was. I could feel him trying to be angry with me but instead directing it inward, injuring himself by banging against the clouds of doubt that were always inside him.

Now, just as suddenly, he made me want to cry. I had never experienced this kind of emotional tossing. It scared me, and at the same time I was grateful for it.

I got up and knelt at his feet. He didn't stop me as I opened his pants. He was uncircumcised and larger than one would expect for a boy his age. He smelled and tasted slightly of soap, and I knew from that as well as from the flash of guilt he felt as I put him in my mouth, that he had masturbated not long before.

Although it took longer than it might have otherwise, I was able to bring him to a full erection. I love the feel of this most vulnerable part of a male getting slowly harder in my mouth. It is one of the most erotic things a man can do to a woman, and that a woman can do to a man. The miracle of fellatio is that it is the one act in which it is never wholly clear who is in control.

I experimented, my abilities telling me what he liked, and then letting me share his pleasure when he came. His ejaculation was innocently sweet, and I swallowed all of it. I kept him in my mouth as he softened, playing with him with my tongue, and as always this reminded me of babies.

I would not want to be a man. Their brief flickering orgasms are seldom as intense or as satisfying as a woman's. Perhaps that is why they feel the need to have them more often.

Finally I put him back and carefully closed his fly. Then I resumed my seat across from him.

"That was truth, not romance," I said, breaking the silence.

He got up to leave, and then turned on the steps. "Ah, but you're wrong," he said. "I vowed I would never have sex except with the one I was meant to love. And that is romance!"

He ran toward the hedges, then stopped and turned and called back to me. "Meet me here at midnight when the moon is full. I will show you a romantic truth that is beyond anything you have ever seen, beyond anything you have ever imagined!"

It was chilly the night the moon fulfilled her promise with her precisely spherical perfection, and I was glad I had decided to wear pants and my jacket.

Paul was already there when I arrived at the gazebo.

"You won't need that," he said pointing at the flashlight I brought.

"I thought we were going into the woods. It's very dark in there."

"It's not as dark as you think. Besides, it will frighten... It'll be okay. I promise."

I left it on the bench, and he took my hand. I could feel his anticipation, bubbling like a spring inside him as we entered the tunnelled darkness.

"Unlike the woods on the other side where you ride, this forest is very old. It is one of the last few patches of aboriginal trees left in the country. No one has ever cut timber or farmed or lived here. That's why they... that's why it's a special place."

All the trees were huge, their ancient mossy trunks twisted from the wind, rain and storms of countless seasons before I was born. The forest seemed timelessly uncaring, and yet I had the feeling that it was aware of me, that I was walking on the breast of a living thing.

Paul was right about the light. It seemed to be everywhere and come from nowhere. Faint pale blueness outlined everything around us, moving with us. I could see every rock and root, every twig and leaf, but only out of the corner of my eye, or if I let my gaze sweep back and forth. As soon as I tried to focus on something specific it would fade and the object become harder to see.

Because the leaves blotted out the sun high above during the day, there was little undergrowth, and walking was easy. We were deep among the wide spaced trees before he spoke again. "This is probably far enough. We'll have to wait now."

"Wait for what," I asked, suddenly unsure of myself for the first time in a long time. It was not an altogether unpleasant feeling.

"Let's sit down and be still. You'll see," he said. Then a moment later, "That is if they want you to."

"Who?"

"The fairies."

Sadly he was serious. I could feel the depth of his convictions, and realized that his firm belief that his delusions were real was what gave him the ability to hide his feelings from me. I took his hand this time, but he was no different inside then he had always been. And now I began to care about him, as I had not cared about any of the boys I'd had sex with.

"There is no one else in the world I would bring here," he said to me. Then he kissed me, and it was as sweet a kiss as I have ever tasted, and I wanted to make love to him.

We sat still for a long time, while I wondered how I could get him to go back without upsetting him.

"What do they look like?" I said at last.

"Like us, except they're always naked. Fairies don't need clothes to keep warm."

"How did you find out about them?"

"Oh, I knew they'd be here. Because of these woods. That was why I did what I did. My guardian is a friend of Doctor Blandon and I was sure he'd send me here when I started dressing up like a girl."

"So you're here because you want to be here?"

"It's not that simple. I had to find out if everything mother used to tell me was true. She used to read me stories about fairies every night. And then, one night after... ah... afterwards, she told me about my father."

"Your father?"

"Yes. You see she believed my father was one."

"Your father was a fairy?"

"My father was a Slovdan, a mischievous fairy, they are as big as human beings and interfere in their lives. She used to say I looked just like him. Whenever she... that is... well, she used to call me by his name sometimes."

He let me feel it now. The love and guilt and desire and loss all swirling together, like clouds being stirred by memories of ghosts, and I knew his mother had seduced him, and that she was dead.

"What happened to her, Paul?"

"She committed suicide."

I was silent for a moment, and then decided that I could tell him. "My father, my real father, killed himself the night I was born. I have never been able to forgive him."

"You will someday. You have to. I'm still trying to forgive my mother."

"At least you knew her."

"I was very close to mother, and thought I knew her, but I didn't. She told me she was going to do it, but I didn't believe her."

"But she gave you a chance. All I know is that mother said I am just like him."

"That explains it. You aren't anything like your mother or stepfather. You must be like him. Maybe you know him better than you think. Or maybe you never know anybody. The note my mother left said she wanted to join my father."

"How awful!"

"Is it? She loved him very much. What is awful is how wrong she was. Fairies are not about death; they are about life. They are immortal, and do not like anything that reminds them of death and dying. In fact by talking about it we are probably keeping them away."

At last he was at least admitting that we weren't going to see them. He had cleverly provided himself with an excuse without harming his delusion. And now I understood his desire to wear girl's clothes. I had always felt that it was only tangentially sexual. What he really wanted was to be his mother, to bring her back.

"Perhaps we should go if they're not going to come tonight. It's getting late, and..."

"Wait, that's it!" he said. "It's all this talk of death, and our clothes!

We have to take them off! Then they'll come, I'm sure of it."

"What about the other times you've seen them? Did you have to take your clothes off then?"

He had already stood and taken off his sweater. "Yes, but only afterwards. You see our clothes are dead, and we've been talking about death, and it's been keeping them away."

He grinned as he unbuttoned and removed his shirt.

If it had been any other boy, I would have laughed. Still, it was far more original than any of the lines I'd heard after "the word" got out at school. All those young anxious boys, many of them eager to lose their virginity, but afraid to say so, and inventing some story to try to get me alone. I had often laughed at them, but then I would pretend to believe them. Why do men think that women have to be given a reason, and why do women think they need an excuse?

I stood and undressed too. It wouldn't take long in this chill before he'd decide we had to go back. But I also wanted to see him nude, and for him to see me.

He was beautiful naked, as only a young boy can be. I took him in my arms, wanting very much for him to want me now. And he put his arms around me, and it was different from the way anyone had ever held me. He did not clutch at me like a hesitant young boy, or embrace me passionately like father or the other older men, attempting to conceal their guilt behind their enthusiasm. Now I wanted him in a way I had never wanted anyone.

Then the blue light seemed to slowly brighten and coalesce around us. I saw the two gleaming, smiling figures out of the corner of my eye. They did not disappear as I turned my head to stare at them.

They were only slightly smaller than I. Their perfect bodies were draped with a diaphanous shimmering material that flowed around them, making them seem more naked than if they had worn nothing at all. The female was voluptuously beautiful and yet as dainty as a white lily, and the male's handsomeness so extreme he seemed almost feminine despite the sculpted masculine contours of his body and his well muscled arms and shoulders. Behind them, their impossibly delicate, almost invisible, veined wings swayed slowly, and it would have been unforgivable to be afraid of them.

"This is Tisha and Obertus," Paul said, gesturing first to the female, then the male.

"Welcome Shellina," said Tisha.

"It is indeed a special night that graces us with the presence of one so lovely," said Obertus, stepping forward.

He took my hand and kissed it, and his warm sensuality flowed through me, making me shiver in the cool night air. Then he put his arm around me, his loose garment flowing around me like a caress. It grew larger and divided, and when he stood back again the living transparency that lightly wrapped me made me feel as warm as if I were in bed.

"You are almost as beautiful as I, Shellina," said Tisha, and I knew there was no greater compliment a fairy could give a human being.

I looked at Paul, and Tisha had done the same with him. He looked as if he should have always been just that way, and I knew that what he had told me about his father must be true.

"Come mortals," said Obertus. "No more talk of death. Tonight is a celebration of life. Tonight there will be only happiness."

He took my hand again, and his touch made me light. I marveled as my feet left the ground, but felt no fear. With a few beats of his wings we were shooting thrillingly through the trees. Paul had taken Tisha's hand, and they raced past us, and his laughter was like a bell leading the way through the forested night.

Even before we were there, I knew we were close. I could see the brightness ahead and hear the music and laughter.

We walked the last few yards through the concentric circles of tall straight trees that looked like pillars holding up the starry sky.

Inside was a magic glen. A small waterfall on one side filled a rippled pool with gin clear water, and in small patches here and there in the carpeting grass grew flowers of unimaginable colors. Everywhere there were fairies of many different sizes, colors and descriptions. Some skimmed the surface of the water like large dragonflies, laughing as they chased each other, and then beating their wings ecstatically, they coupled, hovering in mid air.

In the tall grass around the edges of the pool, miniature porcelain white figures, like perfect dolls, kissed and caressed and played in little laughing heaps, the females often receiving the attentions of several males at once, then flitting to new partners to be pleasured yet again.

Others were larger and less sexually dimorphous, some apparently having the physiologies and capabilities of both genders. These had skins of pale green, and they made love in the hollows of certain trees, or on their wide branches, the trees appearing to have grown purposely to provide them with places to perch and sport.

Paul stood behind me, his arms around me, his hands cupping my breasts and mound as he nuzzled my neck and shoulders and nibbled my ears. Obertus kissed me on the mouth and put his arms around us both. Hugged between them, the feel of their hard bodies made mine melt. I closed my eyes, and for the first time in my life I was alone inside my head. It made me dizzy to feel only my own pleasure, and I went limp as they lowered me to the grass.

Obertus made love to me while Paul kissed me and held my hand. I looked into Paul's eyes as I came for the first time that night, and this time my orgasm was something I was sharing with another. "Thank you," he said when I had come back to myself.

Obertus rose and Paul took his place, and as soon as he entered me the contractions that had not quite died away began again.

Later there were others, sometimes several at the same time. Even Tisha and two other females of her type made love to me, and I to them in a wondrous writhing heap of deliciously feminine bodies.

The orgasmic feeling never went away, but flowed through me like a river all that night, so that I was no longer concerned with having to achieve my own, or my partner's fulfillment. Each encounter was its own pleasure and from each I took new energy.

I never wanted to awaken from the long sensual dream. I realized that I had never really appreciated the power of sex before, that I had given my body freely, but never my heart, that I had enjoyed the bodies of others, but had never asked them for anything more, and that all the time I had thought others were hiding themselves from me, I had been hiding from myself.

When at last we emerged from the woods, the moon hung in her same spot in the sky. I got the flashlight and checked my watch. It still said midnight.

"Did it happen? Was it real?" I asked.

"Do you want it to be real?" Paul replied.

"Yes."

"Then it was," he said.

We walked back to the house holding hands.

It was not necessary to sleep with Doctor Blandon. He released me two months after my night that was not any time at all.

Paul and I made love many times before I left. And I had Vicky join us, kneeling so Paul could enter her while she licked me, or sucking him as I tongued her. Towards the end she could orgasm as Paul spurted into her mouth or her belly, and the pain wasn't as necessary anymore.

Paul and I write each other often. He too was released and is now away at school. He says he will come to visit me when the summer begins. Sometimes he sends me poems. They are very romantic, but now they're also true, and they make it easy to be faithful to him.

Vicky writes to us too. She is still at Greensward, but is doing better. She always sends her love to me and Alfred.

This summer mother, father and I are going to take a real vacation. It will be the first we have ever taken together, a sort of family celebration of my "cure."

I'm not sure what I believe anymore. At Greensward it was easy to believe in the fairies, just as it was easy to believe there was never anything wrong with me.

However, I have learned how to take a certain comfort from the fact that life is uncertain. It is amazing all the ways there are to enjoy yourself and others once you relax a little.

And I do not miss prying into the feelings of other people. My gift isn't gone exactly, in fact I realize that my ability is something we all have but that most of us deny. I just have a little more of it.

I use it differently now, to understand others, and to help them forgive themselves. And to understand and forgive myself.

That, and love, is all life is essentially. At least for those of us who are mortal.

SOMEDAY MY PRINCE WILL COME
Evan Hollander

Once upon a time, there lived a well-hung and vibrant young man named Prince Eros. Prince Eros had almost everything a young man could desire—good friends and wealth, his health, and dozens of beautiful and willing ladies to fuck.

But, alas, young Eros had one rather serious problem.

One night, after sneaking through the dimly lit castle halls to the chambers of Clitora, his sister's busty lady-in-waiting, Eros was made aware of his problem for the very first time.

As he pumped his long, thick cock furiously in the deep valley between Clitora's generous mounds of breastflesh, he found that as much as he wanted to, he could not come. He had been fucking the lady-in-waiting for several hours and although she had orgasmed three times, he had not joined her in that most delicious of carnal experiences.

Now, as the warm glow of the first morning sun peaked over the Kingdom's eastern horizon, Eros had become weary and wanted nothing more than to shoot his white-hot love liquid across Clitora's massive bosom and watch her rub it onto her great dark areola and nipples.

The thought edged him closer, but never over the fine line into climax.

Even as Clitora halted the tit-fuck and took Eros's princely cock in her hands and licked it with long, wet strokes of her tongue, he could not come. Even as she sucked on his cockhead and then took his entire length into her moist, warm mouth, he could not come.

Clitora didn't seem to mind the fact that Prince Eros's cock was still as hard as diamond and she seemed content to continue sucking on it long into the daylight hours. But the young Prince had a prior engagement with Madam Vulva at her country manor later that morning.

"I must go now," Prince Eros said finally as the sun rose fully over the horizon.

Clitora emptied her mouth of cock only long enough to speak. "But you'll be leaving unsatisfied," she said. "I can't possibly allow you to leave my chambers like this. What of my reputation? If others found out, I'd never have another caller."

Eros got up from the bed and began dressing. "On my word of honor, what has happened here—or perhaps I should say what has not happened here—will go with me to my grave."

The ride to Madam Vulva's manor was a bumpy one and the small coach bounced and rocked on the road. By the trip's midway point, Prince Eros's cock had returned to its normal size, but his thoughts were still firmly fixed on his encounter with Clitora. Not being able to come just wasn't like him, he was used to having four to six orgasms per night. Once, he'd come eight times with five different women, an unofficial yet highly sought-after record among male members of the royal family.

While the ability to stay rock-hard through the night at first appeared to be a blessing, there came a point where one wanted the overpowering sexual tension to be released. Furthermore, Prince Eros was of marrying age and his father had been pressuring him of late to find himself a bride. What good would a bride be to him if he wasn't physically capable of fathering children to maintain the royal bloodline? Prince Eros had no answer. All he could do was hope that his problem would correct itself—and quickly

As the coach neared Madam Vulva's manor, the Prince's heart—and loins—began to fill with new hope. Madam Vulva was an older woman and the most experienced sexual partner the Prince had ever had. Madam Vulva had also been the one to take the Prince's virginity (the incident occurring in the back of the coach on a particularly long trip to the

King's summer residence by the sea) and would surely know just the remedy for what ailed him.

The coach pulled up the drive and stopped in front of the front door of the manor. Madam Vulva's chambermaid was there to meet it.

"Madam is waiting for you in the salon," said the chambermaid.

The Prince looked the woman over closely He'd never noticed her before. She was quite beautiful. Her eyes were large pools of sky blue and her hair was a deep shade of red that suggested a healthy lusty fire burned deep within her bosom. The Prince couldn't decide whether she was petite or husky but something about the way she carried herself suggested she was slightly better-endowed than most of the women in the land.

"And what might your name be?" asked the Prince, feeling his cock beginning to swell at the sight of the woman's warm, friendly smile.

"Sensua," she answered, bowing slightly.

"What a lovely name," the Prince said, his gaze fixed on the generous amount of decolletage.

"Thank you," she said, returning the Prince's smile. She led him to Madam Vulva's salon.

"Goodbye, Sensua," the Prince said as the chambermaid left him.

The woman must have noticed the swollen knot of cock between the Prince's legs—the skin-tight leotards not being the best article of clothing for purposes of humility—for she suddenly blushed and put a hand over her mouth. "Goodbye, Your Hardness, uh... I mean Your Highness," she said, turning and quickly running down the hall.

The Prince took a deep breath and opened the door to the salon.

Madam Vulva was lying on the bed wearing black stockings and a bone-white corset that pushed her two mountainous breasts together until they looked to be at the bursting point. Her legs were spread enticingly and her genitalia—proportionally as large as her two huge tits—looked as if it were aching to be fucked. She smiled coyly at the Prince and passed a hand gently over the tops of her breasts and then traced her index finger down the deep valley between them.

"Come over here," she said. "Show me what it's like to be young and virile, and I'll show you what it's like to be mature and wanton."

The Prince nearly ripped his clothes free from his body. Seconds later he was lying next to the woman, sucking on her thumbtip-sized nipples and fingering her sopping wet cunt with four of his fingers.

"How long has it been?" she moaned, tracing a line with her tongue along the Prince's neck and chest.

"Too long," the Prince replied, kneeling on the bed and guiding his throbbing dick into the wanting wet lips of her sex.

He arched his back as the lady took him deep inside her, the muscles of her vagina squeezing his cock and pulling it even deeper. The Prince could feel an orgasm starting to gather strength somewhere down near the soles of his feet. A broad smile broke across his face. Relief at last, he thought, as he placed his palms flat on Madam Vulva's breasts, squeezing them softly as he pumped the entire length of his cock in and out of her cunt.

Hours later, the Prince still had not come. He continued to pump, hard and deep, into Madam Vulva's bucking lovehole, sending her into the throes of yet another wild orgasm, but he was still no closer to coming than when they had first begun.

After Madam Vulva came for the fifth time, she begged the Prince to stop.

"Please, for the love of god...," she said, panting a hard staccato rhythm, her body slick and glistening with sweat. "I'm almost forty years old, have mercy on me."

The Prince complied with Madam Vulva's wishes and stopped.

"It's an odd problem to have," Madam Vulva said later, rubbing a soapy hand across her shoulders and breasts as they bathed together in the large claw-footed tub in the corner of the salon. "I've heard of men not being able to get hard and I've known plenty of men who came too quickly, but I've never heard of a man not being able to come at all. I didn't mind it so much, but I can't imagine what you're going through."

"I suppose I'll have to tell Father. He has expressed a wish that I be married soon," the Prince said with a sigh.

"Well, if you must tell him, I suppose the sooner you do it the better."

"Yes," said the Prince, rising from the tub. "You're right. I must tell him at once."

When Prince Eros told his father of his problem, the King was at a loss over what to do.

"You could not come? Even with Madam Vulva?" the King asked as he stroked his long salt-and-pepper beard.

"Yes, Father. Even with Madam Vulva."

The King took a deep breath and sighed pensively. If Madam Vulva had been unsuccessful, the matter was a grave one indeed.

The King paced the floor of his son's chambers for several minutes, obviously deep in thought. His hand moved from his beard to the back of his neck and once again to his beard as he tried desperately to think of a solution.

"I could see the Wizard, perhaps he has a cure—"

"None of that," the King said quickly "I can hardly imagine what price you'd have to pay for a spell that remedied a problem of that nature." He paced the floor for several more minutes.

Suddenly, the King froze in the middle of the room and clapped his hands together. They made a sound like thunder.

"Consul!" he shouted.

A door at the far end of the room creaked open and an old gray-haired man, bent over slightly at the waist, shuffled in.

"Yes, Your Majesty?"

"I will only say this once," the King said. "So listen closely"

Consul nodded.

"My son is having trouble achieving orgasm." The King stopped to measure Consul's response.

Consul simply nodded, awaiting the King's next word.

"So I make a proclamation to all the ladies in the Kingdom. The first young woman who can make my son achieve orgasm will be his bride... and future queen."

"But, Father—"

"Hush," the King said, placing a hand out in front of him to signify the matter was not open for discussion.

The Prince slumped back in the chair he was sitting in. "Very well."

The King turned to Consul. "Are you clear on what you are to do?"

Consul nodded, and shuffled out of the room.

In weeks the King's proclamation had reached the far corners of the Kingdom and scores of young ladies made the trek to the castle to try their luck. There were lithe blonde maidens, dark, black-haired beauties, busty young redheads, and all manner in between.

The Prince "interviewed" fourteen hopefuls in the first week, twelve in the second. He was now midway through the third week and he was no closer to coming than he'd been at the start of it all.

"Bring in the next," the Prince said, taking a sip of water and lying back down on the bed.

The door opened and a woman more beautiful than any he'd seen before walked into the room. She had waist-length blonde hair that shimmered and shone as it cascaded over her shoulders and flowed down her back. She had piercing slate-gray eyes and skin as light and fair as hand-polished marble. She was dressed in a thin gown of green silk that clung tightly to her body and clearly showed her thick erect nipples as they pressed against the fabric.

"I am the Contessa Felatia," she said in a soft, breathy voice.

The Prince's cock was as hard and as stiff as his broadsword. He pulled aside the covers to reveal his phallus to the beautiful young Contessa.

In seconds the Contessa's gown was crumpled into a heap on the floor and she was crawling across the bed toward him.

The Prince's cock stood erect between his legs like a pike of the honor guard.

The Contessa wasted little time in taking the Prince's cock and running her velvety soft lips up and down the length of it. Soon, it was slick with moisture. Then she clasped the base of it with both hands and took the swollen purple head in her mouth and began pumping up and down on it like the piston of a water-powered grist mill.

The Prince arched his head back and tried to pump his cock into her mouth but he couldn't keep pace with her frenzied sucking. Instead, he leaned back and waited for himself to reach orgasm.

He waited...

And waited...

But he did not come.

He had been sore for some time when he finally had to tell the Contessa Felatia that she had been just as unsuccessful as the others.

With obvious disappointment, she pulled her mouth from his cock with a loud slurp, slowly picked up her clothes, and saw herself out of the room.

The Prince tried to get some rest, but he tossed and turned through the night, never quite falling asleep.

In the morning he was awakened by a knock on the door.

"Come in," the Prince said sleepily.

Consul shuffled into the room. "A woman to see you. She's not a lady, but she says she knows you."

"Tell her to come back later with the rest of the women," the Prince said, rolling onto his stomach.

"That's just it, sir—there are no more ladies. She is the last one. The only reason I considered her was because you still have your... problem."

The Prince sighed. "Very well, let her in."

Consul nodded and turned to leave.

"Do you know her name?"

Consul turned back around again. "She said it was Sensua, sir."

The Prince vaguely recalled the name, but from where he couldn't be sure.

Just then the door creaked open and the woman, Madam Vulva's chambermaid, entered.

The Prince immediately remembered the woman and the memory of her beauty on the morning of his last visit to Madam Vulva's manor quickly had him hard.

She stepped into the center of the room wearing a long black cloak clasped around her neck. The Prince was about to tell her he did indeed remember her when she undid the clasp and allowed the cloak to fall to the floor.

The Prince gasped.

She was dressed in black, wearing shiny black shoes with fashionably high heels. Her stockings were black, held up by lacy black garters. Her underpants were a wispy triangle of sheer black material that only faintly hid her mound of curly black hair and the folds of soft pink flesh beneath. Higher up, her black corset opened widely down the front, showing off her two huge tits to perfection and allowing just a hint of areola to peak out from beneath the thin black fabric.

Without saying a word, the woman pulled aside the fabric of her corset to allow her big breasts to stand free, firm and round on her chest. With the middle finger of her right hand she traced a slow circle over her left nipple until it condensed into a long, hard nub.

The Prince felt his pulse quicken.

Then she took the middle finger of her left hand and repeated the circular movement over her right nipple until they both stood erect like two brown thimbles. That done, she began rubbing her nipples between her thumb and forefingers, squeezing and pulling on them until they pointed at the Prince like a pair of arrow tips.

The Prince unconsciously placed his left hand over the knob of his shaft.

The woman Sensua continued working her breasts, rushing her open hands over the entire area of her globes, making it look as if the massage was making them bigger still.

The Prince's hand began moving up and down his shaft.

The woman stepped closer to the bed, lifting her right leg and letting her knee come to rest on the edge.

With her left hand she traced a line between her breasts down past her belly and on to her dampened sex. With a gentle movement of her hand she pulled aside the material covering her cunt and began to finger her clit, first with the tip of her middle finger and then running the entire length of the finger against it.

With her right hand she hefted her bulbous right breast until the swollen nipple was inches from her ruby-red lips.

The Prince's fist pounded up and down on his rod, faster and faster.

At first she merely flicked the tip of the nipple with her tongue, leaving a glistening spot of saliva on the end of it. Then, as her breath began to quicken and her hand moved harder against her clit, she took the entire nipple in her mouth and sucked on it.

The Prince continued to move his hand over his cock. An orgasm was building somewhere deep within him.

She lifted her left hand from her sopping wet cunt and grabbed her left breast forcefully, squeezing it like a pillow. She did the same with her other hand, turning her head to the side and beginning to moan and gasp as if she herself were about to come.

The Prince felt his legs beginning to tremble.

A few moments later, she let go of her tits, leaving them to heave up and down on her chest with each gasping breath, and moved both her hands down between her legs.

"Oh," she moaned, middle fingers pulling apart the lips of her sex and pressing her index fingers down hard on her clit.

"Oh," she moaned again, almost a scream this time, bringing her arms together and squeezing her tits between them like a pair of water-filled sacks.

The sight was just too much for the Prince to bear.

He grabbed the base of his throbbing, pulsing cock with both hands, arched his back, and let go.

The stream of jism was thick and long and hit the woman Sensua squarely in the chest. Nearly knocked back by the force of the blast, she quickly recovered and began to rub the sticky white liquid onto her sweaty breasts as if it were a salve.

The sight of her rubbing come—his come—onto her tits made the Prince come even longer and harder. He shot bolt after bolt through the air, weeks worth of come coming out of him like a mighty river that had broken through a dam.

When it was over, the Prince fell over on the bed in a heap. He was spent.

When he awoke sometime later, the woman Sensua was lying next to him draped in a robe.

He opened his eyes and looked up at her, smiling. "How did you know what to do?" he asked, giving the nipples of her bloated breasts a lick.

She cradled his head in her hand so he could continue sucking on the nipple.

"Your problem wasn't down there," she said, taking his limp dick gently in her hand. "Everyone thinks this is a man's biggest sexual organ, but it's not. It's this." She pointed to his head. "I knew what you wanted the first time I saw you look at me."

"I'm forever in your debt," the Prince said. "Allow me to repay you in part by taking your hand in marriage."

"I accept," she said eagerly. Then a look of puzzlement crossed her face. "But if that's payment in part, how else will you repay me?"

"Well, you made me come. The least I can do is return the favor."

The Prince rolled over on the bed, took his rapidly growing cock in his hand, and guided it into the warm, soft folds of her cunt.

Needless to say they came happily ever after.

GONE TO THE SPIDER WOMAN

Beverly Heinze

Maxine peered at the neat stack of mummy casings. Quite a collection, she thought. Depressing, though, since more than one of the dried-out husks resembled an ex-lover. She scanned them, searching for Erryl's likeness.

She crept closer. The empty shells, yellowed and dry as parched grass, seemed to represent the forsaken and hollow dreams of their former occupants. With two fingers, she traced the profile of the nearest face, that of a young woman who would now have the perfect nose and finely formed mouth of a goddess. The casings, papery and waxy like insect wings, rustled ominously.

Maxine hung her head. Clearly, it was foolish to have hopes and dreams. The Spider Woman would never break a past client's confidence. But maybe, since she liked Maxine, maybe she would reveal something about Erryl's fate...

"It is taking a little longer for that one," a perfunctory voice stated. Dr. Yu, the famous Spider Woman, was glaring at Maxine with eyes dark and glittery as carbon steel. "She requested, ah... deep changes."

"Deep changes, as in complete changes?" Maxine asked.

"All changes here are complete."

"And then, after completion...?"

Dr. Yu glanced at the small window behind Maxine. "Then she will... fly away."

"Sorry to hear about you and Erryl splitting up, Maxine," Ambassador Lovejoy said. "You two were our top team. The best." He leaned back in his delicate little Hokkidu chair and twisted a lock of frizzy hair onto a finger. He'd gone gray over the years, gained weight, and acquired a battery of vague diplomatic gestures. "She's gone to the Spider Woman, I suppose?"

"Don't they all?"

"Not you. You haven't."

"No, not me," Maxine sighed. As she reached across the desk to pick up the latest gel file, Lovejoy shrank back reflexively, lowering his eyes.

Maxine put on a professional face and made a show of perusing the file. Many years ago, new on Hokkidu, Lovejoy had been a curious and indulgent emissary. "May I?" he'd asked, reaching out to touch the translucent skin. "Beautiful," he'd whispered. "Like stained glass..." He hadn't even grimaced at the mild shock.

Now Maxine stifled the urge to give him an accidental but punishing jolt. Instead, she said, "What's on the agenda?"

"A meeting with the Pribbolites," Lovejoy answered. "They want to negotiate a trade." He formed a tent with his well-manicured fingers and hid the bridge of his nose, appraising Maxine. She knew that a lie would follow this mannerism.

"They're not saying what they want?"

"Of course not. They'll let us stew a bit first." He picked up a pen and lightly aimed it at her. "Word has it they want a nullion."

"What!" Maxine spluttered. "They've never wanted a person before! Mineral rights, trade incentives, tax breaks. But not one of us! They don't even like us!"

"Who does?" Lovejoy answered. "Maybe they want to find out how nullions tick. Maybe you fascinate them."

"Sure." Maxine fought to control her anger as Lovejoy awaited her reaction. "Obviously we fascinate everybody," she stated flatly. "I suppose I'm to discover their motives?"

"Yep. Read the file and go out and see what you can learn on the streets. Your new partner is waiting outside. Noby is her name. Go take a look," he smiled. "Go ahead. I'll see you in a couple of weeks." He stood and swept an arm grandly toward the door. "And again," he added, "I'm sorry about Erryl."

Not as sorry as I am, Maxine thought. Of all the partners she'd had, Erryl had been without equal. Together they'd driven the Pribbolites crazy, disclosing more of their secrets, ruses, double-crosses and Machiavellian twists than any other team. The Pribbolites, who thrived on intrigue, were masters of diplomacy on every planet in the confederation. But here on Hokkidu, where nullions had found a niche in the diplomatic environment, they foundered shamefully. Damn fuzzballs, Maxine swore. She hated them for their self-important strivings. Why did such an eminently protected race crave so much subterfuge?

Meanwhile, her new partner was staring at her, taking in the fireworks. An angry nullion is surely a fearsome sight. While her lungs emanate nuclear yellow sparks, her blood turns a bright crimson and rushes to her vagina, where a dazzling red glow embarrasses one and all. "Are you Noby?" Maxine asked.

"Yes." The woman got to her feet with the grace of a sun-warmed cat. "And you're Maxine Cruz," she stated.

"Yes." Maxine took a deep breath and directed her body to stay cool. "We're to be partners," she said.

"So I'm told."

"I take it you're not too happy about it."

"No."

"May I ask why?"

"Your, ah, reputation as an agent is good," Noby answered. "But for this job, one needs a strong commitment..."

"I've never walked away from a partner," Maxine interrupted. "Or a relationship."

"I know."

They've all left me. A dozen of them. But not because I've driven them away. Maxine sighed. "I guess if you stick with one job long enough, everyone leaves you."

"Could be."

"Well, let's make the best of it," Maxine said, flapping the crinkly gel file at her new partner. "This will interest us both, I'm sure. Let's read it over and talk. Maybe we can figure out what's cooking with those assholes from Pribbolis."

As they walked through the bustling Trade Nexus, the crowds parted like water before a ship's prow. Some citizens smirked, some flinched, but most just moved aside automatically. After all, one inadvertent brush with a nullion could shock them into a seizure or a swooning coma, depending on their own mood at contact. But Noby seemed to have a talent for avoiding the masses: as they streamed past, she left no wake.

But then she did something both surprising and endearing.

From nowhere a group of young Pribbolites had surrounded them, leering and snickering. "What have we here?" the hairiest one sneered. "Gizzards on parade?" He nudged a tawny-furred pal and snorted like a Pekinese dog.

"Walking cadavers," another said.

"Show and tell! Let us see your...!"

Suddenly Maxine noticed that Noby had nulled out. In her place, just about waist-high, jogged nothing more than a column of shit!

"Perfect!" Maxine laughed, unabashed. Then, as the embarrassed boys dropped back, Noby reappeared, straight-faced.

"Breathtaking social commentary," Maxine said. "Now, let's get out of here before those jerks cough up a hairball!"

Noby was still angry. They'd read the file and ingested the gel along with the crackers and beer Maxine had supplied, but her new partner still fluoresced a dim pink glow. "Those pups couldn't have touched us," Maxine said. "They're just kids, after all."

"They're always touching us," Noby spat. "More than we can gauge, they manage to touch us!" Sparks shot from her eyelashes and her fingertips glowed as she reached for her beer.

"Careful. You'll make it go flat," Maxine pointed out.

Noby smiled, showing perfect small teeth. She was a derivative of the oriental stock that had first colonized Hokkidu, a quirk of fate that had lowered her further in the esteem of the Pribbolites, the ultimate exploiters of galactic wealth. To them Maxine was an arriviste, but Noby was a custodian and a servant. That they were both nullions merely accentuated their lowly status.

"Those kids' behavior is just another gimmick," Maxine said. "Meant to unnerve us. It's second nature to them, no matter what age they are."

"I know. Born assholes." Like banked coals, Noby's black eyes had dimmed in intensity. Maxine knew it was time for the test.

"We'll be attending a party at the Pribbolite consulate four days from now," she said. "As partners."

Maxine had attended a thousand such parties, voided to invisibility by her partner, and gathered the state gossip that such exclusive soirees produced. It took a lot of control, a substantial amount of energy, and immeasurable nerve to do it. The penalty for such eavesdropping was retroversion. And no one wanted to finish out her life as a sentient turnip.

"So," Maxine went on. "Perhaps we'd better check the circuits."

Noby's wing-shaped eyebrows peaked. "Sure." She set down her beer and stood up.

Facing one another, the two nullions first blanked themselves out. At close quarters, if in agreement, a pair of them could act much like an anode and a cathode, their sensory output combining to one big zero. "Fine," Maxine murmured. "I can't see you at all, and now I can see through you. Shall we reconfigure?"

There was no answer. Maxine fidgeted, adjusting her image to a faint waver. "Noby?" She waited patiently, as she always did at this juncture. Two nullions sharing one another's energy field almost always end up in bed.

"Why not?" Noby finally answered, beginning to glow a faint pale gold.

Maxine observed her closely, just as she knew Noby would be watching her.

First Noby's skeleton came into view, a bright neon blue. Then her integumentary system, including lungs and digestive tract, became a pale silver color, flat as pewter. Next, her blood vessels and heart appeared, lymph bubbling along like soda water, lime green in color. Her nervous system then showed up, red and glistening like thin lava rivulets. For her finale, Noby's reproductive organs came into sight: Maxine found herself gazing at ovaries like pearly eggs, a womb of black velvet, and a royal purple throbbing tube below.

Holy shit! Maxine was impressed. This woman was a master of self control, and moreover, an artist. "Geez," Maxine murmured. "I hope I don't put you to sleep."

Noby's dark eyes, now glassy carnelian, held no awe as Maxine whipped her body's constituents into a frenzy of whizzing corpuscles and glissading molecules. Then she sent streamers of eerie fire from her fingertips. But not until the fire coalesced into two will-o'-the-wisps that danced about and lit upon her royal purple nipples did Noby smile appreciatively.

"Wow," she sighed, taking Maxine into a loose embrace.

"Absolutely stunning," Maxine uttered. They slid carefully to the thick carpet, pressing close. She barely had time to slip her thigh between Noby's powerful legs before they both climaxed, producing a veritable supernova of white light, shooting stars and frothy comets. "Holy smoke, sweetheart," Maxine gasped. "Who said lightning never strikes the same place twice?"

Noby smiled faintly and lay her head back upon an upraised arm. Maxine turned so that she could see her lover's entire body as it subsided into tranquil repose. It was very much like observing a city at dawn: after the sun chases the stars from the skies, building lights and streetlamps blink off one by one. Then a cityscape emerges, its riches and secrets revealed. But, Maxine noted, this nullion's skin continued to glow and shimmer with all the colors of the rainbow. She dared not risk a caress.

"Did we meet standard?" Noby asked.

"Perfect attunement," Maxine answered. "We'll be topnotch agents. No one will ever see, smell, feel or hear us when we're working together."

"You're the expert."

"Look, Noby. It's true I've been doing this longer than anyone else, and it's true that all my partners have gone to the Spider Woman. But almost all nullions choose that route." Maxine sat up and ran her eyes over Noby's lovely body. Soon, if she slept, all its tissues and wastes would be visible to the naked eye. How many times, as she grew up, struggling to control her own body, had Maxine seen the revulsion in her family's eyes? And strangers' as well. "Face it, Noby. It's a tough, tough life. And when you grow old and careless, it will be an unendurable one."

"And this job just adds extra stress?" Noby's heart-shaped mouth was curled into a sneer.

"It does. I can't help it, but it does."

"Why haven't you gone over then?"

Maxine hesitated. Oh, how she yearned to reach out and stroke Noby's soft, peachy cheek. Instead, she clenched her fists into useless stumps. "I don't want to, Noby," she answered. "When a nullion gets reconstructed, she disappears into the masses of normals and never looks back. No one can trace her origins. She starts a new life."

"So. That's the objective."

"So it is. But I like what I am. And I'm good at what I do."

"The best," Noby smirked.

"I am."

"If you're so good, why don't you touch me?"

"You know we can't, after..."

"We can," she whispered. "We won't self-destruct," she laughed. "I promise."

Maxine extended a hand, fully expecting to be shocked and burnt. But instead she connected with warm, tender flesh, soft as a silken pillow, inviting as warm summer rain. "Oh," she gasped, embracing Noby. "This is unheard of..."

"First time for everything," Noby murmured, guiding Maxine's hand downward.

For all her experience with different lovers, Maxine had never really gotten to enjoy the tenderer aspects of lovemaking, for her close contacts with a nullion were always short, sharp, and explosive. She marveled at Noby's luscious body, running her fingertips over every inch of it.

"Amazing," she breathed. She curled a damp lock of Noby's pubic hair around a finger, then moved down to take a look at the part of a woman's body she'd only glimpsed before. Noby was quite wet. Spying a glistening nub amidst the rosy-brown folds of skin, Maxine gaped. "Why, it's beautiful down here!"

"Oh, Maxine," Noby laughed. "You sound like a tourist."

"But, I've never seen..."

"I know."

Maxine edged a little closer and gently inserted a finger.

"Oh," gasped Noby, lifting up to meet her.

Maxine, still worried about runaway galvanic responses, carefully replaced her finger with a thumb and lay herself fully upon Noby's body, moving very slowly. But within moments, they were both bucking wildly, bodies pressed close and entwined like jungle vines. Soon Noby arched her back and cried out, to be followed immediately by Maxine. For the second time in her life, Maxine saw stars.

Exhausted, she lay limp upon her lover, who had suddenly grown cool and turned a lavender color. "Are you okay?" Maxine whispered.

Noby did not stir.

Maxine pressed her lips to Noby's throat, seeking a pulse. "Noby? Oh, no, I knew we couldn't..."

Suddenly she felt the flesh ripple beneath her, then it shuddered. Was Noby having some kind of fit? "Noby!" Maxine cried. Raising her head, she saw that Noby's mouth was open and she was starting to laugh.

"Oh, Maxine," she gasped. "For a moment I thought you'd expired right on top of me, you were so still, and heavy as a stone!" She cupped Maxine's cheek with a hand. "But then you came back. I'm so glad!"

"Me, too, Noby. Me, too."

The next few days found Maxine out on the street with Noby, mingling with neighborhood nullions and street agents friendly with the Pribbolites. Evenings, Maxine waited anxiously for her partner to show up at her apartment to spend the night in her bed.

All nullions, by their very birthright, were mysteries to most folks. But the way Noby casually surpassed the usual nullion limits left Maxine flabbergasted. Really, she admitted, this woman is unmatched in her ability to control her body, as well as influence mine. Furthermore, as sexual partners nullions generally burnt one another out very quickly, and sometimes literally. But, Maxine thought, that doesn't seem to be happening with us.

She tensed. Noby was approaching. Maxine could feel it in every cell of her body.

"Hi, it's me," Noby called, poking her head through the door.

Maxine stood up, her knees weak. "Come on in, hon." Then her mouth dropped open and her pulse quickened.

Noby had swaggered in and struck a defiant pose, hands on hips, pelvis thrust forward. "Well?" she laughed. Clearly, she was allowing her body to speak for itself.

Maxine gaped. Just behind Noby's left breast a lurid pink rose fluttered rhythmically, as if it had just awakened to the hot sun. And, below her navel, a crimson red barrel smoldered, dripping as if glazed with honey. "Well," Maxine managed to utter. "Thanks be to our ancestors for gifts such as these." She placed the flat of her hand close to Noby's cheek. "Learn anything new this afternoon?"

"Same old stuff, Maxine. The Pribs are leaking a dozen contradictory stories." She looked Maxine up and down slowly. "They do seem to want one of us for something."

"Hm. I wonder what that could be," Maxine smirked.

"I know who knows, though."

"Who?"

"Lovejoy."

"Ah." Maxine felt a flush of anger suffuse her body. Noby leered appreciatively.

"Really, Maxine," she said. "I don't know which is more attractive about nullions: their complete lack of control, or their total control." Taking Maxine's hand, she led her into the bedroom. Hokkidu's periwinkle blue moon was just rising over the evergreen trees outside the window, and a soft breeze carried the mixed scent of bayberries and jasmine into the room.

Lying upon the bed, Maxine pulled Noby into a forbidden embrace, surprised again that no sparks scorched the air. Surely their combined energy could light an entire apartment building. "Amazing," Maxine murmured. Beneath her skin a fizzy current of bubbles steamed from cell to cell, organ to organ, like plasma leaping between all the suns of the universe. "I've never felt anything like this before..."

"You tell that to all the girls," Noby smiled, slowly tracing Maxine's contours with her fingertips.

"Really, I never knew how erotic a touch could be."

"Hm." Noby drew back and gazed at her. "I guess I never did either. This is a first for me."

"Probably a first in history..." Maxine gasped. Noby's fingers were inside her now, moving slowly, searching, caressing ever so gently her most sensitive parts. Soon her head was between Maxine's thighs, resting momentarily.

"Now for another first," she whispered. Her tongue found Maxine's clitoris and grazed it with the lightest of strokes, creating a faint electrical pulse.

"Ah, Noby... What are you...?" Maxine gasped. She reached down to grip her lover's shoulders, but Noby quickly grasped her hands, completing a circuit. "Oh!" Maxine cried out, throwing her head back and arching her spine. She gritted her teeth as spasms rippled up and down her body, and clung to Noby like a motherless child. Then, through red-tinged eyelids, all the stars of the skies plunged toward her and exploded into billions of radiant particles.

Finally, Maxine lay still. From nowhere a lambent breeze came to caress her body, the breath of angels, she guessed, accompanied by the exhalations of all the demons of lust. "Good god, Noby," she groaned.

She opened her eyes warily, fully expecting to find the room in ashes.

Noby's head lay in the little gully between Maxine's belly and thigh, warm and buzzing with tiny lights at the end of each fine black hair. Carefully, she crept up alongside her lover and kissed her gently. "Ah," Maxine sighed. I can taste myself on her lips, salty, pissy, loamy. And maybe a little ozone...

She began an exploration of Noby's warm and supple body. Red ribbons, white strings and blue ropes plied the tender flesh like the lines on a holo-map, while wheels of light lit up her midline from crotch to brow. Cold heat thrilled Maxine's fingertips. "Geez, Noby," she sighed. "You're an amazing woman." Maxine pulled her close, and just for one second, hugged her with all her might.

Driving out to the consulate grounds, Maxine found herself reliving every moment of the night before. Never had she experienced a woman so thoroughly, never had she experienced herself to such a degree. How soft we are, she mused, tender as new buds in the gentle spring. What delicious tastes and scents we have. Truly, interacting with a nullion at a distance, however small, is no comparison to actual physical contact with one. No wonder the normals are so smug, she thought. They're always touching one another, rolling their eyes and grinning, and sometimes they even try to touch us. Until they get burnt a few times.

She glanced at Noby, who was steering the little car down the narrow country roads like a taxi driver, one arm hanging out the window. She must enjoy the wind blowing against her, Maxine thought. Erryl, for all her strength and willfulness, could never have enjoyed herself so patently, would never have appreciated her own body the way Noby does. What was different about this new woman?

Nullions, the result of research on bio-sensitivity, could be traced back to a dominant gene created by the same Dr. Yu who now offered them reconstruction. A specialist in rejuvenation, Dr. Yu herself was said to be more than two hundred years old. And, though rumored to be colder than a popsicle, she never turned down a nullion's request. "Those burn most mournful," she said, "who burn alone." And no one was more alone on Hokkidu than a nullion.

Maxine tore her eyes away from Noby. Did she dare become familiar with the curve of her neck, her graceful hands, her stalwart thighs? Some day those features would all return to the Spider Woman to be made over.

Maxine ached in longing already, knowing this. "Do you see your family very much, Noby?" she asked, trying to change her line of thought.

"No."

"Me neither. They don't spurn me, but they're clearly uncomfortable in my presence. They're always waiting for me to slip up and show them my insides."

"I know." Noby's black eyes were overtaken by a shadow, her jaw grimly set. "My mother is a doctor," she said. "You'd think she could have used me to learn about the human body. From the inside out."

"Ha," Maxine laughed. "A missed opportunity, to be sure."

"Speaking of same," Noby stared straight ahead. "How could you have let Erryl go? You were happy together, weren't you?"

Maxine recalled the last evening she'd spent with Erryl, an evening of anger and recriminations, as she sought to persuade Erryl to forgo reconstruction. "You'll be like everyone else," she'd yelled. "Nothing special!"

"No, Maxine," Erryl had replied. "I'll be accessible." She'd sighed and turned a sad bluish color that Maxine associated with pain. "I'm tired. Tired of being an untouchable."

Maxine longed to reach over and place a hand upon Noby's thigh. "Well," she said, "you're right. We were happy together. And god knows it's hard on a person, to be happy only when in the company of another. It's just grindingly hard."

"Oh."

The party was the usual semi-decadent Pribbolite soiree, with the guests gathering in underlit corners to gossip and practice Machiavellian maneuvers on one another. Maxine, in the state of invisibility that only two nullions could attain, made the rounds, eavesdropping. Annoyed by their thick lustrous pelts and superior airs, she hated mingling with the Pribbolite diplomats. Stocky as furniture and graceless as robots, they took control of every conversation and made it a mission to discomfit the colonists of Hokkidu. Maxine had grown so weary of their posturing that she almost missed the one small group that was quietly not attempting to outmaneuver one another. She and Noby crept closer.

"...for a pet," one creature was saying.

"Really," a large brindle fellow answered. "Fancy that."

Maxine was intrigued by this little group. The males, sleek and robust, were shorter than the slender, blond-furred females. Their eyes and teeth glittered in narrow vulpine faces, their ears, though mostly hidden, stood erectly attentive. And they all wore fancy sashes, armbands, belts and boots of fine cloth. All denizens of Pribbolis eschewed leather.

"Ugh," a regal female exclaimed. "A laboratory specimen is more like it. Really, this is most unsavory."

Suddenly the hair on Maxine's neck stood up. Uh oh. She stifled a gasp as her stomach plummeted like a skylark. What was going on? She scanned Noby for signs of fatigue, but saw nothing.

Then something more inexplicable happened. A young silvery blond female detached herself from the group, turned slowly and stared directly at Maxine. She can see me! Maxine's heart pounded like a kettledrum, threatening to imbalance her perfectly tuned state. Aghast, she saw that the tips of her extremities were taking definition, wavering like guttering flames. Shit!

Another head turned. "Look!" someone cried. "Something's there!"

As one, the entire group spun to stare at Maxine.

"A spy!" a russet male cried. "Security. Get security!"

Maxine raised her arms to ward off the approaching Pribbolites, but her fingertips produced only pale yellow sparks, the weakest of jolts a nullion could muster. She was losing power, fast.

Then, from a doorway, two dark figures lumbered toward her. She heard the whispery buzz of a sump gun, then felt its impact as her nerves caught fire and depleted themselves in an instant. "Ahhh," she sighed, as her lungs shut down and she slumped to the floor in slow motion.

From her new viewpoint Maxine gazed stupidly at the two Pribbolites thundering toward her. With each ungainly step their glossy coats shook like rippling fields of grain, and their breath came in guttural, growling explosions. She waited numbly, resigned to their wrath. But to her astonishment the two guards stopped short. With bulging eyes, they exchanged a brief look of bewilderment, then threw their heads back in an ear-splitting howl.

Cripes! Is that some sort of war cry? Maxine wondered. But then her own eyes popped, for a bolt of crackling blue electricity struck the two Pribbolites and they lit up like arc-lights! Shrieking like banshees, they whirled about the room in a convulsive frenzy, till one bit through his tongue and sprayed the horrified guests with black blood.

"God... damn..." Maxine whispered. How could this be happening? Her eyes rolled back and she sank helplessly into a black void. Where was Noby? And what was that terrible smell?

An eon passed before she awoke, flat on her back upon a cushioned table. She could not lift a limb, turn her head nor move her lips. Yet she breathed. A marionette unstrung, she thought. Then she remembered the Pribbolites, the flames, the screams, and Noby's presence. And someone else's presence, as well! She groaned.

"At last," a voice answered. "I'd almost given up."

Erryl! The face in Maxine's peripheral vision was wrong, but she knew Erryl was nearby. She struggled to speak.

"No, listen to me, Maxine," Erryl said. "You can't move. You've been de-magged and de-juiced. Your lifesigns are nearly flat." Her voice quavered. "You're scheduled to be retroverted. It's not so bad," she went on quickly. "At least you'll still be alive. You'll just be a little less lively."

There was a silence while Erryl struggled to stick a charged patch on either side of Maxine's mouth. "I'm breaking an agreement, but maybe you'll be able to talk a little now."

Maxine managed to focus on Erryl's face. Though still delicately chiseled, it was now covered with fine glossy fur. Oh, Erryl. "You..." she gasped.

"Yes, it's me, Erryl. I knew you sensed me there, at that party, Maxine! It's amazing. Your powers are astounding. Every atom of my body has been replaced."

"Not... your soul," Maxine managed.

"Ah, maybe." Erryl reached out with a silver-blond furred hand, but withdrew it. "Listen, Maxine. I can't stay. I'm only here because Dr. Yu demanded it. You and Noby killed two mercenaries. The Pribbolites insist on retroversion."

"Noby...?"

"Noby's gone."

"Gone?"

"Oh, Maxine. She combusted."

"What?"

"She appears to have blown herself up. There was lightning, smoke, white light."

"When?"

Erryl did not answer.

"When!"

"After her capture. During interrogation," Erryl said. "It was pretty disturbing, apparently. Lovejoy is hopping mad."

Sure. A mistake. The wrong nullion had been given over to the Pribbolites. "Oh, Noby," Maxine moaned.

"Listen," Erryl said again, drawing close to her ex-lover's ear. "Dr. Yu has offered to reconstruct you as a normal human being, not a rejuvenate, not a Pribbolite, not a retrovert." She hesitated. "Though she could get in a lot of trouble for this, she's adamant."

Maxine suddenly recalled what Noby had told her about the Spider Woman. "Our mother, more or less," she'd said. "She created the first one of us two hundred years ago. To her, we are not unlovely. She suffers greatly because no one, including ourselves, finds beauty in us. But she's always willing to change a nullion into whatever we want," Noby had snorted. "Just like a mother."

Noby. Maxine remembered her last few days with her, hours in which she'd learned the exquisite pleasures of the flesh, how to enjoy another body, smell it, taste it, feel inside it.

But suddenly Dr. Yu's stern face was hovering over her, her sharp eyes bearing in on Maxine. "Shall we proceed?" she asked. She lowered the spinnerets for which she'd gotten her name, a jaw-like device designed to weave a silky chrysalis around a body. Then Dr. Yu would pump the genetically altered hyper-viruses and the megadoses of nutrients into it and await transformation.

Dr. Yu's hand trembled as she adjusted the dials. "You were the best, daughter. You and Noby were head and shoulders above everyone else." She reached to remove the electrodes from Maxine's cheeks. "You have decided to reconstruct as a normal?"

"Mother," Maxine managed to utter. The word caused her to remember her own mother's ambivalence, how often her eyes had reflected repulsion. "This body of mine, one you bestowed, was cherished by some," Maxine smiled faintly. "But by none more than myself."

"Aha. I see."

"Then you cannot make it less than it is."

Dr. Yu was quiet for a long time. Then she placed a hand upon a button rarely used by one who specialized in prolonging life. "Yes, daughter," she agreed.

ANTHEM
Lee Crittenden

It's a sin, a crime, for me to be here, but I don't care. The machine room is dark and quiet, the lathes covered in shapeless, ghostly shrouds for the night. The air reeks of oil and metal filings. Somehow the burnt-metal stench remains in the smoky air beneath the distant roof trusses, even though the floor is spotless, the debris swept up carefully by the day-workers and disposed in the massive recycle hoppers. It's a familiar, life-long stink that permeates my being, and penetrates even my dreams.

Other nights there's a second shift here and a third following that, but this is the end of the work-week, and the workers are allowed a two-day free period. It's an old tradition, meaningless, like many of the other things we do. We march in lock step, our identical faces turned toward the future—and it's blank, completely empty to my eyes. Our lives are an endless progression of vacant days, punctuated by the free periods, spent in the identical gray coveralls, the identical gray cubicles. We stand in the chow line with our identical scarred metal trays waiting for bland, over-cooked rice cakes and then a bland rest.

All but me. Why am I so different?

I shiver, touched by the cold fingers of the ventilation, and slide into the shadow of one of the machines. I huddle with my shoulder denting the gray shroud that covers it, watching a vagrant thread flutter in the wind from the vents high above. It's always cold here; the machines require it, prone to overheating, and human flesh has to compensate. The machines are more important, of course, the major capital expenditure for a factory enclave like this. Human flesh is always less valuable, more malleable, more easily replaced and repaired.

That's a cutting thought, and it reminds me what I'm risking here with such a determined sin. Just now I don't give a damn. The sweetness of this crime is what has showed me the sterility of my life here, the possibilities that might exist outside this enclave, outside the empty circle of work and the blank existence we live—something I'd never thought of before. Is that why this act is banned by the managers? Because it makes one think other forbidden thoughts? In a way I'm terrified of doing it, as I always am—but this has brought me a taste of joy, and so I come again to wait every seventh day-period, hiding in the shadows and shivering, thrilling, even though I hate the terror it raises in my breast—hoping she'll come.

I hear a faint scrape, the tiny echo of something living amid the cold silhouettes of the shop machines. I retreat deeper into the shadow, holding my breath. Objectively, I know this wouldn't foil a heat-seeking monitor, but hiding must be an instinct built into me, like the faster beating of my heart, the rush of blood to my belly and thighs—the pulsing of instant arousal.

I dare a quick intake of breath, slide one hand downward over my breasts and belly, down to the throbbing warmth of my vulva. The lips of my flesh are open, pressed tight against the twill of the coveralls, the seam cutting through the center over my clit. The light stroke of my fingers is delicious, exquisite. I lift my hand away, turn my head sharply against the drape of the hanging canopy, scenting like an animal after the interloper.

Another shadow darts between the machines, lithe and furtive, crouches a few feet away.

"Hist!" she says to the darkness.

"Here," I whisper in return.

She moves, and in a second she envelops me. Her body is warm in the frigid air of the shop. Her lips are soft and honey-sweet, and her hands run quickly downward, tracing the path mine took only seconds ago.

"God," I say, as she touches my clit.

"Shh," she says, and pushes me backward. The fabric cover gives behind me, slides over the metal, and then I'm semi-reclined, feeling the smooth base of the machine through the shroud against my back.

I don't have to see the face above me. It's my face, my almond eyes, my short-cropped dark hair. It's my rounded body beneath the sheath of heavy twill coveralls. The only difference between us is the number tattooed in the flesh of her wrist. But still we're separate individuals—and I want her with all of my being.

She jerks at the snaps of my clothing, and the twill gives over my breasts. Her fingers move quickly within the gap, sliding over the coldness of my skin, stroking the sweet hardness of my areolas, the sudden pointing as my nipples rise to meet her palms. I can't help but moan as her lips follow her hands downward, closing around the sharpness of my right nipple like burning fire.

Her clothing is open then, too, and her breasts are thrust into my own hands. They're generous globes with sweet, hard-pointed tips, and they swell and move as she arches above me, straddling my thigh, the tight curve of her belly faintly visible against the exit icons far beyond on the rear wall. Our legs are wound together, and I feel the animal heat of her crotch rubbing against me. The hard seam over my clit is almost painful now, tightened by her rubbing, and I shove her away abruptly, shrug the coveralls off over my shoulders, push them down from my sloping buttocks, kick my heavy boots away. I'm naked then, burning with need for her, reaching, no longer feeling the cold around us at all. She's naked as quickly as I am, and we slide down to curl in the nest of our clothing. We're clasped skin to skin, breast to breast, mouth to mouth, with nothing between us but heat and lust.

I can feel the moisture between her thighs with my hand, the coarse curl of her bush. I probe within its forest and find the hard ridge of her clitoris, the mirror of mine. Beyond it is a softness, a cavern waiting to swallow my exploring fingers. She moans with pleasure as I stab through into her, filling her emptiness, working my fingers back and forth.

Our love-making becomes more violent. Her sucking on my nipple is more amorous, her pelvis grinding hard against me, meeting the thrust of my hand. She abandons my breasts with her tongue, searching for my mouth instead, crushing my lips beneath hard kisses, her fingers working at my nipples now, pinching the flesh. With my free hand I stroke her, massaging her rounded hips, the soft flesh of her thighs. Her nipples slide across my chest as she moves above me, lubed by sweat, and she rubs them against my own, the identical points probing at one another. She groans then, speeding the rhythm, and suddenly tenses, frozen and transfixed above me. I feel the contractions of her orgasm close around my fingers then, and she sinks, gasping, rises again, and then falls a final time.

She rests for a second, and then she's searching for me again, knowing I'm not far behind her. Her hands slide down my body, over my breasts and belly, down to the hunger between my legs. She penetrates me in turn, her fingers forming into a thick rod that strokes the ache within me. The heel of her hand grinds into my throbbing clit, pushing my arousal to utmost. It's nearly more than I can stand. I'm quivering, groaning, thrusting against her hand. I kiss her mouth, her ear, her breast. Then she nips at me suddenly, her teeth sharp on my earlobe, and I'm gone. The convulsion rises and shakes me like an earthquake, an explosion of clitoral pleasure that runs to the tips of my toes and back again. It's electric. I contract beneath her, stifling a scream, and she tugs at my nipples with her teeth, thrusts more slowly, letting me ride it down.

Spent, we lie in one another's arms.

It's a while before we move. She raises her head finally, searching for the time display on the far wall.

"We have to go," she says.

"Yes," I say. I sigh one last time and roll over to see what damage we've done to our clothes.

There's a final rustle of cloth, the faint sound of snaps engaging. Her shadow leans toward me for a final honeyed kiss, and then she's gone, darting away as furtively as she came.

Later we'll disrobe for our rest between the sterile rows of bunks in the dormitory wards. She'll be lost among the identical faces, the identical bodies down the line—but somehow I'll always know where she is.

She's my self, my sister, my clone—only another worker here at Factory Enclave IV, grown anonymously in the vats. We're nothing but cogs in a composite machine, working for the collective good. We know nothing about life outside the enclave, have no future but work, but somehow we've found one another—and this thing between us—something to make life more than it was. Lying on my cot between the sleeping, silent forms, I stare into the darkness, wondering about the state of things outside.

What we're doing is called sex, and the managers say it's obscene for us to have it. Is it incest for me to love my sister-clone, or only masturbation? Dammit, I don't care. Even if they catch us, no one can take this ecstasy away from me.

But still it makes me wonder, what else are the managers hiding from us? Someday I mean to find out.

PIPE DREAMS
Shariann Lewitt

The curl of blue smoke reminded him of the stage, but this smelled
saccharine-bitter while the dry-ice machine filled a club with a
wet, biting, acid stench. This was only one more stage, no more.
And Tim McKeon had been on enough of them he reminded himself,
toured Europe and the whole U.K. and North America.

He shouldn't be afraid any more. The necromantic ritual to call up the
ghost of his favorite writer was really just the creation of his imagination.
There wouldn't even be a crowd watching. Not like when he played death
music in the late night clubs for children with white painted faces and
black-rimmed eyes, when he was somewhere between god and angel.

This was just one more piece of spectacle, cribbed from a book about
ritual magic he had picked up more to impress people at the club than
to actually read. But maybe the whole occult ceremonial would be the
stimulant to get his subconscious on track. Something had to help.
Nothing else had, not the quantities of gin and good hash, not the day
trips from London, not the endless hours in the gym.

There was the room ready with candles and incense already burning,
draped with black cloth and the altar fashioned after the one he had seen
at Jimmy Page's house Boleskin. The house Page had bought because it
had belonged to Aleister Crowley. In fact, it did not look so different from

the set for the past two videos he'd done, both the MTV version and the
one that was too racy for the telly but was well received in the clubs.

They expected this of him. It was just one more element of the col-
lage that went into the product called Tim McKeon. Even outrage had to
be calculated. Though this time there was an edge of desperation behind
the facade, a purpose to the personal theater. This next album was crucial
and he was frozen. The music wasn't there. The words were mud.
Nothing was happening.

Unlike his fans, Tim McKeon wasn't exactly certain that there was any
supernatural. But he had read enough to believe in the suggestibility of
the subconscious, which was where the music came from. If going
through this little act stimulated his ability, unfroze the core that he
couldn't touch, then it was more than worth the charade.

And it would help his credibility, to add oblique references to calling
up the shade of one of his favorite authors to help him out. His fans
would believe it. He made certain to appear the metaphysical high priest
in all his public dealings. It was in his bio and his publicist had coached
him how to hint carefully around the subject in the interviews.

McKeon took another hit off the elaborate antique water pipe. Like
the ritual, this was expected. Fortunately, this was one of the require-
ments he enjoyed. Drugs, sex, rock and roll. The clean and simple things
in life, not all bound up with the dark and twilight. Though it was the
dark that he loved more than the simple.

Two more deep breaths of the saccharine smoke, three. It was just
another kink in the corkscrew life-mythos of Tim McKeon, modern high
priest of Dionysus. He couldn't admit he was afraid that even this
extreme measure wouldn't work. That no matter what he did there would
be no new album and his whole life and career would be defined by
three years and seventeen songs.

Abruptly he put the pipe down. He left the sitting room and went
into his bedroom, stripped and pulled on a single garment of black silk.
Against the fabric his hands were dead blue white like a cadaver. The
scent of frankincense and sulfur and balm of Gilead clung to the robe
from his previous experiments.

He needed the help and he couldn't admit it to anyone. He had told the
others that he was spending the day working on new lyrics for the album,
the one they were due to start recording next month. And he didn't have
anything at all. The well was dry. He was burned out, couldn't write.

The band was just on the verge of a big break. The last two indie albums had done exceptionally well, they were a cult item at home and were starting to sell in the States. The A and R person at Capitol was excited about them, pitching them in the industry as the next big and coming thing. Said he expected music that would shock the world in this next album, said that in some future of the universe this would be important music.

So Tim McKeon knew he had to deliver important music, and knowing that had made life strangely miserable and grey. Even drunk or high he couldn't escape the knowledge in the back of his head. He had to deliver on time, and there was nothing in him. Nothing at all.

The house was silent. Andrew and Gordon were out doing the bars and clubs on King's Road. He'd kicked out the pale, anemic girl with the faintly German accent he'd found in his bed when he woke in the early afternoon. There wasn't even any music from all the speakers wired into every room.

Only breathless anticipation coalesced around him as he stepped into the prepared ritual space. Fear sent shivers of delight through him. He looked around one last time at the fabric draped walls, the altar with its bowl and razor and blood colored rose, the perfection of the whole area. As good as Boleskin, definitely. Better.

And on the altar was her picture. He had cut it out of a book when he couldn't find another. Those overlarge dark eyes and skin whiter than his own watched now from the altar space. She had been dead for a century. She was only the symbol for his own creative abilities, he reminded himself grimly. Just as her book had symbolized the act and the unconscious desires long before psychology tried to strip humanity of its dark and primitive belief. Her book had been perfect, she was perfect, both anima and muse, calling that from his inmost being.

He picked up the sword, held it overhead and began the incantations in Greek. At least he thought they were Greek. He'd spent enough time studying the book and trying out various portions of the ritual before actually attempting it.

Heikas, heikas este babaloi.

But the words didn't matter, only the performance did, and McKeon threw himself into the part the way he always did when he sang. All the way, one hundred percent, and if it killed him then that, too, was one of the pleasures that enshrouded him.

Because he had to believe. The primitive in him had to be called up, assuaged, pampered.

A tay Malkuth, ve Geburah, ve Gedula, le olam omeyn.

Sword extended, he cut a pentagram in the air and imagined it flaming blue. Like the gas hob, like the electrical wires crackling in a storm. The blue burned hotcold over the sword, up his arm like a good hit taking hold. It was strong this time. He'd done it right, really right, and that knowledge excited him far more than any of the girls he'd seen in the club last night.

The opening was finished. He laid down the sword and approached the altar. There was nothing in the huge blue book he had bought at the occult store in downtown York that gave instructions for what he wanted now, but all his doubts were gone. Instinct was his guide, the artistic intuition that somehow made the music work before.

Besides, he had set it up himself. Once he'd written a song about it, about blood and life and walking through the worlds. The fact that he had created a situation where he had to live in that, that teased at the edge of his awareness with the familiar taste of making songs. Songs that felt like clay in his hands, that he could shape but that had their own life and integrity, too. When he could find and express them the way they demanded, when he was flying. When he was creating the music that had taken him out of the ranks of the ordinary, the hopefuls and the bitterly lost.

He smiled and pulled back his left sleeve, then raised the straight razor in salute to the portrait. Like everything else in the ritual, the razor was beautiful. The handle was black mother of pearl and it was tipped in silver filigree. The blade was watermarked blue steel, shimmering like a samurai sword. He looked at the blade for a moment and tasted the fearlust and the power around him. Then he made three neat cuts across the inside of his left arm, matching the precise scars already incised in his flesh.

Blood dripped down his skin and he collected it into the bowl. Blue energy merged with the red and the bowl looked as if it were full of living fire. The blood is the life. Maybe it was Crowley who had said that. He wasn't sure.

There was a perverse excitement in the bleeding, in the incense and her picture and the glittering power that he commanded. He felt detached and floating, watching himself perform each gesture perfectly, each intonation without flaw. Only the energy here was focused and clean, not the screaming raging congregation in the pit, slamming and crushing the life from each other while they paid homage to their own violence.

The crowds had excited him. The blood excited him. The razor was sharp and at first there was no hurt at all, only the disconcerting feeling of the blade moving under his skin. His pain, when it finally came, was piquant and pleased him.

The bowl filled slowly. He didn't need much. When he had maybe half a cup he dropped his sleeve again and left the cuts untended. The photograph he placed in the bowl, bound with life, and raised the sword once more.

More words. Infinitely more words. He used only his right hand on the sword, commanding, his thumb hooked over the guard and placed directly on the steel. He had forgotten who had showed him that trick, probably one of the fever-eyed slamming legions who had invited him to partake of more intimate rites after the shows.

The first few years they were playing out he had done all the rounds. There were the witches, traditional and Gardenarian, the Golden Dawn revivalists, members of both factions of Crowley's O.T.O. fan clubs, and a single alchemist who insisted on drinking tinctures of plants and minerals and poisons diluted in pure vodka. Tim McKeon had participated with all of them, often invited to play a prime role. Everyone knew that McKeon was a magician. He had done it for the excitement, the theater. Even his publicist found McKeon a little too close to the edge for her taste. It was fine and well to cultivate the reputation in the gothic subculture; it was quite another to insist on starting recording at the "correct" astrological hour.

But this time he needed results. It had never mattered before. Always there had been the audience, the fullness of the words and the delicious pleasure of going beyond the rational, breaking all the rules.

He lowered the sword and laid it carefully in place. Now he only had to wait. He sat down on the cushion he had stored under the altar, his eyes focused on the picture and the bowl, trying to focus on one desire. Her. Mary.

Concentration was difficult. His mind wandered off onto the song that was only half finished in his head, that he couldn't quite get to come together. Back, he forced himself. Think about Mary.

He had spent hours reading about her, even about the world in which she had lived. A world that thought of itself as upright and rational and godly all at once. A world that had had a gothic movement all its own, where rebel anarchists and free thinkers and occult charlatans had inflamed the underbelly of the night. He found that world very seductive.

He forced his thoughts back to Mary alone. How she had twisted the creation of life into something dark and shapeless and mute, a monster that was his private self. She would not be horrified by the razor scars that striped his arms. In her soul she had scars to match...

But there was a change in the room. The bluish energy darkened into violet and appeared to hover over the bowl. Then it shivered once, twice.

Tim McKeon strained forward and blinked. He thought it might be his eyes, the drugs, the dim light. But something was happening and it was real.

Girlish laughter broke the silence. "It's only imagination," he heard a young woman's voice say. She laughed again. She sounded muffled, far away, lost in the wires of a transatlantic call.

Then he saw her. She appeared like a hologram made from the violet mist trembling over the bowl. She was not the way he imagined her at all, nothing like the portrait painted when she was in her middle forties, ten years before her death. Although the large, overly intelligent eyes were the same.

This was not the Mary-mother to whom he had intended to bring his sorrows. Instead this was the nineteen year old girl of popular imagination, the one who had run off with a poet to Switzerland and spent a summer on a storm-tossed lake, in a villa where Milton had once stayed. This was the Mary who still had her talent and her nerve, who was not afraid to look at the darkness in herself and display it to the world. Who had the words he couldn't write, the calm courage he needed.

She was him, a creature from the center of his own mind. A projection of the creative within him was the way he phrased it.

It was hard to believe that the creature that stood like a violet hologram, taking more solidity from the blood, was a creation of his own mind. She was not only far younger than he had imagined, but more beautiful as well. Her expression, reflecting the haunted nightmares of her psyche, was the one he had cultivated so carefully and so rarely achieved. And in her hands she held a long narrow pipe.

She puffed on it and then held it thoughtfully away. She looked at him, and those overly large, lipid eyes were alien. She measured him. "I see an illusion," she said quietly. "I think it must be from within my own imagining, a man. But I think he must be myself, a piece of myself. From the opium."

"No," Tim whispered harshly. "You are my dream."

She cocked her head to the side, thinking. "No, sir, I do not believe that is possible," she said. "But I am not certain that you are myself, either. Or my self is bleeding and fearsome, and I do not believe that. Any more than any of us are fearsome, that is." She turned slightly and it looked to McKeon as if she were listening to someone speak. Her lips moved but he heard nothing, as if this part of the dream was barred to him.

"Tell me where you are," she said serenely.

"I'm in a house in London," he said quickly. "A small house near the London Dungeon."

She smiled. "I am familiar with that area. Although I cannot imagine how anyone could tolerate the constant stream of thrill seekers and nannies trying to scare their charges with implements of torture closed away in cases. I have not lived in London in a while. A friend of my father's has offered to introduce me to Society in the season there, but I have always managed to decline. The glitter of ball gowns and titles and vying for invitations is not to my taste. All that matters in Society is making an advantageous match. But, my demon sir, I believe in free love and the natural superiority not of the titled classes but of the creative mind."

"Yes," McKeon hissed. The wild abandon in her words was an anthem that echoed in his own soul, that made the ardent iconoclast in him quiver with desire. "But where are you, and how are you breaking those rules? Because I am doing it by summoning you."

She looked at him quite sternly. "You did not summon me at all," she said. "I smoked the pipe of my own will. It is a journey of discovery, of finding the truth behind the illusion. Though I am not certain that you are any more substantial or have any more truth than do I."

"You are at Villa Diodati on Lake Geneva, where Milton once stayed," McKeon said, almost languidly. "And one night you will tell ghost stories and all try to scare each other. And yours, Mary, yours will be the best. A hundred years after you're dead I will read your book and think of the infinite twistings of my own mind. And because you wrote it I will know that I am not alone. Someone else knows my secrets, my vices. Someone else did not find them too terrible. I am not the only monster."

"But the monster is innocent and beautiful," she protested vehemently. "It is the proper Society man, the doctor, who is evil."

A violet-tinged hand reached out to him and her bottomless eyes showed only calm acceptance.

McKeon tasted the words with disbelief. He had been called beautiful before, but for his face and not for his deepest identity, the self that was too horrific to see in the mirror. But she had seen the very worst, and there was only serene approval in her expression. And she had called him innocent. The depraved, created gothic hero tried to sneer at the word, and shattered.

"Then you think I ought to write it?" she asked.

"You must," he answered, startled. "If you don't then I won't be able to write anything either."

Her smile was grave. "Then we shall both write," she said. "It will be a sacred trust, an agreement. George and Percy do this often, have competitions as to who can compose a better poem about some subject. So you and I shall have a pact. I shall write the story for you. And you must read it and be a fair judge. Although, of course you are only an opium dream." She sighed and looked sad.

"You're the dream," he said, but already her image was fading, the violet fading, separating, and the solid three dimensionality dissolving.

He was aware of the room again. The candles were low and there was a draft coming in under the floor. His left arm ached miserably.

All the books he had ever read on the subject of magic insisted that he had to close the ritual space, no matter how spent it was. He skimmed the book, left it on the floor and picked up the sword again. The closing was almost identical to the opening. He had memorized most of that. But this time the movements felt flat and he was aware that he looked silly, saying words he didn't understand, wearing what amounted to an expensive bathrobe waving a sword around. Tim McKeon swore he would never bother with this magic business again. Obviously it was a complete crock.

His arm was still sore when he woke up. According to the red LED on his clock it was eight in the morning. He groaned. The last time Tim McKeon had seen eight in the morning was when he had gotten lost on his way home from a party in the country and stopped at a local lorry drivers' cafe for directions and ended up buying breakfast for half the room.

He must have fallen out right after the ritual and slept straight through. He was better rested than he remembered being in a very long time. Something, some weight or burden was gone. The ritual seemed part of the night before, a dream perhaps. He'd been toking up, maybe he had been high and imagined the whole thing.

He enjoyed feeling free, feeling alive this morning. He took a shower, let his hair towel dry and put on a clean pair of black jeans. The day was slightly overcast, grey. It made him think of light on a lake, on silent deep water. Lake Geneva, Switzerland, where once three famous writers had spent a summer of wild abandon.

He went down to the basement, to the studio he had set up. The studio he hadn't entered for nearly a year. His hands were flying over the keyboard and the words and melodies were thick in the air around him.

He completely lost track of time, until suddenly he realized he was screamingly hungry and went up to the kitchen. The clock there said it was ten at night. He hadn't noticed. He didn't care.

He brought some provisions down with him, a couple of tins of sardines, half a loaf of bread, two bags of crisps and a large box of chocolate biscuits. Then he went back to work until he fell asleep in the deep carpeting on the studio floor.

He dreamed of Mary. He had forgotten she was so beautiful, so perfectly serene and still like the grey glass water of the lake. Not his anima at all, but his muse. He had never had a muse before and suddenly realized that he was writing for her. Because he wanted to share it with her, because if she saw it then she would know that he was real and worthy, and she would smile at him. He was writing because he had fallen in love with her, with his idea of her. And she was more than a hundred years dead.

The truth did not stop the work, did not impinge on the fevered creativity. Everything and everywhere was music, songs that were impatient to be captured by his sixteen track, to be embellished and supported later with fine production and flawless craft. This was raw, new, but it was all of a piece.

He couldn't stop. The music was greater, stronger than he was. His own lust fueled it, every finished song was one more to play for Mary, to make her see him as himself. To make her love him back. The women he had known in their whiteface and black leather seemed only a pallid imitation of the deep core of brilliance and sadness that he had seen for those few moments in the opium dream. Maybe she wasn't always so grave, so gothic, maybe it was just another illusion. But the doubts were smaller than the songs.

Tim McKeon stayed in the studio for five days, emerging only to use the bathroom and get more food. He was down to the stale donuts when the jag finally ended. After five days he had written nearly seven hours of music, culled down to four hours and twenty minutes of which was positively earth-shattering.

He called the guy at Capitol, who was thrilled. He called Andrew and Gordon, and they listened to his tape twice, silent.

"It's better than good, man, it's bloody insane," Andrew said softly after the second time. "I'm impressed. This is going to blow everyone away."

Andrew normally didn't get excited about anything. Tim was gratified. To celebrate they went out on the town, down to the clubs on King's Road where everyone wore black and the music was loud and harsh and the lyrics were all about death.

Tim stood at the bar, a beer in hand, and surveyed the scene. He'd practically lived in this place for weeks on end, he knew every one of the people here. They were dancing, sweating, trying to impress each other with their chatter, which was all inane. There was Lisa who danced the night to forget the days working as a hotel chambermaid, and Jay-jay who drank and looked cool to be more important than everyone else on the dole. There was Spider the bouncer who was bored to death and read historical romances perched on his stool near the door, and Bajit who walked up to every stranger in the place at least once and told them about her academic career.

It made him sick, suddenly. After the creative glut of the past days he could hardly bear the uninteresting sameness in the lives around him. He wanted to be out of here. He wanted to be in a villa in Switzerland with the Alps high all around, and have Lord Byron and Percy Shelley for conversation over dinner.

He left the club, waved down a cab and went home. The house was silent, almost comforting. He went in, dropped his leather duster on the first chair he encountered, and went to the living room directly to rummage for his pipe. He had to open at least three drawers in the living room side tables before remembering that he had stashed it in the kitchen under the sink.

It was an effort, but he took the large bubble-pipe upstairs to the room that was still set for the ritual. Week old blood clotted and congealed on the picture that had been cut out of a book. Tim looked at that picture and trembled. He had to get back to her. He had to give her the music.

He sank into the cushions and started up the pipe. The water like the blood was stale. It tasted gummy and the pipe took a long time to start. Finally he got it going. He took three, four deep hits off the pipe. It tasted foul, as if it had been left to lie more than a week. More like a century. And then the deep relaxation came, the false sense of drug-comfort that made everything sensuous and secure and perfect. Detached from the causality of daily life, he entered the illusion desperately, praying it was the door he wanted but strangely aloof at the same time. As if he knew, but was afraid of knowing.

He let the drug take him. The thick cushions on the carpet were like a pasha's palace, and he stretched out and felt embraced by oriental splendor. Coleridge had described it all so well. At a wave of a little black box he commanded the music on. It saturated his consciousness, as if it was in his head and his ears at once. He sank into the music until it filled his whole range of perception.

And then he saw her. Her long dark hair was free on her shoulders and she was wearing a white night dress with cascades of lace over her arms and breast like snow, and a single white rose in her hair. White on white, innocent and unredeemed, predator and victim all at once.

She did not appear to notice him at first. She was seated on a large canopy bed with pages in front of her, reading them over feverishly. And then she looked up and met his eyes.

"It is not finished yet," she said gravely. "We have been so busy on the lake and there was the matter of Claire's pregnancy, you understand. But I have begun and am committed to finishing. Even if you are only part of myself, it seems you are a part of myself which must be obeyed."

"You must finish, Mary," he said softly. "We have an agreement, you and I. You promised you would finish the book for me. I finished the songs for you. Listen. I wrote it for you. Because of you."

She cocked her head and her mouth tightened into a line as if she were straining. "It is so distant," she said. "Like the thunder on the lake,

like something from Hell. So perhaps when I think of you as my demon
I am not so wrong."

"It'll go platinum," he said firmly. And then he realized that was not
even close to anything he wanted to say. The words were all for her in the
lyrics he had written down, the words that she could barely hear through
the veil of a century.

"Please," he said softly. "It's my gift to you."

The music embraced them both, relentless rhythms driving it
through them, primitive, free, abandoned and wild. Her dark eyes shone
in the candlelight, tied and twisted on the bed, caught and pinioned and
unafraid all together.

Then she turned as white as her starched lace. "But I was never gift-
ed in music, I could not call up an illusion like this from my own mind.
And you, you seem so very far distant and so real. But I cannot..."

He reached out, desire burning more sharply than the razor ever cut.
He reached toward the white shadowed form, and for an instant he
thought he touched cool yielding flesh. A lock of hair brushed his face
and he was lost in the clean scent of rain.

"I love you, Mary," he whispered into her neck.

Ice ghost fingers snaked through his hair, traced the scars on his arms,
on his chest. She leaned down and kissed the healing cuts he had made
when he had summoned her, cuts deep enough that they were still black
in the center and angry red across the white skin. She smiled at the self-
inflicted injuries like a blessing, then shook the layers of downy lace away
from her own sleeves and showed him neat white cuts that were more
demure from being longer healed than his own. She looked at him, into
him, and she knew him and took possession of his darkness. She
enhanced it, reflected it like moonlight, like the black ink lake under the
stars, like death.

For the first time Tim McKeon truly wanted to die. If the deep slash-
marks of his pain pleased her then he desperately wanted more pain. He
wanted to fling himself into those consuming eyes and drown. He had
given her his music, he had given her his soul and it was not enough.

And then it seemed that she was gone, or translated into the drug
dream that followed. McKeon never was certain if the rest actually happened or was created from his own mind and the pipe. But her presence
had more substance than the girls in the clubs, her breath like the aroma
of poppies filled the room.

Touch surprised him, and yet she was with him, here, draped across the heaped pillows like Coleridge's odelisque. But when he lay a hand against her knee he found her flesh as cold as a November rain. As he lay simply looking into her face and wondering if he could get another key of whatever this was Andrew had sold him, she drew herself upright and leaned over him. She held a small knife in her hand, a pocket knife he didn't recognize. She touched the blunt edge to his cheek and traced the line of his jaw to his ear. Then he felt the point teasing across his skin, down his throat. Not quite cutting. Not yet.

Then she reversed the knife again and caught the blade under his tee shirt. He felt the smooth safe edge glide down over his heart and across his belly as she cut the shirt to ribbons. She moved from his sight. He felt his boots removed, quickly, efficiently, and then the cool path of the knife as she slit his jeans up the leg, tickling his hip and slashing the waist. By the time she shredded the other leg and his clothes, now ribbons, fell between the cushions, he craved release.

The rhythms of his own music pounded in his ears, his blood. Always the blood. She sat on her heels and then moved over him, mounting him without revealing herself. He closed his eyes for a moment to revel in the glory of sensation, feeding on it. But it was not enough. He needed something... more.

He returned his vision to her face. In her face he could see the mirror of his own, desire building in urgency but lacking. Needing. She arched her back and her hands fluttered to her hair. To the white rose tangled in the dark locks. She pulled it down and Tim saw the thorn-decked stem. She lifted just the fraction of an inch and slipped the stem between their joined sweaty thighs.

A sliver of pain pierced the frustration. Mary's lips curved into an incandescent smile. He could taste Paradise; he had never been so high, so torn, so utterly sated and so deeply in need.

The razor was in his hand. Her cold fingers closed over his and she breathed in sharply. He used the razor again, her shining hands on his guiding the blade across both their bodies, pain and ecstacy burning together until the conflagration was all that was left.

But when he woke up amid the silken cushions on the floor he was sad and elated together. There was no soreness, though it seemed like a very old scar was traced across his body that he did not remember.

The sun was setting over London in a glorious array of amber and pink haze. The stones of the London Dungeon were alternately gold and red as the sun stained them with oncoming night. Tim McKeon left his house and started to walk down the street, looking at everything around him as if he had never seen it before. He wondered at the antique shops and colorful but expensive dealers had clustered around the Dungeon waiting for tourists in Mary's London. Some of the shops looked like they might have been there that long.

Maybe it was just a play of light on the display window that attracted him, or the sense of time caught in the sundown in the little antique book shop near the corner. He turned in on impulse. The dark leather bindings with their ribs showing and gilt letters made him think of Mary, of her books. Though he had never been interested before, he went to the S's and began to browse the shelves.

The book nearly jumped into his hands of its own accord, a first edition of Frankenstein, or the Modern Prometheus in the original binding. The leather caressed his hands like her pale flesh. He opened the book reverently. It was his, just as his music was hers, mutual muses through the pipe. No matter if she was merely a creation of his own desperation. She was and always would be his Dark Lady, the inspiration so perfect and glorious and pure that she could not possibly exist outside his own creation.

He looked at the yellowed page, and froze in shock. There, written in ink that had once been black but had faded to deep violet over the nearly two centuries intervening, was an inscription.

> *To the man in the pipe dream, though I cannot believe he really exists, I must express my gratitude and debt for the writing of this book. And for the echoes of the music of Hell that still sound in my sleep and the memory of a night with a demon lover who has never lived apart from imagination.*

> *Mary Wollstonecraft Shelley 1818*

THE JAIL OF HIS MIND AND THE SONGS WITHIN
Eric Del Carlo

D ilating iris. The cell is an orb. White, lacking corners, walls curving, arching. I blunder in—but purposeful in my direction, great lumbering steps from the portal shrinking closed behind me to the stained round hole. My knees go, and my body crumples onto the dais and into the rankness of compounded urine, and my gut lets go. Searing bile coming up in strings. No food in me.

He's watching you. Shaking his head.

My eyes blur. I make hardly a sound. Just the reeking mucous hitting the water. My backbone undulates. The convulsions squeeze my belly, swell my chest. My nose runs.

"Oh."

I saw him as a flicker of shape upright on the foam block as I reeled past. I've seen no facsimile of him before. I do not know the contents of his file. I don't know his name.

Dry heaves now. Not even yellow stomach lining to come up anymore. I wait it out. My mouth tastes profoundly foul.

Finally I push off the toilet and spill limply against the cradle where the wall slides into the floor. I palm both eyes. I make no effort to look at him, but there he is, still seated on the bed, still shaking his head; and

181

his eyes travel me in that circumspect not-looking scrutiny of the cell.

He sees: twenty-five, dark hair grown down wild to the jawline, mild olive complexion, dirty nails, unwashed white loose tights and tunic. Probably I'm very close to what he likes. But the match wouldn't be exact. It would make this game too obvious.

I see: dwindling thirties, face just loosening, not yet sagging, body soft through the middle, limbs more muscular but not especially long, lips compressed and somewhat insolent, sullen blue eyes, clothing less stale than mine. And that head on a brief neck still mechanically rocking side to side.

Don't wait for him to speak.

"The fuck you shakin' your head about?" I swipe my nose along my sleeve.

His mouth moves, and most of the insolence leaves his features. "If I tell you I'm unconvinced, you're just going to try to convince me. You'll be clever about it. You'll use subtle psychological gimmicks. But I'm not in the mood for it. I don't need it. I've got plans of my own."

Don't be hostile.

"Look," I say tiredly, "it's been a bad week. I just puked my brains out for the third time today. If you ain't got anything nice to say—like 'hello'—then leave me alone for now."

"You are clever."

"Leave me alone. Please." I stand, spit several times into the hole and walk to the cell's only other bed. A few personal items are spread on it. His. I wordlessly gather them into an extra sheet and set the bundle on the metaplastic floor between our bunks. Then I settle onto the foam block, face away and eyes shut.

He's looking at you. No expression. Now at the stuff you put on the ground. Now he's picking it up, putting the gear elsewhere.

So he is accepting me as a new tenant—if not an authentic one. I will convince this man of my authenticity as a prisoner.

That is key. It has begun.

I trigger the sac again while he's sleeping; I need only thumb a spot on my abdomen, hard. I shake on my haunches, and this time my retching is loud.

He's awake. He's turning. Frowns. Looks somewhat repulsed.

I'm back to vomiting air. I hold my head.

"Infirmary," he says behind.

"Been there." I gag, spit. "There's nothin' wrong with me."

"Indeed."

"Psychosomatic. Nerves. Whatever."

"I don't believe you."

"I told you to say something nice."

"Hello, then."

"Hello."

Give your name.

"I'm Pedro."

He nods. I go back to my bed and sit.

"We're going to be friends, then, are we?" he asks dryly.

He hasn't sat up.

Say you aren't after a friend.

"I'm not looking for a friend."

"What're we to be, then?"

"Cellmates," I say.

Good.

He shrugs and closes his eyes.

"I'll tell you my name. I'll watch you closely when I say it."

I frown slightly. This has come without prologue on my fourth day in the cell.

"My name is Simon Squall."

I grunt. "It takes you four fuckin' days to tell me your name, man—" I frown again, thoughtfully. I drop my eyes, then raise them into his careful stare from the opposite bunk. "Simon Squall. The Bad Bomber. Right?"

It's correct. Tell him what you know about his case.

"They got you for two years. I caught your whole act on the news. The Bad Bomber. That was crazy what you did. That was some stupid shit to do."

Squall's gaze doesn't flicker.

I grunt-laugh. "Just an ordinary little man. A little job at a little commerce terminal. Just another drone—like everybody else is in the world. And goin' home one day you stop in the middle of a crowd on a rush hour platform and hold up your briefcase and yell you got a bomb inside. And everybody 'course goes nuts and scrambles, and folks get trampled, and legs get broken, and the cops come and take you down, and you got nothin' in that laptop. Nothin'. The Bad Bomber. So you bought yourself two years in here. Stupid. Stupid."

Squall stares implacably. I can feel the careful gauging, the measuring. I haven't acted for him; all I know of Simon Squall and his months-old case comes from my viewing the news.

My responses are genuine. It's why I don't review the file.

The insolence comes briefly to his lips as he purses, then says softly, "That's right. Stupid." He takes a book from his bedside and pours all his attention into it.

He's undecided. He doesn't believe or disbelieve your reaction.

I know I want to tell the voice singing in my head.

I take an unabashed shit on the toilet the following day.

There isn't much in me; I still puke every other meal. Standing, draw-strings undone and waistband stretched between my thighs, I give Squall a good long look between my legs without seeming to maneuver it. Not a classically erotic moment—a half-naked man wiping his ass. But this is Inside, and niceties are done without. Squall's been in awhile. Alone in this cell.

He saw. He liked what he saw.

The seduction has begun.

The light in the windowless orb of the cell goes down to one-tenth at night, and by that I follow the indistinct glint of scalp at the crown of Squall's nodding head. My wrists are crossed at my nape. My hips rise spontaneously to the clutching moisture.

He's ponying up five packs of cigarettes for this privilege —that archetypal convict currency, which Squall has apparently been hoarding. I don't even smoke Outside. The negotiations were unadorned. A funda-mental pragmatic transaction, a naked candid rendering of the unneces-sarily complex stages that allow lovers to achieve this simple joining in the outside world.

He's kneeling at the foot of my bed.

I let go into the bobbing heat.

Afterwards Squall says tonelessly, "You're pretty much my cup of tea, you know, but you're a little darker than I like."

Tell him he'll have to settle for this shade.

"Fuck you," I say to Squall.

I slowly walk the cell clockwise.

"Well," Squall says, and the rueful tone is there, "what are you in for?"

I don't look at him. "Hell, man, there's only two crimes in the world anymore."

"And they are?"

"Throwing bombs and cowboying."

"I didn't commit either of those crimes."

"No," I say. "You're in for stupidity committed on the criminal scale."

"And did you get locked up for the same thing?"

Don't tell him the truth.

I continue walking my circuit. "I wasn't stupid. Just unlucky."

"At what?"

"Humpin' a terminal, tryin' to crack accounts. I was good, but the last system I met was rigged."

"A cowboy," Squall murmurs. "We had trouble with that kind where I used to work. Meddling in our net. Trying to steal confidential information. Scavengers. Rats in the wires.

"Software outlaws—kids wearing dark glasses, flying on speed, skulls strung with monofilaments, living the nihilistic lifestyle, acting like there was something grand about it all—posing. I despised everything about that breed. The radicals out there throwing bombs trying to knock this society off its regimented foundations, they believe. They seek change.

"Although they seek it by the worst conceivable route."

His tone has shifted minutely, and I know he is saying something genuine, unguarded. Is he saying also that he accepts my story?

I pass his bunk again in my circling. He is watching me.

"When I first got in here, you said you had plans. What sort of plans?"

By the book I should wait for a prompt before asking something like that. But it's me in this cell. And I am not a puppet.

That was unauthorized. Don't do it again.

Squall remains silent.

I puke breakfast. The whole thing is taking its toll, and I'm dropping weight.

"That's to elicit my sympathy, right?"

I return to my bed.

"The idea is to cultivate some sort of compassionate link between us—you patient, me nurse."

"I really don't want sympathy," I say. "I wish you didn't have to see this. Think I like hugging the shitcan twice a day...while you sit there makin' smartass comments?"

"Why don't you go back to the infirmary?" Squall asks blandly.

"I been there. I been there so many fuckin' times they won't let me come back. There ain't nothing wrong inside me—that's what they say. Nothin' they can do for me, anyway. It's anxiety. Nerves. I don't like bein' In—hate bein' locked up—hate small spaces—and I get nervous. Can you understand that?

"So I can't hold anything down. I used to be in a bigger cell with two more cellmates. They couldn't stand the sight of me spewin' my food all the time, so they raised such shit about it, beat me up enough times, the screws finally pulled me out. Threw me in with you. So now you get stuck with me. I don't want you feelin' sorry. I don't want you watching. Just turn your head next time you see me make a sprint to the toilet, okay?"

Squall looks away, but there's a spark of some new feeling beneath the surface insolence.

Simon Squall has been expecting me—or someone of my kind.

That's evident. Why?

How expedient it would be to just slap a load of Tell-the-Truth into his arm and get out of him whatever information the DA office wants. But, just as evidently, they can't get the court order to do so. The procedure is notorious for its legal entanglements. So I am put in with him—purposely with no notion of what information I should be fishing for.

Squall is my puzzle. I'll solve him. It is vastly, intimately, privately important to me that he believe I am an inmate as well.

The Bad Bomber. The trial sketched a mousy little man who'd passed some sort of emotional breaking point. No evidence of radical affiliations had ever been uncovered.

Is Squall with the Underground? Is that what they want me to find out?

His cigarettes are cubbied away in a gouge he's dug out of his foam block of a bed. He very deliberately and symmetrically sets the five packs in a file on the floor between us. His eyes are averted, and I sense both solemnity and edginess—the emotions of a ceremony, religious, significant. I know immediately that this is no longer the simple goods barter it has been the past three or four occasions I've sold my cock to him.

He's nervous. Use it.

I stir from the book I've been reading—one Squall's loaned me, a yellowing paperback, a political thriller. I rise on an elbow and glance down at the arrayed cigarette packs. He's got several brands.

"Hey, I haven't even finished the last smokes I got off you," I say, but my tone is soft. The smoking is actually making me nauseous, though it would feel infinitely odd to me now to vomit naturally.

"I know you haven't." Squall's words come lower, almost staccato. "I know you haven't."

I lean over and finger one of the packs.

"I don't care that you're just acting, don't care that your presence in here with me is a lie, that you're a plant, a spy... I don't care about that. Not when we...You're a live warm human body. I am lonely in this place. I like the feel of you. I don't care that you're in here to trick information out of me. Not... not when I've got your human taste on my tongue, Pedro."

And this last comes out in a startling adolescent rush.

This is the first time he's used my name.

He might be trapping you. Trying to rouse sympathy so he can laugh in your face.

The multitudinous hidden monitors in this cell can read any angle in minute detail, but I am with this man, face to face. I can smell him.

"I'm a prisoner, Simon. Just like you."

His eyes have finally met mine, but he remains silent.

I tug at my drawstrings. The insolence is gone from his features, and the softness of his jowls imparts a suggestion of melancholy to the face. He's not an unattractive man.

Be careful.

"Go ahead, man. Fuck the smokes. Just go ahead. Gratis."

Squall wavers, sensing the crossing of an unidentified border—perhaps fearing its inevitability or irrevocability.

Then he comes to me.

I eat the blander portions of the meals we're given, claiming it has a better chance of staying down. I offer Squall my leftovers. He contemplates a moment, then trades; he gets my gluey gravy and fatty meat and I his oatmeal and rice. We talk little, but there is a tacit progression taking place. I've been given the liberty to smoke from his stash whenever I please—or when I feign the desire. He performs fellatio on me about twice a week. I no longer need to populate the scenes with writhing fantasy images in order to get off; it's enough now to simply feel Simon working on me. That link between us is an obvious one—but effective. I play at Mata Hari. He is not open, but perhaps he's ajar.

The voice in my head gives counsel, and I can do nothing to blot it out.

And one day I go to him, and the voice sanctions this move.

Yes. It's time. Do it.

Night in the windowless orb. Fractional lighting. Simon's slight wheeze of sleeping breath. I stand above. I delicately draw away the sheet. I see the familiarity of his shape curled in the shadows.

He faces the wall, and I put my palm across his hip, thinking to ease the figure onto his back gently, but he starts.

"What?" The word is immediate and muddled in his mouth.

I pull at his hipbone, but he abruptly pushes my hand away.

"What are you doing?"

"I want to do something for you. I want to do this for you." I replace my hand, and he allows himself to be rolled onto his back.

"Why?" He almost chokes it out.

"Let me, Simon."

"Why, Pedro?"

"I want to. I know you want me to."

"Taking this thing a bit far, aren't you?" It's meant to be insolent, but the voice is virtually breathless. In excitement?

Fear?

"What thing?" I find his eyes in the dimness.

"The act. You—being in here with me. The act."

"I hate it when you talk that shit."

He goes silent.

I go for his drawstrings. I discover a knot in my throat as the urge to swallow overwhelms me. My body feels heated. I slide fingers into the waistband, and wordlessly he levers hips off the foam. I turn the leggings inside out as I peel them away.

I've seen the organ lolling erect against his pliable belly—and something reciprocal which I don't pause to analyze happens in my groin. But my attention goes elsewhere. To an unexpected sight.

Ask him about it.

"This happen in here?" I ask quietly, almost reverently.

"Yes," Simon answers, and suddenly his tone is matter-of-fact. The secret is out. One of his secrets, anyway.

"Who did it?" But I know.

"I did."

The fresh curling scars are neat and so similar they might've been cut by machine. Around the anklebone. Not wrists.

And somehow the slashing of the ankle is immeasurably more intimate, vulnerable. Deep. The search for the artery. A dull blade. A convict shiv. Some filed scrap of metal. I see the ragged puckering of the wounds; and in that I see the patchwork job done in the infirmary.

"I was in a bigger cell, just like you say you were. My cellmates woke up one morning, saw my bed soaked red underneath me and helpfully shrieked for the guard. Afterwards I found myself lying in restraints and a doctor asking me questions I wouldn't answer at the trial. Then I was alone in here... and you showed up a week later."

"D'you ever think about tryin' it again?" I whisper.

"Yes."

And now I know what plans he has. Plans I am perhaps interrupting. I also know one of the reasons I'm in here.

There's a time limit. A determined convict possesses a preternatural amount of time and patience—a convict's only real possession—and even in a monitored cell it can all be over before those on the other side of the cameras can put down their coffee cups.

So they want me to get whatever it is they need out of Simon Squall before he takes his life in here.

Go to him.

I don't need the prompting. I drift upward, away from the scarred ankles. I am floating. I hear his breath catch and am glad for the pleasure in the sound. Hands trace thighs, following natural lines toward this natural consummation. I will not hurry. I cup his balls, palming, pressing the fleshy pouches. The cock trembles. I perch over his needy body, only my hands working him. My dirty fingernails graze the sides of his shaft, base to head, maddening and lingering.

We shudder as I at last close a hand around him. How hot this organ, how blistering the hunger...

I jerk slowly, torturously, utterly certain of my rhythm. In the dimness Simon's head rocks back, back, chin stabbing ceilingward, backbone arching involuntarily to throw his hips, his cock, his need toward me. I take it. I take everything.

I touch his navel. I stroke his heaving chest. I capture his nipples. I caress his throat.

My pumping has accelerated, and he could burst into my grip, but I won't allow that. This act is to be seen through, to the appropriate end. I shift myself between Simon's raised knees. My mouth goes to him, and it is consumption.

Now we mix, each inside the other's body.

I walk the cell clockwise. He goes counterclock. We continue to divvy up the meals—Jack-Sprat-and-his-wife style.

He loans me books. I tell fictitious but utterly convincing tales about cowboying—the lingo and ambience of the trade I've picked up from inmates; he makes no comment but always listens intently. I puke less often, and my tender abdominal muscles are grateful. I am no longer Simon's five-pack trick. We are lovers. Our cell is a scene of domesticity.

He still will not believe my authenticity. He's been expecting a tactic like this—a plant in his cell to beguile information from him, since he knows he is beyond the reach of a Tell-the-Truth injection—since his attempted suicide. But he cares less and less. He accepts me at the face value for which he can use me.

But I care. I care profoundly.

"I'm a prisoner, just like you."

He looks away.

I see that concealed sadness in Simon more frequently as our days mount. I ask no direct questions about that incident on the crowded plat-form that put him in here. I wait. I know I am now inside of him, but I won't ransack the premises; instead, let him conduct me to the proper room. But I don't know if there will be time. I know—intuitively, read-ing the language of personalized nuances that a monitor cannot distinguish—that Simon is near to an end. He is approaching another border, grimly. I've no doubt that if his bunk were tossed, another shiv would be found imbedded somewhere in the foam.

Night again. The artificial, constructed night of the cell.

I wake in a sudden senseless rush.

He's cut himself.

But the voice in my head registers in no real way. Debris of dreams collides with my dim vision of the cell. I scrabble out of my sheets.

"Simon, man—"

"Listen to me, Pedro." Words composed, controlled, tight.

I am blinking, fumbling. A line of something black streaks the arching white metaplastic wall over Simon's bed. He is sitting up, arms folded firmly against his body.

"What did—"

"Listen."

Listen to him.

I'm on my knees but abruptly afraid to reach for him. The thought of unknown textures—of thick dampness, stickiness— stopping my hand...

"I know you're a spy, Pedro, but I'm going to give you what you want because you've made my time in here easier. And I am appreciative of that. But I'm tired of futility. The futility of trying to wake an entire culture with a few explosions. I was tired of it on that platform, holding up that empty briefcase. I admit I had hoped—remotely, half-consciously— a cop would just shoot me down." He speaks formally. A speech thought out in detail. Perhaps while making the final contemplations of the act that immediately preceded it.

"Did you hurt yourself?" I ask inanely. My throat is clenched, barely allowing sound. I feel my blood pounding.

Blood. Streaking the wall. Draining away.

He wants no interruption. "Listen."

Goddamnit, shut up. This is it.

They can see. They saw. They watched on the monitors as Simon took up the blade, gashed the arteries. They watched—as I must now watch— and they allowed; but the tapes will show this, and an infirmary crew is certainly on its way. I have that small segment of time to extract the information.

"It's about the Underground," he says ardently.

"I'm a prisoner too, Simon." And my hands go to him at last and touch moist clothing, warm flesh beneath—but the seal is broken, the living warmth emptying.

Shut up.

"Pedro—"

"I am. I'm in fucking jail! Believe me. Believe me. Please."

"It doesn't matter."

"It does!" Ranting. It's hammering out of me now, beyond controlling.

Shut up and listen.

My fingers dig in. I jam my forehead against his chest, and sobs burst from me. Everything is gone suddenly behind tears.

"I don't care about it, Simon—the Underground, whatever... that doesn't matter."

I feel his hands in my wild hair. Gentle. Hot blood moistens my right cheek as his savaged inner arm brushes it. He waits. Waits—with life pulsing steadily out of him, he has only patience for my child-like tears and snuffling. And when they subside, I am sedate.

"You don't believe I'm a prisoner?" I whisper, the thinnest upturned imploration.

"No," he says tenderly, tolerantly, lovingly. Then he tells me about the Underground.

Fed, groomed, clothed.

Debriefing. Reports.

I am a numb thing.

Simon Squall was alive but unconscious when the orb's iris dilated and they took the body. The lights came up. Show ended.

There was an incredible quantity of blood on the metaplastic floor. I don't know what has become of him. I know nothing of the men in the cells—any of them—when we meet; I have no knowledge of their fate when we part. Even if I wanted, there are severe regulations governing such things. Simon Squall is dead to me.

I am reprimanded, but the censure is balanced by my record and by the ultimately successful job with Squall. Successful at least in their eyes. A small body of the Underground has been sussed out by my efforts, Squall's minor cadre whose affiliation to he kept so well hidden. A few less bombs exploding in shopping centers and derailing trains. Trying to shake an entire world out of programmed, hive-like, computerized complacency.

Fools... on both sides of the war.

I sit, eyes closed, in the final office. The triggering sac has been removed, and I can think about a genuine meal.

"What're you going to do with your time off?"

I look up slowly. "Go back to New York City and mix bombs in a sink in a basement flat."

"Not funny." It's the voice in my head, sounding strangely lifeless in its full dimensions. She wears a grey suit. In the monitoring chamber—not much bigger than a cell, really—she wears a spidery headset, eye-pieces receiving dozens of alternating images, a microphone hung before her lips. "Not funny—but I don't expect better from you." A mild smirk at this last.

"Do you got leave time coming before your next assignment?" I ask.

"Not me. A new case starts in three days." She shakes her head minutely. This large room is softly furnished. It smells antiseptic. "Barely enough time to get the crick out of my neck."

"Poor you." I stand and leave.

I pass the last checkpoints out of the building. The midday sunlight, as always, seems otherworldly.

I recall lucidly the words I finally said to the man I shared a cell with when I was nineteen. Before the tables were turned. Before I enlisted to have my head wired. A man, a cellmate, one I came to trust implicitly—an act I'd fallen for; and I told him what I'd never told the judge who passed my two year sentence or the prosecuting attorney or even my own lawyer. *Why did you make that bomb? Why did you blow the lobby of that building? You didn't even kill anybody. That's no Underground tactic.*

I was never in the Underground.

To the man who betrayed me, who robbed my trust of the world and left me no real option but to return to that cell where I at least possess the comfort of being on the other side of the deception, where I again and again try to even the score of my original betrayal... to him I said: "I was just angry."

I vanish into the sunlight.

DAY JOURNEY, WITH STORIES
Jason Rubis

I see you standing at the station, waiting for the steamer. It pulls in moments later in a blaze of shifting chrome panels, hot white clouds spouting from its head and sides. Steamers have fascinated me since I was a girl; my cousin Joselle told me once that they ran not primarily on steam, but the combined labour of dozens of slaves kept toiling away somewhere deep in the steamers' bowels. She described the slaves trudging away on gigantic treadmills, their bodies hung with bright chains, or strapped screaming to the inner walls while silver cables robbed their bodies of some form of energy necessary for the steamers' maintenance. "Think of that, Alie! All those poor slaves! All just so people like your papa can get to the City every day...."

Even now, when I take the steamers into the City practically every day myself, I remember Joselle's stories. The basic design of the steamers hasn't changed much, as much as the People in Charge have nattered on about "streamlining" and the virtues of sleek and smooth over ponderous bulk. Of course, nothing much else has changed in the world either in, what now? Five hundred years? A few useful inventions, some stylistic development, then... stasis for another century. I suppose it's comforting, in a way. The steamers are still huge, they still have plenty of room for hidden chambers filled with Joselle's slaves. Now and then I tap my shoe-soles on the carriage floor, just as I did during those infrequent rides in my girlhood. I used to wonder if the slaves below could hear me, and think I was sending them some sort of code—a false message of hope and rescue. I could see them in their secret chambers, straining their sad, beautiful faces upwards, wondering if that day would be the day of their liberation. The cruelty of it frightened and thrilled me.

You've met Joselle; now that she's married she's become properly demure, but when we were both in school she terrorized and delighted me with tales of exotic tortures practiced in far-off (and wholly fictitious) countries. Her favorite characters for these stories were a Prince and Princess, twins, both gorgeous and quite, quite evil.

"What would they do to me if they caught me?" I would ask, trembling. It was a ritual question; I asked it during each of her visits, and Joselle invented a new delight for me each time.

"If they caught a sweet thing like you, well, first they'd make her take off her shoes and stockings. And it'd be no good crying; they're quite ruthless. Then they'd make you sit on a bench in front of a wall with two holes in it, perfectly sized to your ankles. They'd make you put your feet—your bare feet—through the holes, and then they'd lock sort of manacles around your ankles, so you couldn't withdraw them. Then they'd start the torture."

Joselle would stop there to help herself to an apple or a sweet from a bowl on the table and bite into it. You remarked on Joselle's mouth after you met her; it's still a rather pretty, cruel mouth, but then it held an absolutely hypnotic power over me. I'd squirm and watch my cousin's lips with wide eyes, not daring to prompt her, any more than I would have hurried an actual torturer. I was savouring every moment.

"The Princess would have come to sit beside you while the Prince disappeared through a door in the wall. She would inform you that the Prince's menagerie was on the other side of that wall, and that he kept all sorts of ferocious animals in it, all of them roaming free without cages. They'd been brought up from birth to trust him, obey his every command, she'd tell you, but they'd kill anyone else in the wink of an eye."

I couldn't suppress a little cry at that. I'd clench my toes up tightly inside their shoes, imagining them protruding helplessly from the wall, attracting the attention of the Prince's horrible, hungry pets. Joselle would inflict a particularly long silence then, enjoying my nervousness.

"What kinds of animals, exactly?" I'd ask timidly.

"Various species, but all of them ferocious! Wolves and tigers, chiefly. But what would happen next is that you'd feel a long, rough tongue scraping up and down your soles."

"It would tickle," I'd moan, clutching at the rug.

"Yes, tickle horribly," Joselle gloated. "You see—and the Princess would explain this to you as you sat there—the Prince had brought an animal of some sort, most probably a tiger, over to your feet and though the beast was mad with hunger, commanded it to lick your feet rather than simply bite them off at the ankles. But this was a specially trained tiger that would go mad with killing frenzy at the sound of... human... laughter."

"The wall," I said desperately. "The wall would muffle the noise."

"At that point you'd hear something sliding: a small window opening up in the wall just above your head. Any sound you made could easily be heard by the tiger."

"I would bite my lip," I continued bravely. "I wouldn't laugh. I'm not ticklish."

Joselle would reach over then and begin walking her long fingers up my arm. "The Princess would start doing this," she said. "And this" With her other hand she'd take a pinch of her long brown hair and tickle my face with it while I gasped and pursed my lips.

"The Prince would have the tiger lick only one foot at a time," Joselle told me, eyes glimmering. "Leaving another foot free for him to tickle with a long, stiff feather. Up and down the sole, between your toes. How long could you take it, Alie? That feather... and the Princess' fingers... and the tiger's whiskers and tongue, its wet breath on your poor little bare feet, tickling, tickling..."

I'd have to jump up and run up to the lavatory then, and relieve myself. I'd want badly to continue the story when I came back down, but I was too embarassed and Joselle never offered. Besides, there'd be another story next time she came to visit.

No, you'd never imagine Joselle to be capable of that kind of thing now.

You're far enough ahead of me on the platform to make calling out to you impractical, or certainly in poor taste. But I can see you moving towards the same car as me, even though a fair distance will separate our seats. So I content myself simply with climbing aboard and finding a good seat. If you are going to see me, you will see me.

Moments later the steamer pulls out of the station with a wonderful, great roar. I slide my identification card into the slot on my armrest, holding my breath until it clicks Approved and releases the card. I don't know what would happen if it were not Approved. I've never seen anyone Denied, and assuming the possibility even exists (ours is such an orderly society), why do they allow us to wait until the steamer is on its way before we use our cards? It's a mystery to me. I, of course, used to fantasize that if my card were Denied I would be hustled off to the steamer's depths to join Joselle's slaves in a life of desperation and painful toil. In a sense, that very nearly did happen; do you remember the article I wrote years ago that dared make critical remarks about overpopulation of the City, the way everyone has flocked to the Outer Towns and Suburbs? The politicos hated that. If some of my father's old friends hadn't proved so fond of me, I may well have been taken away in actuality. I doubt I would have found prison as romantic as I found the idea of the slaves.

At any rate, here I am, your prim Alie, my little journey begun. I tuck my identification back into my purse and give myself a few idle moments to look around the car. You're too far behind me to glimpse without swiveling my neck around, so I content myself with my immediate neighbors: businessmen and businesswomen properly attired like myself, and several young people wearing their ridiculous, voguish costumes. A boy across the aisle from me sits with his shoes propped up insolently on the seat next to him. His face is painted and his hair coloured and feathered outrageously. He pouts and taps a tune on the window—some music only he can hear. A pretty boy. He fascinates me; it wasn't that long ago I was his age, though of course I was always sweet and well-spoken. As I take out my notes and writer, I wonder whether he would pout and smirk quite so smugly if he found his hands suddenly, magically bound behind his back and if I, sauntering over and seating myself beside him, began kissing him and tweaking the nipples he displays through his artfully ripped shirt. Perhaps I would take a pin from my hair and begin pricking him very lightly about the chest and groin. What's the matter, darling? Why are you crying? Don't you like being mine, belonging only to me, to Aunt Alie? Don't cry, can't you see no one on the car can hear you? They're all reading and looking out the windows. But I'll treat you so nicely.

Joselle and I did something similar to another boy once, a simple boy who worked in my father's gardens. We lured him to the house with sweets and bound him to a chair, he all stupid with fear of these pretty, rich girls, the girls laughing breathless and excited and perhaps a touch frightened themselves. Joselle bent close to me, and her lips wet my ears: "You're the Princess now, Alie. And he's your prisoner. What'll you do to him?"

Of course this was a challenge of sorts; Joselle wanted to see what her little cousin was made of. I wanted to impress her, but I also felt very warm, almost giddy, looking at the gardener boy as he sat panting and staring at me. I took a pin and stuck it into his arm, just above where the rope pressed his skin down in a neat line. "Come on," I whispered to him, "tell me your secrets. You have to tell me. I'm the Princess." I stuck him again and he began to cry in a loud, blubbering voice. When we let him go eventually, we made him promise never to tell anyone what we'd done, and though he gave us that promise readily, I spent many hours sick with terror that my father would confront me one day with my crime. Joselle, of course, never worried for an instant, and in fact the boy disappeared soon after. We simply never saw him again, and when I asked Joselle what she thought happened, she said "Ran away, I expect," into her coffee with a perfect lack of concern. "Unless the real Princess carried him off," she added, lifting her eyes to smile nastily at me.

That was not long ago, but long enough ago to make it hardly worth remembering. I tell myself that I have no time for such reminiscences. I thumb the writer on like a good girl and begin arranging my notes for an article I'm preparing on the restoration of a City monument. Perhaps I sit a little stiffly, absolutely erect, hoping you'll notice my hat (you did buy it for me, after all) and come to me, say hello.

I'm distracted again when a girl emerges from the door at the car's far end and struts up to my fantasy's seat, kicks his feet aside and throws herself down beside him. Her own feet are bare, and when she lifts them to prop her heels on the facing seats, I can see her soles have been intricately tattooed with zig-zag patterns. I look at her; she's even younger and more arrogant-looking than he is, her clothes even more torn and disreputable. Her hair is long, straight and blond. Her eyes meet mine and I smile. She sneers.

"Did that hurt?" I ask, leaning forward slightly. "The marks on your feet?"

"What, these?" she wriggles her toes. "Not hardly. They said they would, but I didn't feel a thing." Such a brave girl.

"I'll bet it tickled," I said, smiling. "I bet they had to strap you down for it while you giggled and giggled." Such teasing familiarities... if I were to make a direct overture to this girl, I could be arrested, such things being decidedly illegal. But the pout on her face gives me considerably more pleasure than the lawmakers could imagine. The boy smirks and she silences him with a glare.

"They use needles, not feathers," she informs me loftily. "And I'm not ticklish. I've been walking barefoot all my life. My feet are like leather."

Her feet are like silk, I thought, looking at them. Soft and white. Spoiled, silly girl, throwing her shoes away in response to some idiotic new fad. She probably stuffed them into the lavatory wastebin just now. As for the tattooing, I'm sure she shrieked and squeaked through the whole ordeal. Needles and ink and blood; I'm sure it was painful, perhaps the only pain she's ever really had to endure. But I like relating her to Joselle's stories; I enjoy imagining the Princess using a quill to scratch the strange patterns on her soles while she giggles and pleads.

I give her a placating smile and go back to my writer. But I've made her nervous, and she's taking it out on her boyfriend, snarling at him for nothing and punching his arm.

Between these two and your unseen presence, I can't concentrate on my writing. It's only minutes now until we reach the first City station anyway, so I put my things away and look out the window, admiring the sunlight glaring on the fields and houses that multiply slowly as we draw nearer to the station.

The City: stone arcs and metal towers, people and people and people. But none of them, not one, your equal. Do you know what I love to remember most? The night we spent in this very City, with you adoring my lips and learning my unfamiliar parts, my geography. The circumstances were so intimate; your heart beating against my shoulders, your mouth nuzzling them, giving me such gentle bites. We had girls from one of the better Houses come in and bind us one on another, then tease our bodies with mourningstones and feathers, tongues and nails and scourges while we gasped and struggled into each other. We were both swollen, both in desire to the point of pain, the philters we had taken staving off and then prolonging orgasm. Do you remember? Do you remember the telepath girl I had specifically requested, because of her storytelling abilities as much as her mental gifts? Do you remember how she teased you with stories that exploited the most secret, delicious corners of your imagination? The boy raped by a woman with eight spidery legs? The woman tied and lowered into a pit of eels? I think she must have liked you. She played with you far more fervently than she did me while she told her stories. I only felt the stroke of her mind on mine briefly, but then I so rarely hide my fantasies; my imagination has none of the enticing coyness yours does. My strangeness and desires are right there on my mind's surface, like colored oil on water. Joselle—the story-girl's predecessor in some ways—brought them up years ago, and they've never sunk back down into my hidden depths.

When you came you screamed, a scream that died away to a slow weeping. I followed you soon after and then we were discreetly unbound and left in one another's arms. That night is my favorite story. I wish I could find a way to tell it to Joselle, but perhaps you would find that indiscreet?

The steamer slows and shrieks and once again exhales clouds as it pulls into the City station. I collect my things and sigh and stand up. The girl is watching me sulkily, arms folded, still wriggling her toes (now rather like an angry cat twitching its tail). Excitement at your presence makes me reckless: I smile sweetly and mouth a kiss at her. It's a risk... no one is watching, but she could call me out, have me arrested and put in chains for real this time, make great trouble for me and you. But though she starts at first her face softens almost immediately and a smile of her own breaks through her sulk, making her unexpectedly gorgeous. I know she's collecting herself to return the kiss, but I turn away (relieved, I'll admit that) and begin walking determinedly up the aisle to you. Always the tease, as Joselle used to say of me. A passive sadist, she called me once, and I rushed to the dictionary.

My heart is beating hard as I approach your seat. Your head is bent over your own writer. Other passengers shoulder past me, I clear my throat, and when you look up at me, things shift, change you into some-one else. A line of throat, a lifted eyebrow. You're not you now. You are Someone Else. You are my mistake. An easy mistake, due to hair color, taste in clothing, approximate height. My stuttered apology is delivered and the you who is not you gets up and smiles and leaves the car.

Disappointment. The possibilities I hadn't known I'd been counting on pour from my eyes: drinks, reminiscences, a walk, another night in this City... re-kindled fires? All of that now gone. And I must walk in not-your footsteps out the train to a cold office and words I never cared about.

But a hand hits my shoulder and when I turn around my blonde girl and her friend are standing behind me. They both incline towards me just slightly and then both deliver an obviously rehearsed, remunerative kiss to the air in front of my face. They stand smirking triumphantly, adorably.

I am delighted. I take their hands and tell them I'm going to buy them coffee. The morning is young, they are young, I am not old, and suddenly I believe again that there are new stories to be made.

THE SPECIALIST
Lauren P. Burka

I ran down to the cafeteria for lunch instead of studying or returning to my room for a nap. This wasn't the first mistake I made that day, nor the last, but the first I had cause to regret.

Two months away from my D.A. certification, I was starting to feel the strain, all the worse because I couldn't complain about it.

"You don't need to be here," one of the instructors had told us this morning at line-up, like they did every week. "All eight of you have Erotic Arts certificates to your credit."

The number had been ten before Kadie quit and nine before Selhahn was dismissed last week. We were far enough into our training that people who stumbled weren't likely to catch up again. They were reassigned to some other specialty, or released to another Band.

"You can expect a salary in the seventy-eighth percentile even if you don't stay with the Adoration. You could make a passable living leaning against a tree in a park two nights a week, for bleeding sake. If you don't want to be here, really don't want to, get out before you get hurt."

My body ached like I'd been turned on a lathe. The finest knives of the Adoration were slicing away physical weakness and shame, rationalizations, delusions, and false pride. They were trying to break me before I broke myself. Or someone else. I didn't quit this morning after line-up, though, and I wouldn't quit now. Even if Gahan had left a cryptic message asking to see me this afternoon. My stomach was snarling with anxiety around my sandwich. This wouldn't be a social call.

"Vri."

"Idran," I replied without turning.

"Hey, slow down." He was carrying a tray of food, a bigger lunch than my own.

"I really shouldn't stay."

"We haven't seen much of you all week."

I sighed. May as well quell rumors now. "You want to know why they took me out of morning class, correct?"

"Ahhh..." He hesitated.

"Then don't be so polite," I told him. "Oh, sit down."

We hooked a table and two chairs on the edge of the dining pavilion. The place was nearly empty, the end of the normal lunch period on a day when most of the standard contracts were on break.

Idran was a year older than I and more poised for it. But then he was slated to become a dom, and he already possessed that aura. His job was so much harder than mine.

I said, "Medical said my skin wasn't responding to surface treatment anymore, and if I didn't stop accumulating bruises, they'd have to grow me a new hide all the sooner." My pale complexion would make me a prize for sadists after I got my D.A., but it required more upkeep.

Idran whistled. "Why didn't they tell us? Trying to keep us off-balance?"

"I think they figured someone already asked me. I've been too busy, though. Tellie has me mornings for a bit, and I've been even more sore, if that's possible."

He grinned. "Don't you like it just a little?"

I picked at my empty sandwich-wrapper. "Women scare me. I don't know what they want because I'm not one of them."

Idran raised an eyebrow at me. "Do you know what men want, then, just because you are one?"

"I like to think so."

"Do you?"

So I was a little slow this afternoon.

"I don't have much time," I said.

"You have enough time," said Idran.

I met his eyes and tripped and fell into that dom's aura.

"Just enough for you," I agreed.

Idran stood and pushed his chair back.

"Aren't you going to eat your lunch?" I asked.

"But of course."

He touched my shoulder, making me shiver as I stood.

I kept my eyes down as I walked two steps behind him like a proper submissive. This would be good, I thought, anticipating a chance to play with an equal, to fuck and not be graded for it.

I thought Idran might paw me over in the lift, but he was keeping reserved in public at least. He possessed a handsome face and long, black hair. I was a little jaded about these by now. Each of us had been recast in flesh for our role, and there were no plain-looking D.A.'s. Idran's eyes were blue, though. I wondered if they were originals.

Back in his room, he ordered me to stand facing the wall while he washed his face and stacked up the junk on his floor. I should be studying, I thought. I had volumes of music theory and political science to pursue, the facets of my education that would make me more than just an excellent lay. I had martial arts practice so that I could throw someone three times my size, or fall safely and make it look real no matter how clumsy the person who wrestled me down.

If I was late, Gahan would hurt me. That was a threat, even for a masochist in training who got beaten to tears every morning before breakfast. And how long did Idran plan for me to stand here? I considered testing his authority.

But before I could, he came up behind me. One hand wrapped around my throat while the other unlaced my shirt and clawed at my left nipple. Subtle Idran, I thought. He knew just how far to push it.

"Of course I do," he breathed into my ear. "I've been watching you every day for the last four months." He pinched my nipple until I mewed.

Gahan said that being wanted was what I did best. At least all of us weren't jaded.

I turned in Idran's arms and tipped my face up. He kissed me, a mere brush of the lips. I stood for a moment more with my lips parted while he smiled down at me. I wanted something in my mouth.

Dropping to my knees, I went for the closure of his pants. He seized my chin before I could begin to tongue that soft piece of his flesh that was even now stirring to weapon-hardness.

"I commend your eagerness," he said, "but that's not what I want from you."

I had no objections. I knelt there on his floor and locked gazes with him, watching his beautiful blue eyes grow narrow and cruel at my insolence. Why not enjoy the struggle before I must surrender? I smiled as best I could around his hand. From the standpoint of technique, I was curious how he would break me if he couldn't whip me.

"That's what you're getting," I said.

"No. I'm getting your ass, and the only remaining question is whether or not I grease it first."

I spat at him.

Idran slapped me across the face so hard that I lost my balance. Well, if my back and ass were too fragile, my face was titanium-reinforced and largely ignored during training. Idran helped my own momentum take me down on my stomach and locked my arm behind me. The pressure on my wrist ground my sigil against my bones. He put a knee on my back.

I tried to twist enough to kick him. But Idran had one hand on my ass, his fingers working deeper and deeper between my legs to that hot spot behind my balls. When he found it I gasped, arching my back against his weight. My penis stiffened under my belly.

"Little slut," he said with a voice like velvet-sheathed knives, "tell me you don't want it, and I'll stop." He was loving this as much as I was.

His fingers worked under my clothes at my bare flesh, one cool finger opening my ass. I moaned into the floor.

Idran said, "You're in danger of boring me."

To hell with technique. "Fuck me," I whispered.

"Are you giving me orders?"

"No! Use me as you wish, sir."

I sensed his surprise and the twinge of fear. The use of titles between students was forbidden. I could be fined for it, I suppose. But I knew both of us were getting off on the broken taboo.

"I am not persuaded." Idran's fingers withdrew from me.

I sighed. It is a truism that good specialists couldn't enjoy their work too much. But in sadomasochism, pleasure is colored with pain and tears. I would never serve a client well whom I did not serve completely. At the least, Idran would not be pleased by my lying here and taking it.

Climbing to my knees, I faced Idran and composed myself in a proper supplicant position, hands clasped behind my back and head down in his lap.

"Please, sir."

Idran picked me up by my hair. I tensed for the slap. Even so it hurt, and the second blow to my tender cheek even more so. I savored the taste of cruelty for cruelty's sake alone, not for my precious education. His hands pushed my head down to his still-stiff penis.

"Suck it," he ordered. "That's the only grease you're getting."

I swallowed, wetting my dry mouth as best as I could. His penis was rather large. My mouth was not, and he didn't let me relax enough to go all the way down on it without gagging, though my teachers say I've the most talented mouth of my class. I've been told too that I look most appealing when I choke and tears run down my face. Idran's hand tightened on the back of my neck, forcing the musky, veined length of cock far back down my throat until my nose met his pubic fur. My own penis swelled.

Idran pulled out suddenly, and I felt a flash of heat from him, so close he was to climax. He pressed my face down into the floor while he pulled at my clothing. I was panting and beginning to tremble as Idran bared my ass.

The head of his penis entered me more gently than I expected. I spread my legs a bit to help him in. Greased or not, I'm an easy fuck, and Idran was impaling me so slowly that it was almost teasing. He brushed the hair off my neck and bit me there. His fingers touched my cheek, drifted to my lips until I could take them into my mouth.

And then the only challenge was not to come before he did, squeezing me in shaking arms and spilling his passion into my guts.

"Good little slut," he said, then gave an unmasterly whimper. "Thank you, Vri."

His body was warmer than a silken blanket. I stirred beneath him, then tensed as a cold fear jolted me fully awake. The clock on his console blinked five minutes to seventeen.

"Oh no," I said. "Gahan."

Idran blinked, then sat up as I climbed to my feet and ran for the bathroom.

"Blood and misery," he swore. "I'll take the blame. I was the dom. I shouldn't have let you sleep."

I emptied my bladder, then washed my face and genitals. "Thanks, but I can't let you suffer for my choices." I started pulling my clothes on and sighed. "It'll do me no good to hurry, either. I can't make it across the Plex before seventeen."

He stopped me at the door with an embrace. I soaked the heat from him, needing it. My next interview would not be so warm.

"Vri, before you go."

"Hm?"

"You felt like you were grading yourself the whole time."

I bit my lip. "Thanks. I didn't realize."

"My pleasure." He kissed me.

I would not run. Gahan had told me if I couldn't be right, be graceful. Of course, it was his displeasure I had to fear now, not some training exercise.

The usual disciplinary measures for a D.A. in training included fines and reprimands, with the threat of dismissal. Mere pain wasn't much of a deterrent for us, given our avocation. The exception was induction wands, used to punish a fuckup during a training session, especially one that compromised safety. Rumor said the course was rigged so that each D.A. will have to live through at least one such session. I had mine already. That was the only time I ever have, with complete sincerity, begged someone to kill me.

But other sanctions were strictly in the domain of "holder authority." After all, one's contract-holder was by definition the person who should know one's weaknesses. If Gahan hit me, it would sting.

I skirted the Plex's huge interior garden and turned south. As I reached the lift, a wall clock was reporting ten minutes after. And, of course, he was waiting by my door, with an air as if this interlude was planned.

I should explain Gahan.

He was twice my age but would never show it. The body shapers gave him an extra eight centimeters of height, a painful process deemed psychologically necessary for many doms. His shoulders were broad and heavily corded under the black silk of his shirt. The sigil on his left wrist glowed red and gold against chocolate skin that would never show bruises. There was a slight curl to his hair, which he kept just long enough to tie back.

It is rumored that the Rausten-Frith empathy scale was revised to accommodate him, though his scores have been bettered since. For twenty years he was a specialist, the most talented sadist the Adoration had ever possessed. When he finally burned out, the Band had retired him to recruiting.

I was but fifteen years old and desperately impressed by the sophisticated creature in black leather behind the desk when I first met him. "My duty is to dissuade recruits from joining the Adoration if they are not truly dedicated, and specifically from becoming specialists," he said. "Most are attracted by the romance and don't understand the dedication required. In your case, however, I can but look at your scores and look at you and know that you were made for this. If you want it, I can hardly stand in your way."

After I passed the first phase of my training, he came out of retirement to hold my contract. There was no more exacting teacher in all the Adoration, no one less likely to be fooled by a half-hearted performance. But then, perhaps no one else could understand what was demanded of me.

As I palmed the door open and he followed me in, I could not help but compare him to Idran. In twenty years of practice, Idran might muster that presence and physical grace. Yet Gahan had no sexual interest in men. It was a shame, really, but I required a holder who did not want me.

My room was large by Adoration standards. The shelves held a few books, precious and beautiful things. I hadn't been there much recently, so it was clean enough.

Gahan took the chair by the window and said nothing at all.

I gave him a half-bow. "I'm late. I will accept such penalties as you see fit, sir." My own rehearsed words sounded painfully inadequate even to me.

"Sit down," said Gahan. His voice was soft and without inflection.

I scrambled backwards to sit on the edge of my bed. He had something else on his mind. For the present, at least, I was spared.

He regarded me for a moment. "Tellie called me this morning on your account."

Oh no, I thought.

"There is nothing wrong with your technique, Vri."

"But?"

"She said your empathic response was sub-standard. You missed most of her prompting, even the more blunt requests."

At last I qualified his demeanor. He was not angry, but disappointed. Excuses slipped from my mouth.

"You know I've been preoccupied this past week," I said. "You yourself ordered my schedule reduced because of medical's report..."

He shook his head. "Vri, that's your skin. I'm talking about your mind."

I unclenched my fingers. "I have more innate talent than any other recruit of my year. If I'm not performing well in one artificial encounter..."

"Innate talent alone may get you through certification. It's not enough for a specialist in sadomasochism." He sighed and rubbed at his eyes. "Perhaps it is time to reconsider your participation."

Quit the Dolorous Arts program? Fall back on Erotic Arts, or take another specialty, like babysitting or bureaucracy or bereavement counseling, something easy? I'd probably have a new holder, and the same hopeless crush on Gahan, but no excuse then to touch him. "Gahan, I reread my entire contract last night. I renewed my consent this morning."

"I do not believe you saw a word of what you read," he said.

I stared. Gahan was my holder. I confided in him. I cried on his shoulder. I took his counsel in my fears and new, strange pleasures. For him to doubt me was like a slap from a stranger.

"Test me," I said.

"Very well." He sighed and shook himself. "Keep a secret from me."

I closed my eyes and formed an image of roses in a market stall by the Canal, the taste of fried food in my mouth, and the smell of something burning. I wrapped it in layers of myself, hid a decoy where Gahan could find it, and buried the true image behind my eyes.

"Open your eyes, Vri. You're no novice to need that crutch."

I locked gazes with him, and felt my secure closure begin to shred.

"Roses in a market stall," he said. "By the canal. The taste of fried food, and the smell of something burning."

I considered my defeat, put it behind me.

Gahan said, "Tell me what I'm thinking."

I measured his steady gaze as I probed at the edges of his formidable mind. I found an entrance and followed it through, evading the traps laid out on either side. Something sweet leaked through. I turned the corner of an emotion and ran smack into a locked door. Retracing my steps, I edged backwards, making a choice where none had existed. As I turned, I was surrounded by iron bars. They closed on me until my hands and breath were bound in iron. I broke the contact with a jolt. I couldn't look at him this time.

"You panicked," remarked Gahan needlessly. "Your perimeter should be more subtle, able to yield to apparent probing and yet reveal nothing. You almost have that down, but your core defenses are tissue paper. Have you been practicing for at least an hour a day?"

"No, sir."

"That's a contract violation."

"I know. Sir."

"Curse you, Vri. You can make anyone within three city blocks want you."

Except you, I thought.

"How will you ever know what else they want if you don't ask? Perhaps I have expected too much from you. If I hadn't let you know your own strength, you might have given your studies half the attention they required." He closed his eyes for a moment, then regarded me, cool once more. "But no, I wouldn't degrade you so by lying. Would that you were so gracious with me. Will you do us both a favor and quit now?" he asked.

Damned if I was going to make it easier for him than it was for me. "No, sir."

Gahan stood. "I'm giving you one day to reconsider your choice. Come to me this time tomorrow, and if you choose to stay, you will receive ten lashes by my hand. Do you understand?"

The skin between my shoulder blades tightened as if touched by a knife point. "Yes, sir."

I sat and thought long after he had gone. Would Gahan have me believe that I failed him when everything I did was by his command?

The sun left my windows. My legs were stiff and sore when I stood, and I decided to take a walk. Certainly I'd get no studying done tonight. I had seen recordings of Gahan at work, with soft floggers and two, three, and five meter single-tailed whips. I might need that new hide after ten lashes. This was no scene, no game of negotiation and consent. No, this would be a true humiliation and pain, given in anger by someone I loved. I should have made him throw me out.

Taking the lift down three floors, I wandered through the public area of the Adoration Central Complex. But through the glass walls I could see lights from Landfall City etching nighttime rainbows, and I decided to go out.

This was a weekend night, but no festival, warm with early summer wind. Two moons were visible on the horizon. I traveled footpaths to wider ways where young people on skates and bikes spun past me, and older men and women flirted, talked, challenged. Two members of the Circle Band were dueling in a park. I watched the vicious gleam of their steel weapons as they circled each other, settling a private dispute with blood. Even their gaudy tempers had a purpose. They kept the skill of armsmanship alive in case our world needed it again.

I checked my credit balance and was mildly surprised. Of course I had been drawing training pay and spending none of it. If I were frugal, I could live for months off my balance and not lift a finger. Reassured of my solvency, I wandered into the tourist district near the Parliament building, where the walkways were mirrored and bright beams of light shot from under my feet when they touched the ground. I found a self-serve cafe, sat down, and ate until I was full. Afterwards I fell asleep under a maple tree in a park and slept until nearly noon.

After a trip to a luxurious public bath, I thought about my free time. I hadn't seen either of my parents in at least a year, though I'd exchanged notes with my mother. They were Bandmates in the Entropic Symmetry, who had argued just after I was born. They stayed together until I turned five and left for school, at which point they split up with relief and never saw each other again. I spent part of the afternoon looking up my father, but as I expected, he had left no public address. I decided not to try to find him if he didn't want to be found, and instead left some messages with the network.

My mother was easy to locate, but wasn't taking calls. Since I had nothing better to do, I walked across town to the same old apartment in a residential district where she'd lived since I was born. The architecture had rounded corners and clever angles that failed to disguise the snap-together construction. Memories bitter and strange stirred in me as I threaded my way between trees that were larger than I remembered, and buildings that were smaller.

I found the apartment, rang the bell, and was informed by message that she had gone away for two weeks to visit a cousin on Crystal of Dawn, Lunar Habitat Three. I thought of leaving another message, and decided against it.

It was sunset. I'd missed my appointment with Gahan, this time more or less on purpose. Every specialist goes through some crisis of obedience, or so we are told. Kadie had, and it was the end of her Dolorous Arts career. But she was still in the Adoration somewhere. I didn't have to stay. What would Idran say to me now that we weren't playing the same game anymore? I couldn't bear the thought of his glances gone from passion to pity. If I wanted my classmate's attentions, I'd have to pay for them.

If I didn't report back in ten days, the Adoration would terminate me entirely. I'd give them back the red and gold sigil from my wrist, cash in all pending bonuses and vacation time, and go shopping for another Band. Like my parents, I could join Entropic Symmetry or some other political, spiritual, and economic unit where one's job wasn't the same as one's identity. I could live off my Erotic Arts Certification and tithe to my new Band. If Gahan thought he was disappointed now, just wait until I didn't come home.

If only I didn't have to wait so long to make it final.

I found a cheap room in a tourist hostel, private but with ceilings so low I had to duck, and no windows. I slept for a good twelve hours, another sinful luxury of dreams after the four or five hours I was used to. I awoke to sexual stirring in my body that I wasn't prepared to deal with yet. I had been kept on the sharp edge of physical desire for a year now. I lay still until my erection subsided.

After a long shower, I considered what to do with myself for the next eight days. No more lessons in anatomy dutifully memorized from color holographs. No human psychology and history. No mornings spent drawing lots with other students to select who would be the victim for some demonstration of technique, and who would practice it under the watchful eyes of instructors. No deep explorations of each human emotion in turn. No more soft hands to massage me when I was sore, hold me up when I was falling, or touch me when I was lonely.

Instead I went to get lunch, then to Parliament to catch up on some recent votes, legislative showdowns between the Adorati and the Charismati. After dinner I caught a new play, then went back to my rented room.

There I lay down and gave in to my pent desires. My own hands were so gentle compared to all those who shaped and used me, and my eventual climax so lonely with no one there to watch.

I made it all the way to the fifth day missing before I checked for messages from the net. There were none. But then Gahan would have figured I needed to be left alone and honored my privacy. Damn him. His silence was more provoking than any lecture might have been.

The next morning I almost returned to beg for mercy. But I could hear Gahan's rebuke: "Vri, don't you dare come back just because you have nowhere else to go."

I grew tired of sleeping. That night I was out late along the Canal, smelling water and apple trees, watching one moon set while the other washed with white the huge, stained stone blocks of the waterway. A young woman, new-made adult of the Circle, came up next to me and leaned on the railing.

"Hi," she said.

"Hello."

I sized up her budding form and the longsword at her hip, the black leather of her armor-like clothes. By now she had seen my sigil.

"Are you... for hire?"

"No."

She took a half-step back from me, but by then my client-negotiation skills had snapped into place.

"I'm an apprentice," I told her. "I may not charge you, but I do have an E.A. I will serve you for free, and you need only ask." That, at least, the Band couldn't take away from me.

She squirmed a bit, the surface of her thoughts transparent. No virgin, I thought, but inexperienced and with no knowing lover to teach her. All of pleasure is not learned from books and self-exploration. I forgot to be a little nervous of the other sex.

"Please?" she said.

"What's your name?" I asked her.

"Silsara."

"Mine is Vri. Would you prefer your place...?"

"Yes," she answered, saving me the embarrassment of explaining my temporary lodging.

Her place was a shared apartment in a Circle complex. She hung her sword on the rack by the door. Her housemate had two friends over playing a strategy game complete with maps and paper markers spread on the floor. They paid us little attention as we stepped over them and entered her bedroom.

"Kiss me," she whispered.

Silsara's hands trembled on my shoulders as I pinned her gently against the wall and brushed my lips against hers. Her mouth opened for me. My hands busied themselves with the laces of her jacket until I had bared the white silk tunic beneath. Small breasts, no bra. I traced them with my fingertips. She moaned into my mouth.

When her knees began to buckle I moved us to her unmade bed. By now she was more sure. Biting me playfully, Silsara pulled at my own clothes and was soon too eager to be shy of my body. Her fingers found my penis and stroked the length. Wetting her hand with her tongue, she squeezed me, playing with the soft fur and the balls beneath. My breath had grown quite ragged.

"Go ahead and come," she said.

I bucked, gasping as I spilled on her fingers. Silsara laughed and tasted them.

"Didn't you want to save that for later?" I asked.

"No," she said. "I'd be most disappointed if you could only come once."

I sighed and smiled. She was right, too. My body had seen little enough attention since I walked out, and was eager for more. I began to kiss her belly, unfastening her tight leather pants and sliding them down her legs. She made her own soft noises when I licked her. Her cunt tasted of leather and her own spice, leaking over the sheets when she came.

When the sun rose I was fucking her slowly, sliding my penis in and out its full length while she rose to climax again beneath me. I kissed and bit her until she gave a stifled scream and convulsed. Sweat was running down my back to the crack of my ass when I finally collapsed on top of her.

I brought us a glass of water from the bathroom and curled up under the blankets with her.

"Was that what you wanted?" I asked.

"Uhm."

As I lay there with her, I probed beneath her surface thoughts for the first time. I found memories of two years ago when she wrestled with friends, one of them holding her down while the other tickled and pinched her. And again of being wrapped up in a bedsheet during the night as a prank, struggling to get free as her compressed hips grew warmer and the juncture of her legs wet and slick. I found the fantasy of being tied down and pinched, and fucked by someone who showed no gentleness at all.

She watched me through half-opened eyes, blushing at the knowledge.

"Silsara," I said, "I'm an apprentice. But I can give you the names of some other Adorati who are far more skilled, who can give you want you want."

"Maybe," she said. "I have to think about it."

A few minutes later she had fallen asleep. I could not, but lay awake and meditated upon my failure. Silsara would be getting a refund, if she had paid me money. I suppose I'd get a lecture, if there was anyone to lecture me.

We said farewell after breakfast. I went to a library to do some more research on Bands, filled out applications, and procrastinated from sending them off. I found my fingers plucking at my sigil, memorizing its shape. Soon it would be gone.

Someone else approached me for hire, but I politely declined and spent the night alone in my room. The next morning would be the last of my long wait. I couldn't sleep, and finally got myself a rare drink of wine from a vendor. When I awoke my mouth was dry and my eyes crusted over.

I dressed and went for a walk. The Canal Bridge was closed to vehicle traffic in the summer. Sellers of trinkets were staking blanket space along both sides. Two Charismati, barefoot in ragged tunics, were handing out inspirational cards. One of them pushed a card under my nose. He tilted it so that the message sprang into three dimensions.

"The world is illusion. The body is exile. Accept the Divine as your savior and be free."

I had no patience for these people. Their band leadership and mine were bitter enemies. The Charismati were instigating legislative assaults on licensed personal services and financial assaults on our other care-giving functions. The Adoration, in turn, had an army of lawyers and accountants investigating certain Charismati charitable donations. Their theology of guilt and penitence and blind obedience, as well as their poor personal hygiene, disgusted me.

"Rejecting the body isn't freedom," I told him. "Knowledge and power are."

He eyed me coldly, and I could smell his unwashed body.

"Despair is the sin of believing that even the Divine, whose benevolence is infinite, cannot forgive you."

"I don't want forgiveness from your dubious god."

"Then beg it from your own," he replied.

He and his companion bowed their heads, dismissing me. The little card, forgotten on the ground, blew over the railing into the canal.

I sighed and trudged back across three quarters of the bridge. The clock on a building above me read only ten. I had plenty of time to make it back to the Plex before I was officially terminated.

Gahan, had I put both of us through this because I was afraid of a whipping?

I took the tubeway part of the way back, then walked. It took me longer than it should have to reach the Plex. I found a console, logged in and checked for messages. There were none, but I had established my presence. I walked to the south end of the Plex to Gahan's quarters. Of course he wasn't in. I should have called first, but no, I had to be dramatic. Even Gahan couldn't be so cold as to absent himself today.

I sat down to wait outside his doorstep. An hour passed. Then another. I got hungry, bit my nails, and tried to doze. At half-past fourteen I saw his familiar figure down the hall and felt a probing mind-touch, quickly withdrawn. He said farewell to the person who walked beside him, and she hurried back the way she had come.

I scrambled to my knees and bowed, pressing my cheek to the floor, so I didn't have to look at him. His mind felt like a block of stone.

"Go to Medical," he said. "They'll be expecting you." The door to his room shut between us with an emphatic click.

Shivering, I climbed to my feet. Medical was another long walk from here and I had plenty of time to imagine what they would do to me. I was hungry, but didn't dare stop for food. Our Medical personnel were the soul of compassion, but a D.A. consigned for corporal discipline was fair game for anything.

The technician who greeted me merely ordered me onto a table and ran a test suite. I heard her voice checking off system functions: heart, brain wave, circulation, reflexes, senses.

"Physical fitness, certified," she spoke into a console. "Psychological fitness, override by holder authority."

Not only my skin, but my sanity was forfeit; one could be patched with no more expense than the other.

The technician handed me to a subordinate who perfunctorily emptied my bowels and bladder, fed me a small cup of glucose solution, then braided my hair. A half hour later I was half-dragged through the door of one of Medical's "wet rooms" and left alone to ponder my fate. The dizziness of hunger had been replaced by fear.

Wet rooms had drains in the floor and ceiling-mounted water sources to rinse the surfaces. The temperature was controlled, and the floors had a bit of give. Students "borrowed" wet rooms for orgies. This one was twice the usual size and possessed a floor-to-ceiling X-shaped rack, anodized black steel, inclined ten degrees from vertical, with soft straps along all four arms and a sensor link dangling from the ceiling. I stood next to it and needlessly confirmed that it had been adjusted down to my height.

The door opened behind me as I contemplated the rack.

"Gahan," I asked, "why all of this for ten lashes?"

"You were gone for ten days. Ten lashes for each day."

I spun to face him. He was wearing a worn leather jacket and a pair of gloves tucked through his belt, next to the three-meter whip. Not the five-meter. I was about to get lucky by virtue of the fact that he was out of practice.

"I was not gone ten days. It was barely nine; I returned this morning. Just because..."

"Make that eleven. Want to try for twelve?"

"No, sir." I swallowed. "Please, Gahan, tell me. When you're done with me, will I still be a D.A.?"

"Beg for it."

I sighed, breathed, and prepared to pay.

"Please."

He stared at me for a moment, then nodded.

"Strip."

I got myself out of my shirt, pants, and shoes. Bare except for my sigil, I leaned face down against the rack. Gahan secured my wrists and ankles first, cinching the straps so that I could not bolt, something I had considered. His bare hands brushed against my skin as he strapped down my forearms, waist, and thighs, and attached the sensor to my right hand. One of the Medical staff would be monitoring its output and would stop Gahan if need be. But I was young and healthy and couldn't expect even that mercy. I squirmed against the cold metal, scraping my nipples. The rack pulled my legs a bit too far apart so that my weight was taken up by the straps. They were benign creatures, though, and would neither hurt nor comfort me.

Gahan stepped before me. He pulled on his right glove, tucking the cuff into his jacket and smoothing every wrinkle. Only a foolish whip master performed without this much body armor. Gahan folded his other glove and offered it to my mouth. Only a foolish submissive refused such a comfort.

I clenched my teeth down on the leather, tasting his sweat, adjusting it a bit with my tongue. I let my head hang and felt my heart pound. Pain is caused by an absence of choices, and now I had none.

Gahan's leather whistled, howled, and cracked against my shoulder. The force of it took me right off my feet so that I sagged in my restraints. I blinked tears, chewed the glove, and reminded myself I had one hundred and nine to go. I hoped Gahan remembered to count. I sure wouldn't be able to.

The second blow clipped my ribs just as I got my footing and almost caused me to fall again. Hot liquid trickled down my back. Sweat or blood? If it wasn't blood yet, it would be soon, a bitter substitute for orgasmic fluids that neither of us would spill.

Blow three scored both my thighs.

At the rate of two per minute, I'd be hanging here for over an hour bleeding on the floor. Gahan was giving me time to appreciate each and every cut. Blow four... or was that five? Did I forget to count one? I wept. Part of my mind was still trying to break the experience into pieces small enough to bear.

The whip caressed me, wrapping a bit on my legs and ribs to sting me even harder. The blows grew further and further apart, or at least it seemed that way. When I opened my eyes, I saw red spots, and then realized that they were my blood on the opposite wall.

My teeth nearly met through the leather of his glove. If this were an ordinary scene, I could start begging now.

The next blow snapped through the air. I heard it, but felt nothing. Gahan gave one startled breath, clipped short. I knew in an instant that he had missed me and cut himself, right through the armor of his jacket. Even as the next blow fell I laughed in silence. Gahan was pushing himself with the three meter, and would share a little bit of my pain. If he was that far out of practice, how were his mind-walls holding?

He knew I was laughing. His attentions grew sharper, more intimate, closer together, until I regretted my mirth three times over. Over-reaching, he missed again, and this time cursed out loud.

And then there was nothing. I scrambled for a grip on reality. No lash to tear my heart out, no sound but Gahan's breath and mine. We were only half-way there. Was he that rattled, or did he plan the dramatic pause for my benefit?

Someone else was crying.

It could not be true, that I could take more than he could give.

I spat out the glove.

"Finish me, Gahan!"

No answer.

"Curse you for being less than perfect!"

This time the whip took me right between the legs. I had nothing left to stop the screaming.

I awoke still strapped to the frame, a taste of blood in my bitten mouth.

"You fainted. We've eleven more."

Of course he waited for me to come around. How courteous. Eleven more and I would snap like an over-wound spring.

Crack.

I groaned, spat, tried to stand and take the strain off my limbs. No use. One shoulder was out of socket. I couldn't feel my hands.

And then the last ten came down on me like a rain of fire with no pause even to scream.

Gahan sighed. I heard the thud of his coiled whip hitting the ground.

The door opened. Through haze I saw two medical technicians entering. One wrapped a blanket around me while the other sprang the straps and let me down. A water bottle was pressed to my lips.

"Keep him on ice for twenty-six hours before you start repair procedures." Gahan's voice was steady and devoid of tears.

One of the techs chuckled. "Wouldn't want to erase your artwork too quickly."

The other's gloved hands probed my dislocated shoulder, then popped it back in place. I tried to scream, but the sound came out weak and tired.

Gahan was gone.

I spent the following day on a nerve induction platform in a darkened room while fluids were pumped back into my body. The induction field stilled my motor nerves, but not my senses. I lay in the dark and considered the twin purposes of punishment: deterrence and retribution.

Neither was I anesthetized for the dermal repairs. Getting flayed and grafted hurt, of course, but it provided some relief from boredom. Medical didn't mess with my mind like they could have, but left me isolated for the next two days while the grafts took. That was worse.

When they finished there were no scars, no changes in pigment, no sign of what must have looked like raw meat. I couldn't tell looking over my shoulder in the mirror that anything had happened to me. On the outside. Medical threw me out with a bottle of analgesics and instructions to drink lots of water.

I met no one I knew on the way back across the Plex. The rest of the class would be carefully avoiding me for a couple of days, gathering at meals to mutter "There but for the grace."

My room was untouched, and still mine. I took a book at random from the shelf and read it until I fell asleep.

The door chimed, waking me. I pulled on a robe. According to the console, this was the third chime. I had not heard the other two. The clock read twenty-five hundred, and the windows were dark.

"Come in," I said.

Gahan stepped through my door and shut it behind him.

I sat down on my bed and tucked my robe around my knees.

"Hello," said Gahan, as he dropped into my chair. For the first time I thought he looked every year of his forty-five.

"Hi."

"Do you blame me for your pain?" he asked.

I didn't answer.

"Don't compel me to do it again," he said.

"I didn't choose the hundred and ten," I snapped. "Are you afraid I'll tell someone you cried? I didn't make you do anything."

Gahan stood. "That was unfair, uncalled-for, and wrong." He stepped towards the bed.

I tried not to flinch. "What are you going to do, hit me?"

"No."

Gahan sat on the edge of the bed. His fingers stroked the sides of my face. "I ran your big rebellion scene exactly the way you wanted it. I let you transgress. I let you repent. I led you through the fires of purgation, and I gave you absolution. Do you think I've ever cried for a paying client? I may not fuck you, but I still love you." He laughed. "I never would have made it through the last year otherwise."

And I had believed him less than perfect.

"I'm sorry, sir..."

"Just shut up," he said, and kissed me.

I shouldn't have been startled, either that he would do it, or that he was clumsy and uncertain, and I had to show him how to do it right.

To hell with technique, I thought, and held Gahan with all my strength.

BURNING BRIDGES
Lawrence Schimel

The bed was on fire. I jumped up, pulling the blankets with me. Reflex made my fingers shy away from the heat. By force of will, I grabbed the burning linen, flipped them over, and smothered the fire.

My heart was racing as I sat naked on the floor amid the smoldering bedding. The smoke detector still cried overhead. I forced myself to stand and reset it. I looked at the bare mattress and burnt sheets and stumbled into the living room, where I flopped down on the couch. I winced as I landed on my stomach; I still had a hard-on from my dream and had bent it in my landing. I wondered what I had been dreaming as I rolled onto my back and tried to fall asleep. In the early-morning light, I could see smoke still drifting from the bedroom.

I have a spark, a tiny flame inside my mind, like the spots that dance before your eyes after you've looked at the sun. Sometimes it gets loose.

I closed the lid of the toilet and sat. The ceramic brought goosebumps to my skin as I leaned against the tank, pressing up against it to absorb the cold into my shoulderblades, the small of my back. October and it was still as hot as August or July, the sun blazing during a drought. They promised me it never got this hot when I first moved to The Bay Area from New York City. But then, a lot of promises had turned up empty, I reflected, as I stood and turned on the tap. I dipped a wash cloth into the sink, soaking up the cool liquid. Elliott... I held the cloth up to my lips, letting it drip against my neck and chest, cold. Oh, Elliott.

I hadn't seen him in months. I had moved to Oakland so I wouldn't run into him accidently on the street, had given up all that was familiar so I wouldn't see him at our favorite haunts in San Francisco. I knew he probably had my address, my phone number, from Walter, who I still saw occasionally for a beer and chat. It was too lonely otherwise, always remembering my old life and friends and never seeing them, never doing anything at all. But Elliott hadn't called since the night I walked out on him, when I found him in bed with someone else.

I ran the towel under the tap again, and pressed it against the back of my neck, reveling in the feel of the cold, wet cloth.

My rage knew no bounds that night. It welled up inside me, a searing pain in my gut, burning like I was on fire. And suddenly my anger burst free, my spark, setting fire to items at random as I ran from the apartment. The thought of someone else making love to Elliott, other hands running across his body...

I leaned forward and stuck my head under the tap, but the image of Elliott's body stayed before my eyes. I imagined they were my hands pressed against his flesh again and opened my mouth to nuzzle one of his large, dark nipples. I bit down on my shoulder, running the cold cloth down my body, between my legs. I cupped my balls, remembering the feel of his mouth on my cock, our bodies pressed together in ecstasy.

I grabbed the bar of soap from its dish and pressed it to my groin, rubbing it back and forth along the length of my cock until it had produced a lather. I remembered when Elliott and I had showered together the first night we slept together. He was in New York on a business trip. Was it two years ago, already? I remembered every detail: our first lovemaking, deliciously awkward as we explored each other's bodies, uncertain of everything but our desire for each other. I let the soap slip between my fingers into the basin, and reached for my swollen, lathered cock instead. I remembered the taste of Elliott's skin, the salt of his sweat under his armpits, his balls, the sweet flesh of his cock. I remembered the feeling of being inside him, the half-closed look on his face as he lay below me, his hands on my hips, pulling me towards him.

I could not hold back any longer and sat down, hard, on the toilet as

I began to come, shooting pale white arcs against my chest and stomach, legs. Beside me, the roll of toilet paper burst into flames. I ignored it, still stroking my cock as it spasmed with pleasure.

I walked outside to the mailbox, squinting in the bright sunlight of a Saturday morning. I rented the second floor of a small house and shared the box with my landlord who lived downstairs. I didn't know why I bothered; the last thing I needed was to see one of those yellow change-of-address labels on a bill, reminding me that I was no longer living with Elliott. I almost turned back, but I would've felt too foolish, suddenly changing my mind without any apparent reason like that. A man was sitting on the porch next door, watching me as I walked to the road. The box was still empty; the mailman hadn't even been through yet.

As I walked back to the house I looked at the man on his porch, shading my eyes against the sun. He wasn't wearing a shirt, and I couldn't help looking over, even though I wasn't at all interested. Once, perhaps, he had been in good shape, an athlete in college, but that had been years earlier. Now, he had a beer belly, coarse dark hairs against darker, sagging skin. I imagined him to be mid-50s, maybe a little older. At least he still had all his hair, short spiky curls, grey-white like old cotton.

Trying to be neighborly, I smiled at him. He ignored me, continuing to scowl. I shrugged, turned, and walked to my door.

"Why don't you go home, Faggot?" he called out to my back, just before the door closed behind me. "Why don't you go back across the Bay where you belong. Go back to your ghetto."

I stood on the bottom step for a long moment. Why didn't I go back? Elliott... Oh, Elliott... I sighed. "It's a beautiful day in the neighborhood," I muttered, and began the climb up to my apartment. "Oh, won't you be my neighbor."

I am lying in the top bunk. They are the bunk beds I had as a child. I look about me and find that i am in my room at home, except everything looks odd. I step on the ladder to climb down, when the rung snaps under my weight. I fall, snapping each of the rungs as my legs push towards the floor. Am I grown so big, since last I slept here? I catch my breath, then lean down to pick up one of the broken ladder pieces. They are candy canes. I lick one to prove by its peppermint taste that I am right. This is what is odd: everything is made of candy.

I walk into the hall and hear noises downstairs, follow them into the kitchen. My mother is cooking. She is dressed all in black and has a big wart on her nose. On her head she is wearing a large, black witch's hat. "Good morning, dear," she says. I'm making myself some breakfast." She points to the corner near the stove. "Would you like some?"

Elliott is chained to the refrigerator. He is naked, gagged, his hands and legs cuffed. I cannot help thinking he looks like he's ready for a B&D session, even as I open my mouth to protest. "You can't eat him," I say

"What's the matter?" my mother asks, cackling like I have never heard her do before. "Don't you want to share with your mother? His flesh is sweet enough for you to eat, isn't it?" She crosses to where elliott is bound. He tries to shy away from her, but the chains prevent him. She turns to look at me and grabs him by the balls. I know it hurts, because Elliott stiffens, his back suddenly hunched. "You eat his meat, don't you?" She shakes his flacid penis for emphasis, violently tugging it. "You eat his meat all the time."

Suddenly, my mother throws open the door of the oven. It is enormous, like a huge, gaping maw. Inside, the coils are so hot that flames leap up from their orange filaments. I rush forward to stop her, but she throws Elliott into the oven and shuts the door. I try to open the door, but it will not budge. The light is on inside, and I press my face against the glass, desperate to at least see him one last time before he burns. Behind me my mother cackles on and on, her voice as high and nasal as a smoke detector.

A blanket of smoke covered the room. I was afraid my spark got loose early in my dream. Frantically, I looked about the room, wondering what was burning, and for how long? Was it too late?

Everything in the room was fine.

I jumped from bed and ran through my apartment. There was smoke everywhere, but nothing was on fire. Downstairs, I wondered? Outside? I struggled into a pair of jeans and ran down the stairs.

Fire raged up and down the street. I cringed from the heat, awed and overpowered by the strength of my spark. Everything was on fire, from my block all the way to the Hills!

I felt my insides wrench with guilt, and began to run toward the flames. I had to make sure everyone got to safety. It was my fault if they died!

I heard shouts for help to my left. The neighbor's house was on fire, the roof crumbling in. I rushed into the building without hesitating, following the shouts. The heat was incredible, like standing in an open furnace. My spark was no help in protecting me from fire. All it did was cause damage, cause harm.

Even with Elliott. Elliott was afraid of my spark. Afraid of me. That's why he hadn't called. He was too afraid to face what it meant, my love for him.

The shouting woke me from my memories. I rushed upstairs and into a bedroom filled with smoke. "Over here!" a voice shouted, "Help me! Over here!" I stumbled towards him. It was the man I had seen on the porch yesterday. He was trapped beneath a fallen beam. I struggled to push it off of his legs. Come on, I berated myself, lift! You caused this fire! Adrenaline surged within me and I managed to lift the beam, holding it on my shoulder as he scrambled out from underneath. I reached out with one hand to help pull him free.

"Get your hands from me, Faggot," he shouted, swinging a fist at me.

I dropped the beam, ducking the blow. I felt a chill in my bones, as the adrenaline burning along my muscles froze.

"You're disgusting. Take advantage of a man trapped in a fire." He stumbled toward the door, turned and spat. "Pervert," then slammed the door behind him.

I was in shock. Why had I bothered? I had saved his life, and all I got in return was hatred. I wished for a moment that I had left him trapped beneath the beam.

No. This was all my fault! As full of hate as he was, I wasn't ready to kill him, wasn't prepared to be responsible for his death.

His, and how many others?

I saw Elliott's face before me, inside the oven. I tried to reach him, but the glass was in the way. I banged against it with my fists, but it would not budge. I cast about me blindly, looking for something, anything, to break the glass. My fingers closed on a pipe, and I swung it desperately at the oven, hoping I wasn't too late.

I choked suddenly, as I gulped in huge lungfuls of smoke. I stared blankly at the wooden door in front of me.

Elliott? Where had Elliott gone?

I was still in the burning house. Elliott wasn't there. He hadn't been there at all, but was safe from the fire, miles away.

But I still heard his voice, calling for me.

"I'm coming!" I shouted, my voice tearing my throat. Panic surged through me; I had to get to him, save him from the fire. My spark burst forth, incinerating the door. I could feel the intense heat as I ran through the now-open frame, but I didn't care. I had to find Elliott, I had to save him. I ran down the stairs, out into the street.

Where was he? I heard shouting to my left, turned towards my own apartment. I saw the man I had saved, ignored him. I could still hear Elliott calling my name; where the hell was he?

Suddenly, the door to my building flew open and Elliott was there, shouting for me. I rushed to him, practically threw myself at him. He held me in his arms, arms that were so comforting and familiar I couldn't help but believe he was real.

"You're safe," he said, hugging me so tightly my chest hurt. "I'm so glad your safe."

I began to cry, an overflow of fear and frustration and happiness, and then passed out.

I could feel the flames licking at my skin. I was on fire, burning up, but I had to go on, I had to save them. This was all my fault. I had to find Elliott, I had to save Elliott.

And suddenly he was there with me, holding me, cradling me in his arms, shielding me from the flames. His hands were deliciously cool, draining away the heat.

"But we have to save them," I said, trying to push him away. "This is all my fault!"

"Shhhh," Elliott crooned. "You're safe now. Nothing is your fault. It was an electrical fire. Up in the hills. You had nothing to do with it. Because of the drought, it got out of control."

I stopped struggling. Electrical fire? Not my spark. Not my fault at all. I wanted to laugh with relief! I thought of the neighbor I had saved. Did I regret it? Risking myself for the sake of preserving his hatred?

No, I realized. I didn't.

I opened my eyes and looked at Elliott. His concern was obvious as he stared down at me, as he held me against him. I never wanted it to end, wanted to remain frozen in that moment, forever the object of his full attention. I was afraid that if I looked away, even for a second, everything would fall apart and I would suddenly wake up from a smoke-induced hallucination and find that I was still trapped in a burning building.

But I could feel cloth beneath me, and finally I tore my eyes away from him to look at my surroundings. I was in Elliott's bed. In our old bed. Everything was as I remembered it. He hadn't changed a bit. I even pressed myself up onto my elbows to peer into the corner by the closet and laughed when I saw his dirty socks and underwear in a pile.

I lay back against the pillow again and closed my eyes for a moment, simply for the pleasure of opening them again to find Elliott before me. He really was there, still holding me, still running his cool hands along my body, draining the heat away. We were both naked, I realized. I wondered what had happened between the fire and waking up here, wondered if perhaps the last few miserable months had been nothing more than a nightmare. But then I coughed, my throat still raw from the smoke, and I knew that Elliott had found me in the fire, had brought me home and nursed me until now. I knew that he still loved me.

Tentatively, I reached out with one hand and pressed it against his chest, over his heart. His skin was as cool as marble, or perhaps it was that I was burning up. I let my hand drift, luxuriating in the cool feel of his body as I explored its familiar planes, in the feel of his hands along my body, my chest, arms, thighs, draining away the heat. It was as if he was absorbing my spark, all my built-up anger and frustration. And I surrendered to the sensation.

I sat up, pulling him towards me. My tongue was stone-dry as it entered his mouth, but he didn't care and, after a moment of kissing, it was soon wet. My hands ran up and down along his chest, which felt like a Grecian pillar, solid and safe; I clung to him. He pulled away for breath, and I kissed my way down his smooth neck and chest to his nipples, those large, dark nipples that had haunted my dreams. I ran my tongue around them, moving from one to the other in figure eights. Small tufts of hair grew in rings at their edges, the only hair on his smooth chest. I let my hands fall into his lap to his cock, swollen with desire and anticipation. His hands ran through my hair and down my back. I licked the strong muscles of his abdomen, working my way towards the sweet flesh of his cock. I felt his mouth wrap around my own cock, moist and tight. I wanted to consume him with my passion, to devour every last piece of him.

Unbidden, my mother's voice from my nightmare echoed in my mind as my tongue was about to touch his cock: His flesh is sweet enough for you to eat, isn't it? Don't you want to share with your mother?

I shook my head, trying to clear the voice from inside my skull.

Elliott sat up, concerned. "Are you okay? Did I hurt you?"

I looked into his face, at his loving concern and felt there could be nothing wrong with the world. I pulled his head towards me, kissed him deeply, my tongue pressing far into his mouth. "I love you," I said, grinning like a baby from happiness.

He smiled back at me, and winked. "Likewise."

I laughed out loud. He hadn't changed one bit!

I turned and eagerly buried my head in his crotch, licking my way down his shaft to his balls. My tongue thrilled at the familiar taste of his skin. I could hear Elliott's catch of surprise as I took one testicle into my mouth, which turned into an almost-purr in his chest as I began to suck on it gently. I let it drop from my mouth and rubbed my face back and forth along the length of his wet cock, letting it slide against my cheeks, eyes, chin, neck. With one hand I reached for his nipples, teased them with pinches and twirls. With my other hand I lifted his cock to my lips. Even his swollen, throbbing cock felt cool, inciting my own desire as the heat of my spark drained away.

I felt Elliott's mouth on my own cock, pumping up and down its length, his lips tightly clamped. It felt like Elliott was going to suck the fire from me. We fell into a rhythm, in unison in sex, life, everything. I tried to hold back, to make the moment go on forever, but I crested over the wave into orgasm, crying out in pleasure. A moment later, Elliott came too, come shooting up at me; I bent my face to catch his warm seed on my nose, eyelids, chin. We shuddered, and I felt an intense fulfilment that was soured by only one thing.

I looked about me nervously, wondering what my spark had set on fire. But nothing in the room was burning. I smiled, turned around towards Elliott, kissed and held him tightly.

We walked down to the Embarcadero and stood at the water's edge. The Oakland hills were foxfire, luminescent, winking in and out of existence.

The water drew my eyes away from the flames themselves, to follow the will-o-wisp path of its reflection. The smoky moon was shattered into a hundred partial images that could not be made to form a single picture, shards overlapping in the lapping of liquid obsidian, soothing and cool and translucent.

I kicked off a shoe, let it drop, splashing water onto the image of the flame. I stepped from Elliott's embrace and dipped a toe into the water, to prove to myself how cool it is, how wet it is, orange and red from the fire and the lights. I had to prove to myself that I had escaped the flames, that the fire cannot cross the black oil-dark liquid, cannot pass along the airy filaments of the bridge, pulsing like an artery through the ebon night.

A sailboat passed beneath the latticework of struts and lights, the arch of its sail billowing like the curve of a cygnet's neck. Its slow, majestic gait was faster than the cars overhead, stopped to gawk at the view from the Styx as they fled. The orange flames leapt up to lick the underside of the bridge, trying to incite the cars to faster motion. Seagulls wafted upwards from the dock in calculated arcs, like pale white fireworks.

I thought of my life on the other side of the Bay, in Oakland. I was perfectly happy to step back into the life I had left behind when I ran away instead of staying to talk. Life seemed so perfect right now, I never wanted it to end. It didn't have to, I thought. All I needed to do was forgive Elliott. He had proven himself when he came searching for me in the middle of the blaze. And he had forgiven me, for leaving him, for my spark.

To my left, three people conversed in French, leaning against the rail and smoking. Ash drifted before me, dropping to the water. One of the tourists laughed loudly and I began to shake.

Elliott put his arm around me and turned my face towards him. "Likewise," he said, and kissed me deeply.

When we came up for air, I focused on the tip of the tourist's cigarette, and let go of my spark, forever.

Our arms around each other, Elliott and I turned our backs and walked home.

AUTOEROTIC
William Marden

She was silver in the moonlight, all curves and light glinting off her white body as she glided down the night road. Fargo thought he could almost smell the woman smell of her, the mixture of sweet perfume and the crisp new-metal of her chassis.

He had ridden the night roads for two hours now, waiting for her, or someone like her, feeling the asphalt fall away from him like fog in the spring night. Feeling the restlessness building until his pulse jumped, but he had waited for a woman.

Who saw him now. As he rode along at a comfortable 50 he paced her, watching the needle edge upwards towards 60 and then 65, then 70. He kept a hundred yards between them, not trying to close on her now. Let her run first, let her play her own games before the two of them played his.

With one set of eyes he watched the road wind out in front of him, the city a grey cardboard prop under the spell of the moonlight. With the other, in his head, he stood above the highway system and watched the chase begin.

He played with her with his eyes, running metal fingertips up and down the curved hind end that dipped down to what appeared to be diamond faceted exhaust pipes. No spew out the back of course, the new pollution laws had put an end to that.

It was a beautiful job, probably a Contessa '34, only a year or so out of style, but it was and probably always would be a classic. It was made for nights like this, made to shimmer and ride the pavement like a transparent wraith, her feminine lines seeming to shift as she passed under first one and then another streetlight.

The bubble top, over the small but powerful engine section, was artfully frosted to go with the ghost-like image the Contessa cast. The driver, even to a person standing only a foot away, would be an indistinct blur, a dark shape against the snowflaked glass. The driver, though, could see through clearly.

The blur of her after-image across his field of vision brought the two halves of him together and he cursed himself for a day-dreaming idiot as she screamed on two wheels across four lanes from right to left exit ramp.

"Dammit!" he shouted, knowing she could not hear him. He cursed himself for his slowness, and for being caught unawares. Some of the women who rode the Hot Strip just came out for an easy uncomplicated Link. And others, like this bitch, made a man work for his fun. The bad part was he wasn't at all sure he was good enough to catch her.

He manhandled his Piledriver across one lane, from second-to-left to exit. He couldn't make it.

She barely did. Whipping the shadow car around as light as though it were truly a creature of fog, she evaded the steel waist-high guard rail, ricocheted off the far side of the exit ramp without scraping metal, and somehow brought the Contessa under control.

The Piledriver had its advantages. With its monster motor, the largest allowed under law and even that under attack, it was faster than anything else on the road. Cops used Piledriver motors for their hotshot jockeys. But the Contessa had a ton of advantage, and here it made all the difference in the world.

Somehow he swung out from the exit ramp and onto the main drag, but the scream of the car told him he'd have a repair bill in the morning.

Knowing it was useless and juvenile, he steered with one hand, stomping down on the accelerator and watching the needle go crazy while he smashed his fist against the padded dashboard. Right now he knew she was laughing at him, and in the morning would tell her girlfriends about the stud she'd shaken so easily on the Hot Strip.

And the cost of repairing what must have been a good sized chunk of metal torn from the left fender of the Piledriver would be salt rubbed in the wound. It was hard enough for him to be one of the few working stiffs who owned one of the almost legendary cars. It was hard enough to scrape together the money for the accessories necessary if you were going to make the Hot Strip run.

The only thing that would make it worthwhile would be a Link, and tonight, and with the silver bitch, if he could ever find her again.

He knew this area of the Strip, knew the streets surrounding it. From the exit she'd taken there was only one direct way to re-enter the system. There were two other round-about routes, but they led through gutted areas where snipers, years after the Burn-Out, still occasionally went hunting for motorists.

If she took it she'd come out behind him, and think he'd have gone ahead and forgotten about her. The only way to fox her would be to take to the jungle, the no-man's land that remained from the riots, and swing around to meet her.

Two miles ahead he took a right exit and entered World War III. The rioters, the looters, the Army had been systematic during the Burn-Out, and what was left was less than the shell of what had been inner-city.

Burnt out hulks of autos, and here and there a tank or two, made the streets obstacle courses. He had to slow back to 30, and switched on ultra-bright. It would make him a target for anybody within a mile, but anything caught in the glare of those beams wouldn't be giving him any trouble for a few minutes.

It was only a few minutes, but it felt like hours, before he made another turn and saw the entrance ramp sign. He could understand now why the cops had given up even the pretense of patrolling the area. He'd gotten his knowledge from old street maps of the city, and if the crazies had blocked a street completely, he'd have been pig meat for sure.

Swinging onto the Hot Strip again he felt the fear leaving him and reflected that the Burn-Out did have its advantages. It had left the old highway system that serviced the city a no-man's land during the night. And that had made cruising what it was.

Knowing now that he would come upon her in a little while, he loafed along, checking his watch. Only 3 a.m. Still time for a good ball-rattling Link that the silver tease would remember for the rest of her life.

As he rounded a curve he saw the silver form ahead of him and laughing, stomped down on the accelerator again. It was time now to go to

Complete Driving, and he flicked the electric system on.

It was like a kick in the stomach that left him reeling and the car wobbling at 90 until he made the adjustment to the new world he'd entered. He rolled on rough-smooth tires that padded the asphalt like furred paws on stone ledges.

The throbbing of the engine was the growling inside him and the piston became his heartbeat. He was looking out the window at the road and feeling it at the same moment, hearing the engine roar and hurling the sound out at the night in the same moment.

Just for the hell of it, he swerved suddenly toward the steel guard rail and at the last moment turned away, feeling the new body he'd acquired moving like the wind, like thought, like smooth metal muscles under synthetic skin.

He played up and down the lanes, bearing down on the white ghost who must have seen him by now. He felt the way he knew a male lion must feel when it sights a female. He savagely smashed the accelerator and roared a warning to her.

"Run, baby, run as hard and fast as you can. Make it last, make it good, because tonight your shiny silver ass is mine."

The silver shadow flickered and faded as she put her own foot down on the accelerator. She must be making 75 now, 80, 90, 100, coming close to the limits of her speed.

The feel of the road at 120 was something he had no words for, hard and dry and fast, like rubbing his skin with burning sandpaper. But it was good, good in a way nothing had ever been—except for one thing.

The hundred yards was narrowing now to 80, 70, 60, while he laughed and almost reached down to handle the enormous drive shaft, the metal rod that was growing from his groin, joining him to the metal beast he now was.

The electronic analogue system was worth every cent. For these few moments all the months and years of working and scrimping was worth it. He wondered for just a second if the old jet and space pilots who'd developed the electronic man-machine hookup had ever felt anything like this.

But they had been strictly in the business of becoming better rocket jockeys. The doctors had whipped up the instruments that would feed mechanical sensation into the human brain and nervous system, but they'd never, he knew, foreseen what it would really be used for.

She was hitting 120 now, as fast as she'd ever go, without a little help. To Fargo the world was a smear of gray against silver, only instinct holding the faded fragments of conscious control that saw the road through two eyes to the heart-pounding, piston-jamming creature he had become.

He was on her tail now, and there was a temptation to Link. He almost snapped open the compartment and plugged himself in, but held back again. She had teased him, now it was time to tease her.

She swerved violently into the next lane as he tried to touch her rear with his front grill. He shot past her and was instantly clamping on the brake. Not before she had nudged him with incredible delicacy into the other side of the guard rail.

He brought the Piledriver back as she tried to swing behind him. As she came up on him he braced himself and at the last moment stomped the brake. With a wild wailing she teetered back and forth to avoid the demolishing of her pretty toy.

Now she was in front of him again and he pulled into the nearest lane and paced her. The dark shape behind the frosted windows turned to look at him, then accelerated with a sound like a woman's sigh. She swung to the left and he followed her.

The porn books had been right about it, he thought, without using words, the memories of the climaxes achieved while reading of metal phalluses shuddering through him. Even now he could feel the power building in him like lightning, waiting for the moment when he would discharge it into the silver, oh-so-bright-and-hard-and-shiny body ahead of him. No other sex could compare with cruising the Hot Strip.

But lust and mind were one now, and he caught her ploy the second time. He followed her to the left, but waited until the right exit-ramp swung into view and then cut over just a second ahead of her. As she screamed her hoped for triumph he followed her down into the night.

As he'd been forced to, she slowed into a comparative crawl down the darkened city streets, lights long ago shot out during the hot summer night that started like any other and then spread a shadow over the city that had never been lifted.

He nudged her gently, the pressure and scratching metal painful and exciting at the same time—a love bite. She shied away but could not pick up her speed so he stayed behind her.

Playtime was almost over. When they returned to the Strip there would be time enough and room enough to Link safely. He tortured himself by refusing the urgent demand of his body to plug into the Female analogue.

The first drops hit him as they approached the entrance and the world blurred and ran down before his eyes. He flicked on the air clean compressed air system and the rain was blown out of his vision before it could break and streak down the glass.

They were back on the night road again, this time a rainbow world of light haloing around streetlights, as though fire danced around the glass encased filaments, the wind hurling the drops at the bulbs from every direction.

She put on one final burst of speed and when he easily matched it he slowed to a comfortable 60, and he knew she was his. He clamped the Female analogue around his swollen shaft and felt the soft, liquid core of it drawing the power out of him.

He pressed a button on the panel and the center grill slid back, the Connector Rod sliding out. In front he saw the license—sheathed for the rare instances when the law might be on the strip—slide upward to reveal a dark cavity beneath.

He was moving to bridge the chasm between when the haloed lights suddenly tore themselves away from the streetlamps in his rear view mirror and became five hungry pairs of eyes that wanted him and his prize of the night.

He accelerated behind her but she swung to another lane and slowed. Losing valuable time he slowed again and came up behind her, trying the same tactic. They might yet lose them if they could reach an exit and hide in the jungle.

When she pulled the same trick again he knew. The bitch wanted the pack to catch up to them. She wanted to go to the strongest metal stallion on the strip, wanted to see twisted metal and flame and blood all over the road for the cleaning crews to remove during the day.

The burning sandpaper sensation came over him again, and the pistons pulsed wilder. He was scared shitless, there was no point in denying it at least to himself. He had dreamed of the battles that won red hot Links, had read of them and seen them in the video dramas.

But it was a completely different thing to be here, to feel the wet strip underneath him, to feel his claws scrambling for a hold on the world that was streaking by, to see those unwinking eyes like hungry wolves coming closer—and closer.

She was beside him and gently swung one wheel over to scrape his own, taunting him as he passed her, running for safety and leaving her to the studs behind. She was laughing at him now, not in her own triumph, but in contempt for a coward—a man who didn't deserve a Piledriver.

They were close enough behind him now to make out the individual members of the pack. There was a pair of Scorpions, small and fast and equipped with illegal dueling blades on their hoods, a Mako with the black fin at the rear rising above the bubble top, a Bomber, and a Piledriver.

The first four together could be dangerous, but singly none could match a Piledriver. The Scorpions didn't have the power or size or speed, while the Bomber and Mako were closer to Piledriver range but neither close enough.

And the Piledriver was an old model. It wouldn't have the speed or maneuverability of his own. But there were five of them, and almost in fighting range, if he decided to fight.

He looked again at the silver form now behind him and shoved himself up harder into the sucking maw of the analogue. He breathed in the night rain and felt it cool the fevered metal skin over his pounding heart. It was not Fargo the man that stepped on the accelerator for a brief second to roar a challenge to the pack. Just for this night, for this one moment, he was as hard as steel, as strong as the engine inside him, and he could not die.

He faded back to cut off the pack before they could reach her, pushing every thought of fear out of his mind. Now that he'd made the decision he felt fantastic.

The Scorpions roared up on either lane beside him as if to get around him to the Contessa, but he didn't give them the chance. He felt the crunch of metal against metal and glass as pressure and pain, and wanted the blood to flow to match the pain.

As the Scorpions had closed in on him, aiming to sideswipe and slash at him with their three-foot long blades, he'd rammed one from the side. The blade shattered his side window, but the Scorpion was hurled into the guard rail.

At the speed it was traveling it could not stop, and ran the rail, sparks shooting up along the length of its passage until the night was lit by a fireball where the small black car had been. The Bomber, coming up in the lane nearest the rail could have avoided it if it had the speed and weight of a Scorpion, but it only had the speed.

It hit the fireball, pushing the blackened core a few hundred feet further along the rail until a second massive explosion rocked Fargo. Stunned as he was he was able to slow to a point where he was riding just behind the surviving Scorpion.

The driver sensed his damage and was changing lanes to get away from Fargo when the Piledriver hit it from the side and the rear. It hit the rail and the driver, frantic to avoid the fate of his partner, jerked free.

And careened across the four lanes, smashing into the other rail. Fargo managed to swing around it as it crossed his path and saw it teeter, then roll as it came off the far rail. The Mako, unable to tell where the Scorpion would end up, had to swerve violently to the right as it ended up squarely in front of him at 110 mph.

About the fourth flip brought it into the guard rail where it lay like one of its beached namesakes, fin snapped off at the base, wheels pointed toward the sky, spinning helplessly.

Fargo had no time to gloat as the rain slick road tore itself out of his grasp and he felt the massive weight of his body—the mass that had killed at least two men and maybe two more—fighting against him, pulling him toward the deadly guard rail.

Flame burned his ribs, tore at his guts as the guard rail bit deeply into his side, gouging out metal and glass. He ducked his head to avoid the spray of glass inside the car.

The world swayed and danced sickeningly as he fought to hold onto consciousness. The pain wasn't real, he told himself. The doctors had proven it was just a psychological reaction. All he felt was pressure. But there should have been blood pouring out of his side, doctors or no doctors.

He escaped the grip of the rail, and the world steadied as he looked back through the rearview mirror. And didn't see the Piledriver until it was almost too late.

As it was he could only position himself so the big machine glanced off him and he was hurled again into the guard rail. Again the flame and the agony. In it he saw the older model swing back from the middle of the strip and aim itself at him like a bullet.

The world centered on his engine, straining as if it would burst, while he tore his body away from the rail again and struck out across the strip.

In the rear view mirror he saw the older car, slower and unable to pull out, hit the rail and hang there for a moment.

In the next instant it was gone. It was several seconds before he heard the explosion from the ground 40 feet below and saw the funeral pyre roaring up to strip level.

He fought the wheel and his body until he was in the center lane steadied again. The rain now soothed his hurt instead of oiling a pathway to death.

After a while he could think and he catalogued the damage. Both side windows gone, with a large crack in the front window. The driver's door would probably have to be pried open and re-welded, plus most of the driver's side where he'd ridden the rail would need welding and painting.

The passenger side would also be bruised, although nothing to compare with that on the driver's side. The car rode as if the wheels and the metal surrounding them hadn't been damaged. The motor still purred smoothly.

As the reality of what he'd done sunk in, though, he realized the damage was nothing. Five pack hunters done in at one time, by one car. He couldn't remember ever having heard or read of anybody doing anything like it before.

Five! The cops wouldn't do anything, the unofficial view was that anybody who was out on the Strip was on his own. Besides, too many biggies and their wives or girlfriends got their kicks on the Hot Strip to really crack down.

He would be famous. Even if nobody knew his name, they would talk of the night that one Piledriver took out a pack. And all he wanted was to ride a silver ass, to Link.

It was only then he noticed he was alone on the strip. Damn the bitch. He felt as though he could pull the steering wheel out of its socket. After all he'd gone through, she had used the fight as an excuse to skip out.

Well, he'd get offers for anonymous books and articles when news of what happened leaked out. That would pay for repairs to the Piledriver. He'd be back on the Hot Strip, and the Silver Contessa would be back too, he was sure of that.

She appeared in front of him like the moon on a cloud-dimmed night. Suddenly she was just there, idling on one of the emergency areas by the side of the strip. He would have slowed but she put on a burst of speed and came around him, then got into the lane just ahead of him.

He'd had the analogue working the entire time and hadn't even noticed it. He was still metal hard and molten and as he prepared for hook-up, he saw her exposing her contact area.

The shock as the two vehicles joined was like nothing else he'd ever known. There was the roughness of the metal rubbing metal superimposed over the wet warmth of the analogue sucking at him. He hammered the accelerator into the floor and jolted the smaller silver vehicle ahead with his surge of power.

Inside the Contessa, he knew, her driver was using a male counterpart of his female analogue, and feeling through her own electronic nervous system the enormous metal prod of the Piledriver hammering inside the Contessa at 80-plus mph.

The pain was far away as he took the curves with her, felt every minute twisting and tensing of metal against metal, while the insatiable female built into the Piledriver drew him closer and closer to the end of all roads—the moment of ultimate power and speed.

As he alternately worked the brake and accelerator to hammer the Piledriver prod deeper into the silver body ahead of him, another moment of his life flooded back into his mind.

He'd been 19 and had bought one of the gadgets called Auto-Suck. Originally conceived as a gag, the actual device had been built. It was designed to be plugged into a car and clamped around a man's organ. He had gotten one through the mail, installed it secretly, and then taken it out on a lonely highway one night.

There had been women before and since, but he had never forgotten the feeling of release and power, of spewing out his strength backed by those tons of metal and millions of pounds of force.

And now, for only the second time in his life, he felt that giant release, as if he were screwing the entire world.

He thought later that his scream of triumph had been echoed by another at the same instant.

Tired and content and proud of himself for making the strip his own, he pulled up alongside the Contessa to take a last look as they approached the new city.

The bubble folded back and the Contessa stared at him from across 20 feet and 60 miles per hour. The wind streamed her golden hair behind her, flushed her fair cheeks and reddened her full lips. She gestured toward the rear of the car and he dropped back.

She touched a control and the cover over her license plate lifted. According to the books this was the accepted signal that a woman wanted to see a man again, away from the strip. With the license number it was an easy step to find a woman's name and address.

Alongside her again he shook his head and after she stared at him for a moment she understood and nodded. At the next cut-off she turned without looking back.

For a moment he wondered if he had been right, then knew he was. They would meet again on some night when the hunger had grown great enough in both of them. It would be better there.

In bed, in that other world, she would only be another woman, while on the strip she would always be silver and oh-so-bright-and-hard-and-shiny.

LIQUID KITTEN
Jamie Joy Gatto

Come, come closer, let me whisper in your ear. Listen, and I will take you to a place, a special place, I've made only for you. Close your eyes and let yourself journey. Fall back safely into the music of my words; allow my voice and only its sound to lift you, to take you there.

I place you on an ice-colored bed where you sink into silken heaps of down-filled pillows. You are naked, clothed only by the energy of a dim saucer moon washing over your flesh, coloring you softly, lucent and pale, like a watercolor painting. You become aware of your skin being absently teased by careless strokes of a breeze slipping in through open French doors. Carried aloft on the wind is the faint, cloying scent of night-blooming jasmine commingling with the crisp scent of salt water.

We are alone, nestled on the coast of the Dark Sea in a large, single room cantilevered high over endless water. From our balcony the sea stretches so far that there is no land, only jet waves illuminated by a moon hung from the sky, so fragile, delicate like a wafer. The air, light and perfumed, caresses your face, your neck; it moves along your meridians. Your peachy nipples rise, transforming into tight, coppery tips. I stand over you, lean close, breathe in your delicate scent along with the smell of sea, but I must cover you now.

"Be still," I say, "It does not feel right to have you so open, not yet."

I dress you carefully in a sweeping, floor-length gown, immersing you in a crisp fabric that moves in whispers. It's so light, it barely exists, until I begin to lace you into the boned bodice. It begins to hug your flesh like fingers made of silk, then it grabs you like a lover's hands winding round your torso, moving across your breasts, almost pushing them out and over the top of the garment.

I cross the laces tighter, tighter, creating little x's from your navel to your décolletage, marking each tiny spot where my lips are prepared to kiss you. The dress becomes one with your body, holding your bones in place, as if it has become a part of you, your own muscles.

I spin you to face me, breathless from your glory. You blush, hiding your eyes from my gaze. I lift your chin with my fingers, "In this place, tonight, I will make you my bride." Your smile moves me to paint your lips. Using a slender brush, I color your mouth an opaline shade of melon, carefully accentuating the fullness of your lips. I offer you a Lucite-handled looking glass, watch as the tiny bow of your mouth curves upward, shimmers in an almost imperceptible smile. "It's good to see you so pleased with yourself," I tell you. "Usually you don't know your own beauty, at least not the way I do."

I lean as if to, but I do not kiss you, not yet. I can smell your breath as your lips part to kiss me, your eyes closed, head back. I can barely breathe. Instead, I gather your hair in my fingers, I lift my silver-handled brush, begin to groom you, adorning your head with long garlands of freshwater pearls, weaving patterns into your hair, close to the skull. Your red hair is wild, garish against the white bed, white skin, white dress. The curls fight me with every stroke as I weave and wind, braid and pull, until they are reluctantly subdued. A tear wells up in your left eye, spills out as a knot too tight to tame is caught in the unforgiving bristles. I wipe it away with my lips, closing each eyelid with a kiss. Finally, you surrender to the repetitive lull of my patient work. You fall more deeply into the bed, letting go, slowly recognizing another scent—the dark flicker of your own musk. I can smell you, too. My hands tremble slightly; the scent of you begins to overwhelm me; my mouth waters, so hungry for you.

"Remember all the secret things you've told only to me?" I say into your ear, "Let me reveal them to you one by one. I haven't forgotten a single thing." I tell you to lie down; I lift the hem of your skirt to your knees, then I open a cobalt vial, pouring a helping of perfumed oil into my cupped palms, I work it into my hands, making it warm. The oil taps at your feet in thick, dense droplets. I begin to knead the slick liquid onto your feet and toes. The sugary scent of violets merges with the lull of lavender, filling your olfactory senses, reminding you of something familiar yet vague, something out of your childhood or maybe from dreams. I lift your skirts, pulling them high above your waist, suddenly exposing your thighs and sex to a rush of cool air. My hands move up your calves, rubbing your taut muscles until they relax into supple, easy flesh. I continue to massage deeply into the center of your thighs, my hands moving closer and closer to the thick tuft of sienna hair between your legs that barely covers pink, swollen lips. You wriggle in response, black pupils dilated, almost swallowing your blue-green irises whole.

"Lie still, my kitten; trust me to prepare you for this night." I smile. "Our night."

Reaching for my ivory comb, I part your labia with my fingers. You hold your breath, look at me with pleading eyes. I begin to pull the teeth of the comb through the thicket of hair, combing you out, one side at a time. You become so juicy, so slick and moist. You let out a little whimper, although I'm careful not to touch any deeper, any closer. I let the motion and rhythm of the comb tug at your hair, in turn your flesh, moving your clit. You open to me like a tender berry, so pink, so ripe, so ready to eat. You lift your hips to me in offering, your head tossing from side to side. You gasp, writhing as I stroke, combing you out. The air, too, is as damp as an oyster. The distinct smell of rain follows an offbeat gust of breeze. You can almost feel the sky thickening, winding swirls of gray, woolen clouds that crowd the lonely moon.

"Ssh!" I quiet you, calmly pulling your arms over your head, stroking your forehead.

You buck and groan, your body begs me to take it further. With one light touch of the tip of my comb, I barely make contact with your clit. It sparks a thousand volts inside you from your groin, up your torso, inside your belly. It spreads to your fingertips and limbs, finally flushing your face beading up with sweat. As you come, the transformation begins; our conjugal bed starts to glimmer, then shine, self-illuminating. Upon it, you glow like seraphim, a hundred points of angel lights; your aura floods the room. As if seeded by your energy, the bed grows four tall posters, it sprouts yards and yards of diaphanous gauze, made fluid by the wind, sparkling, billowing like liquid sails overhead.

"Look what you've done, my love!" But you can barely hear me.

Every pore of you cries out for more physical attention. Like an addiction, it's my touch you crave. I can hear it in your breath, smell it in your cunt, feel it in the power surrounding us. The energy level falls heavily and you float back into yourself, snug into your body, still hot from the feverish heights. The room has grown dim once again and the moon seems to have been swallowed by the heavens. The wind is flexing its phantom fingertips, moving the doors open and shut, drumming over you, carrying a chill and a random sprinkle of rain.

You see a glint, a shiny gleam as I raise my silver serpent-handled knife above your body. You are not afraid, you trust me completely, but in your mind you know that this scene works better with fear. Your breath quickens as I lift your hand, run the blade along and in between your fingers, linger at your wrist; you wince as I slice into the sleeve of your dress and saw a quick line up to your shoulder, tearing the fabric away from your body, exposing your bare arm. I push your head aside and hold the knife under your chin, cold metal presses at your neck. You hold your breath.

"Trust me," I say. You don't nod; you don't move. I simply know that you must.

I tuck the tip of the knife between your breasts, and leave it there, protruding from your luscious cleavage as you breathe in gulps of air. You watch me take a mental picture of you lying there at my mercy; you've never seen my eyes so hungry. With one quick motion, I cut through the string that binds you into the corset; your breasts and flesh spill out in waves from the gown like they've been waiting to be set free for a hundred years. I tear and cut the dress completely from you as rain gusts into the room in spurts and sprays, moistening your cream-colored sea of skin. The fabric banners overhead whip around us like the tail of a kite. I catch one end, wind it round your right arm, then I tie another around your left. I spread your legs, hold you tightly and wrap and knot each ankle. You feel the mattress fall away from under you and suddenly you are suspended in midair, naked, limbs tethered to long white sheets of fabric which fade into the indigo night. You are securely hung, completely supported by the surreal ties. You begin to rock and sway, gently, as I hum a lullaby to you. You can't tell where I am, but you know you're not alone, that I'm with you. You can hear my song softly filling your ears, entering your mind, and you fall down, down into the lightest of slumber, slowly rocking to and fro. The last thing you see is blue, even the moon, everything is a cold, exquisite blue.

You awake to the sounds of heavy wood creaking, the rocking has changed rhythm, has become the tossing of a boat to which you are still tied, still comfortably supported. You hear waves, smell salty air, open your eyes to the even gaze of mine. I am standing next to you, as you hang, hovering spread-eagled on the deck of this vessel. The moon has shifted lower into the black sky, looks as if it will soon dip into the ocean for a night swim. This is the last thing you see before I take away your sight with a dark, silken blindfold.

The texture of the ties becomes brittle, heavy; the soft gauze that once held you stiffens into hard, firm strips of what you discern to be leather. You feel yourself lowered, although you are still suspended, your body feels heavier. The air, still humid, becomes warm, even hot. As your body begins to break sweat, you can actually catch the scent of leather as you sway. Out of nowhere, you feel a prick on the bottom of your left foot; a flinch. You feel a prick under your left breast, then surprise! A twist of your left nipple. You cry out. A sting under you on the right cheek of your buttocks, then hands begin to move behind your legs, under your calves, a prick! A slap on your face! A bite near your navel, a tongue probes it, eats it, so hungry. Behind your knees fingers swirl, linger there in a maddening pattern of ticklish torment. You are helpless: you cannot touch or scratch or shield or guard, you are completely exposed in darkness. I drag a dozen smooth tails across your breasts. You know what this is. I thrust it under your nose. The familiar scent of rubber, exactly like the smell of new tires, fills your nostrils. It's my whip, the flogger you and your skin know so well. I start lightly, whipping each breast in smooth, even strokes. The sting is light like little nips. You feel yourself flush, knowing the heat you feel means your skin is growing pink.

I focus on the nipples, alternating between one then the other, raising them into hard, excited knots. The whipping becomes heavier: it feels like liquid fingers slapping at your skin. When it gets harder, it stings less, but the blows feel deeper, like they are leaving dents in your body, like they are leaving shrapnel in you, like I'm leaving my mark in your soul. The pain is something you are at odds with, for as soon as you think you can't take it anymore, you long for a newer, deeper sensation. Then it ends.

Then I ask you, "Sophie, will you be mine? Will you be with me forever?" You do not answer right away. You are still buzzing, still traveling on endorphins in suspension in the dark void. "Will you take me as your lawful wedded wife?"

I place something tiny, cold and round to your lips. I tell you it's a gift. It's a ring for you, a golden ring, your wedding ring. You kiss it and begin to cry. Your belly shakes and tiny tears roll from under your mask. "Yes!" you say, "Yes. Yes." I tell you that tonight you are mine and I will prove it. I place a smooth cushion supported by what must be a chair or a stool under your ass. You can hear me fussing with various things as I stand in between your spread legs. A latex-covered hand touches your belly as I tell you to breathe. "Just breathe, Sophie," I say, "This won't take long."

You nod. You feel the tight, but gentle grip of a metal clamp at your labia while my latex-covered fingers prod and plan something in the vicinity. You smell alcohol; I mop the cold fluid with a soft pad near the clamp as you wait, unable to move. "When I say 'I Do,'" I tell you, "it will be done. You must repeat after me."

You nod. It seems like an eternity, but in one swift, thin needle stick you feel it in your outer labia lips, then a larger sharp something being pushed through, "I Do!" I say and you shout it out as if it were the last thing you'll ever say. "I do I do I do I do," you continue to mumble over and over crying, joyful, painful, ecstatic tears. You feel my mouth cover yours and my tongue probing deeply; you kiss and suck at my mouth and my lips and I tell you, "You are mine, Sophie. You're wearing my golden ring."

I remove your blindfold and there is no more pain. You see me dressed in pink; everything, for that matter, is pink. Even the wan moon is smiling, clothed in ice pink, highlighting the black sea in rose glimmers. I am wearing a velvet frock nipped at the waist with a full gathered skirt as I stand before you gloved, holding a long ostrich feather, absently teasing my own neck and breasts, running the feather along the curve of my chin, looking at you with an unnerving amusement. You smell fresh roses. The sky begins to rain petals in every shade of pink, mauve and red; they fall and tumble onto your skin, stick in my hair. I smile and raise a tall mauve glass filled with a pink, milky fluid, raise it about a foot from your torso, tip the glass toward you and I let the icy liquid flow onto your skin, onto your navel, onto your mons, drip down into your cunt, following the curves, it reaches into the crack of your ass. You softly dissolve into yourself, into your own skin, into your own voluptuous, fleshy sensations and finally merge into the pink sea of liquid, floating, floating, shimmer and shine.

HEIR APPARENT
Gary Bowen

S tepaan was mad. I looked at where my brother lay drooling in his bed, his once fine warrior's body bent and twisted, face buried in his silken pillow. The form was there, long clean limbs, dark bronze skin, black hair now gone greasy and tangled as it lay about his shoulders. The disease was eating him up, and I doubted he had long to live. Now he raved, wordless long sounds like an animal in labor. The sheets were kicked clear, blue silk slathering over the sides of the great bed that had been the scene of as many triumphs as the battlefield. Alas, if only he had been interested in conquering femi-nine territory, he might have begotten an heir before ruining his health.

"No word," I said to Silvestri, who stood silent at my elbow. "Move him up to the high tower where no one can hear him raving. Make sure he has every material comfort, his silk sheets, a feather bed, his clothes if he wants them, and the opium that blunts his pain. Keep him silent for as long as Prince Vladamin is here. I will see if I can salvage the alliance without him."

Silvestri, grave and grey and old, nodded in agreement. "My lady, Prince Vladamin stands between us and the Ourmani legions. And he is here to auction his loyalty to the highest bidder."

What could I offer Vladamin? Money, and a lot of it. Royal marriage, perhaps, and a promise that—let me be realistic—our children would reign over a united kingdom. Assuming the Ourmani let us live so long. But it was either meet his terms, or pitch for war this very season, and stand hopeless against the Ourmani hordes. Once again I hated Stepaan for going mad and sick, just when his genius was needed.

I retired to my chambers, contemplating the bottles of woman's artifice. I had no great hopes of winning Vladamin's suit based upon my own charms; I was well aware of what they said of me behind my back. Horse-faced, a princess who required an immense dower to outweigh her lack of beauty. Better I had been born a boy, then this stocky, sturdy body might have been put to a work more suitable than the subtleties of womanhood. I decided to wear a red gown cut deeply between my breasts, for though they were small, they were attractive. The skin was smooth and pale and unblemished. The sea-sons of war had not darkened my complexion as it had my brother's. I hung my neck with rubies, hoping to dazzle the foreign prince with an obvious display of wealth. Damn Stepaan. He ought to be marrying Vladamin's sister or aunt or some such thing, keeping the succession where it belonged: in our house.

The maid helped, as much as maids can in these matters, powdering my face, flushing my cheeks with rouge, and arranging artful tendrils of black hair about my face so that I appeared not exactly comely, but tolerable enough. Examining myself in the mirror I was pleased, I was as lovely as I ever had been. I decided to eschew the headdress. Modesty was pointless, and maybe he would spend so much time staring at my uncovered head and breasts that it would be worth it to him to overlook the face in between.

Now, how to complete the picture? Throne room? Tempt him with the power that would be his if he married the sister of the Hero of Ambivalla and begot our heirs? Or seduce him with my womanly beauty? Ha. But he might question Stepaan's failure to appear in the audience chamber, so let it be the garden.

I was cutting roses when he entered. He stopped full in his tracks, and stared at me. I pretended not to notice him even while I regarded him from beneath my lowered lashes. He was tall and dark and slim with slanted eyes—a man of Ourmani descent. His ancestors had married in and out of the Great Horde, and he spoke Ourmani and Belgani and Greek with equal facility. He had even spent time at the Sultan's court in his youth, so I had been told. He was rumored to be apostate, but he had lately endowed a Lady Chapel, so at least he pretended to be Christian. He was a wicked tool, the sort of man who served either side with ease, and though I despised him, yet still I recognized his canny politics could protect us from Ourmani conquest. Damn Stepaan again, that we had to resort to politics instead of honest war.

"Lady Dienna he said, approaching. I had trouble concentrating on my rose cutting, and turned my head away from him.

"My Prince," I replied, curtsying to him, bending far enough forward that my tits nearly popped from my dress. He gave me a hand up, but his eyes did not linger on my bodice. He looked me right in the face. I flushed, I was not used to being stared at so directly.

"You look a great deal like your brother," he commented.

I wasn't sure if that was a compliment or not. I stood with an arm-load full of roses, and felt exceedingly alone. "It is kind of you to call on me," I began.

Up close he smelled of exotic spices. His clothes were a rusty red and cinnamon color, with tight fitting breeches, a bulging codpiece, and a well cut doublet. His almond eyes were liquid and I was sure they would spark to passion with little provocation. "It is kind of you to receive me. Will your brother be joining us?"

"My brother has asked me to entertain you this evening."

He wasn't looking at me at all. Instead he struggled to suppress an expression of disappointment. "I see. I was looking forward to meeting the Hero of Ambivalla. When will he be available?"

"I thought you knew him."

He flushed. "I have seen him, but we have not been introduced. I was at Ambivalla when his brilliant tactics and courage upon the field rallied the Belgans not one, not twice, but three times, and drove off the armies of the Sultan and liberated the city."

I was moderately interested. "I did not realize you had been one of our allies on that day."

He flushed. "I was not. I was a hostage in the palace of the Byi of Carpolo. Your brother rescued me, though he did not know it. There were many Christians in that place who were freed by the victors."

"So you owe my brother a debt of gratitude."

"Yes. I have written him..."

"Will you sit with me a while?"

His eyes picked across my features, and I began to feel that my finery and cosmetics were not adequate to gloss over my imperfections. "Yes, milady." He sighed as if it were a chore. He settled himself upon the turf seat beside me, and the smell of chamomile drifted up. I was glad to discover the House of Florii had some claim to his loyalty, but all the same, my personal confidence was crumbling.

"Do you like roses?" I asked, holding one to my lips. It was as soft as velvet.

"I am a great admirer of the Paradise Gardens," he replied. "Have you heard of them?"

"The Sultan's gardens."

"Indeed. He keeps them well tended, with hundreds of flowering and fruiting plants. He has oranges in winter, kept under glass. Also limes, and cantaloupe. Very sweet and delicious." No gallant comparisons of my form to the well rounded forms of fruit, nor to the sweetness of the flowers. He should have at least made the attempt, even if it was insincere.

"Are you married?"

He stiffened. "No, I am not married."

"I suppose many ladies have cast their eyes at you."

"More than a few. They do not interest me."

"Has no lady captured your heart, even in jest?"

"No, no lady," he said shortly. "I give my allegiance to men."

I buried my face in the blooms, blushing scarlet. 'Hostage' was an exceedingly discreet term for what he had been. Catamite in the court of the Sultan, no doubt. I thought it better to misconstrue his meaning. "It is only proper that a man should respect courage in other men."

"Indeed. And your brother is the bravest of them all."

"He will be flattered to hear you say so," I choked out.

"I look forward to the opportunity to make my devotion known to him in person."

I rose in agitation. What was I to do? This was a disaster. No marriage was going to come out of this, not for anything. "Sufficiently devoted to ally yourself with us against the Ourmani?"

He rose also. "If the Hero of Ambivalla can make use of my humble talents, they are at his service."

"I'll tell him so." I fled.

Silvestri listened as I related all that had passed between us. He rubbed his thin lips and said, "This is not so bad. He is inclined to our house, and all that it will take to win him over is flattery, cash, and the belief that his devotion is reciprocated."

I paced the length of the room, light and shadow alternating across my form as the daylight streamed through leaded windows. "Stepaan is an idiot!"

"Perhaps we should test Prince Vladamin's devotion."

"What do you mean?"

"Have you the stomach for it?"

I drew up my shoulders. "Stomach for what?"

"What will save your house and cement an alliance between the Courescu and Florii?"

"I was prepared to marry the decadent princeling, I suppose there is nothing worse to put up with."

"You will need some education in the matter."

"Teach me."

The maid wrapped the binder tight around my breasts, then stitched it closed. It went over my shoulders and down to my waist—there was no chance of it slipping. I would have to be cut out of it, but that would come later. Next, the leather phallus stuffed rigid with horsehair was buckled around my hips, and I regarded it with faint repugnance. It was huge, huger than even my brother's own considerable member, and broadly flared at the head. Truly it would constitute a test of Vladamin Courescu's endurance, if nothing else. That any man could tolerate such a violation disturbed me, but Stepaan, curse him, had had no problem persuading young men to do exactly that. Hence the pox upon him, and who knew how many of his paramours.

Next I stepped into his trousers, indigo velvet the color of the sky just after sunset. They clung to my legs and spread tight over the phallus pressed against my belly. Next came a fine white linen shirt with full sleeves, a dark navy-purple velvet doublet, stockings, dark blue high-heeled boots up to my thighs with golden buckles across the arches. His purple-black cloak was heavily adorned in gold braid, and fastened with a heavy gold chain, and my own dark hair was cut at the shoulders and tightly curled in the foppish style my brother preferred. The mask concealed the bottom half of my face, revealing only my eyes. The hat with its broad brim shadowed all, three plumes of purple and gold circling the peak like a crown. Stepaan was nothing if not a peacock. I felt the fool, but when I confronted myself in the glass, I gasped.

It was as if my brother had come back from the brink of madness and disease, laughing at my worry as he left to roister in the town again, and to stick his dick into as many male whores as could be gathered together in one place. I looked the part, and for the first time I began to believe I could do it. The maid admitted Silvestri to the room, and he eyed me critically, then nodded. He wrapped a dark cloak about himself and handed me a dagger with a golden hilt. I had no idea how to use a sword and was not foolish enough to cumber myself with a weapon I had no mastery of, but a knife was not so strange to my hand. A woman must defend her virtue. Not that anyone had ever tried to outrage mine, but I had been equipped with the necessary skills in the hopes that it might prove necessary.

At the Sign of the Cat the procurer greeted me by name. "Ah, Prince Stepaan, I am delighted to see you well and on your feet again! We had heard awful news—"

"Ssh," Silvestri hissed. "The gentleman is wearing a mask. You cannot possibly know his identity. Please address him only as 'milord.'"

The procurer grinned and bobbed his balding head. "I understand, sir. Discretion is required. Would you like your usual?"

"Something new," I rumbled. "I'm bored." That was exactly what Stepaan would have said, so I said it, even though I had no idea what had been offered me.

The procurer pursed his lips, then brightened. "I have acquired a virgin from the farms of Threunia. Perhaps you would like to be the first to break him in?"

"That would suit me admirably well," I replied, my voice rasping. My throat hurt because Silvestri had made me inhale a vile cloud of stuff that he had burned. It had made my voice hoarse and I did not sound like a woman. I didn't sound like Stepaan either, and coughed from the irritation.

"Milord is well?" the procurer asked.

"Plagued with an ague," I replied. "I'm supposed to be home in bed."

"You'll feel much better after spending time in one of our beds," he winked.

I grumbled wordlessly.

We blindfolded the virgin and tied his hands behind his back, then tied him over the end of the high bed. We didn't want him grabbing inappropriate things and spoiling my masquerade. The bed was high enough I could stand behind him and mount him, and I suspected that was exactly why the beds in that place were made that way. The virgin complained bitterly and even cried as I defiled him, but I gritted my teeth. That it was hurting him was irrelevant, I had lessons to learn. Silvestri stood at my elbow, coaching me, and holding a jar of lard. After a great deal of lard and a great deal of advice, the virgin stopped complaining and began to moan like a girl. I gripped his hips firmly, just my phallus protruding from my trousers, and thrust in and out of him. It was like a dance almost, one step forward, one step back, pause, repeat. It was pleasant even. I began to see why men might like doing it so much.

Silvestri let me go on that way for quite some time, and I noticed the front of his grey trousers had bulked up. "That's good," he told me. "Now try this."

Following his directions I pulled all the way out and the ex-virgin squirmed backwards. I sank into him in one deep stroke, and he threw back his head and howled. I tried it again, and had the same result. I got curious about the whole proceeding at that point, and experimented with other thrusts, different tempos, different motions, memorizing each gasp and wiggle of my helpless subject. Finally I got tired.

I withdrew. The new whore lay with his chest on the bed, asshole red and gaping. "I think that's about as much as you can learn in one night," Silvestri said. "We'll come back again tomorrow night. I'll make the arrangements."

I put my phallus back into my trousers, glad the doublet was long enough to cover the bulge. I released the young man, who stood up with his erection sprouting between his legs, trembling and pale. I was sorry he hadn't come; obviously, my technique left something to be desired. A few minutes later the procurer was entering the room, and Silvestri was telling him, "Let no one else touch him. I don't want him to even look at another dick. He must be kept for His High—for My Lord." Silvestri handed over a lot of money.

The procurer nodded his head. "I'll tie him to the bed and lock the door to the room. No one shall use him until the Pri—young lord—is finished with him."

We left. Once we mounted our horses and trotted away, I asked, "Why?"

"Because the virgin idiot has never had a real cock up his ass, and doesn't know what we're doing to him. If he services another man, or even gets a good look at a male member, he'll catch on. You've got a lot to learn if you're going to make a demanding prince like Vladamin happy in bed."

"Can't we just tie him to the bedpost and have done with it?"

Silvestri gave me a long look. "Prince Vladamin isn't going to sell his loyalty for anything less than the best orgasm of his life."

"Damn." I savored saying the word out loud. I'd thought it often enough, but actually saying it was reserved for those who wore trousers. "It doesn't sound too promising."

"But it's the only gamble we've got."

Vladamin was in the garden, pacing with his hands behind his back, eyes on the ground. I stopped and regarded him, wondering if he would be pleasing to a man like my brother. Vladamin was tall and muscular, though not too tall. I was almost the same height. He wore a cloth cap on his head with a single pheasant feather; he was dressed today in colors that were inspired by woodland birds. His shirt was ivory silk beneath the brocaded doublet composed of many earthy, rusty colors, and I realized that tint was extraordinarily well suited to his complexion. Which would explain why it seemed everything he owned was some variant of the color of rust. He looked up, and our eyes met, and his eyes were hazel flecked with gold. His complexion was fine, his moustache glossy black. He spotted me. "Prince Stepaan!" He hurried to the gate. I stood silently, frozen in shock as he knelt before me, and bending far forward, kissed the toe of my boot, then the other boot. "I have been waiting so long to meet you," he began almost shyly. "I am a great admirer of yours. I have heard so many things about you. I've listened to every report of your victories, and pored over the maps retracing your routes."

He remained kneeling at my feet. I had to answer, so I shrugged. "Bah. A romp in the countryside. Those Ourmani would rather make love than fight. Of course, I'm better at that, too."

He smiled hesitantly. "So I have heard. I've often wondered..."

"You'll have to forgive me," I said hastily. "I've been ill." I indicated the mask over my face. "You wouldn't want to catch it."

I turned on my heel and walked away, heart hammering. Stepaan would have said something far more gallant, but then again, Stepaan would have had no reason not to take him right there in the garden if he felt like it. I walked up to my room and locked the door behind me, and leaned against it, shaking long and hard.

Damn Stepaan. He could have done it. Vladamin would have let him, and never mind who might be watching out the windows. The Hero of Ambivalla could do no wrong.

I could do no wrong. It hit me hard. I was living my brother's legend. Every prerogative I had ever held against him was now mine. All I had to do was claim it. No one would gainsay me, everyone adored me. My vices were as famous and as admired as my victories. I was a god on earth. As long as I could live up to it.

I yanked open the door and bawled for Silvestri. My voice cracked and scraped, his damn smoke had ruined it. But servants scampered, and it occurred to me I was endangering my deception. "Tell him to meet me in my room," I snarled at them, and strode down the hall to the blue bed chamber.

Stepaan had been installed in his new room in the tower, and so his bed was wide and empty. Royal blue velvet curtains shrouded the window embrasure and the room was amply furnished in the modern style with furnishings imported from Franconia and Italia. Rugs were ankle deep upon the floor, easy chairs flanked the fireplace. A painted wooden screen hid a bathtub. It was mine now. Even the damn cat with the long white hair that shed on everything was mine.

Silvestri arrived. I flopped in one of the easy chairs, and propped my boot on the grate. "I want some new clothes. And more virgins. I need practice. I don't want to go down to that place anymore, bring them up here." Stepaan had had a veritable harem of boys traipsing up and down the backstairs. "Pension off all the old whores, get me some new ones."

"Yes, milord." He bowed.

"And find me a new fencing instructor. For my sister," I added. Stepaan had no need of fencing instruction.

When he left, I mounted the stairs to the top of the tower.

My brother was sitting slouched in an old armchair, gazing vacantly at the fire. He was wrapped in a blanket, and his face was haggard. He lifted his head as I entered.

"Who are you?" he asked.

I shut and barred the door behind me. The room was small, and the rafters supporting the conical roof were plain to see. I ducked under one and joined him before the little fireplace. I pulled the mask down.

"Dienna," he breathed. "What are you doing?"

"Living up to your reputation," I answered. I pulled up the three legged stool and sat down. "What do you know about Prince Vladamin Courescu?"

He passed a hand over his face. "A clever politician, well liked by the Sultan Hadra."

"He admires you greatly."

"Yes, I know. He sent me a case of Rhonish wine after my victory at Salamish. Along with some poetry he wrote."

"Did he."

"The wine was good, the poetry was bad."

"Do you have it?"

"It's with my papers somewhere."

"I need to know everything you have ever said to him."

"I've never met him. I toasted his health with his wine and left it at that."

"Good. Then mayhaps I can deceive him a while longer yet."

"Why?"

"He's downstairs, and wanting to prove his devotion to you."

Stepaan smiled wanly. "I think he will change his mind once he sees what's become of me."

"He's not going to see you at all. I shall deal with him."

His eyes raked me up and down. "You might get away with it, for a little while. But you'll have to either take him to bed or to battle, and then you're undone."

"I'm studying."

He farted and huddled into his blanket. "Don't be an idiot."

"Everything you know, I need to know, now, before it's too late. I'll leave you pen and paper; write down everything that ever happened to you. Every battle, every plan, every scheme, every fortress, every anything. Do it for me before you die. Give me whatever's left of your brain to defend the House of Florii."

He frowned, then said, "I can write, I suppose. Perhaps it will prove interesting to future scholars. But the House of Florii is at an end, unless your offspring prove to be infant geniuses."

I rose. "Just write. Tell me what I need to know in order to pretend to be you. We'll just have to hope your reputation is enough to shield this house."

It was evening, and a single candle burned on the table. The chess board was set up, black pieces and white pieces made of polished stone gleaming by the light of a single candle. The acrid smell of Silvestri's herbs hung in the air, and I was coughing again, my throat ripped raw. I lounged in a blue velvet robe, white fur slippers on my feet, and my points undone. The room was overly warm, the curtains drawn across the windows. To this caliginous and smoky atmosphere Prince Vladamin was admitted.

"It is kind of you to amuse me this evening," I rasped. "I'm afraid my ague has taken a turn for the worse." I had dispensed with the mask, in the dim light and the twisting haze of herbal smoke he could hardly see what I looked like. He waved his hand in front of his face and coughed. "Your pardon, the herbs have been burned to drive off the contagion." I coughed and hacked violently.

"I had heard you were ill," he began timidly.

"I'll be over it soon enough," I replied. He took the seat opposite me. "Black or white?" I asked. I was a good chess player, better than Stepaan, if the truth be told. A good part of his success was due to boldness, rather than long thinking. I thought a game would tell me much about Vladamin's character.

"I readily acknowledge your superiority in all things martial," he replied.

I turned the table so that the black was on his side, and ventured a pawn. "And where does your own excellence lay?"

He blushed. "In bed and in politics," he replied. "I can serve you well in both capacities."

I grinned. "You're on intimate terms with the Sultan Hadra I hear."

"He has shown me favor," he replied diplomatically. He moved a pawn.

I countered, and continued my questioning. "I am not a sultan."

"No." He moved another piece.

"What can I offer you that the Sultan cannot?"

"A place of importance. At the Sultan's palace there are many men who come and go. Not to mention, he has a hundred wives and four hundred concubines. Yes, he has shown me some favor, but he has forgotten my name more than once."

"I've forgotten the names of most of the men I've bedded, too."

He flushed, and the pieces continued moving. "Then I think we have one detail understood: My price includes being remembered."

I studied him from under my hooded eyelids while pretending to study the board. "If you're memorable." Stepaan would not have said such a cutting thing, but there were limits to how far I could submerge my own attitudes.

"I promise you, My Prince, you will not forget me."

"I see. The Sultan's neglect wounds your pride."

He countered my move adroitly, glancing only briefly at me. "A man desires many things. Pride is only one of them."

"In my case, an heir is of greatest importance. I will not live forever." That caught him off guard. "But I am not the marrying kind. Fortunately, I have a sister."

"I have met your sister." Noncommittal.

"I think we have another point of understanding. My sister needs a husband."

"I didn't come to marry your sister."

I smiled faintly. "My sister's husband can live under my roof and enter my service without any hint of scandal. Not that I am overly concerned about scandal, but your reputation has been... more carefully kept than my own."

He flushed. "You impose a heavy burden, my lord."

I glowered at him. "I'll admit that my sister is not the most handsome of creatures, but you will show her proper deference. Take her riding tomorrow."

"My lord?"

I coughed and waved. "You don't think I'm going riding, do you? Talk politics or something. Educate her." I decided it was time for a melodramatic measure. "Rumors concerning my ill health have not been exaggerated. It won't be long until my sister—and her husband—are ruling in my place."

He jumped up and crossed to me, put his hand on my knee. "Let me serve you while you yet live, milord." His hand crept towards my crotch.

"Please my sister. If she speaks well of you, I'll consider it."

He withdrew in frustration. "Must I?"

"Yes."

He bowed, barely concealing his feelings. "As you command, my prince."

"Do you know what I value most in a man, Vladamin?" He shook his head mutely. "Obedience."

He stared at me a long time. "I have been short sighted. Of course a prince of your prowess must think on many things."

I waved my hand at him. "Go now."

He bowed and withdrew.

Once he was gone Silvestri slipped the whore into my room. The young man was Ourmani stock, but not nearly as handsome as Vladamin. Nonetheless, he removed his clothes and bent over, and I mastered him quickly. He even came, his hand working in time to my thrusts in his ass. As for myself, I tumbled into bed and slept poorly, my sex wet with unsatisfied needs.

I bathed and dressed in riding clothes: skirts of brown and gold, with plenty of make up. I bound my hair up under my hat, concealing the fact that it had been shortened to allow me to masquerade as my brother. I took a riding crop in my hand, and mounted the steps to Stepaan's garret.

"Sister," he drooled. His eyes wandered. He was not himself, but several pages of parchment lay at his elbow upon the writing table. He staggered to his feet. "I am not entirely sure that you will be able to make sense of what I have written," he slurred, "but you are welcome to it."

I gathered up the sheets, studied his scrawled hand. I could make it out. I had other details to study. "I have never lain with a man. Have you ever been with a woman?"

"A few times."

"How ought a woman behave when she wants to lay with a man?"

"Boldly, my dear. Boldly.'" He sank into his chair. "Are you trying to seduce Vladamin?"

"Yes."

"Suck him."

"Suck him?"

"It'll make him hard."

"Suck his... manhood?" It had not occurred to me that such things might be done, though now a number of Stepaan's lewd jokes made sense. "Will he tolerate that?"

"Willingly." He tugged his own crotch absently. "I'd like some myself, right now. Send me a boy."

"No. No one must see you like this. Not when I have been success-fully pretending to be you."

He glared at me. "I want it."

"You don't get it."

"Bitch."

I locked the door behind me.

Vladamin cupped his hands, and boosted me into the saddle. I rode astraddle, having not adopted the Western technique of riding side sad-dle. I was not so enamored of Western imports as my brother was. Vladamin mounted the other horse, each of us riding a blooded mare of sorrel complexion. We cantered off, unescorted, as I wished. We weren't going far, just up the ridge above the castle. The woods were neat, cleared of deadwood to feed the castle fires, and presented any number of green glades scented with wood lily and ivy.

Vladamin had adopted a rather drab garb of brown, with trousers instead of hose, and knee high boots. It almost seemed as if he were deliberately trying to appear stuffy and unattractive. If I didn't want to marry him, that would relieve him of having to please me to please Stepaan. I chuckled. I was going to make him squirm.

"This is far enough, I think,"' I said. I turned to him. "Have you ever lain with a woman?"

He blushed red. "No, milady, I have not."

I dismounted. "Come down." He climbed down and followed me with a worried look.

"My brother wants me to marry you and beget an heir."

"I am aware of the needs of succession," he said cautiously.

I wrapped the horse's reins around a branch, and he did the same. I walked uphill, hiking around a patch of ferns and wandering through the dappled light. "I don't want to get married."

"Neither do I," he replied promptly.

"But I am getting interested in the allure of the flesh."

"I see."

I hadn't a clue as to how to seduce him, so I said, "Now."

"Milady?"

I dropped to my knees before him and unfastened his breeches. His manhood fell out and he watched me with worried eyes. I sucked him into my mouth, and the swelling was instant. "That—is nice," he admitted. "Surprising, but pleasant."

I worked him diligently, moving my mouth in the same manner I had learned to move my hips when mounting the whores. Pretty soon he was breathing hard and gasping appreciatively. I lifted my hem and put my hands between my legs, and discovered that I was extremely wet, and not only that, I had an ache I didn't know how to satisfy. A bit of fluid drooled from the tip of his cock into my mouth, and I laid down and pulled him with me. We found the right angle, and he slid in. His face was red, but he humped me hard, and waves of pleasure surged through me. I locked my thighs around him, my spurs digging into his back, and he thrust savagely until I shuddered and broke into a million pieces. He spent himself inside me at the same time, and we lay together afterwards. Then he carefully disengaged my spurs and lifted himself up.

"You have your brother's directness."

We righted our clothes and walked back. "Has he fucked you?" I asked.

He turned bright red again. "No. Not yet. But he will."

I almost laughed. "You think so?"

"That's what I came for." His face was burning.

"He's had a lot of whores. You're expensive."

He grunted. "I'm giving up a lot for it."

"Are you?"

His eyes were dark and wary. "If I do this—"

"Yes?"

He shrugged. "Let us simply say that I do not have your brother's prowess in battle, so I dare not flaunt my... preferences as he does."

"You want him to shield you."

He knelt and offered me a stirrup of his hands, his face bland. "Things are not necessarily what you think."

I stepped in his hand and he lifted me up. I settled in the saddle and headed back to the castle. I was satiated with a limb loosening lassitude

I had not felt before, and puzzled by his remarks and his behavior. Never mind. I'd puzzle over him later.

I practiced again, this time administering to the whore with my mouth and bringing him nearly to the verge of spending. When I thrust my big phallus into him, he did come all over himself. I fucked him long and hard for good measure, and he got hard again. When he spent the second time, I felt my own pleasure peak, though not as completely as when I had demanded Vladamin service me. I liked being Stepaan.

I admitted Vladamin to my brother's bed chamber again. I was dressed in thigh high black boots, black velvet trousers, and a white silk shirt. A black doublet was over all, and gold earrings dangled from my ears. A red sash went around my waist. One foot was propped on the hassock.

"I require personal service," I said without preamble.

His eyes lit. "Yes, milord." He crossed and knelt before me.

"Polish my boots. With your tongue."

He looked at the long, long length of leather. "Why do you humiliate me so?" he asked me, his voice a frustrated whisper.

"Because I am accustomed to having my way in all things," I replied.

"I would happily serve you in more intimate ways."

"You and a thousand others. Do something for me they will not." I was smiling to myself. "Show me that you are different, more dedicated, more—willing."

He bent and kissed my boots, then his mouth began to work. He kissed the boot passionately, face flushing red, working his way from instep to knee, tongue slathering across the shiny leather, hands cradling my calf, licking all around the length of it. His ass bobbed as he licked and his hand went between his legs, and I knew I had read him right.

"Lower your trousers."

He obeyed, and his erection sprang loose. He kept his hands away from himself, and continued to lick my boots, slobbering on them until his cock drooled with pearly fluid.

"You may fuck my boots." I moved my foot from the hassock to the floor.

He straddled my feet and pushed his cock between my ankles, sliding his manhood back and forth between my legs, his arms embracing my knees, his face turned up towards mine, eyes locked on mine, sweat standing up on his brow as he sawed back and forth. I leaned forward to look down his back to the tight globes of his ass clenching as he pushed himself towards climax. I stroked his velvet back, then kissed him on the mouth. His mouth opened and my tongue went in, thrusting hard.

"Make sure you come on my boots, and don't get any on the carpet."

He moaned. He put one hand down low, and when he finally spurted, pushed his cock up to where it splattered the sides of my boots. Without being told he got down on his hands and knees and licked up his mess.

"Put my spurs on," I told him and handed the gold things to him. With his pants around his knees and his flaccid organ lolling, he strapped on my golden spurs. "I'm going whoring," I said. "See that you are gracious to my sister again tomorrow."

He ground his teeth in frustration. I walked out on him.

I fucked three whores that night, and gave each of them a throbbing orgasm. When I returned to my own bed, I fingered myself, then crawled to the foot of the bed and impaled myself on the bed knob, humping it violently until shaken with orgasm.

Soon, I decided. But first I wanted to torture him some more.

Vladamin rode with me. I wore black; I liked it better than the blues and purples that filled my wardrobe. I had read Stepaan's memoirs, and had come to the conclusion that however brave he might have been in battle, he was timid in ruling. He had often granted clemency when he might have enjoyed the power of total tyranny. As beloved as the Hero of Ambivalla was, our house might not have come to such dire straits if he had been more ruthless. I decided to practice on Vladamin. "I've decided to fuck you today," I commented by way of starting the conversation.

He brightened. "I've been looking forward to it... Stepaan," he replied.

I tapped the riding crop against my boot. "Have you? We'll see."

We rode as far as we could on the horses, then tied them to the trees, and I led him up the steep cliff, hanging onto tree branches and shrubbery until we reached the last crag. We climbed hand over hand until at last we came out on the bald head of Mount Kilar. "Take your clothes off."

Had anyone swept the crag with a glass they could have see us clearly. But nobody but the eagles saw. He stripped. He stood in the sun, and it gilded his bronze body. I stood staring at it, admiring the muscles that were covered in a fur of black hair, the fullness of his balls, and the tightness of his chest. His thighs were corded with muscles, and hands were clenched open, his eyes staring at me for any clue.

"Why did you come to me?" I demanded.

"Because you were the only man that could commit the sin of sodomy and get away with it."

"Have you ever done it?"

He flushed. "Yes.'"

"Tell me.

"In the Sultan's household. I was... too fond of it. It's all right for a man to use slave boys that way, but for a man of noble birth to allow himself to be used... was unacceptable. So they used me, and then they laughed at me." He smiled grimly. "And then you laid siege to Ambivalla, and all the Ourmani lords were quaking in their boots. They knew your reputation, see, and they feared that you would do to them as they had done to me." He smiled grimly. "I would have liked to have seen that."

"If I use you, I'll use you hard and expect you to take it without complaint."

He knelt. "Yes, my prince."

"Hold out your hands."

I wrapped the red sash around his wrists, ran it between them to separate and tighten them. Then I took hold of his hair and forced his head down. I tied the sash to his knees, forcing him into a bowed over position.

"Now I'm going to hurt you, for no other reason than I feel like being cruel. And you're going to take it, for no other reason than you want to please me."

I whipped him with the crop, lashing him stroke after stroke, striping his bent back. He gasped, but he did not scream. He braced his hands against the ground, and I moved lower, beating his ass. "Is this what you want me to attend to?" I asked.

"Yes," he gasped.

"Is this the part of you that craves my attention?"

"Yes."

"The part that sins?"

"Yes!" he was twisting under the lashes.

I cropped him harder, cursed him and called him vile names, until at last his ass was red and he was lifting his hips to me, groaning in the ecstasy of pain. His posterior was red and hot, and I ran my hands over it. I slipped my arms around his waist, found his erection straining, liquid leaking from the tip. I unbuttoned my fly then, and slid my phallus into him.

He arched and wept, groaned and shuddered. I moved slowly in him, and gradually he accommodated my thickness. I held tight to his hips, spitting occasionally to slip more freely between his cheeks. "Is this what you like?" I demanded.

"Yes, my prince. Do with me what you will."

"Marry my sister. Get me an heir."

"Yes, my prince."

"I'll expect you to service her during the day and me during the night."

"Yes, my prince."

He was drawing up like a cat that has its tailbone scratched. I sank all the way to the hilt in him, and suddenly he was moaning loudly. I clasped my hands around his cock and balls and felt them pumping, and could almost hear the splatter of seed upon the rocks. "Is this the best you've ever had?"

"Yes, my prince. Thank you. I'll do anything you want."

I withdrew from him, stood up. "Turn around."

He turned, automatically opening his mouth, expecting to service my phallus. I dropped my trousers, and he gaped. I unbuckled the strap and showed him my short haired woman's sex beneath it.

"My brother is a ruined hulk, raving some days and drooling the rest. Prince Stepaan has been conquered by disease."

His jaw was hanging open. I rebuckled my belt, settling my phallus snugly into place. "You've never even laid eyes on him, only me."

"P-p-princess?" he asked.

I slapped his face. "Prince Stepaan, now. Somebody has to save our house from disaster."

His jaw clicked shut and he stared at me in awe. "You are a worthy sister to the Hero of Ambivalla."

"I've acquired some of his vices, too."

His eyes dropped to the immense phallus pointed at his face. "You're equal to his legend in that, too."

"Bend over."

EROTIC FANTASTIC

He bent, and I mounted him again. This time, he cried out when I entered him. I rode him long and hard, until I had exhausted myself.

The wedding was a fine affair. With fine insincerity I promised to love, honor, and obey him as a good wife should, then for our wedding night I ordered him to submit to my every whim. He complied, and after a certain amount of practice, became skilled at administering to both my phallus and my woman's sex. I enjoyed watching him; the rush of power that came from having another man attend my tyrant prick was sweet. Then I made alternate use of his cock and his ass, and we both fell into a satisfied and well earned slumber.

My brother died fourteen months later, but not until after the Battle of Carcoum, in which his advice, transmitted via carrier pigeon, won the day for me. My husband I sent as an ambassador to Sultan Hadra, and with his improved skills, the Sultan did not forget his name this time. Nobody laughed at him either— nobody dared to laugh at the sultan's favorite paramour. As for myself, I missed him for the year the sultan was despoiling him, but I gave birth to our son, and when my husband arrived home, he was laden with all manner of rich gifts showered upon him by the happy sultan.

We reigned long and peacefully after that. And though my brother is buried in the cold, harsh ground, yet still the common folk say the Hero of Ambivalla never died, and that some nights you can see him stalking the old places that knew him well.

THE LIMO
Reed Manning

Vince cruised into the estate via the service lane, past immaculate lawns, retaining walls of natural stone set by hand, and into the lee of a three-story mansion. The elegance visible through his windshield was enough to make him wonder how he could get into investment banking.

The caretaker greeted him by the six-car garage. Vince pointed at the emblem on the side of his truck: SUBLIME AUTO DETAILING. "I'm here to do the limo."

"Right," the caretaker said. He fished a valet control badge from his pocket, keyed in a code, and pinned the device on Vince's shirt. "There. Just let the garage and limo know what you want."

"Great."

"I'll be over there if you need me." The man headed for the rose garden, clippers in hand.

Vince opened the back of his truck, uncapped spray bottles, unravelled hoses, and unlocked the garbage bin. He turned to the garage. "Open." The nearest door obeyed. Daylight fell on an elegant gold limousine.

A Detroit Limited. Vince sighed. They didn't make 'em like that any more.

Setting a marker on the asphalt next to his truck, he said, "Center your front bumper over that, my friend."

The automobile rolled to the designated spot, using its battery-powered accessory drive. To turn on the powerful road engine, Vince would need more than a valet badge.

"Unlock doors, hood, and trunk."

The car obeyed. "Thanks," Vince said, and began vacuuming. Only a little touch-up was necessary. The owner was apparently a tidy sort, and the filtration system had taken care of most of the dust. But Vince skipped nothing. Not only was he trying to impress this first-time client, but he never settled for less than a thorough job.

The Detroit Limited was one of the first A.I. models, available even before the traffic guidance network had fully come on line. Vince aimed to treat this one well. "You know, if it weren't for cars like you, I might be unemployed right now. Some chauffeur would be doing all this." Instead, mobile detailing was an industry that had come into its glory days.

He emptied the ashtrays, wiped them, and began cleaning the upholstery. "How about some music, my friend?"

The sound system woke, the volume increasing gradually, serenading the car's interior with 1970s pop.

"Nice equipment," Vince commented, wiping the speaker grills. "How about something more, um, 21st Century?"

The music shifted to a contemporary hit. A pair of female vocalists belted out a high, soaring harmony that had Vince pausing just to listen. "That's good," he said. "Gets the blood moving. Say, you got a name?"

"James."

Of course, smiled Vince.

A stain on the edge of one of the rear seats caught his eye. He aimed his spray bottle, and paused.

"Looks like a come stain." He chuckled, glancing around the roomy interior, with its little champagne refrigerator, its cushioned elegance, its dark windows. "Bet these seats have seen some heavy action in their day."

The music dimmed. "I can tell you about it, if you'd like," said James.

Vince guffawed. "You're kidding."

The car didn't reply. Vince began to think. How many times had he wanted to know how life was for the people who got to ride in vehicles like this? "All right," he said. "Start with how this stain got here."

James laughed. "My owner's wife was entertaining a friend..."

Rule number one: Don't ignore your young, beautiful, shapely wife. That was Dean's mistake. While he had been off on one business trip after another, his lovely Claudia had been having her pussy waxed and polished night after night. By now, she almost wished he wouldn't come home. Boyfriends were so much more lavish with sexual favors than were husbands.

She wasn't going to miss out on one last chance for some gentlemanly attention before he returned. So as she headed out to the airport in the limo to greet him, she stopped a short way down the road to take on an extra passenger named Nick.

"We've got twenty minutes," Claudia said, pulling his mouth to hers. "Don't bother getting undressed."

They kissed long and firmly, then she pressed him into a reclining position and lowered herself between his legs. "I've been tasting this in my mind all day," she said as she zipped him down. The light of the stars and street lamps filtered through the tinted safety glass, revealing his massive boner—much, much larger than her husband's, and more skilled. Her women friends all claimed size didn't matter; she knew they'd change their minds if they did it with Nick. Not that she'd share.

She licked every part of his cock and leaned back, admiring the way the silvery light gleamed off the wetness. Pumping him with her hand, she was delighted to see a drop of pre-come ooze from the tip. She smeared the natural lube all over the head, using the tip of the finger that wore her wedding band.

"Oh, please," he moaned. "Put it in!"

She giggled. "Sure." Soon his blunt, firm knob was nudging her palate, and her lips and tongue were riding back and forth along the shaft. There was so much of him to pamper that the zipper was distant and irrelevant. He could have been wearing seven layers of Arctic gear and his handle would still have protruded beyond.

Getting head wasn't enough for him. He wanted to touch her. His hands roved down, and after several pauses to appreciate her mouthwork, he succeeded in reaching inside her décolletage. He thumbed her nipples to hardness. She smiled but brushed him off, preferring not to be distracted until she had sucked him to the point of quivering.

"My turn," he said, flipping her over. She spread her legs. Her skirt slid aside, uncovering her crotch. He lit the cabin light for a moment, just to worship the visual she presented—smooth, well-toned skin; tiny, symmetrical, pale tan labia; and just enough muff to accent it all. No panties or hose barred his way.

He licked from her perineum to her clit with one long, feathery stroke. She melted into the upholstery.

"Go for the big one," she urged. "No time to linger." She knew she'd let him dally down there forever if she didn't set some limits. He'd done her for an hour only two nights before.

He ran his tongue over her clit in clockwise strokes. Meanwhile his middle finger traced the outline of her labia and found the moist crack between. He eased the first joint inside, added the ring finger, and spread her flower. She rewarded him with a dainty outpouring of pussy juice.

Her button swelled. Her cunt grew pliant. His fingers wriggled in up to the main knuckles. Pressing the rear side of her pubic bone, he began to rub her G spot.

"Oh, heaven," she murmured.

The orgasm, when it arrived, lifted her off the seat. Nick kept grinding her with tongue and mouth, vibrating his fingers so that her entire pelvis shook. Her heaves sounded like sobs, but in between each sharp intake of breath, she grinned like a fiend.

With a light stroke on his forehead, she pressed him away, sagging onto the upholstery. Lifting one of her tits from her dress, she let him lick there, where the stimulation would prolong the ecstasy without exceeding her capacity.

Sighing as she returned to reality, she tucked her boob away. "Ready to stick it in?" The request sounded more like a plea.

"Yes, ma'am!"

His pole, thick as it was, glided into her cunt with no difficulty. She grunted as she accommodated his girth, then relaxed and raised her ankles onto his shoulders, making the fit even more snug. Juice flowed down the crease of her ass; she used it to massage, and tickle, her anus. Already she was regretting that the short car ride didn't leave them enough time for some backdoor pleasure—she needed tons of foreplay to prepare her sphincters for a partner as endowed as he was.

It was only a small regret, and it vanished from her mind as he humped her. He unbuttoned his shirt and slid his pants down to his thighs in order to pound her without encumbrance. His pelvis met her thighs, her crotch, and the smooth globes of her rump, transferring sweat and heat and getting the same in return.

A dreamy expression came over his face, but she trusted his control. He kept fucking as the miles wound down.

They exited the freeway and began to approach the air terminal. "Now!" she said. "Fill me!"

Nick obliged. With an enthusiastic groan, he pressed deep into her and let himself go. His hips shuddered, lifting her off the seat with each thrust. "Yes! Yes! Yes!" Claudia cried, milking him with her thighs.

Spent, Nick withdrew. He beamed at her, wiping off his swollen wand with his handkerchief.

"Providence Airlines," announced the limo, filtering through a maze of taxis toward the curb.

"Quick!" urged Claudia. Nick had just time to restore his clothes before they stopped. He slid out, pausing to kiss her farewell.

"Dean goes out of town in a week," she purred into his ear. Then he was gone.

As the car proceeded from the departure level to the baggage claim/arrival area, she straightened her dress, arraying herself so as to hide the fact that nothing lay between the seat and her naked bottom.

There was Dean, standing at the curb, his luggage at his feet. The limo pulled up. A sky captain placed the bags in the trunk.

"How are you, darling?" Claudia asked as her spouse plopped onto the seat beside her.

"Exhausted," he said. Just as she had anticipated, he lay his head back, patted her thigh, and started to doze. She merely smiled as hot come trickled out of her onto the seat, mere inches from his resting hand, hidden by her skirt and by the night.

"That was pretty hot," Vince said as the limo finished its account. "And the husband never found out?"

"Dean is much too busy with his own affairs to pay attention to what his wife might be doing."

"Lemme guess," the man said. "You could tell me about his adventures, too?"

"No. He never fucks in here. I just know from all the phone calls he places to his girl friends using my cellular rig. But if you want more juicy stuff, I belonged to a rental company for my first two years of operation.

You might say I've been used."

"Yeah?" Vince scratched his chin, intrigued. "What's your favorite incident?"

Keith knew his fiancée would get a full report on what happened after the bachelor party. But with luck, she'd never think to wonder what he did on the way to the party.

Crystal and Ashley nuzzled on either side of him as the limo sat on the freeway, caught in a traffic jam. Keith hoped the gridlock lasted forever. He'd done his share of fucking in his life, including a few times with Crystal, a dozen occasions with Ashley, but never two women at once.

"Marina's a lucky gal, getting you all to herself," Ashley said. "After tonight, that is," she added, her envy turning to glee.

The ladies slid out of their dresses and hung them from the built-in clothes rack. Ashley wore bra cups only; as she peeled them away, Keith pondered how they had stayed attached. Velcro tits? Not by the looks of all that smooth skin. Crystal wore a silk chemise, her small, high boobs wafting the garment away from her waist and ribs. No need for a bra. Her nipples swelled outward as she lifted the silk away from them.

They posed for him as if he were a camera. His eyes roved over four fine breasts, one pair capped in oval circles the color of creamed coffee, the other decorated with pert nipples the shade of peach blossoms, with areolae so pale the edges vanished in the subdued light.

His cock bulged against his fly.

Down came the panties, which they tossed aside as if nothing could be more irrelevant. First Crystal spread her legs, showing off her light, soft pubic curls, then she picked up a flashlight and pointed it at Ashley's crotch. No hair at all. Smooth pubes, waxed to perfection. Keith scanned her twat—every last crinkle was visible—and imagined wrapping his mouth around it.

Ashley turned around, bending over. A cord with a pull-ring extruded from her tiny, pursed asshole. Crystal grinned and bent over as well, redirecting the beam of light. Her anus, which Keith remembered fondly from a night spent in the Edgewood Motel over on Route 4, also clutched a string.

"We dare you to pull these," Crystal said. "But do it slowly."

Keith obliged. With Crystal providing the spotlight, he tugged gently on Ashley's line. Soon her sphincters began to bulge from within. Out popped a bead the size of a ping pong ball.

"Oh!" Ashley said. She shuddered from the release.

More cord trailed up into her crack. Keith pulled the length taut. Another sphere birthed into freedom. Ashley thrashed again.

"My turn," Crystal said. Ashley took the flashlight, and Crystal positioned her ass right in front of Keith's face. He pulled. A bead eased out, but though it was smaller than those that had come out of Ashley's back entrance, it set her to moaning just as loudly.

Keith's prick was throbbing now. The gals had found an ideal way to remind him how sensuous each of them was, how far their erogenous zones extended. They weren't after orgasms yet, they just wanted something to awaken their juices. And they'd found a way to do it that was a visual feast for him, and delightfully nasty besides.

He alternated the tugging, until the fifth and last bead emerged from each set of buns. Then, with impish smiles, the women shoved them back in.

"You have too many clothes," Crystal said. In seconds, they stripped him bare.

"You liked this so far, yes, you did," Ashley commented, grasping his achingly rigid pole.

They went down on him simultaneously. Long after the car had resumed travel, their tongues and lips slid up and down either side of his shaft, taking turns for full-mouth indulgence.

When he started to tremble, they switched to fucking. Keith didn't have to do any of the work—groom's treat. First Crystal ground her cunt along his hard-on until, hair in sweat-drenched ringlets, she was trembling with the need to come. Then Ashley took over, fucking herself to an equal frenzy. A feral need brightened Keith's pupils.

"You need to shoot your wad, don't you?" Ashley cooed.

"Yeah," Keith murmured, barely able to form a coherent reply.

"We want to make you come a special way," Crystal said.

Ashley lifted off, faced away from Keith, and reimpaled herself. Lodging him deep inside, she began to rock her hips.

Delirious, Keith hung on to her waist.

Half-panting, Crystal knelt between both sets of legs and ran her tongue over Keith's balls, over Crystal's twat, and along his dick as it pistoned in and out. She twiddled Crystal's clit with one hand, and her own button with the other.

It was like nothing Keith had ever felt. So much moisture. So much stimulation. And all he had to do was sit back. It was a blow-job and a fuck together.

As Ashley pulled him out, deep-throated him, and shoved him back in for the tenth time, he couldn't hold back. Thrusting his cock upward as much as possible, he unloaded into Crystal's pussy, Ashley lapping away in a manner that made his gushes feel twice as powerful. Both women began to heave in time to his spurts: A triple climax. Could it be? He certainly wasn't going to ask if they were faking.

They sprawled over the seats, panting, happy, satisfied. Keith saw that some time during all the activity, the beads had been pulled out again. "We'd let you keep these as souvenirs," Ashley said, waving the attached spheres, "but if Marina stumbled across them, it could be incriminating."

The women lovingly wiped Keith off, combed his hair, put him back in his tuxedo, and stroked his face until the car reached its destination.

"Remember us," Ashley whispered. The ladies stayed in the car, arm in arm, to be delivered home by James while Keith celebrated the end of his bachelorhood.

"The nice thing is," said James, "Keith is still married. His wife must be one hell of a chick that he doesn't miss what he got that night."

"Oh, man," Vince moaned. "The Autobiography of a Limo. I can't take much more of this."

"Why?"

"Do you know how long it's been since I've been laid?"

"A long time?"

"Seven months. My dick's been dating Rosie Palm so much it's about to fall off! I've been working too much to meet any eligible women."

"I could help you," the car said.

"You could help me get laid?" The cartridge of replacement air freshener fell out of Vince's grip. "How?"

"Well, I can't guarantee you'll get any action, but this other limousine I know has a cute owner named Traci. Just your age. I could set you up."

"You cars talk to each other?"

"Sure. Through the traffic guidance nets. You could say this other limo is my girlfriend. I wish I could give her a lube job."

"You learn something new every day," Vince said, shaking his head.

"But I don't know—that would be one weird blind date."

"Got something against rich girls?"

Vince hesitated. "Cute, single, and rich?"

"A widow. Her husband left her a bundle. Only nice thing he ever did for her. He was an older guy, treated her like a trophy. Last thing she wants is another one like him. She's craving a chance to meet a wholesome, athletic, blue-collar type, but she doesn't know quite how to locate one."

"Like me."

"Exactly like you."

It sounded too good to be true. "Are you being her pimp or something?" Vince asked.

"Ahem. I prefer the term 'matchmaker'. Look, you're a nice fella. You treated me like a person, not just an A.I. I'd love to do this for you. My friend would love to help out her owner. That's all that's happening here."

Vince shrugged. "Well, I guess I've got nothing to lose by checking it out." He closed the door, and ran his chamois cloth along James's roof one last time. "Anything I can, uh, do for you?"

"Let me know how it comes out, will you?"

"It all came out well, don't you think?" James asked the classy green limousine beside him in the driveway. They were parked next to one another, directly below the second-floor master bedroom of a mansion belonging to a certain rich young widow.

"I'll say," answered his companion. "If they stay up there much longer, they'll scorch the sheets."

Vince and Traci were still fucking each other's brains out after six months of courtship. No engagement had yet been announced, but the widow had gone to the trouble of purchasing James from the investment banker for Vince's exclusive use. Traci's garage could hold four or five limos.

"I would say 'drench', not 'scorch'," replied James.

"Eeeuuwwww."

At last, Vince emerged, hopped briskly down the portico steps, and settled into James's lush passenger compartment. The man brimmed with Just-Fucked Glow.

"I take it you enjoyed yourself tonight?" the car asked.

Vince chuckled. "You could say that."

"You know, one of these times, you two are going to have to do it in here. How about on that nice straight stretch of freeway just past the bridge? You could bring some champagne, slip a CD-Rom in the video player?"

"Dream on," Vince said amiably. "Doing it in here would be like having someone watching."

The limo uttered a vocal raspberry. "Inhibitions. Let it all hang out, Vince my boy. Live life to the fullest."

Vince just smiled. "Home, James."

Sighing, the car started its engine.

CONSUMPTION
Mason Powell

Richard was supposed to be dead. Jared has seen him die, had cried, had been to the funeral, which, despite the ravages of the disease, had been an open coffin ceremony. There was no doubt that Richard was dead: but there was also no doubt that the young man at the automated teller, not five yards away, was Richard. It wasn't a trick of the lights; they were bright and clear, in the hope of driving away muggers. And the pale coloring, the elegant black suit, the touch of make-up: all so uncharacteristic of Richard: that couldn't fool Jared either. They had been lovers for too long for little things like that to deceive. The way the hand moved, slipping in the plastic card, punching the code buttons—it was Richard.

"Richard?" Jared asked across the short distance, his voice suddenly harsh in the night air.

The man did not turn, but the tiny jerk of his movements betrayed him. It was Richard, not quite fumbling, stuffing the card and the receipt into his wallet, shoving the money into his pocket and turning to leave.

"Richard, it's me, Jared!"

Richard turned, their eyes met for a moment, then Richard spun and ran.

"Wait! Please, what's going on?"

Jared took out after him, throwing every last bit of his failing energy into the effort, but it was hopeless. His lover, dead barely six months now, ran too fast. Faster than Richard had ever run, faster than Richard had ever been able to run. In a matter of seconds Jared found himself sinking next to a light post, his breath wheezing in and out of his lungs, the sweat pouring down his face, his heart pounding.

Is this it? he wondered. Was the Grim Reaper about to claim him? Was that what the vision of Richard portended?

But what kind of vision was it; to see your dead lover at an automated teller machine? Was the next life going to be as crummy as the current one? Did one have to work and scramble to survive, use money and credit cards, cope with all the same crap? Were the Ancient Egyptians right? Would there be a White House in the next world, and a National Debt?

Jared tried to laugh, but he choked instead. He wondered what would determine who occupied the White House of the Dead. Did you get stuck with the president who was president when you died? But no, that couldn't be it: the president would likely still be alive when you died. As would several others.

Jared did laugh, choking as he did so, at the absurdity of such thoughts passing through what might be his last moments.

A woman appeared at the corner. She was tall and beautiful, with glossy black hair and pale skin. She wore a long, tight black dress and black shiny shoes with stiletto heals. Her eyes were black and piercing as she walked slowly toward him, and they looked down on him with frank appraisal. As she came abreast of him she stopped. He noted that she had a cigarette in a long, thin, cigarette holder dangling from her hand. She slowly lifted it and took a puff, then let it fall carelessly. She looked like a vision from a silent German expressionist movie.

He thought for a moment that he knew her. Was she Lady Death, come for him in such a form?

"I'm just sick," he gasped out.

"Honey," she said, "if you keep using that kind of shit you're gonna' stay sick!" And then she laughed, throwing her head back, the sound like a window breaking; and without another word she walked away, her heels clicking on the pavement like a tiny drum beating out a slow march.

Jared slumped where he lay. His heart was slowing a little, so maybe, he thought, this would not be the end. Maybe this would be just another of the interminable episodes where his strength gave out and it felt like the end. One day, the doctors told him, it would be fatal. But maybe not just yet.

His mind returned to Richard, who had died of the same fatal sickness, a new form of mutated tuberculosis that was mercifully still rare. Which of them had given it to the other, or whether either had, was irrelevant. Richard had died, he, Jared, was supposed to die—but Richard had just taken money out of an automated teller, and though he had looked a little strange, he had not looked dead.

Jared let his mind run backward. To the last days with Richard: further back, to before the diagnosis, to the time when they had first been lovers. He had done it before while waiting to get his strength back. There wasn't a lot more that he could do. Besides, the past was strong for him. He could draw from it, draw the strength that the future did not hold.

There was a deck, built of redwood and perched on a cliff above a little cove. When the air was still the scent of pine needles, like incense in a temple, drifted from the hills that tumbled down to the Pacific. When the breeze blew, the cool smell of the ocean made it like the prow of a sailing ship on mythic ancient seas.

Richard lay on the deck naked, his body bronzed and hard as bronze, his hand slowly sliding up and down on his hard cock. He hadn't heard Jared come back from the store, walk across the carpet, stand in the open doorway; or maybe he had. There was a part of Richard that liked to play games on the edge. A slight cruelty without malice.

Jared waited for his own cock to be at full hardness, straining against the rough mesh insert of his lime green trunks, before he slowly peeled off the yellow tank top, let it fall silently to the carpet, then slid the trunks down and stepped out of them. He slicked his hand with the sweat off his chest, then began pumping in the same, steady rhythm that Richard was using.

Even when they were together, touching, there was a distance between them, so this sex at one remove, the distance between them physical rather than psychological, was not strange or unusual; just another permutation of the uniqueness of their relationship.

The sun moved slowly up the sky and beams reflected from the cove below dazzled Jared, flakes of light like mica chips shattering in his eyes as his orgasm came upon him, wracked him like a storm-tossed ship, broke him on the shoals of his body's release. He panted with the heat, broke like a wave on the rocks, shot spume high like ocean water against stone, then receded.

Richard's hand continued to move, slowly, steadily: and then Richard's dark eyes snapped open, locked with Jared's pale ones, and Richard shot silently, the whiteness falling like drops of rain upon the bronze of his chest and belly. He smiled.

"There was fresh abalone at the market today," Jared said. "I got some for supper."

"Good," said Richard. "Shall we go swimming or shooting?"

"Let's continue shooting."

They both smiled.

The cove above which their house was built was an anomaly: warm Pacific waters. The way in which the land curled around, nestled, enclosed, made for a shallow place with pale blond sands. In late summer and autumn the sun, coupled with the shelter from the Pacific winds, was enough to warm the water and make it pleasant for swimming. There was very little warm ocean water for swimming in California; not until Mexico. This little cove on the Mendocino Coast was worth much more than anybody could have ever paid for it.

But the pine woods were almost an equal attraction. They were old enough to be clear beneath, so one could walk through them without tangling on undergrowth. Jared had set up an archery range through the woods, with all different kinds of shots and targets. There were long shots down deep avenues and across ravines, and there were shorter, sometimes easier, sometimes more difficult, shots.

The first target was a life size picture of Jesse Helms, the notorious bigot and hypocrite. It was the first target, and an easy shot, because nobody wanted to miss the opportunity of putting an arrow through the bastard; and most of the guests who made the trek up during the summer knew little or nothing about shooting a bow.

Jared had taken up archery in junior high. He had been terrified of getting an erection in the showers, not knowing that it was usual, and not just a symptom of his youthfully painful homosexuality. Archery gave him a sport without showers, and besides, he had an aptitude for it. He had continued it in college and had been on the team. He had even studied a little about Zen archery, but he knew that he wasn't ever going to devote his life to it, so that had not continued.

The two pastimes which the house provided were emblematic of the two men. Richard was a swimmer, and a good one. He loved the sun and would lie in it for hours, jumping up periodically to run naked down to the cove and dive through the waves. He was even good at the butterfly. Jared preferred the cool shadows of the forest, and the still, intent moment of the shot. It was all precision, and letting go at the right moment. He sometimes thought of it as being like golf, in the woods, in the shade. He sometimes wondered what he looked like, pale, blending in with the shadows just before sunset, moving quietly with his bow and quiver.

"Hey! You! You all right? You drunk, or on something?"

Jared opened his eyes and saw a policeman, squatting down in front of him. He took a deep breath.

"No. Thank you, Officer. No, I just have this lung condition, and I'm afraid I over did it. I think I'll be all right now."

He started to climb to his feet. The officer took his arm and helped him up; still watching him carefully. There were lots of new drugs on the streets, and more than one cop had been killed helping someone who was on something strange. Jared moved carefully, not wanting to provoke an unwarranted response.

"Do you want a cab?" the officer asked.

"No, I don't live far. I just saw someone I thought I knew, and like a fool, I started to run after him. I tend to forget that I can't run anymore, at least not safely."

"Well, you take care of yourself," the cop said, friendlier than Jared had expected him to be. "And don't worry about the kids in the weird outfits, or let them startle you. They're harmless enough."

"Weird outfits?" Jared asked.

"Yeah; lots of black, dead-looking makeup, that kind of thing."

Jared thought of the woman who had passed and stopped, the one with the stiletto heels and the cigarette holder. He also thought about Richard, who had never worn any makeup; at least not until tonight.

"It's a Gothic Club," the policeman continued. "They only do it once a week. Other nights they share the building with other groups."

"I don't understand," Jared said.

"I guess you could call it Rock 'N Roll, though it doesn't sound like the stuff bands played when I was a kid. Kind of medieval rock. They all dress up in black, makeup, looking like death warmed over, and they go and listen to their bands, and, as far I know, I guess they dance, too. I've never been in the place. I just know about it because it's on my beat. On Thursday there's an Old Folks Club and they do jitterbug to old Sammy Kaye tapes. Well, you're looking a little better, and I've got things to do. Take care of yourself."

The officer gave a little one-finger salute and sauntered off, and Jared stood watching him go. The quiet and the night closed in, and memories welled up out of the darkness.

The bar had computerized lights built in everywhere. Lights flashed out of the ceiling, lights ran in strings under the transparent dance floor, lights made dizzying, ever-changing, patterns on the walls. Behind the bar itself there was a mirror with a one way surface. Presumably one could go behind it for some reason, but the main thing was that complex lights could shift and change and appear where no lights should be, reflected in empty space behind and through the customer sitting on a stool with one drink too many in his hand.

The music was deafening, but nobody was there to listen. Perhaps everybody was there specifically not to listen. The air pulsated with the beat and the bodies pulsated in the hot air. It was a steam room heated with pheromones, and the whole tone of the room was male.

Jared sat at the bar, casually cruising the dancers. He was drawn to a wild figure in jeans and green tank top, dancing alone like a madman under the lights. Black hair, smooth body, his face contorted in ecstatic frenzy, his eyes clenched tight like someone forcing his way into another reality.

The music changed and the dancer kept dancing, on and on, one dance after another. Jared felt his testosterone storm building to the point where he thought lightning might strike out of his cock; he finally pressed out onto the floor and danced, making his way near the intense young man, inhaling the smell of his sweat, almost gasping with the want of him. When the music shifted into something slightly softer he reached out and touched a bare shoulder.

Black eyes snapped open and transfixed him. Jared licked his lips, tried to speak. The dancer's lips smiled.

"I'm Richard," he said. "You've been watching me a long time."

"Yes," said Jared, breathing hard.

"Can we go to your place?" Richard asked.

Jared nodded dumbly.

In Jared's apartment Richard had simply walked across the room, looked out the window at the cityscape, then turned and peeled off the tank top. Every lean muscle was delineated on his golden torso. He undid the big, Western belt buckle, pulled open the buttons, and bent, pushing down the jeans and stepping out of them. Somehow his sneakers were already off.

Jared stared at him, his eyes moving quickly to the patch of crinkly black pubic hair, the smooth, half hard cock, the general perfection of a dancer's lean body. Then, as if time had vanished between desire and consummation, he was on his knees and the scent of Richard's sweat was like a cloud surrounding him.

But later, when he stood and turned Richard around, to face out the window; preparing to take Richard in turn: he saw the welts.

His fingers traced them gently across Richard's back, and Richard flinched. They had not been visible under the tank top.

"I shouldn't be here," Richard said softly. "I have a lover. A master."

"And he did this to you?" Jared asked.

"Yes," said Richard. "He'll do it again when he realizes I've been with you."

"Do you have to tell him?"

"He'll know. He always does. I think he sees it in my eyes."

Jared moved his hands away, but still stood close enough that the heat of their bodies blended.

"Do you want to go?" he asked.

"No," said Richard. "I want you to take me."

He leaned back and their bodies touched, and Jared's arms slid around him, and Richard was taken, standing looking out on the cityscape.

The policeman was gone and the street was empty. But there was a kind of thread of sense that ran from Richard's appearance at the automated teller through the memories that Jared used to hold himself together, to what the policeman had said. If Richard was alive after all, then he would be dancing. If there was dancing at the Gothic Club, and all the people

dressed in black and makeup, then there was a likelihood that Richard
could be found there, dancing.

Jared turned in the direction the policeman had indicated and began
to walk. He had no idea what he would do if he found Richard. What
could he say? Clearly if Richard didn't want to see him, then that was
that.

But why would Richard have staged his own death so elaborately, so
convincingly, if all he wanted was to leave Jared behind? Was a lover such
a hard thing to ditch?

Well, sometimes, yes.

It had been inevitable that Jared should meet Ronk. The affair had
become too intense, too consistent, to go undetected.

At first Ronk had assumed that his boy was simply going out on him,
and had beaten Richard. Richard was able to handle that. It had been part
of their relationship from the beginning.

"I don't exactly like it," Richard told Jared, "but then again, maybe I
do. I feel wanted; cared about; cared for; owned. You know how people
always say 'be mine' or 'I want to be yours alone' and things like that?
Well, I do belong to Ronk. He lets me know that. He said he ought to
make me wear my collar full time."

"Your collar?"

"Yeah, it's a chain dog collar. I have to put it on when I come home at
night. He said the other night, after he had whipped me, that he ought to
weld it around my neck so that people would know I am his property."

"Then you're a slave."

What had been obvious was not really obvious. When Richard was
with Jared he had not seemed in the least subservient. Jared wondered
how different it might be with Ronk.

"I try to be," said Richard. "But I'm not really good at it. I want more
than that. I want more than Ronk. I have my own needs that extend
beyond his."

"Why don't you just leave him?" Jared asked. "Are you into him for
money? Are you afraid of being without a lover? You know that I want
you. If you have no place to go you could certainly move in here."

Richard smiled oddly, tenderly.

"Thank you, Jared. No, I am not into him for money. In fact, I have
enough money that I will never need to work. My parents are well off.

They've always been too busy with the business to pay much attention to me, but when I came out of the closet they let me know that they would see to my welfare, but that they would prefer me not to hang around and be an embarrassment to them. They're Republicans, and I think my father wants to run for office someday."

"Then what is it?"

"Ronk is a good master. He loves me. He loves to take care of me."

"But you don't love him?"

"I suppose I do, in a way. He excites me. He turns me on. When he looks at me I shiver and get afraid, and want him to take me and do whatever he wants with me. I like being his boy. But—it's as much like an addiction as it is love. When I'm away from him I want tenderness, affection without discipline... Oh, I don't know how to explain it! I want what you give me. But when I see him..."

Jared took a deep breath.

"Do you think he would accept your loving both of us?"

Richard was silent for a long time, then replied: "I don't think so. His ownership is important to him. The whole point, to him, of me going out with others, is to provide a reason for punishment. And besides: I think, Jared, that I want to be with you; and only you. But I know that if he walked into the room and told me to follow him, I would have to."

"Suppose we just moved away," Jared said, thinking it was truly a crazy idea. He would have to find work, they would have to find a community where they would not have to fight bigotry...

"It might work," Richard said, startling him. "But we would have to tell Ronk straight out. I owe that to him."

Jared could hear music now. Not loud; at least not in comparison to what he remembered from the bars of ten years earlier. A couple hurried past him, their arms locked, their hair black as night and long, their faces white, their lips painted red. He was not sure whether it was a boy and a girl, two boys with willowy mannerisms, two Lesbians, whether one was transsexual, or what. They seemed very happy.

He hurried after them.

Ronk was not as big as Jared had expected, but he was big. Six feet tall, with short blond hair and massive shoulders. He was smooth shaven with roughly handsome features and he lounged in a big, old fashioned leather chair, with one leg thrown over the arm. He was stripped to the waist, which exposed his hairy, muscular chest, and his hand rested on his crotch, massaging it gently, as if his crotch were the unquestioned mediator of all actions in his universe.

"So you're the boy my boy has been seeing?" he asked, puffing on a long, thin, cigar.

"Yes," Jared said.

"That's 'Yes Sir!'" Ronk snapped.

"No, it's just yes." Jared said evenly, concealing his nervousness. Ronk did exert a great force of personality, a masculine dominance that was easy to feel; but Jared had not come to the place for sex, he had come for a showdown.

Ronk stood up, threw out his aura of command, of power. His eyes bored like twin drills.

"I respect your relationship with Richard," Jared said, "but it is no longer working out. Richard and I have fallen in love, and we want to be together. I guess I would be willing to share him, but he says that wouldn't work for you. So I am here to say that I want him, and that we are going away together."

Ronk's face didn't change. He did not unlock his gaze from Jared's, but his attention moved, nonetheless, to Richard, who stood a couple of paces behind Jared, as if Jared was there to protect him.

"Is that true, boy?"

"Yes Sir," Richard stammered out. Jared knew that Richard's eyes were on the floor. Richard had said that Ronk never let him look up at him except during certain kinds of sex. Jared had counted on that.

"Do you really think you can get along without me, boy?"

"I... I want to try, Sir," Richard said.

Jared knew how hard it was for Richard to say that; but they had discussed what it would take to break the bond, and how it would have to be Richard's decision, even if Jared was there to help.

Ronk snapped his fingers, down next to his crotch, and before Jared could speak Richard was hurrying across the room, sinking to his knees in front of his master, clasping his hands behind him.

"Richard," Jared said, "you don't have to..."

"Just a fair test," Ronk said casually, grinning maliciously. "To see if he really can leave."

Jared held his peace. Much as he didn't like it, Ronk was right.

Richard had to make the break on his own or it would never work.

Ronk reached down and pulled open the buttons of his fly.

"One last time, boy," Ronk said. "Just to see if you can do without it. Suck it!"

Jared swallowed hard. He wished that something would distract Ronk; so that he could blink, so that the staring match between them could end as the little drama of dominance played out; but he knew it would not happen. He knew that he dared not let his eyes stray, nor blink, nor change focus, lest Ronk gain the absolute control of the situation he so desired.

Richard made a little mewling sound in his throat, then, obediently, he pulled the pants open all the way and did as Ronk had ordered. The wet sounds filled the air, and Ronk, now even more confident of his power, lifted the thick cigar to his lips and puffed away, casually, right through his orgasm.

Still, their eyes were locked, and still Jared held on, not betraying the loss he felt inside. Ronk stuffed his cock back into his pants and buttoned them, then fastened his belt.

"You still want to go off with this wimp?" Ronk asked.

"Yes Sir," Richard answered.

That broke Ronk's gaze, and gave Jared the victory.

There was a single floodlight, bent to shine down on a nicely lettered sign proclaiming The Chartres Club. It was an old brick school building, no doubt abandoned after the changes in building codes brought about by the earthquake of '89, and the sign was hung from masonry nails driven into the mortar. The stairs ascended under an archway, characteristic of old, poor, city schools, and at the top was a woman in black satin with a roll of tickets such as Jared had seen many times at carnivals. She took his $10 and gave him a stub, then pushed the other part of the ticket into a small wooden box with a slot in the top.

"Siouxsie is God," she said casually, an affirmation of a faith Jared did not understand, much less share.

He went through the door and into a hallway. It was dim and lacking any distinction, but the music provided a guide and eventually he found a double door to the left that gave access to what had once been a gymnasium.

There were small cafe tables set around the sides of the room, each with a blood red tablecloth and a cheap, pressed glass, vase with a single red rose. The walls were hung with commercial tapestries and elaborately framed prints of paintings by Medieval and Early Renaissance masters: mostly crucifixions and martyrdoms. The lighting was dim, shadowy and cool, and there was a smell in the air that was all too easily identified with the cloying sweetness of a funeral: lilies, Jared realized.

The center of the room was the dance floor. It was defined by the presence of four huge angels which Jared knew could not really be made of stone. Nine foot angels made of stone would have weighed tons. They could not readily be moved aside for the Jitterbugers on Thursdays.

The giant papier mache figures in the Exploratorium came into his mind. They, too, looked like stone.

The light over the dance floor was slightly brighter than that which illuminated the tables. It was white light, with just a touch of blue, and it came from directly above, an illusory miraculous luminescence breaking through dark clouds. It made the dancers look like figures from an old black and white film as they moved to the music.

It took a moment for Jared to recognize the song. He had not kept up with the fashions in music, which had become so diverse that perhaps nobody could keep up with them anymore; but it was a song that he had heard on the radio more than once.

"In the deep of the flood,
In the beat of your blood..."

Who was it who sang that? What group had that dark, mysterious undertone?

"When the light disappears, as I sink in the mud..."

He had it: Premature Burial.

"When I give up and die/As I hope that this time/Love is not just a lie..."

Yes, he recognized it now. Stained White Flag by Premature Burial.

The dancers danced alone under the blue white light. No couples, no pairings, just single dancers locked inside the music world of individual dreams.

Richard was there, his eyes closed tightly, his body moving with the same smoothness it always had.

Jared's eyes stung. His nose filled with the scent of Richard though he knew he could not really smell anything over the heavy perfume of death lilies. His mouth went dry and his feet moved of their own volition, one heavy step after another toward the dance floor.

He entered the white light of the charmed circle encompassed by the towering pseudostone angels. He wondered if he could dance. He wondered if he would stand out, a stumbling zombie moving toward a figure from the other side of grave.

Richard's black eyes snapped open, blacker than night under the white light.

The music changed. Richard walked calmly toward him, took him by the arm, and led him out of the light; past the tables, past the roses, into the dimness and through an exit. Down a stairwell and out a door, into an alley.

"You should not have come," Richard said simply, turning to face him full on.

The spell broke. From the moment when he had seen Richard at the automated teller machine he had been ensorcelled by possibilities, by dreams, by faint hopes and chances, but now that all shattered.

"Should not have come?" he said. Then anger boiled up in him. "Should not have come? Richard, you were my lover! I sat with you through sickness, and, I thought, death! What do you mean, I should not have come? Richard, look at me! I've got what you had. Even if I didn't love you, do you think I could walk away without wondering what's going on? How you come to be roaming the streets, alive..."

"Jared, I'm not alive," Richard said.

Jared stopped talking, the silliness of the statement throwing his brain out of gear for a moment. Richard reached out, took Jared's hand, and held it to his cheek, which was cold.

"Feel the chill, Jared. Feel the tomb in my face and my hand."

Jared let his hand perceive just how cold Richard was, then he slowly withdrew it.

"This is stupid," Jared said. "If you didn't want me for a lover anymore you could just have said..."

"I don't want to do this, Jared, but I must. I'm sorry."

Richard's face changed, swiftly. His eyes changed. Then his lips curled back, and there were teeth, large canines, sharp teeth... Jared felt himself falling...

It was gone. They both stood as before in an ordinary alley in the dark.

"I did die, Jared," Richard said. "But not before Ronk heard that I was sick. While we were living on the Mendocino Coast, Ronk was being bitten, sickening, and dying the death that gives immortality. You know that he loved me, in his way. He came to me by night, in the hospital. He made it possible for me to go on, maybe forever: certainly until someone stops me. But now I am his boy again, and this time it is forever."

There was a very long moment of silence.

"It is far from a perfect lifestyle," Richard continued. "We are predators. We prey on humankind. You cannot imagine the shame of needing what you do not wish to take."

Another very long moment as Jared tried to digest what Richard was saying. Then Jared said: "Very well. If that is how it is, then that is how it must be."

Jared reached up, very slowly, very deliberately, and loosened his tie. He unbuttoned his collar, then the first three buttons of his shirt. He pulled the collar back, exposing his neck, and leaned his head back.

"Jared, no! You don't understand!"

"I don't care! I am going to die anyway. If you have any love for me, then take me with you. If you have not, then simply take me, and let me die with one special kiss."

A cold laughter knifed between them. They turned, and Ronk was there, his Levis black, his denim shirt black, his face pale: but it was the same Ronk.

"Go ahead, Richard, suck him!" Ronk said. "Last time it was me you sucked, but this time it will be a little bit different."

Richard turned toward Ronk.

"I won't kill him!"

"And you can't bring him over!" Ronk responded, laughing harshly.

Jared saw Richard's fists clench.

"What does he mean, Richard?"

Ronk came closer, his movement smoother than Jared remembered it.

"What I mean is this," Ronk said. "We are predators, just as my boy told you. That means we are part of the ecology; always have been. But like any predators, our numbers are limited by the possibility of prey. Our survival depends on there not being too many of us. We have to remain unnoticed. That means we have a strict code about bringing in converts to the faith. I had to wait a long time for the Community to approve my bringing Richard over. I nearly lost him because of that. But there are no exceptions. There is only so much blood in the bank, and you can only make limited withdrawals. The community has got pretty good at survival over the millennia, so I guess the plan works."

Richard turned slowly, and from the look on his face, Jared knew it was the truth that Ronk spoke.

"Now," said Ronk, "if my boy don't want to suck you, maybe I will; since that's what you want, eh?"

Richard stepped between them.

"Keep your hands off him, Ronk!"

Ronk slapped Richard hard across the face.

"What is this? My boy rebelling against his Master?"

"We made a deal, Ronk," Richard said coldly. "I am your boy, but you leave Jared alone. You remember that?"

Ronk relaxed, his muscles unbunching.

"Yeah, I remember it. But your former boyfriend is sick like you were. Don't you want to help him out of his misery? How about letting him make the decision? Only a minute ago he was begging you to fang him. If you ain't got the guts to do it, maybe he'll let me."

Richard looked at Jared and suddenly the curtain that had always been drawn between them was down. For the first time Jared felt total communication with Richard; he knew what Richard was thinking, knew why there was such pleading in his glance.

Richard wanted to save him, but like Ronk, he had to wait for the opportunity.

"Maybe I'll just wait, Ronk," Jared said. "Maybe Richard will change his mind. It just wouldn't be the same with anyone else. You understand?"

For a moment Ronk's demeanor melted, and he allowed just the slightest trace of understanding to show through. Then the iron mask of macho flashed back into place.

"Sure, kid," he said. "But if it gets too bad, and you can't find him, there's a lot of hungry people who hang around this place. Think of yourself as a donation to the homeless."

"Jared, will you please get out of here?" Richard pleaded.

Jared smiled and nodded. He wanted to reach out and touch Richard once more, even though the flesh was cold. But the curtain was drawn again, and he sensed that it would be dangerous for Richard if Ronk sensed what had passed between them. He turned and headed back into the building.

"Now, boy," Ronk said to Richard, behind him, "you are going to discover why eternity is just the right amount of time for learning a little discipline."

Jared climbed the stairs, re-entered the Chartres Club, and moved around the edge of the dance floor toward the exit. A raucous cut by Nine Inch Nails was playing, but neither the volume nor the intensity of the music served in any way but to bolster the illusion of death: it was the perfect soundscape for Bruegal and Bosch.

A week later Jared knew who Siouxsie was. He had given up the apartment in the City in which he had entombed himself since Richard's death and returned to the Mendocino Coast house. Certain rituals of passing which he had delayed were now performed and finished. Richard's clothes had all been cleaned and packed and given to charities, and his own wardrobe, an assortment of bright hues, had been replaced. His closet, once a kaleidoscope, was now a sepulcher of greys and blacks. He had even exchanged the brown leather belt sheaf in which he kept his small pocket knife for a black one.

Anyone might think that I have, at last, gone into mourning, he thought, smiling to himself as he left the bedroom, walked across the living room, and slipped a CD into the player. But what anyone might think would not be what is true. It seldom is.

The slow, dark music of Lycia's Granada welled up, loud enough to be heard throughout the house and into the piney woods. Jared went down the stairs, got his bow and quiver from the cabinet Richard had built him, selected an assortment of target arrows and fierce, barb-headed hunting arrows, and headed toward the archery range. It was almost dusk now, the blue hour, and one's vision would have to be sharp to hit anything. But Jared had shot through the course a thousand times. The repeatable pleasure of slaying Jesse Helms was always a satisfying form of relaxation.

It was the third evening in a row that he had performed his little magic. A glass of red wine drunk slowly in the bedroom where they had made love so often. Then the grey shirt with the poet collar, open at the throat, and the black cotton trousers, and the silly old penny loafers he had found in an antique store.

"Only in California would you find shoes in an antique store that you can remember seeing on sale; and at six times the price!" Richard had laughed.

Then the music, the strange and intense Gothic Rock, with its sound quality like a great hollow cathedral and its fevered beat anticipating apocalypse.

Jared had never believed in magic, but he knew plenty of people who did, and it had been simple enough to pump their brains for a spell of attraction. He had even spent a few bucks for a bottle of bath oil that was supposed to help the spell along. It was pleasant enough.

Removing all the garlic from the house had been obvious.

He released his first arrow and it got Jesse right between the eyes. It was Jared's personal opinion that Jesse Helms never looked so good as with an arrow sticking out of his head. But in the course of his magical researches he had heard a lot about intent and similarity, so for the moment he did not retrieve the arrow. Let Jesse have a headache at least for the night.

The second shot of the course was slightly tougher, but not really any great difficulty for a man in good shape. Tonight, however, Jared's strength seemed to be waning. The illness had phases, and on this night it seemed to be building for one of the weak and tired swings. As he nocked the arrow and drew it back his forearm started to shake. His hand weakened, the strength flowing out of it like water down a drain. The arrow escaped and went astray into the woods. He felt the sweat break out on his forehead, then all over his body. He sat down on a rustic bench that Richard had made and took deep, deep breaths.

In the old days, back in the Nineteenth Century, when tuberculosis was both rampant and fashionable, they had called it Consumption, because it slowly consumed the victim, like a banked fire eating away until there was only the vibrant, glowing shell, waiting for the last crackle that would collapse it into ash. It had almost been wiped out with the introduction of wonder drugs: but governments, which made much of how they protected the populace from various shadowy menaces, were not interested in an aggressive, and likely successful, war against a mere disease; and so tuberculosis, syphilis, gonorrhea, and a host of other ills to which the flesh was heir, marshaled their forces until ready to strike back.

While Russia fell under the dinosaur weight of bureaucracy, Plague led back the Horsemen, with Famine close behind him.

Poor War! Once so proud, now an also-ran.

And what of Death?

Above Jared the dusky blue deepened and the stars found their way into the sky, a few at a time, beyond the fine black shadows of the needles of the pines. There would be a full moon in a little while. Only the mountains to the east kept it from appearing with the sun's setting. The music from the house played on—an odd effect, really: one was used to rock music filling up all the space it occupied, but in the pine woods it was only a part of the volume. It was not a sheet of sound but a veil that drifted like tendrils of tule fog.

The weakness passed and Jared stood, nocked another arrow, and shot directly into the target. It was now a little too dark to actually see the flight, but the satisfying thunk of the arrow as it pierced the hay was quite distinct. He walked along the trail until he came to the target and retrieved his arrow. It was not a bullseye, but it was a pretty good shot for the level of darkness.

He had gone far enough into the night for the music to fade when he heard the sound of the wings. It was enough like the soft beating whir of an owl at the hunt that he could not be sure; but the fine hair on his arms stood up and a chill made him shudder. He stood still and waited for what seemed hours before Richard came walking silently through the darkness toward him.

"I heard you call me," Richard said.

"I had to," Jared responded.

"Yes, of course. But—But the odds are against us. Very few of our kind pass these days."

"I suspected that. And I know the danger of being near you, or at least I suspect it."

"Yes. Jared, I know what it looks like from your side; but please, I don't want your blood on my teeth."

Jared was struck by the idiom and laughed. If he made it to the other side, he realized, there would be much to learn.

"May I assume that you are forbidden to kill one another?" he asked.

"We cannot kill one another," Richard said emphatically. "The nature of what we are would make us a pack of vicious animals if we could. Our loyalties to those alive would destroy us."

He looked down at the ground, a gesture which in life had always been accompanied by a deep blush.

"So, you do still love me?" Jared asked.

"You know I do."

"Do you know that I will fight for you?"

Puzzlement crossed Richard's face. Jared clarified.

"Back when we were first together I fought for you, against Ronk. I backed you when we went to tell him that you were leaving. Our weapons were only our eyes, then. But Richard, I love you, and I will fight for you with whatever weapons I can muster."

"Jared," Richard said, tensely, clearly worried, "you can't fight him now! Don't you understand? If you meet his gaze he will have you, be able to hold you, bend you completely to his will!"

"I won't fight with my eyes this time." Jared said.

Richard took his meaning and stared at the bow and the arrows.

"It won't work," he said after a moment's thought. "He's too strong now, and too swift. He can see in the dark better than you can in the day. He can smell you, so you can't hide. You'd be a rag doll up against him. And besides, Jared, I also love him, in a different way."

"I know about that," Jared said. "He is your Master. He cares for you. But if that is something you need, Richard, I will provide it. If I have to own you to make you mine, then I will. And if I have to win you in battle, I'll do that, too. I never thought I would think in these terms, Richard; you know that. But I lost you. I have been in Hell for six months without you. There were nights when all that I wanted in the world was a clean death, so that I could be with you again. I learned that I would do anything to have you back, no matter how imperfectly I might achieve it. Better to die in a fight with Ronk than live without you, Richard."

The velvet darkness was warm for a moment, then it ripped open with a slow, loud clapping, from the path in the direction of the house.

"A wonderful little speech," said Ronk, standing not far away and applauding. "And at last, Jared, you and me can see eye to eye on something."

"Ronk, no!" cried Richard. "You promised!"

"And you promised that you would not see him again," said Ronk coldly. "Here you are, and all debts are canceled. It is time to settle accounts and give Jared what he wants."

Ronk walked forward and his face began to change. Jared wrenched his eyes away, knowing what would happen if he allowed Ronk to seize his gaze.

"Ronk, I won't let you hurt him!" Richard said, and threw himself between the two men, grabbing hold of Ronk.

Jared reached into his quiver and pulled out one of the barbed hunting arrows, swiftly nocking it and preparing to draw. But now Richard was between them!

"Get out of my way you little scumbag!" Ronk snarled, and hurled Richard to the side.

Jared drew, aimed for Ronk's heart, and released.

But Richard threw himself between them again, and the arrow pierced his shoulder, pinning him to Ronk's chest.

"Bastard!" Ronk howled, struggling.

The arrow had not gone into his heart, but the barb held it in his flesh, and held Richard to him, so that he could not rush forward, try as he might.

"Jared, as you love me, run, for pity's sake!" Richard cried, trying to hold on to his Master as Ronk struggled to pull the barb free.

Jared turned and ran, deeper into the forest, away from the house.

Close, he thought. Close, but it's not over yet!

Ronk might have perfect night vision, but these were paths which Jared had trod thousands of times. Ronk could see, but Jared knew.

Around a curve, around another curve. Jared had no delusion that he could merely stand and shoot. If bow and arrow could bring one down, then they'd have died out early on. The stake, driven through the heart, implied that the creature had to be held down with the wood through him long enough to die altogether.

He came to the target. It was his favorite shot, really. Back where Richard and Ronk were struggling there was a clearing. From there the trail wound back and forth, but from the clearing to the target it was a clean shot, straight through the trees, like a long, thin tunnel.

He yanked open the snap on his belt sheaf and pulled out his pocket knife, fumbling desperately to open it. The blade flipped out and with no hesitation at all Jared slashed his left wrist: once, twice, deep cuts that made the blood flow. He folded the knife against his arm and thrust it back into the pouch, snapping it shut.

A howl of anguish came from behind.

"Run, Jared, run! He's loose!"

Jared smeared his blood all over the target, then moved quickly, around and behind it. He drew a hunting arrow and nocked it, then held the bow by the arrow and string and pushed his bleeding wrist up against the hay, directly behind the blood-smeared target.

Bait!

But again, as the blood flowed, he felt his strength draining.

Not now! Not now, please!

The sound of wings came like hurricane fury, and then a powerful shock threw Jared to the ground as Ronk slammed into the other side of the target. An animal howl filled the night, and a sound of licking.

Jared didn't waste his strength getting up. From his knees he drew the bow, aimed it at the back of the target, and released. The arrow, from such close range, pierced the hay bale.

Another howl, this time of pain mixed with fury.

Jared climbed to his feet, fighting the dizzying weakness, and dashed around the target, staying well out of reach. He was already drawing another arrow as he saw, by the dappled light of the rising moon, Ronk pulling back from the target, the barb sticking out of his back just down from the shoulder.

Jared took careful aim and shot.

It had not occurred to him that he would have to shoot Ronk in the back: or that the spine might get in the way of the arrow piercing the heart.

Ronk pulled the first arrow free of the target and spun to face him, hate and blood lust making his eyes glow.

Jared shot another arrow, and this one hit its mark, going right through Ronk's heart and into the target behind him. By now, however, he knew not to stop. Another arrow followed it, and another, even as Ronk struggled to free himself.

Richard appeared, an arrow still sticking out of his shoulder.

"Jared, no, please!"

Jared shot another arrow into Ronk.

Richard ran to Ronk, made himself a shield, struggled to pull the arrows free.

"Master, don't leave me!" Richard sobbed.

Ronk stopped struggling. He put his big arm around Richard and his face changed again. He looked at Richard tenderly, then kissed him, with great gentleness.

"I won't leave you, my loyal little slave," he said.

Then he died.

Jared wished desperately that life was a movie. In a movie Ronk would have crumbled to dust and blown away. In the movies death was

clean and septic and dramatic and clear. Bad guys were bad guys and
good guys were good guys. The credits would flow as the wind cleared
away the last traces of what had once been a man, and only the stake
would remain.

Ronk hung there looking like a crucified gladiator, Richard clinging
to him and weeping.

It was not the happy ending Jared wanted.

But sometimes you have to make do. Sometimes you have to save
what you can, and change unhappy to bittersweet, as second best.

"Richard," Jared said, "I'm sorry. I had no choice."

"You could have left well enough alone!" Richard snapped.

"I would have died. I did what I had to."

"You still might die!" Richard snarled. "We cannot kill one another.
Don't you understand?"

"When I am one of you I will not be able to kill any of you. But I am
not yet one of you. I would have been happy to share you, but he refused
it..."

Richard continued to weep, but his body slumped and Jared knew
that his anger was passing, leaving only his grief.

The moon rose higher and higher and the dappled light became clear
and cold as it cleared the pines and shone down. The scene, so obscene
now, was limned with light that made grey and black and white the only
monochrome realities. Jared's mind, unable to silence its pragmatic parts,
went rattling on, wondering where in the woods to bury the remains,
what rites were appropriate to those of the tribe he sought to join.

At length Richard pulled away from the body and stood, looking at
Jared defiantly, as if he wanted to re-kindle his anger, but also as if he
wanted to move forward, into the safety of another pair of protecting
arms. Jared realized that it was Richard's uncertainty, his ambiguity about
courses of action, that had always given him that strange attraction, that
quality of playing games on the edge. It was not a cruelty without malice that had governed his actions, but rather an innocence without decision.

"I don't want your blood on my teeth," Richard said, and his eyes did
appear to be firm, and decided; but Jared knew better.

Slowly, deliberately, Jared took out his pen knife again. He opened the
blade and carefully curled his lip in just the contemptuous way he had
seen Ronk do it. He took the sharp blade in his left hand and held it up

to his throat, to where he felt the jugular vein pulse with impending fear, excitement, tension. He cut, feeling the warm blood flow. Then he raised his right hand up, next to his throat, and snapped his fingers.

"Suck it!"

SOUL OF LIGHT
Catherine Asaro

The two Jagernauts were watching Coop. He didn't understand why he had caught their interest. He had a permit to display his light sculptures in the plaza. Although he had applied for the permit six months ago, he had no connections to speed its acceptance, so he had waited, striving for patience. Today he finally had a licensed place under the airy colonnade in this plaza known as Plaza, in the even more inventively named city of City. And now two Jagernauts were watching him as if he didn't belong here.

Coop tried to ignore them. Maybe they were only enjoying the gorgeous day. It was perfect. But then, so was every day on the Orbiter space habitat.

Graceful buildings surrounded the plaza, luminous blue or violet, with elegant horseshoe arches. A rosy bridge drifted to the ground from the upper level of a radiant white tower. Gold, blue, and green mosaics tiled the courtyard, and a colonnade of blue columns bordered it. The sky arched above him in a dome, far above, four kilometers to be exact. The Sunlamp hung low in the west. A group of people were hiking across the sky hemisphere, which everyone called Sky. Their bodies were hardly more than specks from this distance.

Coop looked around his exhibit, all holo-sculptures of exotic worlds.

These pieces showcased his best work, much better than the military holo-banners he designed to support himself. He loved making the sculptures. Unfortunately, they didn't pay his rent. He smiled to himself. Maybe if he renamed all his pieces Art, the Orbiter citizens would buy more of them.

The Jagernauts, however, were still watching him. His smile faded. What did they want?

The male Jagernaut was standing across the plaza, shadowed in the colonnade's overhang. Coop couldn't tell much about him, except that he was huge and wore a uniform. He drew Coop's attention like a magnet. It took a conscious effort to pull away his gaze.

The woman was in the other direction, leaning against a blue column, close enough that he could see her well when he snuck glances her way. Although her clothes resembled black leather, he had heard that the synthetic cloth and implanted web systems of a Jagernauts uniform protected a person far better than real leather. Her snug pants tucked into black knee-boots, and the sleeveless vest fit her like a second skin. She had gold bands on her upper arms, indicating she was a Primary, the highest Jagernaut rank. Her black hair fell to her shoulders, framing a face with strong beauty. Like all Jagernauts, she was in excellent shape, her well-curved body taut with muscle.

Pedestrians flowed through the plaza, coming and going, or browsing exhibits. Coop turned to a woman admiring his sculptures. He didn't make a sale, but when he glanced at the Jagernaut again, she had focused her interest elsewhere. His tension eased. It must have been only coincidence that she had been watching him.

Just as Coop convinced himself that he was safe, the Primary turned back to him. He struggled to quell his surge of panic. Jagernauts were officers in Imperial Space Command. They served as intelligence operatives, Jag fighter pilots, and military advisors. Her rank indicated she stood high in the hierarchy on the Orbiter, this idyllic space habitat called home by the Imperialate's elite. Coop was here only on the sufferance of the politicians, VIPs, and nobles who dwelled inside the habitat. Had he offended someone? He couldn't imagine what he might have done, but his low status left him vulnerable to the caprices of the Orbiter's citizens.

Stop it, he told himself Why would they send the equivalent of an admiral to apprehend a nobody like himself? It was absurd, really. Surely she had no interest in him.

Suddenly the woman pushed away from her column and headed his way. Coop froze. He couldn't run; he would rather face a marauding Jagernaut than abandon his treasured sculptures. So he stayed put, surrounded by the waist-high crystal columns he had set up to display his work. Stay calm, he thought. You've done nothing wrong.

The Primary stopped a few meters away and studied one of his works, a starscape he called The Eternal Shore. It rotated above its column, a spiral galaxy aglitter with gem colors, superimposed on a seascape with waves tinged red by an impossible trio of setting suns.

Doing his best to look innocuous, he walked over to her. "My greetings."

The woman glanced up. She stood half a head taller than Coop and moved with a grace that suggested martial arts training. Next to her muscled beauty, he felt self-conscious about his lithe build, which made him a good dancer but would never confer much strength. The exercises he did every morning gave him flexibility rather than bulk.

"This sculpture is incredible." Her voice was low and throaty. "Are you the artist?" She indicated his light signature in the starscape. "Coop?"

"Yes. That's me." He almost winced at his stilted tone. "Is there a problem?"

"Problem? No, I don't think so."

His shoulders relaxed. Maybe she just wanted to look at his art, perhaps even buy a piece.

"Do you have permission to sell your work here?" she asked.

Something was wrong. "Yes. Of course." Coop's pulse jumped. He had heard the horror stories about Jagernauts taking away hapless citizens who trespassed on unwritten codes of Orbiter life. What lay in store for him now?

Then again, those stories might not be true. At times he suspected it entertained his new friends to tell him tales of dire shenanigans committed by purportedly depraved Jagernauts. This one hadn't actually done anything more nefarious than ask if he had a permit.

Coop unhooked the cube on his belt. As the Jagernaut took it from him, her fingers brushed his hand. He wasn't sure if her touch had been intentional or an accident.

When she clicked the cube into the gauntlet on her wrist, lights glimmered on the gauntlet, and a holo appeared above the cube, showing his head and shoulders. Coop flushed. Images of himself always embarrassed him. Rather than a grown man of twenty-four, he looked like a boy, with yellow curls spilling down his neck, large blue eyes, and a face too angelic for people to take him seriously. The diamond ring in his ear sparkled. He supposed if he wanted to look more his age, he could cut his hair or wear clothes more severe than the blue trousers and billowy white shirt he had on today. He felt comfortable this way, though, so he had kept his style.

The woman studied his holo. Her gauntlet would be reading the cube and sending data to the biomech web within her body, which interacted with her brain. It gave him an eerie feeling, knowing she was part machine.

Finally she gave him back the cube. "It looks like everything is in order."

He began to feel more comfortable. "Yes, ma'am. I followed all the procedures."

"Did you now?" Her gaze traveled down his body, then came back to his face. "I think you break rules just by standing there."

He almost dropped the cube. "What?"

Her smile flashed with mischief. "I had more pleasant arts in mind."

Ah, no. So that was it. He had so far avoided Orbiter citizens with amorous intent, but one this powerful had never approached him before. Although he could admire her beauty in a theoretical sort of way, he doubted he could give her what she wanted.

"Trouble here, Primary?" The deep voice came from behind them.

Coop jumped, spinning around. The other Jagernaut stood only a few steps away. The impact of his presence hit Coop like a tidal wave, almost physical in its intensity. The man towered, over two meters tall, with a massive physique. He had classical features, stunningly handsome, chiseled from gold. His metallic gold hair curled close to his head, glinting in the light from the Sunlamp. Metallic highlights gleamed in his skin. His eyes were large and violet, and fringed by gold lashes. Coop's startled surge of admiration had nothing theoretical in it this time. A thrill of excitement raced through him.

"No trouble, sir." The woman saluted, making two fists with her wrists crossed, then raising her arms to the Jagernaut.

The man grinned. "Relax, Vaz." He spoke with a cultured accent Coop couldn't quite place. "We're both off duty."

The woman, Vaz apparently, lowered her arms. Although she smiled at the man, Coop had the impression she was sending the fellow a less friendly message: Get lost. I saw him first.

Coop considered trying to slip away while they argued over him. He could vanish as if he had folded up into one of his holo screens like a flick of laser-light. He discarded the idea, though. It wasn't only that he couldn't leave his work. He also doubted he could hide from two Jagernauts.

Besides, he wasn't sure he wanted to hide.

He didn't know what to think about these two. Vaz had one of the highest possible ISC ranks. If she saluted this man as her superior officer, what did that make him? He had a Jagernaut insignia on his chest, but his uniform was gold instead of black. His tunic went over trousers with a darker gold stripe up each long leg, and his heavy boots came to his knees. The uniform had almost no markings, only two gold bars on each shoulder. Maybe he was a Jagernaut Secondary. But no, Secondary ranked lower than Primary, which meant he would have saluted Vaz, not the reverse.

The man looked around at Coop's work. "Did you do these?"

"Yes, sir," Coop said. The shorter he kept his answers, the less likely he was to say something awkward. He couldn't stop staring at the Jagernaut.

"They're well done," the man said. "I'm surprised I've never seen your pieces in a gallery."

It flattered Coop that the Jagernaut liked his sculptures. "I don't have any contacts." He wanted to shut up, but he was so nervous he kept talking. "I've only been on the Orbiter a few months. I support myself designing holo-banners for Imperial Space Command."

"ISC propaganda banners?" The man shook his head. "An appalling waste of your talent."

Coop almost said, It really is boring, but he held back, doubting it was a tactful response under the circumstances.

Vaz was watching them. "It's almost time for you to close up," she told Coop. "Your permit says you have to be gone by the evening shift."

Coop realized then what they had been waiting for—the time he had to leave. He blushed, feeling his face heat. The male Jagernaut regarded Vaz with a speculative gaze. Again Coop had the sense that a message passed between them, this time an agreement in their dispute over him.

The man gave Coop with a slight smile. "Have you had dinner yet?"

This was going too fast. Coop could barely push out his words. "I wasn't planning to eat."

"You have to eat," Vaz said. When Coop turned all the way toward her, she looked him over with unabashed appreciation. "Keep that beautiful body of yours healthy."

Startled, he stepped away from her—and backed right into the other Jagernaut. The man caught Coop's upper arms, holding them in his huge, muscular grip with unexpected gentleness.

"Vaz, slow down," the man said with a hint of exasperation. "You're scaring him."

"Don't be afraid, beautiful boy," Vaz murmured.

"Just come to dinner with Vaz and me." The man's voice rumbled behind Coop, deep and husky. "That's all. Just this one night. We won't hurt you."

Coop stood still, acutely aware of the man's massive height at his back, like a wall of muscle. Coop didn't even come up to his chin. Contained energy. A fantasy flashed in his mind, those powerful arms embracing him. He didn't know whether to be aroused or alarmed.

The Jagernaut rubbed his hands along Coop's arms, his touch alive with a controlled, seductive strength that made Coop's breath catch. He stared at Vaz, wondering what messages she and the man were sending each other now. Jagernauts had infrared units implanted in their bodies, which meant their biomech webs could communicate with wireless signals. They blurred the borders of humanity; were they augmented humans or human-shaped machines?

You're so far out of your league, you're drowning, Coop thought. He had never before met anyone even approaching the status of a Primary, let alone whatever rank this man claimed. The two Jagernauts also seemed to know each other as friends, which suggested they moved in circles he couldn't imagine. He would be crazy to become tangled up with them. But if he told them no, he might spend the rest of his life wondering what he had lost.

Vaz was watching him with a curious gaze. "You're so quiet. What are you thinking?"

"I'm not sure." What would happen if he turned them down?

"It's your choice," the man said. "No repercussions if you say no."

Coop tensed. Did they know his thoughts?

The woman's voice softened. "Just your moods." She smiled, her eyes glossy with desire. "Except when you shout your thoughts at us. Like you just did. We can't usually pick up even that much, unless the sender has the same neural augmentation as we do."

The man bent his head, his breath stirring Coop's hair. "Come with us. I'll take you to the Regency."

The Jagernaut's exhalation against his neck made Coop's skin tingle. So did the thought of the Regency. Its clientele were so far above him, he couldn't imagine being in the same building with them. Interstellar leaders and royalty dined there. Maybe the offer was a lie, so Coop would go with them. For all he knew, these two would sell him as a pleasure slave or do some other harm.

But why would they lie? They could have their choice of companions. They needed no deception. Nor did his fear about their selling him have a logical basis. Imperial Space Command existed to protect Skolian citizens against the Trader Empire, with its thriving slave trade. It would make no sense for these officers to sell him to their enemies. Besides, didn't ISC expect Jagernauts to live by a code of honor? Certainly his health would be safe with them; ISC officers had to pass strict medical exams to keep their jobs.

The man brushed back a wayward lock of Coop's hair. "Take your time to decide."

Coop couldn't think straight now, with the male Jagernaut touching his arms and face, and Vaz gazing at him as if he were a delicious meal. He had no referent to judge their tantalizing invitation. On his home planet, Phosphor, he had lived a sheltered life, going to school and working on his sculptures. For a time, his parents had pushed him to marry, but they had finally accepted he would probably never take a wife.

The Phosphor settlement was a small frontier colony, inconsequential in the greater scheme of Imperial politics. But a traveling diplomat had noticed Coop's work and given him a letter of introduction to the Orbiter Arts Council. To Coop's surprise, the OAC granted him a visa to live on the Orbiter for a year, as an artist in residence. When he had arrived six months ago, he had viewed the Orbiter with naive wonder, envisioning it as a place where he could swim the heady waters of culture in a great center of Imperialate civilization.

It hadn't turned out that way. He struggled to support himself, far out of his depth in every facet of Orbiter life. In some ways, he had less status than the maintenance droids. But now that he no longer sought mir-

acles, he enjoyed his life here and knew he would return home filled
with inspiration. Certainly he had never expected anything like this. If he
said no to this invitation, would he be losing a night of fantasy or saving
himself from grief?

Vaz walked over to him, watching his face as if he were a bewitching
puzzle. "Your moods are like clouds scudding across the sky Are you
afraid? Or excited?"

Coop spoke in a low voice. "Both."

She cupped her hand around his cheek. "Don't be afraid. We'll treat
you well."

"I don't know what to say."

The man slid his arms around Coop's waist, pulling Coop against his
body "Say yes."

The embrace sent a swirl of heat through Coop. He took a deep
breath. Then he said, "Yes."

The flyer's cabin defined the words "subtle elegance." The craft had come
to the Plaza in response to a summons from the male Jagernaut. Gold carpet covered the deck, as soft as bliss. The walls glowed white. The three
of them sat on white divans that molded to their bodies. The air had the
barest trace of a scent, perhaps an exotic flower with a name Coop
couldn't pronounce.

He still didn't know the man's name either. The Jagernaut sat sprawled
on a couch across from him, drinking wine from a ruby goblet, his legs
stretched out long across the deck. In the subdued light, his handsome
face brought to mind an ancient god carved from gold. His broad shoulders sunk into the divan, and it adjusted to accommodate his bulk.

Vaz reclined on a couch at right angles to them, drinking from another ruby goblet. Coop sipped his own drink, painfully self-conscious. He
had never tasted such fine wine. It made him feel guilty to consume it.
He kept his holo-case on his knees, clutching the tube until his hand
ached. The holographs for his art were rolled up inside. He wished he
could go to his apartment and leave his work there, but he was too nervous to ask.

The man took a swallow of his wine. "Have you been making sculptures for long?"

"Most of my life," Coop said.

"You have talent."

Vaz smiled. "Your sculptures are like poetry, but in light instead of words."

"Thank you." Coop wished he didn't sound so stiff.

"Your style reminds me of Tojaie's approach," she said. "I like your choices of color more, though."

Her knowledge caught Coop by surprise. He appreciated that she compared him to Tojaie; Coop considered him one of the great names in the field. "His work had a big influence on how I use light."

The man raised his eyebrows at Vaz. "I never knew you studied art."

"I haven't." She sipped her wine. "I just like light sculpture."

Suddenly it hit Coop why he recognized the man's accent. It was Iotic. Almost no one spoke Iotic any more, only the ancient noble houses. Although they held less power now than in earlier eras of the Imperialate, they still lived in a rarified culture. Was this man of noble blood? That might explain why a Primary deferred to him. But no, she had given him a military salute.

So ask him. Coop started to open his mouth, then lost his nerve and closed it again.

The man smiled. "What is it?"

"Sir?" Coop asked.

"You're so tense." He laid his hand on the divan next to him. "Come sit with me."

Coop swallowed, trying to steady himself. Then he stood up and crossed the cabin. As he reached the other divan, the flyer swayed and he lost his balance. With a cry, he toppled to the deck.

The Jagernaut moved so fast, his body blurred. He caught Coop around the waist before he even finished falling. Lifting Coop easily the man set him on his feet. Then he let go and settled back on the divan on if nothing had happened. It all took only seconds. The man hadn't even spilled his wine.

Gods. Coop stared at him. He had known Jagernauts had enhanced strength and reflexes, but it hadn't seemed real until now.

The man tilted his head, a hint of amusement in his gaze. "Are you going to sit?"

"Oh. Yes. Of course." Knowing his face was as red as a sunset, Coop sat by the Jagernaut, on the edge of the divan.

The man trailed his hand through Coop's curls. "You have beautiful hair."

Coop averted his gaze. "Thank you."

"Do you ever use yourself for a model?" Vaz asked. "For your sculptures, I mean." Relaxed on her divan, she watched him as if he were a wild and beautiful animal they had coaxed into their lair, but who might bolt if they weren't careful.

"I don't do self-portraits," Coop said. "I don't like the way I look."

"Good gods, why not?" she asked. "You're gorgeous."

A chime came from the flyer's computer. Then a mellow voice said, "We're coming into the Regency."

"Ah. Good." The man sat forward. He put his arm around Coop's shoulders and pressed his lips against Coop's temple in an unexpected kiss. "She's right, you know You're as much a work of art as your light sculptures."

Coop blushed, embarrassed, but also flattered. As they stood up, a portal shimmered open in the hull. He expected to see a landing area outside, but instead he looked down a corridor with luminous sea-green walls. A line of people stretched along the hall, and a man in an elegant black jumpsuit waited outside the flyer, the Regency logo gleaming on his shoulder. Coop marveled at it all, wondering if his friends would even believe his story, that a Jagernaut had invited him here, to a private entrance no less, with humans waiting on them instead of robots. Dire shenanigans indeed.

The male Jagernaut disembarked first. Coop followed and Vaz came last. The gravity had decreased; he felt about half his normal weight. The rotation axis of the spherical Orbiter pierced the hull at both poles and gravity always pointed perpendicular to that axis, so as they moved closer to a pole, the ground sloped more and gravity decreased.

The man in the jumpsuit bowed to the male Jagernaut. "It is good to see you, sir. You honor my establishment."

Coop blinked. He must have misunderstood. Surely the Regency's proprietor himself wouldn't come to meet them. But no, the man had said "my establishment." Coop wondered at the sir he used for his guest. If the Jagernaut came from a noble House, wasn't the proper title Lord? Or the proprietor could use a military title. Coop had heard that some nobles preferred "sir" because they considered their titles an anachronism. He had little idea how these matters worked; they went too far beyond his experience.

The proprietor accompanied them down the corridor. He and the male Jagernaut went first, and Coop walked behind with Vaz. The people in the hall bowed as they passed. Coop felt suitably intimidated. Vaz fell silent too, but the male Jagernaut was unfazed. He nodded to the Regency employees as he passed, seeming to take their behavior for granted.

At the end of the corridor, the Jagernaut tapped the wall on his right. It rippled into a view screen, which showed a dining room. White carpet sheathed the room's floor in glimmering opulence, sparkling with pearly highlights. The far wall consisted of a window with a spectacular view of both Sky and Ground. It spoke volumes about the wealth of the Orbiter's population, that they could waste an entire hemisphere of their habitat on an essentially useless sky. In the distance, City gleamed in ethereal splendor, its towers radiant in the evening.

"It's beautiful," Coop said.

"It is indeed." The Jagernaut was studying the guests in the dining room. "So. Barcala is here."

That caught Coop's attention. Following the Jagernaut's gaze, he saw Barcala Tikal seated with several dignitaries by the window. Tikal was the Imperialate's civilian leader. He governed the Assembly. The military leadership went to a different person, Imperator Skolia. He commanded Imperial Space Command.

Tikal had won his position through election, whereas the Imperator had inherited his title as a member of the Ruby Dynasty. Technically, the Ruby Dynasty no longer ruled. In theory, the Imperator answered to Tikal. But in practice? Coop had often heard the words military dictator used for Imperator Skolia. It had relieved Coop to learn that the Imperator based his operations on a planet rather than here on the Orbiter. A person might see Barcala Tikal in the Regency, but not the Imperialate's alarming dictator.

"I wonder what they're discussing," the Jagernaut mused.

The Regency's proprietor spoke in a low voice. "Perhaps how to vote on import tariffs in tomorrow's Assembly session."

Coop froze. That sounded like restricted information, the kind that you went to prison for revealing. Or hearing. Glancing at Vaz, he saw she had carefully composed her face into a neutral expression.

"An interesting topic," the Jagernaut said. "I wonder what they will decide."

"Who can say?" the proprietor murmured. "Perhaps an affirmative vote."

The Jagernaut continued to watch the diners. "Indeed." He turned to the proprietor. "Well, Jaron, do you have a private dining room for us tonight?"

"Of course, sir." Jaron waved his hand, and the end of the corridor shimmered into a horseshoe arch. They walked into a sumptuous chamber. Blue silks with subtle designs paneled the walls, and a lush white rug carpeted the floor. A low table made from diamond occupied the room's center, with velvet cushions strewn all around it. Diamond goblets glistened at three place settings. The plates were mirror-china, white with blue edging. Someone had already laid out a steaming dinner, the platters piled high with delicacies.

"Is this acceptable?" Jaron asked the Jagernaut.

Acceptable? Coop wanted to laugh, more from nerves than humor. That was like asking if the galaxy had a few stars.

"It will do," the Jagernaut said. "We won't need anyone coming in."

"Of course, sir." Jaron glanced at Coop and his eyebrow quirked. Coop's face burned. Was it that obvious why the Jagernauts had brought him here? He felt as if he were adrift in a sea of social clues he only vaguely understood.

The male Jagernaut spoke to Jaron. "I heard that your daughter graduated from the design school. Congratulations."

"Thank you," Jaron said. "It is kind of you to mention."

"Has she taken a job yet?"

"She applied to the College of the Arts on Metropoli," Jaron said. "They expressed interest, but unfortunately her letters of introduction lacked sufficient... stature."

"Metropoli." The Jagernaut nodded. "I know the school."

Jaron bowed. "Thank you, sir." Then he discreetly withdrew. The archway shimmered and vanished, leaving a luminous blue wall.

Coop wasn't sure what had just happened, but he suspected the Jagernaut had offered to make sure Jaron's daughter received her acceptance, probably in return for Jaron's information on the Assembly vote. Envy surged in Coop; he would give anything to study at Metropoli's College of the Arts. Of course, he had neither the connections nor the funds for such a dream. A wild thought came to him: ask this Jagernaut to send him too, in return for a night of pleasure. As soon as the idea formed, Coop pushed it away, angry with himself. He hadn't come here to use anyone. That would be like expecting payment for a gift. It would tarnish the gleam of this spellbound night.

Vaz was walking around the room, studying the silks. "These are incredible." She turned to the other Jagernaut. "You have good taste, Althor."

Althor? Coop barely held back a startled exclamation.

Then he took a calming breath. Many people called their sons Althor. This man could be anyone. The name had become popular in honor of Althor Valdoria, the Imperial Heir, successor to Imperator. That Althor was a prince of the Ruby Dynasty Someday he would be Imperator.

The name could be coincidence—except everything made too much sense: Althor's Iotic accent, Vaz's attitude toward him, their private entry into the Regency, Althor's casual acceptance of everyone's deference. The two bars on his uniform didn't mean Secondary—they meant second in command of ISC.

Coop sat on the floor at the table, surrounded by pillows, his mind reeling.

Althor sat next to him. "Are you all right?"

"You're the Imperial Heir." Tell me I'm wrong.

Althor smiled, crinkling the age lines around his eyes. "Well, yes, but I don't bite."

Vaz laughed softly. "That's disappointing."

Stunned, Coop looked up. Vaz was standing across the room in front of a silk panel, her sensuous leather-clad figure a striking contrast to the airy hanging.

"Come on, Vaz," Althor said. "Sit down."

She obliged, settling at the table near them. Then she flopped down on her back, making pillows jump around her. "Gods, I'm tired." With a heave, she pulled off one boot, then the other. "Ah, yes. Much better."

Althor laughed, and Coop smiled despite his shock. The idea of an intimate dinner with the heir to an interstellar empire left him dazed. It made Vaz seem less intimidating in comparison. Now that he knew she wasn't going to konk him over the head and carry him off to a cave, at least not literally, he was beginning to enjoy her unabashed joy in life.

Althor took a platter off the table. Coop recognized neither the food nor the gold tines set to the side. He figured out the tines when Althor used one to spear a square of some undefined substance, then offered it to him.

Flustered, Coop ate the square. It was delicious, melting in flavors of meat and nuts. He couldn't believe the Imperial Heir had just fed him.

"Like it?" Althor asked. When Coop nodded, Althor fed him another.

Vaz sat up and zestfully heaped herself a plate full of food. Watching her devour it, Coop marveled that she could eat so much and stay so spectacularly fit. Althor ate even more, demolishing a giant steak. Yet their comments suggested they were having a lighter meal than usual. Coop wondered if their huge appetites came from the biomech within their bodies. From what he understood, an internal microfusion reactor supplied most of the energy a Jagernaut needed to run his or her systems. But that probably couldn't account for every last calorie.

Coop didn't eat much. He couldn't calm down. He drank a lot, though, draining his goblet each time Althor filled it with wine. The others also drank, especially Althor, but with his large size he hardly seemed affected.

Finally Althor leaned back in a pile of cushions. He reached out and slid his hand through Coop's hair, his fingers brushing Coop's neck. Then he pulled Coop down, laying him on his back. Half buried by pillows, with Althor leaning over him, Coop felt as if he were in a nest.

Althor gazed at his face. He traced his finger along Coop's cheek, his expression gentling. Then he lowered his head. Even knowing it was coming, Coop wasn't ready when Althor kissed him. He slid his arms around Althor, overwhelmed, but pleased too, unable to believe he was in the embrace of the Imperial Heir.

When Coop felt Vaz settling against his other side, at first he didn't understand. It wasn't until she started to unfasten his shirt that he realized they both intended to play with him at the same time. He wasn't sure how to respond; this was already well beyond his slight experience with intimacy. At first it excited him to have two such compelling people take him so far outside his unsophisticated fantasies. When they pressed in closer, though, he began to feel suffocated.

"No." Coop broke away from the kiss, aware that Althor could easily hold him down if he wanted.

"It's all right," Althor said.

Vaz tickled the sensitive ridges of Coop's ear with her tongue. "Do you know, beautiful artist, your hair could put the Sunlamp to shame with its golden light."

Althor smiled. "Poetry, Vaz? I didn't know you had it in you."

"Ah, well." She put her arms around Coop's waist. "I'm inspired tonight."

Coop began to unwind. He liked Vaz's sweet-talking. Althor must not be in Vaz's chain of command, if he could spend time with her this way. But wasn't Althor in everyone's chain of command? Whatever the rules on fraternization, they didn't seem to apply here. He gave up trying to sort it out. Tipsy enough to loosen his inhibitions, he couldn't keep straight which of them was doing what to him. He swam in a sea of sensations: Althor's lips against his skin, Vaz biting his neck, an arm around his shoulders, someone stroking his chest. Now they were taking off his shirt. Althor's uniform scratched his skin and Vaz's leather felt smooth.

Then Vaz slid on top of him, gripping his leg with her muscular thighs. Both Althor and Vaz were larger than him, and stronger. It was too much, too fast. Coop turned his head, straining to breathe. His cheek brushed Althor's chest and he inhaled the crisp scent of Althor's uniform.

Taking hold of Coop's chin, Vaz turned his face back to her. She kissed him, tenderly at first, then with more passion. He began to struggle, trying to pull away

Vaz raised her head. "I won't hurt you," she said softly "It's only a kiss."

"Only." Althor brushed his lips across Coop's forehead. "Except you've never kissed a woman before, have you?"

"No." Coop's voice was barely audible.

Vaz blinked. "Really?"

Coop averted his gaze. "Yes. Really."

"Then I'm your first." She smiled when he looked up at her. "I like that."

"Vaz, give him more time," Althor said. Then he put his big hand behind her head and pulled the Primary into a kiss himself, deep and full, capturing her attention.

After Althor distracted Vaz, Coop no longer felt so trapped. He wanted to embrace Althor, but Vaz was the one on top, so he put his arms around her. It felt strange, but sexy in its own way. He smelled a tantalizing hint of spices.

While Vaz and Althor kissed, Coop explored Vaz's body. When he ran his hands over her breasts, she sighed. They seemed too large to him, a contrast to the muscled planes of Althor's chest. Curious about how they felt without material covering them, he fumbled with the catches on her vest.

Vaz drew away from Althor, regarding him with a heavy-lidded gaze. Then both she and Althor turned their attention to Coop. With their hands moving on him, their bodies pressed against his, and both of them kissing him, he became so distracted that he didn't realize they were undressing him until they had his clothes off. He shivered, but it wasn't from cold.

Althor was moving against his hip, a steady rhythm, pressing his pelvis forward, then tilting it back again. At first it stimulated Coop, but when he felt the full size of Althor through his uniform, he almost panicked.

"I'll be careful with you," Althor said in a low voice.

Coop tried to relax. Vaz was rubbing on his thigh, her hip brushing his erection. He cupped his hands over her behind, enjoying the way her muscles flexed. Althor slid his hand between her legs, and she groaned as he played with her.

Then Althor pushed his hand further and stroked Coop the same way. With both of them touching him so much, Coop knew he couldn't last much longer. Closing his eyes, he let himself build to a peak.

Before Coop could climax, though, Althor took his hand away. Stymied by the sudden loss, Coop opened his eyes—just in time to see Althor put his arm around Vaz and haul the Primary off Coop, bringing her against his massive chest with a thump.

"Hey!" Vaz made a throaty protest. "Let me go!"

Althor spoke near her ear. "Keep that up, and he'll shoot off like a firecracker."

Coop turned on his side, dazed with alcohol and craving release. He pressed against Vaz and tried to reach around her to Althor.

Althor nudged Coop onto his back again. "Not yet."

Suddenly Vaz moved fast, far quicker than an unaugmented human being could ever achieve. She lunged across Coop, flipping over his body in what he thought must be a combat roll, though it happened with such speed he couldn't be sure.

Althor reacted even faster. He reached out and grabbed Vaz even as she started to roll away Then he heaved her back over Coop, her breasts rubbing Coop's chest. Althor pinned Vaz against his body, her back to his front, his one arm trapping both of hers.

Coop barely had time to blink. His body tingled where they had touched him. If he hadn't been lying under the fighting Jagernauts, he probably wouldn't have even known what they were doing, it all happened with such fleet grace. They made beautiful, deadly blurs.

"Let me go," Vaz growled.

Althor laughed, then scooted aside enough to let her roll onto her back between him and Coop. He grinned at her. "I've never seen you like this, Primary." He slid his hand between her legs, stroking her back and forth. "You're usually so cool and collected at your command."

"Pah." Vaz glared at him, then laughed and put her arms around his neck. She drew his head down until his lips met hers.

Coop lay with his head propped up on his hand, fascinated, watching while Althor freed Vaz of her vest and the metal and leather halter that held her breasts. She helped him take off her gauntlets, using care to disconnect them from the sockets in her wrists that linked to her internal biomech web. He left her Jagernaut bands. They glinted gold on her upper arms.

Vaz gave Althor the full force of her sultry gaze. "What are you doing?" She tilted her head toward Coop. "I thought you wanted him."

Althor's face gentled. "I'm slowing you down, Vaz, so you don't terrify this beautiful boy."

Coop smiled. Terrify indeed. Captivate was a better word. Worse fates existed in the universe than having the Imperial Heir and a Jagernaut Primary desire him.

As Althor caressed Vaz, Coop laid his palm on Althor's hand, feeling the roughness of his knuckles, the weathered skin, the blocky muscles. He imagined what that hand could do to him and his body grew warm.

Then Althor folded Coop's palm around Vaz's breast. After a hesitation, Coop gave her a caress. She sighed, so he kept playing with her breasts, curious. Although she didn't stir his response like Althor, her vibrant sensuality intrigued him. The more he stroked her and tweaked her nipples, the more she groaned. He hadn't realized that seeing someone respond so much to his touch would turn him on as well.

As Althor kissed Vaz, he tugged off her pants and the scrap of black leather she wore for panties. Coop wondered if those were ISC regulation underwear. Somehow he doubted it.

Coop wasn't sure what to think of Vaz's sculpted curves. He had friends he knew would give anything to be here now, holding her spectacular body, enjoying all that gorgeous sexuality. Watching Althor handle her excited Coop more, though. He couldn't have Althor yet, so he put his arms around Vaz and rubbed against her thigh.

Althor slid his hand into Coop's curls and pushed his mouth to Vaz's breast. When Coop tried to pull away, Althor held him there.

Coop spoke softly "I don't..."

"I know," Althor said. "That's why I like to watch you do it."

Coop blinked, trying to fathom why it aroused him to know that it turned on Althor to see him with Vaz. It was too complicated to figure out. So instead, he drew Vaz's breast into his mouth and suckled, pulling on her nipple.

"Oh, yes," Vaz murmured.

Coop moved his palm down to where Althor was stroking her. He slipped his hand under Althor's and they both pressed against the folds between her legs. It startled him how wet she had become; his fingers slid inside her before even he realized what happened. She sighed, rocking against his palm. Every time Coop bit her nipple, she moaned deep in her throat.

Then she stiffened under the pressure of their hands and cried out. Althor suddenly pushed Coop away and lifted his body on top of Vaz, settling between her thighs. He had his hand under his own hips now, unfastening his trousers. With a great thrust, he entered Vaz, pushing her into the cushions. She held him close, pressing her body along his. Lying next to them, Coop watched with aroused fascination as Althor moved inside her. The powerful drive of Althor's hips made his muscles flex like a erotician's holodream. Coop laid his hand on Althor's thigh, shy even now, but unable to stay away.

As Althor surged in Vaz, he put his arm around Coop, holding him tight against them. Vaz strained up to meet Althor on each of his thrusts. Suddenly she cried out and went stiff, arched against him, her head back, her glossy black hair spread out on the white pillows. Coop felt the climax shudder through her body.

Althor groaned, his voice low and deep, like the rumble of a starship engine. With a huge thrust, he shoved Vaz deeper into the cushions and held her there, pumping his life's fluid into her.

Gradually Althor and Vaz stopped moving. Then they lay still, breathing deeply, Althor's arm still around Coop.

After a while Vaz said, "You're a dream, Althor. But you're squashing me."

He gave a low laugh and slid off her, lifting himself over Coop as well. He grabbed a cloth napkin off the table and cleaned himself, then stretched out on his side behind Coop, his chest against Coop's back.

Languid now, Vaz turned her head toward them, her eyes closed. A bead of sweat rolled down her temple and into her tousled hair.

Achingly aware of Althor lying against him, Coop felt like a string on a finely-tuned instrument, pulled too tight, ready to snap. He didn't realize he was still rubbing against Vaz's thigh until Althor caught his hip, covering it with his big hand, stopping Coop's motion.

Vaz opened her eyes, sprawled on her back, looking sated and warm. "Let the boy enjoy himself," she murmured.

Althor bit at Coop's earlobe. "We have all night."

Vaz yawned. "I'm on duty in the War Room early tomorrow morning." Her fingers drifted to Coop's erection. Folding her palm around him, she slid her hand up and down.

Coop moved in her grip, relieved. But then Althor nudged her hand away. Frustrated, Coop caught Althor's hand and put it on his shaft.

"Is this how you would like your first time?" Althor handled him with expertise. "Like this?"

Coop felt his face turn crimson. Was his lack of experience that obvious?

His cheeks burning, Coop nodded.

"No wonder you want him to yourself, Althor." Vaz sighed and closed her eyes again. "The beautiful boy is a virgin."

Coop had no answer for that. On Phosphor, he had never had much opportunity for partners; colonists married young and had children right away, to keep the settlements robust. Although he had long known his preferences lay in other directions, it hurt to be different than everyone else. But he couldn't force himself into a mold he didn't fit. Orbiter society was far more open to alternate lifestyles, but he felt out of his depth here, afraid to respond to anyone. If Vaz and Althor hadn't made such an effort, he probably wouldn't have gone with them either.

It was worth waiting for, though, to lose his virginity to the Imperial Heir. And now that he understood Vaz better, he was glad she had joined them. With the women on Phosphor, he had to put up a front, straining to fit roles of masculinity defined by a frontier culture that valued aggression and ridiculed artistic sensitivity. With Vaz, he could be himself.

Coop's lips quirked in a smile. The women on Phosphor would love Althor. He was the ultimate Phosphor male. Coop could almost hear the girls chiding him back home: Why can't you be more like him, Coop? But guess what? He was the one Althor wanted.

As Vaz dozed, Althor explored Coop, his motions slow and drowsy. Coop closed his eyes, submerged in the joy of being held, wanted, and pleasured. But gradually Althor's hand stilled. Coop felt the Heir falling asleep, though he couldn't have said how he knew. As Althor's breathing deepened, Coop held back a sigh. He wasn't the least bit sleepy

After a while, though, Althor murmured, You make me feel almost human.

Coop rolled onto his back so he could look at him. "You are human. You're incredible."

Althor's opened his eyes. "I didn't say that out loud."

Coop wasn't sure what he meant. He also wondered if he was fooling himself, thinking Althor's voice had held affection. "You're so full of strength and beauty."

"Beauty?" Althor gave him a wry smile. "I don't think so."

Coop touched his cheek. "And sad."

"Sad?" His voice was a low rumble. "Why do you say that?"

Coop tried to put into words the pain he sensed behind Althor's shields. "You know you're strong. But that's not enough. Not for you. Strength isn't serenity."

Althor spoke quietly. "I'm a machine. Don't romanticize that."

"Your mind and body may be augmented, but you're still human."

"Am I?" His voice had a shadowed sound. "Link me into the Orbiter War Room and I become a primary node on the web of Imperial Space Command. A machine dedicated to destruction. It has nothing human in it.."

"No," Coop said. "You're magnificently human."

Althor's face gentled. "And you, my golden beauty, are deluded." But he spoke with tenderness.

Vaz curled against Coop. "It doesn't feel human."

"But why?" Coop asked. If anyone could be called human, surely it was the vibrant Primary.

She spoke softly. "When we fight, our minds and bodies become part of the ISC machinery. Jagernauts are empaths. We have to be, to link to our weapons, our ships, and one another. Our biomech webs augment our ability to make those links, but we have to start with something to enhance. Empaths. Designed to kill. Do you have any idea what that does to a person?" Vaz shuddered. "Althor is right. Don't romanticize that life. It's hell."

Coop pulled her close, offering the only comfort he had to give, the warmth of his body. He felt protective. It was an odd response, given that she was the Primary, larger and stronger than him. What he felt, though, concerned emotions rather than physical defenses.

Althor spoke near his ear. "You're a harbor of light." The touch of his breath stirred reactions all over Coop's body. The Heir began to move his hand again. He brought Coop to the edge of orgasm, then backed off before Coop found his release, keeping him in a sensual torment of pleasure.

Vaz slid away from them and sat up, her hair swinging around her shoulders, black and lustrous in the muted light. She could have been a holovid sex-dream, leaning on one hand with her legs stretched to the side, and her glorious body nude except for the gold bands on her upper arms. Although she looked about thirty, she had to be older if she had the rank of Primary. With all her enhancements, and probably nanomeds in her body to delay aging, she might live for decades with this robust, strapping health.

"She's fifty-five," Althor said against his ear. "I'm fifty-seven."

"But you seem so young," Coop said.

With amusement, Althor said, "So do you." He bit at Coop's earlobe, manipulating the diamond earring with his tongue. Vaz watched them, drowsy and curious. The lights had dimmed, leaving only a faint glow that softened the lines of their bodies.

Coop tugged on Althor's tunic. "I'd like to see you." He hesitated. "All of you."

At first he thought Althor would refuse. Then the Heir sat up, shifting his long legs. The shadows enhanced the classical lines of his face and made his violet eyes look almost black. As he unfastened the high collar of his tunic, he glanced at Vaz. "There's a sapphire vial with a gold top."

She nodded, seeming to understand, and turned to sort through the remains of their dinner. Althor slid his hand down the front of his tunic, opening it up. The metal mesh shirt he wore underneath gleamed gold-black in the dim light. Metallic gold hair covered his chest, glinting, curling around the mesh. As he pulled off the tunic and shirt, his chest muscles flexed. Coop couldn't stop watching him.

Althor set aside the clothes. Then he indicated his knee-boots. "Take them off."

Self-conscious, Coop sat up and grasped one boot. After straining for

a few moments, he managed to pull it off Althor's leg. He ran his hand
along Althor's calf, savoring the ridged muscles under his trousers. Althor
was leaning back on his hands, watching, his lashes lowered halfway over
his eyes. Too shy to speak, Coop struggled with the other boot until it
came off. Then he set the boots far away in the pillows, so Vaz could lie
with him and Althor and not get a heel in her back.

Althor pulled his legs under him, getting up on his knees. His belt
was already undone. He pulled it off slowly, then held it in both hands
and snapped the leather, idly, as if he had done it so often he no longer
noticed.

Coop's pulse lurched, not with anticipation but in fear. He backed
away, sliding in the cushions.

Althor caught him around the waist and pulled him back. "What's
wrong?"

He took a deep breath. Yes, he wanted Althor. But not that way. Maybe
some people liked that belt; he had too little experience to know. But he
had no wish to feel it. Was that what Althor wanted?

Althor brushed his fingers across Coop's cheek. "For some, it's a form
of consensual play. I would never touch you that way without your consent."

"Do you always know what I'm thinking?" It made Coop feel even
more vulnerable than before.

"I get more from you than with most people." He set down the belt.
"It's part of why I noticed you in the Plaza. Your innocence. It's so fresh.
Did you know you're an empath?"

That caught Coop off guard. Empath? "People say I'm too sensitive."
Was that why he always felt defenseless?

"You can learn to guard your mind. Some of us build such strong
shields, we become fortresses."

He had no doubt Althor maintained prodigious defenses. Yet Coop
was picking up some of his emotions. He wanted to believe Althor had
eased his mental guards because he hoped to draw Coop closer to his
emotions. But Coop knew that was unrealistic. More likely, Althor simply
didn't feel the need for as many defenses right now. Coop wished he had
even a fraction of Althor's mental strength, so he could protect his own
mind. Maybe then he wouldn't always feel as if he were living without
his skin, his emotions raw to the world.

Althor was watching his face. "An unguarded empath can seek the help of someone more powerful. A protector. Your guardian would build a shield in your mind with his strength. It would leave you unguarded to him, but your mind would otherwise be barricaded."

Coop couldn't meet his gaze. "I wasn't guarded at all when you saw me in the plaza."

"And in that," Althor answered softly, "you gave me a gift. If you had been guarded, I would have never sensed your radiance in the darkness."

Would you give me your protection? Coop thought. But he said nothing. He feared the almost certain rejection far too much to ask such a question of the Imperial Heir.

As Althor finished undressing, Coop watched, mesmerized. "You're beautiful," he whispered. And it was true. His body was perfectly sculpted and proportioned, but larger than life, a study in power. Coop didn't say what he feared, that Althor would end up hurting him no matter how much he intended otherwise.

Althor set his clothes aside, then drew Coop into his arms, holding him against his chest with his legs on either side. He spoke in a low voice. "Trust me."

"Hey," Vaz said. "I think I found it." She closed a drawer in the table and turned, showing them a blue vial. "Is this the one?"

Looking over Coop's head, Althor nodded. "Yes. There should be a sapphire dish with it."

"What are you going to do?" Coop asked.

"Here." Althor laid him down in the pillows, stretching him out on his stomach.

Coop clenched his fists in the cushions. Lying this way, he felt helpless. He looked over his shoulder to see Vaz holding a gold cloth and a blue dish. Althor took the cloth and soaked it in the bowl, which held a fragrant oil. The musky scent tickled Coop's nose.

Vaz slid over to sit at Coop's other side. She seemed content to watch now, but he could feel her growing hunger. She was going to want him again, and this time he didn't think Althor would distract her. He hoped he hadn't gotten himself into more than he could handle.

Althor stroked his knuckles against Coop's cheek. "You'll be fine."

Coop made an effort to relax, putting his head down and closing his eyes. As Althor stroked his buttocks with the cloth, a pleasant shudder rippled through Coop. But when Althor started to rub the cloth down inside him, Coop tensed, fighting a swell of panic.

"The oil will just cause some numbness," Althor said. "To make it easier on you."

Easier? It had never occurred to him that Althor would try to mitigate the pain. Nor was this a last minute concern; Althor must have considered it ahead of time, or he wouldn't have had the dish of oil prepared. Coop heard Vaz open the vial, then felt her massaging a gel into his shoulders. The release of tension in his muscles came like bliss.

"What is that?" he asked. "It feels wonderful."

"It's a nanogel." Althor kneaded some of the gel into Coop's back. "The nanomeds diffuse into your body They affect neurons in your brain and nerves in your skin."

"Wait!" Coop pushed up on his elbows. "What are you doing to me?"

"Shhh." Vaz nudged him back down. "It won't harm you. It's an aphrodisiac and a muscle relaxant. It just feels good."

Althor took Coop's hand and folded it around the vial. "Here. Use it on me."

Coop rolled onto his side to face him. He blushed when he realzed what Althor wanted. But he poured a dollop of the gel into his palm, then used his hand to pleasure Althor—and discovered that touching his lover aroused him just as much.

Althor drew in a sharp breath. He pulled Coop into a muscular hug that could have crushed him if Althor hadn't restrained his strength. Chills spread through Coop, maybe from the embrace, maybe from the nanogel, he didn't know, only that he didn't want it to stop.

This time Althor lay Coop on his back and stretched out on top, supporting his weight on his elbows. Vaz stopped playing with Coop's hair and started to draw back, giving them room. When disappointment swirled through Coop, she paused, then came back and ran her fingers through his curls again. A smile touched his lips. Making love with empaths had advantages.

Althor slid his arms under Coop's thighs and lifted his legs, bringing Coop's knees almost to his chest. Coop managed, easily limber from his dancer's exercises. But he felt suddenly afraid, knowing it was too late to stop.

"It's all right," Vaz soothed. She kept stroking his hair, her touch softer now.

Althor joined with him as gently as possible, but Coop still clenched his hands in the pillows, trying not to cry out. Then the pain receded, surprising him. Sensations rolled over his body: muscles flexing, hands stroking his skin and hair. He pressed against Althor as if he could lose himself within his lover. He had thought he would come right away but he stayed on the tantalizing edge, unable to sail over the top. With their bodies buried in the pillows, Althor took him, his immense power almost devastating, but contained and controlled so he gave ecstasy instead of pain.

Later, after Althor finished, he let his full weight rest on Coop. As they readjusted position, Coop brought his legs down. It could have been suffocating with someone so large covering his body His head barely came to Althor's shoulder. He had to turn it to the side to breathe. But rather than confined, he felt protected.

Still restless, Coop slid his hand up Althor's back. His palm brushed across a small indentation in the Jagernauts spine at the waist. He discovered another at the base of Althor's neck. It took him a moment to realize what he had touched. Sockets. Ports for hardwire jacks.

Althor stiffened, but then he exhaled, as if resigned to Coop touching his implants. Coop picked up complicated impressions from his mind. Part of the reason Althor hadn't undressed earlier came from his unconscious tendency to exert the control that defined his life as the Imperial Heir. But Coop sensed another reason now, Althor's wish to cover those aspects of himself that he thought made him less human. Cyborg. He hadn't wanted Coop to see or feel the sockets. Yet Althor still seemed human to him, maybe even more so, because his greater differences made his need for human contact that much greater.

Althor stirred and caressed Coop's arm. Then he subsided back into his doze. Coop wondered if the Jagernaut was always this careful with his lovers. The thought of Althor holding someone else bothered him far more than he wanted to admit. He had no claims on the Imperial Heir. Althor had already told him, in the plaza, that he could expect no more than this one night. Coop wished it could be different.

Vaz tweaked Althor's ear. "Don't go to sleep."

"Hmmm?" Blinking, he lifted his head. "Why not?"

"If you plan to sleep," she said, "then move please, so I can have him."

Drowsy, Althor said, "You can't have him." He rolled onto his side and pulled Coop into his arms, spooning him into his body his front to Coop's back.

Vaz folded her hand around Coop's erection and gave Althor a wicked grin. "He isn't done, your royal somnolence."

Althor kissed Coop's cheek with unexpected affection. Closing his eyes, Coop lay still, content to let them argue over him as long as one of them eased his needs. Vaz took him into her mouth and used her tongue with an unexpected shyness, as if this wasn't usual for her. With a groan, Coop moved in her. He didn't think he had ever been this stimulated before.

Vaz lifted her head. She nudged him onto his back, then came up and straddled his hips. She had already slid down onto him before he realized he was inside of her. Startled, he opened his eyes. "Wait."

"Coop, you'll be fine," she murmured, stretching out on top of him. Althor had fallen into a doze, but now he stirred. "Coop?" he asked drowsily "Is that your name?"

Coop was so startled, he forgot to be disconcerted by Vaz. It was true: he hadn't told Althor his name. The Heir had never asked.

"Yes," he said. "It's my name."

"I like it," Althor said. Then he went back to sleep.

Coop bit his lip. Every time he started to relax tonight, another emotional jolt hit him. He knew he had no right to hope Althor would consider him special, but it hurt to have that made so blunt.

"What's wrong?" Vaz rocked her hips on him.

He shook his head. What could he say? *I want him to care for me as more than a beautiful body in his bed for one night?*

"Is it really so bad this way?" she asked.

At first he didn't understand. Then he realized she thought he was upset because he didn't want to make love to her. "Vaz, no. You're incredible." He rolled her over in the cushions, covering her body with his.

Coop moved languorously with her. Even now, he couldn't come. Vaz closed her eyes, matching her rhythm to his. He knew she was lovely, her body lush, her passion strong and sweet. And he even appreciated it, the way he would enjoy a beautiful painting. He liked her. If he ever had the chance to know her better, he might like her a lot. But she wasn't the one he wanted to love him.

After a while she moaned the same way she had when Althor made love to her. No, not love. She and Coop were fucking. It was good, very good, sweet and wild, but it wasn't love.

She murmured his name, and her muscles inside contracted around him until he thought he would go crazy. He felt so close, poised on the edge, but he couldn't go the rest of the way.

With a cry, almost of protest, Vaz pressed against him. Her whole body shuddered, then stiffened for a long moment. Finally she gave a sigh of relief and went limp.

Coop wanted to keep going. She didn't ask him to stop, so he continued. But after awhile he eased into stillness. Lifting his head, he looked down at her face. In repose, her ardent sexuality had softened into an unexpected sweetness.

"Did you like that?" he asked.

She gave him a contented smile. "You're wonderful."

He tried not to think about the sleeping warrior at their side. "You too."

"Don't be angry with him, Coop." When he just averted his gaze, she spoke gently. "He lives with pressures no one should have to endure. He wages war against the Traders every day, as second in command to his brother. The Traders are stronger than us, much stronger. We only survive because of Althor's family. They're protecting almost nine hundred worlds and habitats. Someday Althor will have to shoulder all that responsibility. If he seems distant or cold, it's because he has too much to hold inside."

"I understand." He didn't fully; he couldn't imagine the nightmares Althor lived with. But he appreciated Vaz's words. He lay his head next to hers and she held him close. She didn't ask him to move, as she had with Althor, probably because he weighed so much less.

He didn't realize he had dozed off until a pressure around his waist woke him. He was still lying on Vaz, still inside of her, still aroused. Althor had put his arm around them both and was pulling them back to himself. As the Heir nestled them against his body, he opened his eyes as if to assure himself he had them both. Then he submerged back into sleep.

Held within the circle of Althor's arm, Coop began moving in Vaz again. She stirred, mumbling a protest. "Can't you?"

"No. I don't know why." He kept going, caught in an agony of pleasure, rising closer to his peak, only to find it out of reach. He groaned in exquisite frustration.

"Althor," Vaz muttered. "Wake up."

"Can't," he mumbled.

"Come on." She shook his shoulder. "Did you give Coop a suppressant?"

Althor opened his eyes, his long lashes glinting in the dim light. "The wine had a mild one. It should be wearing off now."

"A suppressant?" Coop asked. "What is that?"

Vaz sighed. "You are such an innocent."

"Why do you say that?"

"A suppressant acts on the neural centers in your brain that process an orgasm," she told him. "It suppresses them."

Coop blinked at Althor. "Why would you do that to me?"

"It makes it that much more intense when you finally go." He gave Coop a sleepy smile. "It feels good."

Vaz frowned at Althor. "It's also illegal."

"Why?" Coop asked. It did feel good. Besides, if Althor hadn't done anything, Coop knew he would have shot off within moments after they had begun making love. And he couldn't help but think of it as love, no matter what it meant to Althor and Vaz.

Althor rubbed his eyes. "The Traders use suppressants on their slaves. They get them worked up with aphrodisiacs, then don't allow them satisfaction for days, maybe longer."

"It's cruel." Vaz glared at Althor. "You shouldn't be doing that to this sweet boy."

"I'm not a sweet boy," Coop grumbled. "I'm a grown man."

"And charming," Vaz said. "But Coop, I need to sleep."

"I don't understand why it didn't affect you and Althor."

"I can have the biomech web in my body nullify the effects," Althor said.

Vaz nodded. "Mine probably kicked in automatically."

Althor slid his hand between Coop's thighs, brushing his shaft where it entered Vaz. "Pull out."

Coop didn't want to stop. But he wasn't about to refuse the Imperial Heir. As he pulled out, Vaz sighed, a sound half of relief and half of regret.

"It's your turn," Althor told him. "Both Vaz and I had you. Now you choose how you want to finish. And with who."

"Don't tease him," Vaz said. "You know you won't do what he wants."

Althor didn't answer. Instead he watched Coop, waiting.

Coop hesitated. "I'd like for you to—to use your mouth. On me."

"He won't." Vaz closed her eyes. "He never does. Only has his lovers do him..."

Althor laid his hand on the pillows near his head. "Slide up here."

Coop slid past Vaz. Then he sat back on his haunches.

"Vaz," Althor said. "Wake up."

"Aw, no," she protested. "I'm tired."

"I want you to sit behind Coop."

"Whatever for?"

"So I don't knock him over."

Grumbling, Vaz pulled herself up and knelt behind Coop. She put her arms around his waist, her front against his back, her knees on either side of his body. Then she nuzzled the top of his head, taller than him even now. "You smell good," she said. "I love your hair."

Coop smiled, still watching Althor. The Heir rolled onto his stomach and levered up on his elbows so his head was over Coop's lap. Then he went down on Coop.

"Ahhh..." Coop groaned. He hadn't actually expected Althor to honor his request; he had no doubt that what Vaz had said was true for Althor's other lovers.

He submerged into a sensual daze. Althor used his expertise just right, sensing what Coop liked from his mind. Finally Coop began to build to a climax. It took forever, slow and maddening, more intense than he could have imagined. Nothing had ever felt like this. It was agony, it was heaven, and he never wanted it to end.

Just when he couldn't take any more, when he thought he would surely pass out from the intensity, he began to climax. Waves of pleasure spread from his groin throughout his body. It caught him in a tidal wave. He arched against Vaz, his body straining. When the full force of the orgasm broke over him, he screamed. He was dimly aware of Vaz murmuring to him, of Althor holding him, but only through a lush fog of uncontrolled sensation.

Eons later the waves subsided, until finally he sagged forward. If Vaz hadn't been holding him, he would have collapsed.

"Better?" Althor asked.

"Gods," Coop whispered. "That was incredible."

The Heir grinned. "Good." He put his arm around both Coop and Vaz. "Now you two come back down here and sleep."

So they lay with him, Coop sandwiched between the two Jagernauts, facing Althor. Vaz fell asleep right away, her front against Coop's back, her arm draped over his waist. Althor slid his arm around both of them, as if to assure himself he wasn't alone.

Coop's final waking thought was that he didn't want to waste his last moments with them sleeping.

The flyer landed on a balcony of Vaz's estate in the hills. The robot staff at the Regency had laundered their clothes while they ate breakfast, but Vaz still decided to go home before she went to work.

Coop stood with her in the hatchway, their bodies bathed in the streaming morning sunshine.

"Good-bye," he said, not wanting to let her go. They hugged each other, holding onto their last moments.

Then Althor shifted behind them, in the flyer. With a sigh, Vaz released Coop. She cupped her hand around his cheek. "Be well, beautiful artist." Softly she added, "Your work is better than Tojaie's sculptures. You remember that."

"Thank you." He kissed her. "You be well."

Then they separated and Vaz walked onto her balcony. As the shimmer began to form in the flyer's hatchway she turned and waved to him.

"Good-bye," he murmured. He set his hand against the shimmer and felt the membrane of a molecular airlock. Then it solidified into the flyer's hull.

Coop turned to see Althor relaxed on a divan, drinking a mug of steaming khava. The Heir nodded to him. "I can let you off at your apartment. Or at the Plaza, if you're showing your work today"

Coop swallowed. This was it. The end. "I guess my apartment. My permit only lets me set up on the afternoon shift."

Althor spoke to the air, giving the flyer Coop's address. The craft lifted so smoothly Coop didn't even lose his balance.

"Sit with me," Althor said.

Coop settled next to him on the divan. "How did you know my address?"

Althor tapped his temple. "I checked my memory files for the city."

Just like that. I checked my memory files. Coop wondered what it would be like to have a computer enhance his mind.

Althor indicated the holo case Coop had left on the deck. "Would you mind showing me your work again? I enjoyed it yesterday but we didn't have much time to browse."

Coop almost made a joke about how Althor had used his browsing time to seduce the artist. But he held back, too aware of Althor's rank and title to dare teasing him. He picked up the narrow case. Holoscreens lay rolled up inside, each in a protected slot. He withdrew his favorite and unrolled the screen on the deck. Then he activated the holo. The image of an ocean ship appeared, all light and color, deep blue, vibrant. It was sailing through a sapphire sea frothed with white caps, stirred by a storm. Lowering sapphire clouds swirled in the sky. The dragonhead at the ship's prow suddenly roared, fire curling from its nostrils and mouth.

"It's gorgeous," Althor said.

"Thanks."

"People with artistic genius have always astonished me," Althor said. "I'm like my brother Kurj. Literal. Your gift seems to me an inexplicable magic."

Like my brother Kuri. Coop wondered if Althor had any idea how unsettling it was to hear him make such casual reference to the military dictator of an empire.

"He named the places in the Orbiter, you know," Althor said. "City. Plaza. Sky. Ground."

"Ah." Coop didn't know what to say. He doubted Your brother lacks imagination would be appropriate.

Althor smiled. "Tell me something. If you didn't have to make holobanners, what would you most like to do?"

"Work on my light sculptures."

"Suppose you had a patron?"

Coop swallowed, suddenly nervous. "A benefactor?"

"I know of an apartment available in the Skyway Building. It has a ballroom you could adapt into a studio."

Coop was sure he had heard wrong. The Skyway was to City apartments what the Regency was to restaurants. He didn't even have the status to set foot in its lobby. "I can't afford it."

Althor laughed. "Coop, when you have a patron, he takes care of that."

"I couldn't let you spend so much on me."

"Why not? It's nothing to me."

Coop stiffened. Nothing to me. Once again, he had begun to hope he meant more, only to have it thrown back at him. Then he became angry at himself. Here Althor was offering him an incredible apartment, and he was unhappy because Althor didn't also offer himself. Ungrateful clod, he thought. "I don't deserve your generosity."

"Yes, you do." Althor tangled his fingers in Coop's hair. "What amazes me is that it never occurred to you to ask, and you were actually ashamed when you thought of asking for my help with the school on Metropoli." He rubbed his knuckles along Coop's cheek. "I'll arrange a stipend for you, so you don't have to design holo-banners any more. And I'll have your visa changed to permanent residency."

Althor would let him stay on the Orbiter? "I don't know what to say. It's so much."

"Credit and housing are nothing." Althor regarded him. "What goes beyond that, though, does matter."

Coop hesitated. "What do you mean?"

Althor started to speak, then stopped. For the first time a hint of uncertainty showed on his handsome features. "I'm not an easy person to care for, Coop. And my schedule is a killer. Yesterday was one of the longest breaks I've had in years."

Although Coop heard all his words, his mind stopped working after care for. Afraid to hope for the impossible, he only managed, "I don't understand what you're saying."

"The apartment and stipend are yours no matter what you decide. I don't want you to think they're conditional on your pleasing me in bed." Althor's voice gentled. "When I saw you in the Plaza yesterday, an angel surrounded by those ethereal light sculptures, I couldn't believe that someone so beautiful could be that way inside, too. But I felt your mind, untouched by the ugliness I live with every day." He paused. "I would like for us to take some time together, if you agree, to see if we suit each other for something more permanent."

Coop wanted to shout it from the towers: Yes! He managed more decorum, though. "I would like that."

"How would you feel if I asked Vaz as well?"

Uncertainty rippled over Coop. "You like her?"

"As a friend." He smiled slightly at Coop. "I can tell how much she wants you. And her happiness is important to me. We've known each other for decades, since the academy, though neither of us would choose the other for a partner." He traced his fingers along Coop's chin. "You're the one we each want. Can you handle that, two people expecting your affections at the same time?"

The idea both excited and disconcerted Coop. It also told him a great deal about how Althor felt toward Vaz, that he would trust his lover with her. But Coop didn't know if he could handle it. Although he liked Vaz, it wasn't in the way she wanted him. Last night had gone well, yes, but she had been new and different, he had been stoked up by the nanogel, and most of all, Althor had been there.

"I'm not going anywhere," Althor murmured.

"I don't think I'm enough for her."

The Heir gave a low laugh. "I think she likes it, knowing she has to work for you. It's a challenge." His voice turned pensive. "Why do you think she and I don't suit, despite our friendship? She doesn't want a warrior, Coop. She wants the beautiful, gentle artist with the radiant soul." Softly he added, "And so do I."

Coop spoke shyly. "It would be wonderful, then."

Although Althor's face didn't reveal his relief, Coop felt it from his mind. It astounded him to think that Althor had feared rejection, even knowing how Coop felt about him, as he must have known, given that he was an empath. Strange how life worked, that such a powerful man, one considered more machine than human, had such a poignantly human response.

Machines don't doubt themselves, Coop thought. They didn't love or need to love, nor question how they expressed that love. What he, Althor, and Vaz gave one other, both the questions and the answers, was achingly human.

He and Althor sat together, content, while the flyer hummed through the clear morning air.

Althor and Coop also appear in the Skolian Saga novel The Radiant Seas. *Family trees for the Ruby Dynasty and a timeline for the saga appear in* The Last Hawk, The Radiant Seas, Ascendant Sun, *and* The Quantum Rose.

CONTRIBUTORS

Laura Antoniou is best known as the author of the Marketplace series—*The Marketplace, The Slave, The Trainer, The Academy*, and *The Reunion*. She is also author of the novel *The Catalyst*, and the editor of *Leatherwomen* volumes 1-3, *Some Women, No Other Tribute, By Her Subdued*, and *Looking for Mr. Preston*, among other anthologies. She lives in Queens with her lovely wife Karen S. Taylor. "Shayna Maidel" first appeared in *Ritual Sex*, edited by David Aaron Clark and Tristaon Taormino, Rhinoceros Books, 1996. The story later appeared in *Things Invisible to See*, edited by Lawrence Schimel, Circlet Press, 1998.

A challenger of rules since childhood, Catherine Asaro regards those who constrict literary genres with a why-not gleam in her eye and a talented hand. That's why the sexy stories from this Harvard Ph.d and owner of Molecudyne Research draw reviews and praise from readers of science fiction, romance, action adventure, and suspense, and from men as well as women. Among the many honors earned by the Columbia, Maryland author are The National Readers' Choice Award for Best Futuristic Fiction for *The Veiled Web* and *Romantic Times* magazine's Reviewer's Choice Award for Best Science Fiction Novel. "Soul of Light" first appeared in *Sextopia*, edited by Cecilia Tan, Circlet Press, 2001.

Francesca Lia Block is the author of over a dozen novels, including *Echo, Violet and Claire*, and *The Hanged Man*. Her best-known work is the Dangerous Angels series: *Weetzie Bat, Witch Baby, Cherokee Bat and the Goat Guys, Missing Angel Juan*, and *Baby Be-Bop*—all books that follow the adventures of a group of friends living in a place she calls Shangri-L.A., otherwise known as Los Angeles. "Milagro" is one of the stories in her book of erotica for adult readers, *Nymph*, published by Circlet Press in 2000, and in paperback in 2003.

Gary Bowen is a gay, lefthanded writer originally from Waco, TX. He is the author of *Diary of a Vampire, Man Hungry* and *Queer Destinies*. He is also a prize-winning poet, an anthologist, and activist. "Heir Apparent" first appeared in *Genderflex*, edited by Cecilia Tan, Circlet Press, 1996.

Lauren P. Burka's Tarot cards told her she would never get a normal job. She is the author of the S/M erotic chapbook *Mate: And More Stories* (Circlet Press, 1992). Her stories have appeared in *Absolute Magnitude, By Her Subdued*, and in various Circlet anthologies. "The Specialist" first appeared in *S/M Futures*, edited by Cecilia Tan, Circlet Press, 1994.

Reneé M. Charles's work has appeared in *Best American Erotica 1995, Symphonie's Gift, Dark Angels, Women Who Run With The Werewolves,* and Circlet anthologies too numerous to mention. Her stories have received Honorable Mention in *Year's Best Fantasy and Horror.* She lives in the midwest in a big Painted Lady house with her many cats. "Like a Reflection..." first appeared in *Selling Venus,* edited by Cecilia Tan, Circlet Press, 1995.

M. Christian's work can be seen in *Best American Erotica, The Mammoth Books of Erotica* series, *XX Magazine, Taboo, Quickies 2,* and over 100 books and magazines. He is the editor of the anthologies *Eros Ex Machina, Midsummer Night's Dreams, Guilty Pleasures,* and (with Simon Sheppard) *Rough Stuff.* A collection of his short stories, *Dirty Words,* was published by Alyson Publications. He also writes columns for www.scarletletters.com, www.bonetree.com, and *Playtime* magazine. "State" first appeared in *Selling Venus,* edited by Cecilia Tan, Circlet Press, 1995.

Lee Crittenden currently lives in Florida, teaching at a community college on the East Coast, and she's currently very interested in sports and music. She has been writing and publishing science fiction and fantasy stories for several years and has previously had erotica published by Obelesk Books, as well as by Circlet Press. "Anthem" first appeared in *Sexcrime,* edited by Cecilia Tan, Circlet Press, 2000.

Reina Delacroix is the pen name of a shy, quiet librarian, living in Northern Virginia with her cats, George and Shen T'ie, and her precious pet, Michael. "Wilderland" first appeared in *The Beast Within,* edited by Cecilia Tan, Circlet Press, 1994.

Eric Del Carlo's short fantasy, horror, sf, and smut have appeared in *After Hours, Figment, Aberrations, The Leading Edge, Pandora, Talebones,* and *Options* magazines. He tells us "This story was written in New Orleans where I shall now and forever dwell." "The Jail of His Mind and the Songs Within" first appeared in *Wired Hard 3,* edited by Cecilia Tan, Circlet Press, 1997.

Jamie Joy Gatto is a sex activist, a widely published author, and Editor-in-Chief of the erotic webzines www.MindCaviar.com, www.OpheliasMuse.com, and *A Bi-Friendly Place.* Dozens of her short stories are included in projects such as *Best Bisexual Erotica 1 & 2, Best SM Erotica, Ripe Fruit, Guilty Pleasures, Of the Flesh, Love Shook My Heart 2, From Porn to Poetry,* and many more both on and off the Web. She writes a quarterly SM column for T.E.S.'s *Prometheus* and for Greg

Wharton's *www.suspect-thoughts.com*. Jamie Joy has authored the poetry book, *Unveiling Venus*, the ebook *Suddenly Sexy* (available at www.katyterrega.com), and is coeditor of M. Christian's *Villians and Vixens* (Black Books). "Liquid Kitten" previously appeared in her collection of erotic short stories *Sex Noir*, Circlet Press, 2002.

Beverly Heinze lives in the Santa Cruz mountains, where, earthquakes notwithstanding, she enjoys writing science fiction stories. She has worked as a research biologist in genetics and radiobiology (six years with NASA), a teacher, and a group psychotherapist. She loves writing science fiction because it allows her to use her imagination and get away with it. "Gone To The Spider Woman" first appeared in *Worlds of Women*, edited by Cecilia Tan, Circlet Press, 1993, and was reprinted in *The New Worlds of Women*, 1996.

Evan Hollander writes fantasy, science fiction, and erotic stories and is best known for combining all three in men's publications such as *Gent.Virtual Girls*, a collection of his best erotic science fiction was published by Circlet Press. He also has stories in the Circlet anthologies *Technosex* and *Selling Venus*. "Someday My Prince Will Come" previously appeared in *Of Princes and Beauties*, edited by Cecilia Tan, Circlet Press, 1995.

Shariann "S. N." Lewitt is the author of numerous science fiction novels including *Interface Masque*, *Songs of Chaos*, and *Rebel Sutra*. A native Manhattanite, Lewitt now lives in the Boston area with a spouse and two parrots. A slightly expurgated version of "Pipe Dreams" first appeared in *All Hallow's Eve*, Walker & Co., 1992. This version later appeared in *SexMagick*, edited by Cecilia Tan, Circlet Press, 1993.

Raven Kaldera is a pansexual pagan leather priest with an attitude, the co-editor of *Best Transgendered Erotica*, author of *Hermaphrodeities*, and co-author of *The Urban Primitive: Paganism in the Concrete Jungle*. His erotic fiction has appeared in many, many Circlet anthologies. "Cyberfruit Swamp" first appeared in *Genderflex*, edited by Cecilia Tan, Circlet Press, 1996.

Robert Knippenberg—A 16-year-old trapped in a much older body, he writes obsessively, consumed by such questions as "How come aliens haven't abducted anybody kinky, who might really like all that stuff? Or is it that the only ones we see on TV are their rejects...?" "For The Mortals Among Us" originally appeared in *Mind & Body*, edited by Cecilia Tan, Circlet Press, 2002.

Reed Manning is the author of *Earthly Pleasures*, a collection of erotic science fiction stories publishd by Circlet in 1995. He writes prolificly for men's magazines like *Mayfair*, *Club International*, and *Lui*, and loves to sneak in some science fiction to those publications as often as he can.

William Marden is a veteran newspaper writer who has occasionally let loose in fiction. "Autoerotic" has been reprinted various times, but had its first appearance with Circlet Press in *TechnoSex*, 1993.

Mason Powell was born on a cable car. His mother was a professional woman—his father was the Pacific fleet. He has appeared as a serious actor in some of the worst porn movies ever made. He is the author of four published novels, one published work of non-fiction, and some forty published short stories in such places as *Drummer*, *Mach*, *Manifest Reader*, as well as numerous science fiction magazines in both the USA and abroad. His most famous work is The Brig. "Consumption" first appeared in *Wired Hard*, edited by Cecilia Tan, Circlet Press, 1994.

Thomas S. Roche's published books include seven volumes of erotica (*Noirotica 1, 2,* and *3*; *Dark Matter, His, Hers,* and *Best Men's Erotica*) and four volumes of horror and fantasy fiction (*Sons of Darkness, Brothers of the Night, In the Shadow of the Gargoyle* and *Graven Images*). His work has also appeared in several volumes each of the *Best American Erotica* series, the *Best Gay Erotica* series, and the *Mammoth Book of Erotica* series. He is currently the Marketing Manager at San Francisco's Good Vibrations. "Temporary Insanity" first appeared in *Black Sheets*, Issue #4, 1994, and reappeared in *Selling Venus*, Circlet Press, 1995.

Jason Rubis' fiction, poetry and articles have appeared in *Aberrations, Variations, Leg Show, The Seattle Weekly*, and *Industrial Decay Quarterly*. Jason Rubis lives and works in Washington D.C. "Day Journey, With Stories" first appeared in *Fetish Fantastic*, edited by Cecilia Tan, Circlet Press, 1999.

Lawrence Schimel is the author of hundreds of short stories and dozens of books, including *His Tongue* and *The Drag Queen of Elfland*. His works have been translated into a dozen languages. "Burning Bridges" first appeared in *Honcho* magazine, and later in *Wired Hard*, Circlet Press, 1994.